Nash Falls

BY DAVID BALDACCI

Travis Devine series

The 6:20 Man • *The Edge*
To Die For

Amos Decker series

Memory Man • *The Last Mile*
The Fix • *The Fallen*
Redemption • *Walk the Wire*
Long Shadows

Aloysius Archer series

One Good Deed • *A Gambling Man*
Dream Town

Atlee Pine series

Long Road to Mercy
A Minute to Midnight
Daylight • *Mercy*

Will Robie series

The Innocent • *The Hit* • *The Target*
The Guilty • *End Game*

John Puller series

Zero Day • *The Forgotten*
The Escape • *No Man's Land*
Daylight

King and Maxwell series

Split Second • *Hour Game*
Simple Genius • *First Family*
The Sixth Man • *King and Maxwell*

The Camel Club series

The Camel Club • *The Collectors*
Stone Cold • *Divine Justice*
Hell's Corner

Shaw series

The Whole Truth
Deliver Us From Evil

Other novels

Absolute Power • *True Blue*
Total Control • *The Winner*
The Simple Truth • *Saving Faith*
Wish You Well • *Last Man Standing*
The Christmas Train • *One Summer*
Simply Lies • *A Calamity of Souls*
Strangers in Time • *Nash Falls*

Short stories

Waiting for Santa • *No Time Left*
Bullseye • *The Final Play*

Vega Jane series

Vega Jane and the Secrets of Sorcery
Vega Jane and the Maze of Monsters
Vega Jane and the Rebels' Revolt
Vega Jane and the End of Time

DAVID BALDACCI

Nash Falls

MACMILLAN

First published 2025 by Grand Central Publishing, USA

First published in the UK 2025 by Macmillan
an imprint of Pan Macmillan
The Smithson, 6 Briset Street, London EC1M 5NR
EU representative: Macmillan Publishers Ireland Ltd, 1st Floor,
The Liffey Trust Centre, 117–126 Sheriff Street Upper,
Dublin 1 D01 YC43
Associated companies throughout the world

ISBN 978-1-0350-3445-1 HB
ISBN 978-1-0350-3446-8 TPB

1 3 5 7 9 8 6 4 2

A CIP catalogue record for this book is available from the British Library.

Printed and bound in the UK using 100% Renewable Electricity by CPI Group (UK) Ltd

MIX
Paper | Supporting
responsible forestry
FSC® C116313

Visit **www.panmacmillan.com** to read more about
all our books and to buy them.

To the memory of Art Collin, you will always remain in our hearts

Nash Falls

CHAPTER

I

WALTER NASH DID NOT WANT to attend the funeral. Who wanted to bury their father, even if the two were not close? Yet when he had been a little boy the pair had experienced many wonderful times together, the stuff of Hallmark movies and greeting cards.

Then, as the years crept by, Nash had the misfortune of becoming someone that his tough-as-nails, take-no-prisoners Vietnam veteran father had been unable to respect, or apparently even like. After that, his father, Tiberius—universally referred to as Ty—had led his life and Nash his, and the two never saw one another for the most part, although they resided in the same town: his father in an ordinary cluster of old homes, Nash behind a security gate that kept out all others, including probably those who lived in the ordinary cluster of old homes.

Nash worked on his tie while he appraised himself in the mirror. Forty years old, a stitch over six feet three and lanky, but too thin with a bony, undeveloped chest and lackluster shoulders, and stick arms and legs; he'd never focused on muscling up. Unless you were an athlete, soldier, cop, or bouncer, what was the point? His brown hair was still thick and wavy, although graying slightly at the temples.

He and his wife, Judith, and their nineteen-year-old daughter, Maggie, lived in a sprawling nine-thousand-square-foot, two-story, stone-and-stucco house with a finely appointed finished lower level, and a total of five bedrooms and seven bathrooms for just the trio of them. There was also a three-car sideload garage, with his big burgundy Range Rover, Judith's silver Mercedes-Benz S-Class sedan, and Maggie's forest-green BMW convertible occupying the bays. The property was completed by a large, landscaped backyard anchored by an in-ground pool with iridescent tiles.

Maggie had been a college pregnancy, compelling Walter and Judith to hasten down to the local courthouse to say their wedding vows with a judge they did not know, and in the absence of both their families. A true honeymoon had never followed. They'd purchased a condo instead. It made far more sense, Nash had decided. For him honeymoons were simply very expensive photo album fillers. He had later sold the condo and paid off both their college loans with the profits.

Nash was a senior executive VP at Sybaritic Investments. He had risen to that title after years of hundred-hour weeks and brief or no vacations, and living at thirty-five thousand feet as he went from one state or country to the next, crunching numbers, analyzing business opportunities, negotiating terms, and putting together complicated deals that required legions of lawyers and mounds of paper, and a cool hand while under enormous pressure.

All of his hard work and sacrifice had paid off. He now earned a seven-figure salary plus substantial bonuses.

Although he adored them both, Nash was not overly close to his wife or daughter; it was simply not in his nature to be particularly intimate with anyone. They did not seem put off by his aloofness. Indeed, his wife and daughter welcomed him on those occasions when he did join in.

The truth was he had never made friends easily. An introvert, he was proficient and talented with numbers and moving money from here to there, and assembling business prospects together in ways that were visionary and value enhancing. He could articulate all sorts of substantive and meaningful things having to do with such tasks, and also be a motivating and fair leader with his team. However, in truth, he preferred to be alone.

He had had one friend, though, one that he missed terribly to this day. He was a labradoodle named Charly. They'd gotten him from a breeder when Maggie was four. A year ago, as age and illness had robbed the senior dog of any quality of life, they'd had to put Charly down. Nash had become so disoriented and breathless during the procedure that he had thought he was having either a panic attack or a heart attack.

Did that make me pathetic? Shedding tears for a dog when I didn't come close to that level of grief for my father's passing? Yes, it probably did.

Yet, in Nash's defense, Charly had demanded nothing of his owner other than the ability, time, and space to adore him. And Nash's father? Well, the man had done pretty much the opposite of that, much to his only child's continued bewilderment.

Nash did take pride in providing his small family with a prosperous living. Judith had gone to college to study to become a teacher. However, with the pregnancy they had decided that she would stay home with Maggie. But now that their daughter was grown, Judith had talked about getting her teaching certificate and maybe starting out as a substitute teacher before seeing if she wanted to go full-time. Whether it was teaching or something else, Nash supported her a hundred percent.

A lovely, tall, and athletic woman, she kept fit and healthy, optimistic and energetic. She liked to garden, and was an excellent cook. She had been an attentive and hands-on mother to Maggie, volunteering liberally at school, being a member of the PTA, and also being steadily active in neighborhood functions, all while Nash was in London, Singapore, or Doha negotiating and closing yet another deal.

He knew he couldn't have done what he did without her support. Nash had always considered theirs a true partnership. Judith had also been a game participant in all the corporate functions and other duties expected of spouses whose significant others were climbing what could be a very slippery business ladder.

A weekly cleaning crew looked after the house, and they had people to maintain the pool and yard. Judith also went on fun trips each year with her girlfriends. He and Judith occasionally went away on their own, or with Maggie, and when they did, it was always quite pleasant. Their sex life was right where it should be, he thought, for people of their age with two decades of marriage and a child behind them.

He had sensibly started Maggie's college fund on the very day she had been born, but his daughter had decided to take a gap year after graduating from high school. She had been accepted at a handful of quality universities. However, Maggie had recently informed her parents that she wasn't even certain that she wanted to go the college route.

She had started to make noises about becoming an *influencer* and a *creator* on social media and using some of her college funds to do that. Nash knew that she spent a lot of time in her room on her computer, like most people her age. She also had a sophisticated digital camera and an expensive Yeti microphone along with some editing equipment. He could hear noises coming from her room at odd hours.

He did not mind helping his daughter realize her dreams. She was full of positive spirit, and was also tall, like both her parents, and lovely, having taken after her mother in that regard. However, the parade of boyfriends that had come through their home during her high school years! They had run the gamut from cocky jocks to awkward nerds, and even some well-past-college men whom Maggie had met in ways she had never fully explained. Nash had sent the older gents away using his executive voice to let them see the potential liability of dating someone so much younger than themselves.

So if this influencer thing was partly a popularity contest, then Maggie might have a shot. But he also didn't want to support her to such an extent that she ended up incapable of supporting herself. Relying on others was not a good idea.

Before their falling out his father had once told him: "You rise or fall on your own, sonny boy. Then you have no one to blame or thank except yourself."

This made Nash think of the titular head of his company, its CEO, Everett Temple, who was five years younger than Nash. His lofty position was due entirely to his father, Barton Temple, who had founded Sybaritic and many other companies over the decades. Everett was worth at least $200 million, again solely due to daddy.

And Everett, who insisted on being called Rhett, thought himself the very smartest person in the room, because to see himself as anything less would be akin to confessing that his "success" had nothing to do with him. At least that's what Nash conjectured, and he doubted he was wrong. Because very often Nash *was* the smartest person in the room, even if he never intimated that he was.

I surround myself with people just as smart or even smarter than me. That way, they collectively make me look brilliant.

But who knew what tomorrow would bring?

2

As NASH FINISHED GETTING READY, he thought about his mother and the breast cancer that had taken her five years before. And long before Nash had been born, Agent Orange in Vietnam had gotten its miserable clutches into his father, filling the man with carcinogens that had, for decades, wreaked havoc on his once powerful body.

His father's first wife had killed herself for reasons that had never been explained to Nash. He had married Nash's mother when he'd been thirty-seven and they'd had Nash a year later. As an Army brat Nash didn't have to move around much, because by the time he had come along his father was navigating the downhill portion of his enlisted ride to a full military pension. They had come here when Nash had turned three, and he had been here ever since, except for when Nash had left to attend college.

When Nash was a child, he and his father had spent a great deal of time together, doing things that fathers and sons normally did. Years in Little League baseball where, due to his clumsiness brought on by growing too much too fast, Nash played outfield and his father called out advice nonstop, or else screamed at the coaches, the ump, and other parents, sometimes throwing fists as well as insults. They had gone canoeing a few times and camped out once, but not for long as poison sumac waylaid Nash and nearly sent him to the hospital. By the time he was thirteen his father had taught him how to shoot like a pro and handle firearms exceptionally well. Nash, though, had absolutely refused to go hunting with his father. He could never see himself killing another living thing.

They also attended sporting events together where his father sucked down beers and Nash a soda. His father was the sort of fan who shouted and gesticulated no matter how well or poorly his team was performing. During these times Nash ate a hot dog and cheesy fries, and thought of other things. For the most part those times had been good; his father had been a fun, willing participant in the important moments of a little boy's life.

As a child Nash had attended his father's military retirement ceremony. He had experienced great pride during the ceremony as he watched his father in his full military regalia, his chest brimming with hard-earned ribbons and medals, being celebrated by other brave, tough, and strong men.

He'd also seen, when they would go to the beach on vacation, the permanent wounds grafted onto his father from his combat days. He had felt proud of his dad and sorry for him at the same time, that he'd had to go through that and suffer so.

These blissful times had ended when Nash had opted to play tennis instead of the manly sport of high school football. It had been for a simple reason: While already over six feet at age fourteen, Nash was very thin and underdeveloped, and he didn't want to get his head knocked off. Playing a sport that could damage your brain for the rest of your life, for no compensation in return, had never struck him as a productive or intelligent use of his time.

His father, who Nash knew had been a football legend back in Mississippi, had completely changed toward his son after Nash had made his decision not to pursue football. There were no more fun times. No more father-son outings. There was only a wall between the two that Nash had never really understood because he couldn't believe something so frivolous as choosing one sport over another could have such drastic and inane consequences.

Then high school was done, college had begun, and then Nash had married, become a dad at a young age, graduated with high honors with a degree in business, and begun forging his identity as a husband, father, and businessman extraordinaire.

His widowed father, who had lived only eight miles away, in the same little vinyl-sided house in a hardscrabble neighborhood where Nash had grown up, had not spoken to his son right up until the day he had died. He hadn't even allowed Nash to come to hospice to say his goodbyes. He had never even told his son he had been taken to hospice. In fact, Nash had only heard of his father's death from the man's elderly neighbor.

So today was here and goodbyes would be made, and then what exactly?

His black dress shoes polished, his hair combed, and his slender jaw set as firm as he could manage, he walked out the door to join his family. Then they would drive off to pay final respects to a man who, for decades, had not respected his son in the least.

He was actually looking forward to tomorrow coming as quickly as possible. Then it would just be another day at the office where he could be reasonably sure of what to expect, for Nash was a man who, for the most part, loathed surprises.

And another day of his predictable life left on earth would be checked off to be followed by another day that was pretty much a facsimile of its predecessor.

Or so Walter Nash thought.

CHAPTER

3

THE INCENSE SURPRISED NASH BECAUSE this was a non-denominational church. His mother had been raised Catholic and she had done the same for him, so he was well used to the smells and bells. His father had not attended Mass with them. He had explained to his son that the concept of God was for those who chose not to think for themselves.

"When you need to look to the sky for guidance, sonny boy, it's time to call in a damn shrink," he had told Nash, well out of his devout mother's delicate earshot, for Ty Nash tried mightily not to upset his beloved wife.

Nash was also surprised that there was even a church service being held for his father. Or a casket. He had also assumed his father would go the cremation route, the pathway that his mother had chosen. Her funeral service had been the last time father and son had occupied the same space. A devastated Ty Nash had perched in the front pew, staring at the floor and looking like all substance and soul had left him. Nash had been three rows behind and sobbing heavily, as his wife and daughter took turns consoling him.

He had kept in touch with his mother throughout the estrangement with his father. She had been there for the birth of Maggie and later attended his college graduation. They would see each other for dinner occasionally, or she would come to his house for birthdays and holidays and the like, but he never went inside his childhood home. When they were together, they never spoke of his father, although Nash could tell, in his mother's looks and the questions she sometimes phrased, that she wanted to broach the subject. Yet Nash knew a reconciliation was not possible. Unbeknownst to his mother, he had attempted one, soon after she had been diagnosed with the disease that would later claim her life.

While his mother was in the hospital for treatment, he had shown up unannounced on his father's doorstep, with a hot takeout dinner for them to share in one hand, and a six-pack of his father's favorite beer in the other. His father had taken one look at the offered food and his son's sympathetic features, and then knocked the food out of Nash's hand and grabbed the beer. He followed that up by violently sending Nash off the porch with a vicious right hook to the head that his son had never seen coming, because Nash had ventured there to make peace and break bread with his dad, not pummel him. His jaw and back had ached for a month.

The church crowd today was fairly large, and somewhat rowdy, the latter condition due entirely to one set of mourners. The Harleys he had seen parked outside had portended the presence of Ty Nash's Vietnam veteran chums. His father had been a founding member of this motorcycle group, which they'd called the "Fuck Off" club. They'd even had leather jackets made up with that phrase stitched on the back.

The vets sat together, their suits mostly ancient and rumpled, but their hair combed and their faces clean, and none of them seemed to be too stoned. But he was certain they would all get shit-faced afterward and go on ad nauseum about the exploits of Ty Nash, soldier, husband and...father. Now they were talking in voices that carried and their words were not all that appropriate for a house of worship. However, Nash was sure no one had the guts to tell the battle-hardened wild bunch to knock it off. He certainly didn't.

The Nash family sat in the second row of pews, behind a woman who was the only one perched in the first row, which had been marked as reserved. She had been introduced to them as Rosie Parker by Harriet Segura, a longtime friend of the family. Segura had also been the elderly neighbor to alert Nash to his father's death. Parker was in her sixties, tall, thin, and big-boned with a long, flattened face, and eyes that seemed to bite into Nash's flesh like no-see-ums. Her dress was ill fitting and seemed decades old. After the introduction to the Nash family, she mumbled something incoherent, seeming to tremble with the slight effort.

What the hell was that about? thought Nash. His wife squeezed his hand in support and sympathy; his daughter was glued to her phone while she twirled a strand of her bouncy blond hair.

Harriet Segura leaned forward from the row behind and said quietly into Nash's ear, "She's been living with Ty for the past couple of years or so, his girlfriend of sorts. Least he held her out to be that." Segura, a grim, matronly sort, had added, "Ask me, she's a damn gold digger and your father too sick to notice."

Nash was blithely unaware that his father possessed any gold to dig, nor did Parker look remotely like a gold digger, but he decided to table that, for now. He tried never to draw conclusions without sufficient data.

He had not been asked to speak at the service and was glad of that. He *was* startled when Parker rose and went to the altar after being called on by the minister. She quietly and haltingly read a psalm, and then spoke more forcefully about Ty being a wonderful partner, and lover. Nash gasped at this last word, although there were hoots and catcalls from the Harley section of the church.

Judith's fingers tightened around his.

The final speaker called upon was a mountain of a man whom Nash knew well from his childhood.

Oh shit.

His name was Isaiah York, but he was universally known as "Shock." Nash had never known from where that moniker had originated. As a boy he had once asked his father about it. Ty Nash had growled, "Maybe I'll tell you at some point, sonny boy, but you have to *earn* that right."

Apparently, Nash never had, and thus the genesis of "Shock" remained a mystery.

The size of a Mack truck, the Black man had been Ty Nash's best

friend growing up in Mississippi, and then his chief mate in Vietnam, although Nash senior had not been the most enlightened when
it came to race relations. As a child Nash had even heard his father
call Shock the N-word, but the enormous man seemed to somehow
take it as a sign of respect or affection, or something. Maybe it was
an Army or perhaps a Vietnam thing, Nash didn't know. He just
thought it was weird as hell.

Shock, stylishly attired in a dark pinstripe suit that fit his enormous body well, reached the lectern, turned to face the crowd, gave
his old comrades a thumbs-up, and, in a voice that mirrored his size,
boomed, "Some folks here who should be here all right." Hoots and
hollers came from the Harley club. Shock let it quiet down before
turning to look directly at…Walter Nash.

Oh, for the love of God, thought Nash as he sensed what was
coming.

"Then you got you folks never should be sittin' their damn asses
down on these fine pews to send off this man's man to his eternal
rest and reward. No sir. To hell with 'em, I say, right, crew?"

The Harleys all started to clap and hoot their agreement.

As Shock's gaze bore into Nash he closed his eyes for a moment
and felt his wife's fingers clutch ever tighter over his. When he
opened his eyes, Maggie was no longer manhandling her phone or
playing with her hair. She was staring up at Shock, along with everyone else.

The elderly minister had looked like he'd been electrified when
Shock had cursed from the altar. "Sir, really, that is hardly—"

"Now," boomed Shock. "We here to see us off a good man, a
brother, in peace and war. Die for the dude and he do the same for
me. In Nam. And right here in the good old US of Fuckin' A." He
held up a knotty fist the size of a pineapple for emphasis. "Truth.
No lie."

More hoots, hollers, and claps came from the Harley crew.

The now red-faced minister rose and made a few tottering steps along an altar that had been verbally desecrated by a man who did not look remotely finished F-bombing out.

Shock swiveled his gaze to the flag-draped casket, which stood on a wheeled platform in the center of the aisle.

"Ty, you be gone but I'mma tell you somethin'." Shock pounded his beefy chest. "This Black ass is gonna miss you, Ty, like I ain't never missed nobody in my whole goddamn life. No lie. No lie!"

Nash glanced at the minister, who had now frozen in his walk.

Shock first pointed to the sky and then to the floor. "Ty, ain't sure where your ass be endin' up there or down there, just like my ass when it be my time to kick off." Shock looked back at the fine coffin. "But wherever you be, Ty, I'mma always have your back, man. When I get there, you see. We endin' up in the same place, that be for damn sure." Shock pounded the lectern. "God or the devil, here come Ty Nash, right to your sucklin' breast."

Nash again eyed the minister, who still seemed rocked by the *goddamn* comment, but the *suckling breast* reference appeared to have scored an impact, too.

Shock glanced at the shocked minister. "Okay, Man 'a God. All yours, baby. Let's finish this thing. Ty got to get on goin'. No lie! But first things first. Men! Tention! Forward, march!"

The Harleys stood as one and lined up in formation like the fine soldiers they had once been. They trooped single-file to the casket. There, Shock joined them. And each man took a turn pounding on the casket three times. Six men, eighteen blows. And then Shock finished it off in a voice that boomed like cannon fire: "Can I get me an Amen for this man gone to his eternal *salvation*, or *damnation*? Can I, people? Come on now! Do your duty!"

Everyone in the stunned crowd, including Nash, his wife and daughter, and even the stricken minister, joined in with a hearty Amen.

Shock then marched over to where Nash was sitting, pointed a long finger at his head, and bellowed, "He thought you was the biggest stuck-up prick in the whole goddamn world. And I'mma tell you what. Where I lookin' from, man be right on the money. Just like always. Ty know. Ty *know*. No lie. No lie!"

"Good God!" exclaimed Nash. "My choosing tennis over football in high school? *That's* the reason for all this!"

Shock eyed him steadily. "If you think that, you ain't nearly as smart as your daddy said you was."

He then glanced at Judith and Maggie and said tenderly, "Ladies, my heartfelt condolences on your loss."

Shock looked once more at Nash and mouthed one word: *prick*.

On that final note, Shock turned and walked out with his crew.

A minute later, the Harleys powered up, and they all listened to the throaty roar of side pipes and rubber winding up across asphalt. Nash thought he could hear Shock scream above all this cacophony of baffling noise, "Bro!"

4

To HIS CREDIT, THE MAN of God finished the rest of the church service in one minute, fifty-three seconds flat. Nash knew this because he was staring dead at his watch the whole time, the blood drained from his face. He was paralyzed by what had just happened, but not just for the verbal abuse he'd endured.

My father called me smart?

His wife rose and pulled him up for the closing hymn. Maggie stood next to him, while again hammering away on her phone.

Later, Rosie Parker accompanied her dead "partner and lover" out to the hearse and then climbed into the sleek ride provided by the funeral home. She was apparently more family than Ty Nash's actual family.

Nash led *his* family to the Range Rover.

At the cemetery they stood under a small, mildewed tent as the rain splattered down. The still-frazzled minister speed-sermonized through his remarks, ending with how inspiring it was that death was surely to be followed by rebirth. When he was done no one else came forward to speak. Shock had apparently said all there was to say, the Harley crew had not bothered to come to this part of the service, and Nash was still in such a muddle that he could not form words.

As they were heading back to their vehicle, a small, wiry man in his seventies and wearing a decades-old three-piece gray suit walked up to Nash.

"Mort Dickey, Mr. Nash. You *are* Walter Nash, son of the deceased, Tiberius Nash?"

Nash had not heard anyone refer to his father by his full name since the man's retirement party, where it was made good-natured fun of by Shock and the other storm troopers.

"I am," he replied.

"I was, or rather still am, at least for a little while, your father's attorney." He held out a card, which Nash took. "Give me a call when convenient. Terms of the will, estate matters, that sort of thing. Being a businessman, I'm sure you understand."

Nash shook his head. "No, I *don't* understand. I know my father left me nothing. And I'm certain he did not make me his executor."

"Well, then you would be wrong on *both* counts, wouldn't you?" He tapped the card. "I'm in the office all week." Dickey nodded at Judith and Maggie and strode off.

Nash pocketed the card, got into the Rover, and drove on autopilot all the way home.

By midnight the rain was still pouring and Nash had finished more scotch than was good for him. Judith had stayed up as long as she could before he had emphatically—and a bit drunkenly—sent her off to bed. Maggie had gone to her room as soon as they had returned from the cemetery.

Nash took a full bottle of brandy and his favorite cut crystal snifter glass, which he'd gotten in Spain, and walked out to the roofed-in and comfortably furnished back patio. He stood and drank the brandy and watched the rain fall, and Nash wondered if the dead really could come back to life.

Oh, and by the way, Shock, and *Dad, I am not and never have been a stuck-up prick. And it* was *my decision to play tennis over football that started this nightmare.*

He swallowed more brandy and pulled out the lawyer's card and looked at the address. Not the best side of town, but his father's side. Nash would have to make sure the man was actually a lawyer. He wouldn't put it past Shock and the other meatheads to pull a final, stupid prank on him in his father's *loving* memory.

He abruptly turned to the side and threw up first the brandy and then the scotch and then what else he wasn't sure. Some splashed on his pantleg, and his first thought was the dry cleaner. He would have to drop them off. And they were relatively new, a nice, lightweight gray summer weave, not pleated or cuffed, but with a subdued taper at the ankle, as was the style now.

And why in the hell are you even thinking about that?

He bent down and put the brandy and snifter on a low table.

As he straightened he nearly toppled back over when the man stepped out of the gloom of shadows and rain with an umbrella shielding him from the downpour.

"Holy shit," exclaimed Nash, nearly vomiting again. "Who in the hell are you?"

The man stepped next to Nash and out of the rain, reached into his jacket pocket, and produced something that looked like a black leather wallet. When he dexterously opened it and held up one half and then the other, Nash saw by the dimmed overhead light that it was not remotely close to being a wallet.

The impressive badge was shiny, even in the gloom, with the gold bird with wings spread at the top, and something else the woozy Nash couldn't make out down below. The ID card on the other half read Special Agent Reed Morris.

"I'm with the FBI, Mr. Nash. I'd like to have a chat if that's okay."

A white-faced Nash, teetering between more nausea and what he knew to be the coming mother of a hangover, exclaimed, "Now? You want to have a chat now? I just buried my father, for Chrissakes, it's after midnight, and it's pouring a shitstorm."

"I take it you've been drinking?" said Morris, who looked to be in his forties, short and compactly built, with salt-and-pepper hair. He looked tough and confident in his off-the-rack suit and sensible rubber-soled wingtips. The FBI agent made a show of glancing at the snifter and the bottle of brandy on the table.

Nash, who had clearly reached the limits of his ability to remain civil, barked, "No shit, Sherlock. And I don't see how that's any fucking business of yours."

"I'm thinking of the cognitive issue, sir, nothing more. We need to be clear on things, you see. Might we go into the house? Where it'll be private? We'll stay on the lower level. I would not want anyone else aware of this meeting."

Nash stared at him in an uncomprehending swirl of tipsy.

Morris said, "The temperature really dropped. Doesn't feel like June, does it?"

Nash did his best to focus. "You want to come inside?"

"For a chat. Lengthier talks will follow, of course."

Something finally managed to weave its way through the scotch and brandy and into Nash's normally logical and focused mind.

Words then poured out like confetti at a wedding. "Oh, God, this has to do with my father, right? What laws did he break? He's dead now. I don't see what I can do. If there's a problem, I have— And I'm *not* a prick. I don't give a damn what Shock—"

"It's actually nothing to do with your father, sir," broke in Morris.

Nash, in his diminished capacity, did not seem to grasp the man's response.

"I have a lawyer, a good one, but I have no liability. As I said, my father—"

Morris gripped Nash's forearm. "And as *I* said, it's nothing to do with your father."

"But what then?"

"Shall we step inside? I think it best. For everyone."

CHAPTER

5

NICE PLACE," SAID MORRIS AS he looked around the spacious and tastefully decorated lower level of the Nashes' elegant home.

Nash did not hear this because he was in the bathroom wiping off his fouled pants with a wet towel. After he had finished, Nash, using the same towel, also quickly cleaned his vomit off the patio's stone floor.

Then, pale and unsteady, he eyed the FBI agent.

Morris said, "How about some coffee? I see a fancy machine over there." The agent pointed to a fully equipped bar area next to three tall Sub Zero wine chillers.

"I can make you a cappuccino," said Nash, sounding put out by the prospect.

"Only if you'll have one too, sir. Might set you . . . a bit better for our conversation."

Nash pulled out the ingredients, nimbly operated the machine, and produced two cups of steaming, foamy liquid.

They sat around a small, leather-embossed table where Judith would play cards with her girlfriends. Behind a nearby door was a fully equipped gym that his wife frequented daily. Maggie faithfully used it, too, telling her father that physical appearance was critical to her product and brand. Nash would open the gym door on occasion and idly look at all the ways to improve one's "appearance," and then he would wander off and finish his potato chips and ice cream.

And still, he never put on a damn ounce.

"Excellent cappuccino, Mr. Nash, thank you," said Morris,

wiping the foam off his lips with a paper napkin taken from a holder on the table.

"What is this about if it's not to do with my dad?"

Morris slid a notebook and pen from his jacket pocket. He opened the notebook. "Oh, I *am* sorry for your father's passing."

"Thank you. So why is the FBI interested in *me*?"

"Sybaritic Investments. You're head of acquisitions."

This opening salvo gave Nash pause. He had been deposed many times during civil lawsuits filed in connection with his work; it just came with the territory. He had been taught that *yes*, *no*, and *I don't recall* were the only three acceptable responses in such a situation.

"Yes."

"Been there since college?"

"Yes."

"You like the work?"

"Yes."

"Ever think of leaving?" Morris asked.

"No."

"Get along okay with the top brass?"

Nash frowned. "Meaning who exactly?"

"Just in general."

"Yes."

"Know the Temples?" asked Morris.

"Yes."

"Everett *and* his father, Barton?"

"Yes, in fact, Barton hired me right out of college."

"I looked up the term *sybarite*. It means 'lover of luxury.'"

"Yes, it does."

"Odd name for an investment firm, don't you think?" said Morris.

"Actually, I think it's quite apt. You invest so you can afford a life of luxury. You know. To…make…money." He said the last part as though speaking to an idiot.

Or an FBI Special Agent.

"Ah, never looked at it that way, but then again I don't see a life of luxury in my future. So how would you characterize your relationship with Everett Temple?"

"In what way?" said Nash.

"In any way. Your words, please."

"Wait, do I need a lawyer?" asked an ever more cautious Nash.

"Not currently, no."

"'Not currently'? What does that mean?" Nash said, clearly startled by this.

"It means, right this very minute, no ... you ... do ... not ... need ... a ... lawyer."

Funny, thought Nash irritably. "But that could change?"

"In life everything is subject to change, sir, is it not?"

"I don't need you waxing philosophically, Agent Morris. I just need to understand what is behind your being here tonight asking these sorts of questions."

Morris made a show of symbolically closing his notebook and capping his pen. He did it so fluidly that Nash suspected it was part of the man's art of negotiation.

"I believe you to be an honest, hardworking person, Mr. Nash."

"Well, you're right, because I am."

"But that does not mean that everyone at your firm is, does it?"

"Hardworking or honest?" asked Nash.

"Either or both."

Nash felt a flutter in his chest. "But you're here about the *honest* part?"

"Laziness is not a crime, at least not to the FBI."

"But dishonesty is," noted Nash.

"It probably won't surprise you to learn that I've built my entire professional career on that one precept."

"And who at Sybaritic is dishonest?" asked Nash.

Nash was now wracking his brains to find an answer to this before Morris could provide one. Had he missed something, or done something that could come back to—

"Everett Temple likes to be called Rhett, correct?" asked Morris.

"Yes," said Nash, who was caught off guard by this odd query.

"Do you know why?"

"I've... I've never really thought about it."

Morris gave a hollow chuckle. "Oh come now, Mr. Nash, a smart, observant man like you? Yes, we have done some digging on you, sir. The Bureau would not just pick you out cold turkey."

"Okay, I assumed he was a fan of *Gone with the Wind*. You know, Rhett Butler, the virile, swashbuckling sort who builds an empire and gets the beautiful girl at the end?"

Morris shook his head. "But the thing is, Scarlet and Rhett part ways in the end."

"If you say so. I never finished the book or saw the movie, actually. And why the hell are we even talking about this?"

"Let me cut to the chase. The FBI strongly believes Rhett Temple to be a criminal consorting with some very dangerous people over some highly illegal business." Morris leaned in. "That's why I'm here, to recruit you as our inside person to build a case against Temple and his partners and tear down the whole nefarious enterprise, brick by brick."

As Morris was speaking, Nash's mind began to shut down. When Morris was done, it started working again.

When the FBI agent had appeared in front of him, Nash had truly thought it had something to do with his father. When told it had nothing to do with his dad, Nash had had several thoughts about what it could concern. None of them came close to this.

"W-wait, you're saying that Rhett Temple is a criminal?"

"Yes."

"Rhett Temple the CEO of Sybaritic Investments?" said an incredulous Nash.

"That is the only reason I'm here."

"And he's consorting with dangerous people?"

"Yes, Mr. Nash he is. Very dangerous."

Now, Nash had the thought that Shock and his band of idiots

had hired this man to impersonate an FBI agent to scare the shit out of him one last time, in honor of his father's passing.

"Mr. Nash? Sir?"

Nash was staring off into space, contemplating how badly he wanted to strangle Shock if he—

"Mr. Nash?" Morris jerked on his arm, bringing Nash back in focus.

"You cannot be serious," said Nash.

"I am very serious, sir."

"Look, did Shock put you up to this? Because I am tired and in no mood for this bullshit. So if Shock did orchestrate this, you can just fuck off, right now."

"Who is Shock?"

Nash eyed him closely, but then dread started inching up his back as the man stared stoically back at him, with an expression as serious as Nash had ever seen.

He said, "But Rhett is rich. Why would he—"

"All will become clear if you agree to help us."

Nash refocused on what Morris had originally said about him working for the Bureau. "You want me to be your…spy?"

"Perhaps *whistleblower* is a better term," suggested Morris.

"I thought whistleblowers came to the authorities, not the other way around."

"Then *spy* is fine. Or *mole* or *undercover agent*. Same thing really."

"For the record, I've agreed to *nothing*," exclaimed Nash heatedly. After what seemed the longest and most demeaning day of his life, *this* was now happening to him? "And, dammit, you can't just barge in here and drop a nuke on my life like that."

Morris said smoothly, "Frankly, we don't expect you to willy-nilly jump on board our mission bandwagon. And we can't force you to cooperate, because this is a free country."

"Exactly," said Nash primly.

"But please keep in mind that this is an extremely high priority for the Bureau. We will bring these people down, with or without your help. Now, if you don't agree to work with us, but then are somehow implicated in the wrongdoing?" Morris shrugged his shoulders and gave Nash a glum, resigned expression.

"Are you threatening me?" snapped Nash.

"I am being *realistic* with you. When a criminal enterprise tumbles under a wave of indictments, lots of people lose out, some unfairly. But with your financial resources I'm sure you'll be able to hire the best criminal defense attorneys, so you may get off with a lighter prison sentence."

Nash blanched. "You just said you believed me to be hardworking and honest."

"And I also said that in life everything is subject to change. And while right now *I* believe you to be honest, the facts may differ from that. And facts are funny things. They can be massaged very carefully to point in a variety of directions."

"So you're going to force me to help you, is that it?" Nash said quietly even though he wanted to scream at the man.

"I prefer the term *persuade*."

"So this actually *isn't* a free country then?" observed Nash.

"Your words, sir, not mine."

"I take it freedom is now also subject to change?"

"Now who's waxing philosophically?" observed Morris.

Nash sat back, desperately trying to process the situation. "Look, I need time to digest all this. It's a lot."

"You strike me as a good man, Mr. Nash. Good morals, *principled*."

"I have never done anything dishonest in my life, at least of which I'm aware."

"And I think you, above most people, would want to do the right thing."

"Of course, but—"

"And wanting to do the right thing means taking certain risks, deciding things under pressure, and having the courage of one's convictions. I think you are that man."

"But...but I just need a little time. I need to think about what you're asking of me. The pros and cons. The downsides. It's just how I'm wired. My God, wouldn't you, if the roles were reversed?"

Morris looked like a salesman who had failed to close the deal. "All right, Mr. Nash, take a *bit* of time." He rose. "We will be in touch, very soon, to hear your...decision. And then we will go from there. With you." He paused and added ominously, "Or without you." He placed his card on the table. "If you need to reach me in the meantime. And, though it goes without saying, tell no one of this. Not even your family."

"But—"

"No one," broke in Morris. "But if you agree to help us you will assuredly *not* be going into this alone. We will also provide protection for you and your family. But I would also ask you to look upon this as an opportunity to get out of your comfort zone, all while doing enormous good and really being a patriot for your country."

"Yes, yes, of course, jumping into the pit with dangerous criminals, always a bucket list item for me," Nash retorted angrily, because he was angry.

"If good men stand by and do nothing? You no doubt know the rest." He looked over at the wine chillers and the expensive coffee machine and the tasteful and original artwork on the walls. "And after all, there *is* more to life than luxury."

"And if I decide to do this and dangerous people go to prison, but others get away? What happens to me and my family? You said you'd protect us?"

"If necessary, you can go into WITSEC, Witness Protection."

"And my wife and daughter? Don't they have a choice in all this?"

"Everyone has a choice, Mr. Nash. And every choice has *consequences*. But they, if necessary, can go into WITSEC too."

"And what will our lives be like then? I suppose we'll have to move somewhere, have new identities? Will we lose all our wealth as well?"

"Those details will be gone over once you've agreed to work with us, Mr. Nash. But please keep in mind that we will bring your company down with or without your help. And much of your wealth may go away anyway because of that. I'm sorry."

"But I've earned what we have! For over twenty years, I've busted my ass. And I've never done anything wrong."

"That may well be true. But I can tell you that the Department of Justice will go after anyone who has profited off a criminal enterprise even if they did so unknowingly. You may win that court battle, but the attorney's fees and the negative publicity? Well, you may well wish for the anonymity and the lesser living standards of Witness Protection over all that."

Nash had one final query for the FBI man. "Why me, Agent Morris?"

"Look at it this way. We are giving you a chance to be a hero, Mr. Nash. To serve your country. And to right a terrible wrong. We would not have approached you if we didn't think you had the strength, fortitude, and skill set to bring this investigation to a successful conclusion. We are putting tremendous faith in you, and we at the Bureau believe it will be rewarded."

He then vanished into the darkness from which he'd first appeared.

As soon as he was gone Nash slumped to the floor of his beautiful home and contemplated how his entire life could have gone to absolute shit in the span of a mere twenty minutes.

6

RHETT TEMPLE DRIFTED IN AND out of lanes on the freeway in his customized Porsche convertible. At this time of night there was little traffic. It had been a hot day early on and then the rains had come hard and heavy, collapsing the temperatures. As he wound along to his destination he could see the line of blackened clouds rumbling off to the east, resembling a fluid mountain range.

He felt a sudden overwhelming urge and pulled off at an exit, skidded to a stop, rolled a hundred-dollar bill, cut the powder, and did a line of coke straight off the dashboard. He rubbed at his nose and snorted, sending the last few grains of the pure stock up his nostrils and rocketing into his bloodstream.

You had to pay extra these days to make sure your pills and powders weren't laced with fentanyl or some other new synthetic, which could carry you away from this world in a nanosecond. So he got his stuff from a man he trusted implicitly—an old frat brother of his—who did a fine side business in the drug trade, and also had a fridge-size pill press housed in a cheap storage unit. The man also minted money as a concierge doc to rich hypochondriacs.

The wealthy wanted to live as long as possible for a simple reason—they were having way too much fun.

He drove on to his father's sequestered compound in the hills. It was gated but he had the code—unless his father, Barton Temple, had changed it on him. Again.

He just likes to screw with me because he can. I'm only rich

*because of him. But when he croaks I'm finally my own boss. So
here's to croaking soon, Dad.*

As he got out of the car Rhett hocked on the aged cobblestones
that had been shipped over from Prague or Budapest to finish off
what his father called a *motor court*, but which most people would
merely term a driveway. He took a moment to stare up at the colossus
his father built because he'd been bored and had a spare $40 million
in cash burning a hole in his portfolio. Rhett didn't know how large
it actually was, but the place looked like it deserved its own zip code.
His downtown penthouse, which took up the entire top floor of his
skyscraper, would have probably fit in the kitchen of this sucker.

During a break in the rain, he ran to the covered stone entrance,
where he was greeted at the cathedral-size double oak doors by an
authentic English butler named Herbert or Harold, or something
like that. The man had been brought over from the Savoy Hotel
in London and looked wide-awake at two in the morning. Rhett
assumed the quarter million the gent was paid annually plus benefits, along with free five-star food provided by the live-in chef, and
luxurious accommodations, justified losing some sleep.

The liveried British robot eschewed the elevator and led Rhett
up a series of staircases wide enough to accommodate a semi, then
knocked on a door at the end of a hall that was so long Rhett had
nearly gotten all his steps in for the day. The servant received autho-
rization to enter from the deep voice inside and he opened the door,
nodded at Rhett, and marched back to his upscale hidey-hole.

Rhett fixed his shirt cuffs, adjusted his jacket, smoothed down
his hair, and entered the room feeling like a truant summoned to the
principal's office.

His father was sitting in a chair by the window wearing a luxurious white cotton robe with his monogrammed initials woven into
it. As Rhett approached, he caught the image of a young, blindfolded
woman clad in a tight black minidress being led away through
another door by a member of his father's security team.

"Missus Number Three not home tonight?" observed Rhett.

Barton Temple had two inches on his six-one son and about a hundred pounds, none of it muscle. His curly silver hair implants seemed to quiver with amusement.

"Mindy took one of the jets somewhere. Cannes maybe. She used to be in the film business, you know."

"Yeah, as a hair and makeup artist."

"Which means she knows how to make herself look good, boy," his father shot back. "Only reason I married her. She looks good on *me*."

"You *summoned* me," said Rhett. "And I'm here. So what's up?"

"The funeral?"

"What?"

"How did the funeral go?"

"Who died?" said Rhett, dipping his head as the pulse of the coke pop wore off.

"Christ, boy, when are you going to get a simple message through that tree stump you call a brain? Walter Nash?"

"Walter is very much alive."

"I meant his *father's* funeral."

"What about it?" Rhett asked.

"I told you to attend."

"Hell, I thought you were joking."

His father shook his head in frustration, turned to a fully stocked bar against one wall, and mixed himself a whisky soda without asking if his son wanted anything.

"Walter Nash is the best damned hire I ever made, and that includes you. He is the only thing standing between you and that sinking ship you call a company. Which, by the way, was a great business until I let you run it. Into the ground."

"Come on, we're doing fine."

His father turned to face him. "I don't call profits and revenue being down fifteen percent each *fine*, especially when your industry benchmarks are all the other way. And on top of that your free cash flow is for shit. But for the success and savviness of Nash's acquisitions, you'd be down fifty on both, and your cash flow would be pennies instead of dollars. Bottom line, the man is carrying your water, and a dozen other firms would do anything to poach him. So you go to his father's fucking funeral."

"Okay, okay, I'm sorry."

"You *are* sorry, but not in the way you mean, boy."

Barton lit up a cigar pulled from an inlaid walnut humidor. Rhett saw that it was a limited edition Montecristo that cost over $500.

Barton Temple had been to over 120 countries. He was intimately acquainted with kings and dictators, titans of industry, and the monied generational wealth from all four corners of the globe that shaped much of life for the other eight billion people on planet earth. He'd dived off Mexican cliffs in his younger and fitter days, and shot bull elephants and lions on savannahs in Kenya while Rhett was still in diapers, or so Barton liked to brag. He'd made shady fortunes in Africa and South and Latin America and parlayed that into even greater wealth in European corridors. There had also been rumors of his doing deals with Middle East arms dealers when they were still a thing. He'd bought up skyscrapers in New York and oil refineries in Texas and a ton of land and businesses in between. He was a welcome visitor in the homes of other billionaires as well as in the power corridors of world capitals, because he greased palms with the best of them. The carried-interest tax loophole in the U.S. tax laws still survived principally because of his lobbying efforts, allowing the super wealthy to pay even less in tax than the staff they employed to change their kids' diapers, or theirs, when they became too aged to do it themselves.

But he was one bloated SOB now. And he didn't look so invincible to his son.

He can't last much longer.

"Look, I'll send him a nice card and flowers to the house and I'll offer my personal condolences, blah-blah."

"You are one heartless prick." But then Barton smiled. "Just like I raised you."

"You *didn't* raise me, Mom did, in case you don't remember. And it wasn't as a heartless prick. For that, it's all thanks to you."

"I was there for all the important moments. Like when I handed you the keys to Sybaritic for no good reason other than you're my flesh and blood. You weren't boo-hooing about me missing your ball games and science fairs then."

"Is that all you wanted to ask me? About the funeral? You ever heard of *texting*?"

When his father didn't answer, Rhett glanced at the doorway through which the masked woman had disappeared. "Oh, I get it. You wanted me to see you can still get the job done with the young ladies? Never doubted it, Dad. I mean, you did marry a twenty-nine-year-old just last year. What was tonight's model? Sixteen?"

His father drained his drink. "We *do* need to go over a few things."

"Like what?"

"Your expectations for AB," said his father.

"AB?"

His father shook his head impatiently. "Keep up, boy. After Barton."

Rhett decided candidness was the order of the day and said quietly, "I guess I always assumed as the eldest child the lion's share would go to me along with the running of the companies. Beth has no interest in business."

Barton studied him from under hooded eyes, his expression unreadable. "In addition to your younger sister, you also have two half sisters who are considerably older than you."

"Right. But Angie has autism spectrum disorder and lives here with you. And DeeDee is a trust fund adult who lives in luxurious splendor in Paris, has never worked a day in her life, and wouldn't know an LBO from a Ho Ho."

"Autism spectrum disorder, my ass. Angie's over fifty with the mind of a toddler."

Rhett stared at his father, incredulous that he could speak about his special needs daughter with such callousness.

But then again, why the hell are you surprised? He's the world's biggest asshole. And you're not far behind him.

"She's also the nicest person in the entire family," said Rhett emphatically. "But she's not going to be running any of your businesses."

Barton took a cigar puff. "It was her mother's fault. I did nothing wrong. I mean, look at DeeDee. Girl's got all her brains."

"That's debatable," replied Rhett, who found it disgusting that his father never accepted responsibility for anything that went wrong. He only took credit for the successes.

His father eyed him over the cigar smoke. "FYI, Mindy has been making noises about wanting to hear the pitter-patter of little feet."

"You'll be past eighty before they're in pre-K. And isn't four kids enough?"

"Quality over quantity, boy. How many times have I told you that?"

His father rose and walked over to the bar to refresh his drink. "And when are you going to get married and have kids of your own? You can't be chasing ass all your life."

When Rhett didn't answer, his father turned to him with hiked brows. "Jesus Christ, please do not tell me you really like men and not girls?"

"Look, leave me everything, nothing, or something in between. I don't really care."

His father smirked. "What? You'll fend for yourself then?"

"I have, for a long time."

"Then you need to knock off the coke. I did it for a few years. It'll mess you up."

"I don't do drugs."

"Then what's the white crap on your cheek, boy? You can't even lie worth a shit."

Rhett rubbed at his face. "I'll do the mea culpa with Nash. Are we good here?"

"Yeah, you better get on back to that *penthouse* you earned all by yourself," Barton snapped, tacking on a snort of contempt.

As Rhett walked out, his father called after him, "And get yourself a damn wife and start making some babies, boy. You still won't be an alpha but you can at least pretend you're one."

Rhett hated being called boy, which was why his father only called him that.

He stopped at a powder room and cleaned his face, then made a detour on his way out and popped his head into a bedroom on the second floor.

Angelina—Angie—Temple was sitting up in her bed and staring at the ceiling, which was littered with pasted-on stars. The whole room was a nod to her perpetual childhood, filled with dolls and stuffed animals, and old Disney movie posters. Her hair was cut in bangs and was nearly all gray now.

Her gaze dropped from the ceiling to him.

"Et?"

She had never managed to pronounce his name, so *Et* had stuck. Doctors didn't use the term *low-functioning* anymore, but Rhett knew that Angie would fall into that category. Yet she was kind and gentle, except for the occasional outburst because of a loud sound or a bright light. Sometimes nothing at all would set her off, but those times were now rare. Rhett knew this was because she was on a litany of medications to moderate her hyperactivity, control her ritualized behavior and irritability, and reduce her anxiety. She seemed happy, he thought.

Lucky her.

"Hey, Angie."

He pulled up a chair and sat down next to the bed.

"Et?" she said again, her mouth wide with smiles. She leaned over but did not hug him. She did not like to touch or be touched. "Et, Et, Et, Et," she said in a singsong voice.

Angie had been his big sister growing up; they had played for hours at a time. She was the perfect companion to an energetic little boy because she never tired of having adventures, or doing goofy stuff that children did. But as a little boy he had also witnessed in terror her uncontrollable tirades. As a man he just felt sorry for her.

Back then he had been closer to Angie than anyone else in his family. But then Rhett had grown up and Angie couldn't.

"Why aren't you sleeping?"

In answer she pointed to the ceiling. "Tars. Pretty."

He looked up, too. "Yep, the stars sure are pretty. But they'll be there when you wake up tomorrow, okay? So, night-night-night." This was a phrase indoctrinated into Angie's mind by her therapists; it worked like clockwork to get her to go to sleep. His father had insisted on something like that to control her. Rhett had understood his desire to have a tool such as that, but part of him loved to see Angie rebuff the old man.

"Night-night, night-night, Et, Et, Et, Et." She lay back and closed her eyes. She was asleep by the time he reached the door.

He looked back at her resting peacefully, and then Rhett went on his way wishing he were a little boy again, playing with his big sister.

But that wish was never going to come true, so he trudged back into the world that his father had fashioned for him.

CHAPTER

7

"LET ME GO! GET OFF me, you jerks!"

Rhett had walked outside in time to see his father's sex-mate for the night being forced by two men into an SUV, with her eyes still blindfolded.

"Hey," he called out.

"Yeah?" said the biggest of the men, who was the head of Barton Temple's personal security team.

"Where are you taking her?"

"Back to where she came from, *sir*," said the same man.

"And the blindfold?"

The man looked at Rhett like he was an idiot. "Protecting the boss, sir."

"I'll take her back," said Rhett.

"No can do," said the man. "Our orders—"

"The 'boss' just told me to come down and see to this. Care to go upstairs and wake him up and ask him?"

None of the men looked remotely willing to do that.

Rhett gripped the woman's arm. "Let's go."

She immediately started to struggle until he leaned in and whispered, "I'm getting you out of a tight situation. Trust me."

He guided her to his Porsche, and got her settled and buckled in.

As he climbed in next to her he said, "What's your name?"

"Can I take off the blindfold now? They said if I did it before I wouldn't get paid."

"When I get to where you're going you can. What's your name?"

"Laurel."

"How did you come to be here tonight?"

"I work...for people. *They* set it up."

"How much of your fee goes to the *people*?"

"Seventy percent, I keep the rest," replied Laurel.

"You need to work a better deal."

Frowning she said, "Just drop me off, okay?"

"Where?"

She gave him an address and he put it into the nav system.

He studied her. She *was* young. Maybe jailbait young. His father had to be slipping to play things that close to the edge. "Did he treat you okay?"

She shrugged. "I was thinking of other things. That's what I do."

"He pay well?"

"Yeah. Real good."

"You mind my asking how much?"

"Two thousand," she said in a tone that was full of both pride and wonder. "Two grand for ten minutes' work," she added, which made Rhett snort.

"I'm surprised he could satisfy you."

"He couldn't. But I satisfied *him*."

It took Rhett a moment to understand what she meant. "Right. Well, he is pretty old."

"Whatever."

"But you only get thirty percent. That's six hundred bucks."

"Still a lot for ten minutes. Per hour that's like—"

"—thirty-six hundred."

"Yeah, way more than doctors and lawyers make."

"You been with him before?" he asked.

"Three times before."

"How can you tell with the blindfold? His voice?"

"It's his smell," she said, wrinkling her nose.

This piqued Rhett's interest. "So what does he smell like?"

"Old. Mothballs, and something else I can't quite figure out."

She turned to him again as they sailed around a curve. "So you think I should get more than thirty percent?"

"Well, you *are* doing all the work."

"You're rich, right?"

"How can you tell that?" asked Rhett.

"You were at the guy's place. His goons called you sir and let you take me away. And your car smells and sounds expensive."

"You could be a detective."

She said in a coy voice, "Look, you wanna do it with me? It's not like I got any personal satisfaction from him. And I get to keep a hundred percent."

He looked her over. "How old are you?"

"Twenty-two."

"No, really, how old are you?"

"Nineteen, I swear."

"You got ID?"

"Left pocket of my dress. Why don't you pull it out?" she added coyly.

He leaned over and snagged it, feeling the softness of her hip at the same time. She smelled good, honeysuckle and coconut.

The driver's license showed her name as Laurel Burke, age nineteen, and it looked legit. At least it would give him plausible deniability. He took a picture of it with his phone, slipped it back into her pocket, this time stroking her hip and thigh.

"And don't worry, I'm on the pill. Of course with the old guy it didn't matter. You can't get pregnant *that* way."

Though he was certain his father had never told Mindy, Rhett had found out his dad had undergone a vasectomy a while back. His father would probably just keep having sex with Mindy and blame the lack of offspring on *her* inability to conceive, since he'd already successfully fathered four offspring.

"Sometimes the pill fails. So I *will* be using protection."

"Where do you want to do it?" she asked.

In answer he found a dirt road, where he pulled to a stop in front of a thicket of wild butterfly shrubs that drooped with the weight of the recent rain. With the break in the weather he put the Porsche's top down so they'd have more room.

Rhett had her keep the blindfold on while he slid down his pants and underwear and put on the condom. He then put the seat back as far as it would go and helped Burke climb over the console and sit astride him.

She slipped her dress off, revealing only a thong underneath. He tugged that aside, and the Porsche rocked for the next half hour.

"Can't I take the blindfold off?" she gasped.

"It's more fun this way," he countered. "You can imagine me any way you want."

"Kinky."

Finished, he slowly stroked her hair.

"Better than the old sack of shit?" he whispered.

She moaned throatily. "Oh, yeah. Lots."

When the rain started to fall again, Rhett started the car and put the top up, to keep them from getting doused. They put their clothes back on, and he drove off. A half hour later he slowed to a stop in an area of the city far away from the penthouse crowd. He peeled off a huge wad of hundreds from a stash he kept in a custom lock box under the front seat, then grabbed a small, zippered vinyl bag from the console and put the cash in there before handing the bag to her.

"Five thousand cash."

"Shit," she said. "Seriously?"

"You want to count it?"

"No, I'm good. I trust you."

"And like you said, you get one hundred percent. Thirty minutes of work, so that's *ten grand* an hour."

She smirked. "Thanks for the raise."

He helped her get out of the car and looked around. "You close by?"

"You see a red door?" she asked.

"Yeah, number twelve, on the left."

"That's me."

"You got a key?" he said.

"In my other pocket."

"Count to five and then take off the blindfold."

"Maybe we can do this again."

"Maybe we can."

He got back into the car. "So, what do I smell like?"

She turned toward the sound of his voice. "Not old, for sure. No mothballs."

"But?"

"But—and don't take this the wrong way, mister—you…you smell a little like the other guy."

CHAPTER

8

Nᴀsʜ ʜᴀᴅ ᴅʀᴀɢɢᴇᴅ ʜɪᴍsᴇʟꜰ ᴜᴘsᴛᴀɪʀs at two in the morning. The slumbering Judith was breathing deeply, her face partially obscured by a sleep mask. Nash stood there for a bit looking down at her and wondering how he was going to deal with all this. With her.

He changed into his pajamas, flossed and brushed his teeth, and also gargled with mouthwash to get the remaining vomit out. He slept on the couch in the sitting room just off the bedroom. When he awoke the rain had passed and the sunlight was slanting in the large window. It was like a buzz saw to his skull. That was when he noticed Judith standing over him wearing only a sheer, clingy lace nightgown.

"Walter? Are you okay?"

He rubbed his eyes and nodded. "Sure, why do you ask?"

"Well, why did you sleep here for starters?"

"Came up late, didn't want to wake you."

"I'm impossible to wake," she reminded him.

It was true. She fell asleep *before* her head hit the pillow.

Judith had majored in English Literature in college, with minors in Spanish and art history. Nash sometimes thought she had married him because none of those fields would necessarily support the lifestyle to which she aspired, while his degree could, and had.

And she said she was on the pill, but then Maggie…

But still lucky me, he thought as she bent down to kiss him, her hand reaching to his crotch and staying there.

"I was so worried about you after yesterday," she said, sliding her fingers up and down the lengthening part of his groin. "Is there anything I can do to make it better?"

"I think we'll figure out something," he said, sliding down his pajama bottoms.

She slipped off her nightgown, moved the chain necklace with the attached locket so that it hung across her back, and pushed him flat on the sofa. She climbed aboard, and for the next twenty minutes Nash forgot all about FBI Special Agent Reed Morris. Although he might have taken out his fury against the federal agent in the form of his lovemaking, because when they were done, his wife fell off him, sweaty and breathless.

"What got into you?" she gasped.

"You just know how to press all my buttons, babe," he replied, tacking on a pained smile, because what he was keeping from her was burning a hole in his gut.

They bathed together in the walk-in shower, the floor of which was done in river rock and pebbles, so their feet got a nice massage too.

Judith went to her closet to get dressed, and Nash ventured to his to do the same.

Her much larger space, full of custom cabinetry, looked like a haute couture clothing and accessory boutique after an earthquake had struck. His looked like a haberdashery run by a longtime obsessive-compulsive off his meds.

His tailored suits were arranged by color, purpose, and season, as were his shoes on a section of slanted shelves. Drawers with dividers contained folded socks and underwear, fancy knit sweaters, pocket squares, belts, and cuff links. Shirts were sorted by office or leisure. He had a section for casual wear like jeans, shorts, and chinos. A pullout rack held his ties, of which he had more than a hundred, although he generally selected from the same half dozen or so.

He had a watch winder box for his timepieces, a thoughtful Christmas gift from Judith; he tended to wear the same TAG Heuer because he liked the heft and how it felt on his wrist. At one point he'd wanted to purchase a Patek Phillipe but could not justify paying more for a watch than he had spent on his first home.

As he sat in his underwear on the upholstered chair in his closet, he thought back to what Reed Morris had said: *There's more to life than luxury.*

Nash's father would have hated his son's closet, along with pretty much every other facet of his life. Ty Nash had basically worn the same four sets of clothes during the whole time Nash had lived with him. And he had purchased them all at Walmart, just as they had purchased all of Nash's boyhood clothes from there as well.

Judith popped her head in. She was already dressed and looking radiant, the gentle sheen of recent sex imprinted on her high cheekbones.

"Thanks for the workout, big boy, I can skip the gym today."

He knew that Judith would never skip the gym, great sex or not.

"It *was* wonderful."

"I'll get the coffee on. Can I make you breakfast?"

"No, I'm, uh, not really hungry."

"Try to have something, honey, you really can't stand to lose any weight, you know."

"Yeah," he said, his tone now depressed.

Judith seemed to note this, so she perched on his lap, and played with the locket hanging off her chain necklace.

"What happened yesterday was so unfair to you. That...man who said those awful things to you?"

"Shock," he noted.

"Yes, it was completely shocking, all of it."

He took a few moments to explain the man's nickname. "I don't know where it came from, but that's what my dad always called him."

"And the language he used," she continued. "I thought that poor minister was going to have a stroke."

"Yeah, me too."

"Are you going to contact your father's lawyer?"

He had forgotten about that. "I'll call him today."

"I wonder what all that's about. It's not like your dad had much."

"Yes, that's right," he said absently.

"That woman he was living with? She seemed quite odd, almost frightened of you."

"Yes, she did," he agreed.

Judith seemed to sense his absence from the conversation and gently tapped his forehead. "A lot going on in there, right, mister?"

Oh, you have no idea, thought Nash. He said, "Yes. But I'll get through it."

"You always do." She jumped up. "Coffee in five minutes. Chop chop."

She disappeared out the door and Nash suited up for another day at the office, which now would be unlike any other day at the office ever.

CHAPTER

9

NASH WAS IN HIS STUDY packing his briefcase when Maggie appeared in the doorway. She had on a velour warmup suit in a muted shade of rose. Nash could have sworn his mother had worn a similar outfit thirty years ago. But somehow his daughter looked *hip* in it, he concluded.

She waved a folder at him. "Here it is," she said.

"What?" said Nash distractedly.

She carefully laid the folder down in front of him with exaggerated solemnity. "My business proposal, Father dear."

"Your what?"

She became all serious in a single beat. "For my social media influencer platform. I told you I was putting it together. I've worked on it for weeks now, staying up late and everything, drinking espressos and Red Bulls. My business plan, all the numbers, projections. And I was conservative in my forecasting," she added with a knowing look. "Because I know you like *conservative* estimates."

He opened the folder and saw colorful charts and graphs and what looked to be budget and revenue and income projections.

"Okay, I'll take a look at it later."

"Dad, I really need to get going on this."

"I *will* look at it…later, okay? I've got a busy day."

"It's something I'm passionate about. And you always told me to follow my passions."

"But I also said that you had to find a way to pay the rent and utility bills. And food would be good, too. If your passion can do that, great. If it can't you have to pursue your passion in your spare time just like pretty much everyone without a big trust fund."

"I think this can both be my passion and also allow me to pay the light bill."

"And the rent," he pointed out. "And food. Not much works without food."

"I thought I'd live here until I got things really rolling."

Of course you did, thought Nash.

"So you'll look at it?"

"I said I would, and I will. But not now."

Her pouty look vanished and she assumed a genuinely worried expression. "You…doing all right, Dad, after yesterday? I mean that—"

He cut in, "I'm fine."

"Are you sure? Because that was the most unusual funeral service I've ever been to. And *I* felt weirded out, so I can only imagine what it did to you."

"I went to funerals like that all the time when I was your age," he lied.

"Wow, okay. But who was that big Black guy with the foul mouth? He, like, just took over the whole thing and was just spouting stuff. I think he was high on something."

"He was my dad's best friend."

"But he didn't have to do that stuff in front of everybody. It was embarrassing."

"Well, my dad was that way to me, too, so there is that consistency."

Nash could tell that she was having a hard time figuring out his bizarre attitude on this, and, truth be known, so was he.

In a calmer tone he said, "Look, I'm sorry, Maggie. I know I'm not making much sense, and I don't mean to be so short with you. I…I just have a lot going on right now."

"I get it." She looked up at him with a timid expression. "So, is that why I never met your dad? Because he didn't like you?"

"Pretty much, yeah. He wanted nothing to do with me or my family."

"Well, his loss." She tapped the folder. "Whenever you can get to it." She leaned over and gave him a peck on the cheek. "And thanks for being a great father, unlike the guy we just buried."

"Uh-huh, yeah."

With a confused and somewhat defeated expression, Maggie left him alone.

When he saw the velour suit disappearing out the door, Nash thought, *I wonder how she'll feel about zero funds for her influencer/ creator platform when we all go into Witness Protection?*

But then Nash reminded himself that he had not agreed to help the Bureau. Hell, he had no evidence that Rhett or anyone else at the company had done anything wrong. He had to believe that the FBI did not make it a policy to just make unproven statements about such serious matters, but still.

How can I agree to help them unless I'm reasonably sure what they're telling me is true?

He drove to the offices of Sybaritic Investments, which occupied the four top floors in one of the tallest buildings in the downtown area. The place was expensively built out and had all the bells and whistles that the monied field of private equity typically offered their employees: a subsidized dining room, a gym, an on-call massage therapist, and free dry cleaning (up to a limit), because when you worked twelve or more hours a day, who had the time to run errands, eat, or work out? Nash was also on the company's board of directors, and he knew that the current financial situation wasn't the best it had been. Total revenue, profit, and free cash flow were all down, but his division was making money hand over fist.

But if Agent Morris is to be believed, my business home for nearly twenty years is a house of cards about to come tumbling down, and they want me to help them do the tumbling.

He pulled into his reserved space in the parking garage, hefted his briefcase, and headed to the twin glassed-in elevators. He got off on his floor and nodded at the woman who sat alone behind a futuristic-looking, wood-and-metal receptionist's station in a spacious and elegantly decorated reception area. Ellen Douglas was a prim and proper woman in her fifties who sometimes brought cookies to the office. She smiled at him and said hello as he passed through the secure door by swiping his badge on the port sensor.

His office was adjacent to Rhett Temple's. The man's door was closed and Nash couldn't see a light on under it. Rhett didn't usually come in early, but he normally stayed quite late. He worked hard, Nash had to give him that. If he didn't have such a chip on his shoulder because of his daddy issues, he might actually make a good executive one day.

But that point was moot if he was a crook.

Nash shut his door behind him, sat at his desk, placed his palms against his blotter, and stared at the opposite wall. Whenever he'd had to make an important decision in his life, he'd followed the advice laid out by his mother to him when he was thinking about colleges. She'd said to take out a piece of paper and make two columns. On the left were the pros of a decision and on the right were the cons.

For obvious reasons Nash did not want to commit anything to paper, so he did this calculation in his head.

Okay, if I'm convinced what Morris said is true, let's walk through this.

The pros of working with the FBI: One, avoiding criminal prosecution if they found someone else to be their spy and he got caught up in all the indictments. Two, knowing that he did the right thing to bring down bad actors. Three...Nash couldn't think of another reason.

Then the cons of working with the FBI: One, he could be killed while snooping. Two, he could still be swept up in a criminal prosecution if the FBI decided to screw him. Three, his wife and daughter would never forgive him for upending their lives and being forced to go into Witness Protection. Four, he could be killed *after* he went into Witness Protection by the dangerous people who got away.

Nash could think of a half dozen more, but what did it matter?

He loosened his tie, collected all the air he could in his lungs, held it for four seconds, and blew it out for the same span of time. When he was a child, his father had taught Nash how to do that when he was nervous or anxious about something, which was almost every minute of his young, angst-ridden life.

Ty Nash had lectured, "Everybody gets scared, sonny boy. But you can control your fear. You got the keys to the car, so to speak. Suck the air in for a count of four, hold that baby for four seconds, and then let it out for another four, hold it for another four, then do it all over again. See, that gives you control back. Pulse goes down, blood pressure goes down, clammy skin goes away, upset stomach no longer upset. Your brain is telling its little scare demons to back the hell off and let the adults control the room again, you got that?"

A young Nash had nodded and said yes he had got it.

"And you keep on doing it until those bad boys go back to sleep. It worked for me in combat, so it'll work for you with whatever crap's going on in your life."

And it *had* worked for Nash. Through all the traumas boys normally went through while they were navigating puberty and girls and, well, everything.

The only times it *hadn't* worked was when his father had cleaned his clock after the tennis-football thing, and then every time after that with anything having to do with Tiberius Nash.

Nash finished his breathing exercises, and he did indeed calm.

Seeking a distraction from the momentous decision he was going to have to make, he pulled out the card from Mort Dickey, picked up his phone, and called the man, wondering if he had two possible catastrophes to deal with instead of merely one.

CHAPTER

10

I THINK IT BEST IF WE meet in person," said Mort Dickey over the phone.

"I have a busy week," said Nash. He glanced at the calendar on his computer screen and his spirits fell. He had to travel out of town in two days' time. "If we can't talk now, how about a Zoom?"

"I'm an old-fashioned lawyer, Mr. Nash. I don't really like being on camera. So, for me, *zoom* can remain a verb."

"All right. How about tomorrow morning at eight?"

"You can't do later?"

"Eight thirty. That's the best I can do," said Nash. "I'm scheduled to travel out of town early the next morning and I have a full calendar tomorrow."

"Eight thirty then. Your father said you were some sort of bigshot money guy."

"I'm surprised he knew anything about me," replied Nash tersely.

"Oh, he knew a lot, Mr. Nash. A lot."

Nash did not like the sound of that. "You intimated that my father had left me something and I was his named executor?"

"Correct."

"What does the estate consist of?"

"Tomorrow, Mr. Nash. As you said, you're a *busy* man, and I don't like conducting business over the phone any more than I do over *zooms*."

Dickey hung up on him and Nash slowly set his phone down on his desk.

Someone knocked on his door. "Yes?"

His heart skipped a beat when the door opened revealing Rhett Temple.

He rose so fast he smacked his knee on the desk's edge.

"Rhett, what…I mean, how are you doing?"

Rhett came forward, looking deeply embarrassed. "First I want to apologize for missing the funeral. They screwed up my calendar and had the wrong day listed. I'm really sorry. I hope things went as well as possible under the circumstances."

"Yes, yes, they did," answered Nash, who was actually thankful that his boss had not been there to witness the personal insults his executive VP had suffered. "And it's no big deal."

"It *is* a big deal, Walter. It was your father. Were you two close?"

"We sort of drifted apart as the years went by."

Rhett perched on the edge of Nash's desk. "I also had flowers delivered to your house this morning. They must have missed you?"

"Yes, but I'm sure Judith or Maggie was there to receive them. Thank you."

"And how is that daughter of yours doing? I remember when she interned here one summer. She is smart, very quick to pick up on things."

"Maggie wants to be a social media influencer and online content creator instead of going to college."

"She'll do great. And let's face it, Walter, appearances count. And she's got all that, just like her mother."

"Well, we'll see how it turns out."

Rhett looked around Nash's office. "I wish my space were this tidy."

"I like things to be organized. Makes me more efficient."

"Speaking of, your earnings quarter is shaping up to be a blowout one. Thanks for all the hard work and contributions to the bottom line."

Nash managed a smile. "That's what you pay me for. And the work is…challenging, and I like a challenge."

Like maybe bringing you and this place down brick by brick, he thought.

"Well, carry on, and, again, my deepest condolences."

"Thank you."

Rhett turned his back on Nash, gave an exaggerated eye roll to the wall, and left.

Nash stood there rubbing his knee and wondering what the hell all that was about.

It was clear to him that Rhett had never intended to go to his father's funeral. So, what were the apology and the flowers for? Wait, did he know the FBI was sniffing around and he was wondering if they might have contacted Nash?

The weight of all of this collapsed his slender legs, and he fell heavily back into his chair. He looked at his phone, where Reed Morris's number was listed under *X* in his contacts. Should he call him? And tell him what? That his chief target had apologized about the funeral and sent flowers? Why would Morris give a crap about that? The federal agent probably wouldn't see any connection or threat to his case from flowers and apologies.

Maybe I'm just being paranoid, but who the hell can blame me?

He concentrated on his work, which included a slew of brief in-person meetings with various members of his team, emails to read and write, Zooms, and phone conversations in different time zones going over a dozen pending deals, and a host of early due diligence work on several potential acquisitions. Before he knew it, it was well past lunchtime. Nash normally had his secretary call something in for him and then ate at his desk. But today he decided to stretch his legs and go for a walk.

He headed to a deli a few blocks from his office and got a pastrami and rye, some Old Bay chips, a giant pickle, and a cup of black coffee. He ate at a white plastic table in the back of the shop while brooding over his predicament.

A titan of investment eating a pastrami and rye and a fat pickle on a plastic chair.

Normally, Nash would have laughed at this silly thought. But not today.

After coming back from the restroom, Nash saw his bill was waiting for him. He saw another piece of folded paper tucked under it. Nash looked up quickly but saw only two customers who weren't paying him the least bit of attention, the waiter, a woman at the cash register, and the short-order cook in the back. There was no one else in the place.

However, there was an address on the note, walkable from here. Whoever it was wanted to meet with him, in ten minutes.

Trying to remain calm, Nash paid his bill and got a fresh coffee in a to-go cup. He walked at a leisurely pace, but every step felt like he was hauling a ton of bricks on his back.

Someone is obviously watching me. It has to be Reed Morris. When he said a bit of time, he apparently really meant it.

When he rounded the last corner and approached his destination he started to do his breathing exercises. Nash had not made a decision, and he didn't see how he could without first finding out if there *was* criminal activity at his company. And if he did decide to work with the FBI, he needed to make a full disclosure to his wife and daughter.

He was so absorbed in these thoughts that he nearly bumped into someone.

"Excuse me." But then Nash froze as he focused on the tall woman with the long face.

What was the name again? Right, Rosie Parker, partner and lover to my late father.

"Mr. Nash?" she said tentatively, her features full of the same heightened nervousness he had observed at the church.

"Yes? Wait, did you leave that note with my bill?"

"I did," she conceded.

"How did you manage that? I never saw you."

"Your bill came right after you went to use the restroom. I slipped it in then."

"So you were following me. Why?"

"I saw you leave your office. Um, have...have you talked to that lawyer yet? I saw him give you his card at the cemetery."

"Mort Dickey? Yes, but only to make an appointment to meet with him. Why?"

"Your...father promised me certain things, Mr. Nash."

She wants her piece of the pie. "What did he promise you, Ms. Parker?"

"Please call me Rosie."

"And I'm Walter."

"He, well, he said I could stay in the house."

"All right. Is that also in his will?"

"I don't know. I never saw his will."

"Do you have some proof that that was his wish?"

Despite his natural suspicions, Nash couldn't help but feel sorry for the woman. Her clothes suggested extremely limited means, something he had earlier noted at the funeral service. And she was very thin and just looked worn down.

"No," she said softly.

"Okay, well, if you can find some proof that would be good. I will learn the details of the will when I meet with Mr. Dickey. What is your cell phone number?"

"I don't have a cell phone."

That wasn't unduly surprising to Nash. His father had never had a cell phone, at least that he knew of, though Nash had bought his mother one.

"Okay, but my father had a house phone. Is that still active?"

"Yes."

Nash recalled the number from his childhood. He repeated it to her to make sure it hadn't changed and she said, "That's the number, yes."

"Okay, I'll call you after I've met with Dickey. I have to travel out of town shortly, so it might be after that." When tears started to well up in her eyes he said firmly, "Rosie, if my father wanted you taken care of, you will be taken care of, all right? I give you my word."

"Yes sir. All right. Thank you."

He stood there looking at her for a moment, his curiosity ratcheting up. "How did you and my father meet?"

"I work at the VA. He came in for treatment for his…troubles."

"I see. And what do you do at the VA?"

"I…do the bedpans, turn the patients on their backs and stomachs, pick them up when they fall. I help them safely walk the halls during their rehab. Whatever they need. I'm very strong and I work hard. I really do, sir."

To Nash, it seemed Parker wanted to communicate that she was no freeloader.

"That *is* very hard work that not many people would be capable of doing. I'm sure you have helped a great many people who needed it."

She glanced at him. "You're nothing like Ty said you were."

"And what did he say I was like?"

"He said you were one mean bastard. That was why I was so nervous at the church."

"I am many things, but a mean bastard is not one of them."

"What Shock said to you at the church? It wasn't right," added Parker firmly.

"But he *was* a wonderful friend to my father. Especially after my mother died."

"How did you know that? Your father told me that you two weren't close."

The information about Shock's consoling his father had come from the neighbor, Harriet Segura. She had told Nash that she had seen Shock over there nearly every day for six months after Nash's mother had passed away.

Out in the backyard, holding Ty in his arms while the man was sobbing his heart out. Never seen two men, especially two men like that, act that way. What friends are supposed to be. That Isaiah York—love him or hate him, he's the real deal.

"I had ways of keeping tabs on my father," he replied. "Though I didn't know about you." He appraised her. "But you were clearly very important to him, Rosie."

"He was a complicated man, your father. But he was real good to me."

"Do you have any idea why he would have made me the executor of his estate? Did he ever mention me other than to say I was a mean bastard?"

"A few things here and there," Parker said cautiously.

Nash checked his watch. "Look, when I get back to town we can meet."

"You can come by the house. I mean, it's your house now."

"We won't know that until the will terms are disclosed. But that would be nice. I haven't been there...in a while. I'll give you a call."

"Thank you, Mr. Nash."

"Please, I said it was Walter."

"I...I know. But—"

"But what?"

"You just seem like Mr. Nash to me. I know you're quite important."

"Who told you that?"

"I've got to go. I have to catch the bus."

"Do you need a ride? I can call you an Uber."

"No, I...no, the bus. I prefer it. Goodbye."

Her long legs and powerful strides ate up the pavement in huge chunks. No doubt her physical labor at the VA kept the woman strong and vigorous. And thin.

Nash walked off wondering who in his father's world would ever have considered him important.

II

Nash took an unplanned yet significant detour on the way home that night.

He passed old houses that had been on his morning paper route when he was thirteen. His mother had fretted over him disappearing alone on his bike into the predawn hours. His father, unsurprisingly, had said it would put much-needed hair on his chest. He'd actually made a weapon for Nash out of a short, thick rubber hose with a half-pound slug wedged inside one end. His father had then capped and secured that end with black electrician's tape.

"Anything weird, you hit first and ask questions later," his father had instructed him.

Their next-door neighbor had owned a dog named Rusty. He was a messy-looking mutt with short legs and a bark that would freeze you in your tracks. But he was actually a lovable, friendly canine whom Nash had wanted to adopt because he didn't think the neighbors took good enough care of him. The animal was always chained in the backyard, and its home was a small wooden hovel that was covered with snow in the winter and like an oven during the summer. Nash would bring Rusty water every day when it was hot and he would haul over old blankets in the winter so the dog would be warm enough. Nash would lie face down, partially inside Rusty's doghouse, lay his head against Rusty's mangy fur and…dream.

Then one day Rusty was gone. The neighbors said he had run off. But Nash had seen the chain with Rusty's collar still attached. A distraught Nash had gotten his mother involved with Rusty's owners, an unfriendly couple named Donohue. After his mother could make no headway his father had taken up the cause. Nash had watched anxiously while his father trudged over and knocked on the Donohues' door. He stood there talking to them. When he came back, his father would not meet his son's eye.

"They gave Rusty away, to a farmer with a lot of land where he can run and have fun."

Nash did not believe a word of this. Why would Rusty's collar have been left behind? When he asked his father this very question, his dad had gotten upset and told Nash to man up.

Nash had waited until dark, then slipped over the fence with a flashlight and investigated further. When he'd found blood in Rusty's doghouse and bits of fur that looked like it had been torn away from the dog, he had gone back to his room and sobbed the night away. Something had clearly attacked and killed Rusty. And the Donohues, who had never loved or properly taken care of the animal, had probably chucked his carcass in the trash.

And worse still, his father had lied to him.

As Nash turned the corner onto his old street he wondered if the falling-out between him and his father had actually started then, and not with the tennis-over-football decision.

I guess he didn't think I could handle the hard truths, wimp that I was.

He slowed as he approached his old home and was startled to see that it was in far better shape than he would have thought. When his mother had been alive she had done her best to keep the property in decent condition. And Nash had provided funds for her to hire people who could help her do so. To keep his father from the truth, they had worked out a cover story of his mom's having inherited from an elderly relative.

The old siding had been replaced, the porch redone, and the roof looked to have recently been reshingled. The house had no garage, but there was a carport on the side. However, there was no vehicle there. The last time Nash had checked, his father had still possessed his battered Ford Bronco, a relic from the 1990s.

His dad also had his Harley, but he didn't see it anywhere on the property. It was possible that when his days were growing short Ty Nash had sold it or given it away.

Nash pulled to the curb. The houses on either side of his father's place were not in good shape. Old cars with missing tires and doors were up on cinderblocks at both residences; the screen front door was hanging off one, and the other one's front door was absent its glass, the hole covered over with gray duct tape. The general air of neglect and poverty permeated the entire street.

Even the widowed Harriet Segura's home, nicely kept up when he'd been young, was now showing its age. A few flowers had been put in cracked plastic tubs on the front porch but now drooped in the heat. The chain-link fence encircling her backyard was leaning over in places, the poles' cement footers having given up the fight to weather, gravity, and time. Her siding was dented and stained with dirt and algae. The years left their mark on all things, he knew.

Nash watched as two young men completed a drug deal involving small packets of white powder exchanged for cash; a young woman dressed in next to nothing vaped away and checked her phone as two ogling teenage boys followed her like lovesick puppies.

The other homes appeared to have young families living in them, no doubt the only residences they could afford in a country where decent homes in safe neighborhoods for hardworking people apparently couldn't be had for reasonable prices. Banged-up bikes, tattered Big Wheels, plastic toys, and rusty play sets were scattered all over the browning grass. A bicycle jump—improvised from a long, curved plank, a couple of sawhorses, and a dented fifty-gallon drum lying on its side—took up much of the front yard of one home, which was also flying a DON'T TREAD ON ME flag.

Two bare-chested men glistening with sweat labored over a jacked-up Dodge Charger parked at the curb, their heads and torsos leaning into the engine compartment and only surfacing for a beer or a tool. When they threw unfriendly glances Nash's way, as he sat there in his suit and tie and fancy foreign ride, Nash quickly put the Rover in gear and pulled away.

This trip down memory lane had been a complete waste of time when he didn't have time to waste. He drove across town to his gated community and walked in from the garage to receive an embrace from his wife.

"Look at these flowers, Walter. They're from Rhett. Came this morning along with a wonderful sympathy card." She pointed out a large glass vase full of red, yellow, and purple blossoms that were quite lovely.

"Yes, he mentioned to me that he was sending them. He apologized for missing the funeral. Some calendar mix-up."

"I didn't really think Rhett had that side to him. He's handsome, and rich of course, with a certain charm. But there's always been something about him. A level of—"

"—disingenuousness?" suggested Nash.

"Exactly." She smiled. "Here I'm the English Lit person and you the business side, and you came up with exactly the right word."

"That's because some businesspeople are quite disingenuous."

He again felt his gut burn. *Just tell her, for God's sake. You've never held anything of importance from this woman. You've made every major decision together.*

But his abject fear simply would not let the necessary words form.

And what if the FBI lied to me? What if there is no proof of wrongdoing? How can I blow up my life for that? And Judith's and Maggie's?

Judith said, "Dinner will be ready shortly. Line-caught salmon in a nice white wine reduction sauce I've been itching to make, broccoli, couscous, and my summer starter special: feta, watermelon, arugula, and blueberries with lemon and olive oil dressing. Oh, did you talk to the lawyer, what's-his-name?"

"Mort Dickey. Yes. We're meeting tomorrow morning. I'm going over to his office." He added in a nervous tone, "I...I went by my old neighborhood today."

She turned back from the stovetop, where she had multiple operations ongoing. "Feeling nostalgic after your father's passing? That's perfectly natural."

"Dad's house looks, well, like he put some real money into it."

She glanced curiously at him. "Really? I didn't think he had the funds to do that. Unless...you?"

"I helped Mom with funding maintenance and such, but nothing to do with renovating and fixing the home's exterior—the roof and siding. That must have come from Dad."

He perched on one of the stools set around the large granite-topped island. "I also...ran into Rosie Parker."

"Who? Oh, your father's...*friend*? Another odd bird, if you ask me."

Nash decided not to tell her of the *odd* circumstances of how they had met today; it might upset his wife to know that a stranger was inserting cryptic messages in his deli bill. "She said that Dad wanted her to be able to stay in the house."

"Is she named in the will?"

He grabbed a handful of raw almonds from a bowl and popped one into his mouth. "Don't know. I'll find out tomorrow. She seemed pretty desperate. They met when he was at the VA hospital for treatment. She works there."

Judith eyed him sharply. "How desperate?"

"I don't think she has much."

"Okay, but don't get sucked in by some sob story, Walter. I know people look at you and see this hard-ass businessman. But I also know how kind and generous you are."

"I don't intend to get sucked in by anyone," he said emphatically. And now he was not simply referring to Rosie Parker, but also FBI Special Agent Reed Morris.

After dinner he went to his study to finish reviewing some profit projections, budget forecasts, and other essentials for his upcoming trip when there came a tap on his door.

Maggie poked her head in. "I got your text. So, you read it?"

He nodded and motioned her in. As she sat across from him he pulled out her proposal, which had his notes scribbled all over it. This had taken up a chunk of his afternoon because he knew it was important to her.

I really hoped it would be…better than it is. Well, here goes.

She smiled. "So what do you think? Be brutal, I can take it."

"Okay, you have $201,670 in your college fund and you need that *plus* another three hundred thousand to *initially* fund your business? Jesus, Maggie."

Her pleasant look faded. "Well, I want to hit the ground running. If I build up enough momentum I figure I can hit positive cash flow in eighteen months."

"Almost all of these expenses are for first-class air and train travel, hotels, restaurants, concerts, clothes, shoes, and third-party vendors. Not a single appreciating asset or an asset of any kind at all. Just outflows to other vendors, leaving you with zip. You even have trips to the Cannes and Sundance Film Festivals in there."

"Right. But my whole influencer market segment is lifestyle, Dad. Fashion, film, food, music, going places, experiencing cool, transformational moments in time."

"In addition to France and Utah, you also have Milan, Tokyo, Paris, Hong Kong, Abu Dhabi, Stockholm, Santiago, and some place in Vietnam I've never heard of."

"Hoi An. It's like the coolest clothing mecca. Have you ever been to Vietnam?"

"No, but my father went there. Only it wasn't for cool clothing. And then there're tickets to see Rhianna in Rio, Taylor Swift in Singapore, and Billie Eilish in London."

"Those are some of the events I'll be reporting on. Local flavor, food, music, the vibe on the ground. It's an experience guide for my generation. Even if they don't get to ever go to those places or attend those concerts, they can see them through my unique prism."

You mean your bubbled, pampered, entitled, paid-for-by-somebody-else prism? mused her father. *And whose fault is that?* he also thought.

Nash said, "It sounds to me like a yearlong vacation that adds up to half a million bucks."

Her look transformed from pouty to angry. "You obviously did not get my point. The numbers are all there. You like numbers, right? So there they are."

"I *appreciate* numbers that make sense. These do not. And I can't let you waste your college money on something like this. You will come out of this with no funds for your education, leave me in the hole for three hundred grand, but you will have had a really great twelve months of first-class fun and no responsibility."

"You don't know the influencer world at all."

He glanced at some notes he'd made on a legal pad. "I actually did some digging into that today. The competition is fierce and the platforms have gotten a lot savvier about how much they pay and how they hold creators accountable. Every industry has that Wild West phase initially, where absurd amounts of money are thrown at anyone with a heartbeat and a half-assed concept, but then the easy times are over. That's where your space is currently. It's matured to the point where fundamental metrics now rule the day."

"Fresh content is always going to be needed," she retorted. "And I have a runway to making substantial profits. It just takes time. And I'm not counting on one revenue stream. You always taught me to not put all my eggs in one basket."

"That's all good, Maggie, it really is. But even if you have over 500,000 followers and you post *daily* content that routinely achieves over 100,000 views, you'll be compensated less than $60,000 annually. Now keep in mind that's *gross* revenue, not profit. And you have no guarantees you'll consistently hit those numbers. And many of your competitors are posting multiple videos every day. That is one hell of a workload, especially when you're traveling all over the world. And to keep your product fresh and professional looking you're probably going to have to hire contractors to help you. That's another expense that will come out of your revenue. You might actually end up in the negative when all is said and done."

"But there are multiple revenue streams, Dad, like I said," protested Maggie. "And I know other people who have started these lifestyle-focused platforms and they're doing really well. It's all about building up initial subscription bases, and eyeballs to get ad revenue, providing cool and exclusive content that will lead to premium paying viewers, and cultivating sponsorship relations. And I picked my subject matter because people are huge fans of entertainment, travel, food, and high culture."

"Granted, you can earn direct revenue, tips, and the like from the paying subscriber base of your platform, as well as monies from sponsored content, brand partnerships, and also commission sharing from both digital product and merchandise sales, as well as affiliate links. But fully half the creators online now make less than $15,000 annually. There was one creator I looked at who has nearly two million followers and posts content that routinely gets hundreds of thousands of views. She was paid a little over ten grand last year. And on top of that you get no paid time off and have no health care or retirement benefits. It's a recipe for disaster, and I can't support it."

He looked up from his notes. "Well, Maggie, you asked for brutal. There it is."

"So your answer is no?" she said quietly.

"I want the absolute best for you, honey. I would support you if I thought this had any chance of having a positive outcome. But the odds are just not with you. You might as well go play roulette in Vegas with your college fund."

"So, in other words, you have no confidence in me? You just lump me in with all the other losers out there, is that it? You don't think I can beat the odds?"

"I do not consider you in any way to be a loser. I just think that your talents can be pointed in other directions. If not this or college, perhaps another business idea?"

"What, a dog-grooming business? Or how about carpet cleaning?"

"People do need their dogs groomed, and their carpets done. And both are respectable ways to make a living. And you can get into both for less than a half million in cash—and you'll be buying assets with that cash, not paying other people so you can run around the world and have fun."

She got up, snatched her proposal off his desk, and slammed the door behind her.

Nash sat there with his eyes closed.

Was I too harsh? Would I have come down that hard if it hadn't been my flesh and blood? No, I actually let her down easy, only it sure doesn't feel like that right now.

He opened his eyes and stared at the door through which his angry and bitter daughter, no doubt hating the thought of him right now, had disappeared.

What if Maggie and I fall into the sort of relationship I had with my father?

He refocused, finished his work, and then made the call. He was now doing what he should have already done. Not finding out if his company was engaged in criminal activity, but something even more fundamental: seeing if Special Agent Reed Morris really was who he said he was.

CHAPTER

12

Hello, Hal, Walter Nash. You got a few minutes? I'd like to pop over. Great, thanks."

Hal Rankin lived on the next street over. A former FBI agent, he had cashed in by starting his own private security consulting business. Nash had met him at several neighborhood events and he seemed like a rock-solid guy; he had regaled Nash and other neighbors with tales from his federal law enforcement days.

Rankin greeted him at the front door with two glasses of red wine in hand, one of which he passed to Nash. He suggested they take a walk in the backyard, which, like Nash's, had a large pool and immaculate landscaping. This was the sort of community where keeping up with the Joneses had been taken to a high art form.

Rankin was medium height, stockily built, and about twenty years older than Nash. He didn't look like much of a tough guy, but Nash supposed modern policing required far more brains than brawn. Nash wondered how long before the day came when all cops would be superstrong and hyperintelligent robots that could not be killed or outwitted by humans.

Now that *should be a wake-up call to us all.*

"So, what's up, Walt?" said Rankin as they stopped for a moment to admire a stone waterfall set in the middle of the yard right off the pool. Its water cascaded down a slope and collected at the bottom before being recycled back to the top to repeat the process.

For a moment Nash saw an image of his own life in that Sisyphean endeavor.

"Walt?" prompted Rankin.

Nash had worked up what he hoped was a plausible cover story to elicit the information he needed.

"As you know, I'm in the investment business. Normally, it's cut-and-dry, the sorts of things we buy and sell, I mean. But occasionally we get something out of my comfort zone and I just wanted to check in with you on one of them."

"I don't know much about your field," began Rankin doubtfully. "I'm just a former federal cop who advises folks on how to keep safe and out of trouble."

"Yes, and you obviously do that very well. But you *would* know something about this potential investment, with which I have no experience whatsoever."

"I'm officially intrigued."

Nash said, "We've been presented with an offer to invest in an independent film."

Rankin looked surprised. "Okay, not what I was expecting. FYI, I know less about making films than I do about investments."

"The thing is the script deals with a man, an ordinary sort of person, who's approached by an FBI agent. Late at night, in the man's home. That's why I thought of you."

Rankin looked interested once more. "What does the agent want?"

"Apparently there's some skullduggery going on at the man's company and the agent wants the fellow to become the Bureau's inside person, like a spy. If he helps bring down the company, he'll go into Witness Protection or some such. And if he doesn't agree to help, well, it might be rough going. They say they have two well-known actors lined up to play the man and the agent. The agent is a woman, and then you get the whole sexual-tension dynamic."

Rankin said knowingly, "And the audience is on tenterhooks waiting to see when they'll fall into bed together?"

"Exactly. But I just found the whole idea sort of unrealistic. I mean, would one meeting be enough to get the man to totally upend his life? And if an audience doesn't believe the basic premise, then the story just doesn't work. And there goes our investment."

"Doesn't the man check out the agent's story to make sure it's authentic?"

"No, and that's what I believe is missing. And how does the guy even know the person who made contact with him is an actual FBI agent? And without that, I just think the story fails."

"Can I have a gander at the script?"

"I'd love to, but I had to sign the mother of all NDAs."

"Of course. Well, there's an easy enough solution you can suggest to the writer."

"There is?" Nash said innocently.

Rankin smiled. "Walt, the FBI's not some clandestine organization keeping the identities of its agents a top secret. We leave that to our brethren at the CIA. In the script I presume the agent left the man with his business card?"

"Yes, that's actually on page four," lied Nash.

"Then your man can check online to verify the phone number belongs to the local FBI office, or another office if the agent is not from the area. He can then call that number and ask for the agent."

"Even though it's all hush-hush?"

"I don't mean scream to the world that there's an investigation ongoing with the man's company. But if the person purporting to be an agent is actually an agent, they will verify his status with the Bureau. And if the writer wants to really make sure, he can have the character request a meeting with the agent's associates and/or superiors to ensure that this is not some sort of scam. They'll need to do that anyway to prep the guy for what they want him to do. Then the audience will follow the rest of the film while gorging themselves on popcorn and Junior Mints until the guy and the gal escape death and jump into bed."

"Does the Bureau even do that sort of thing? Enlist people on the inside to act as, well, a mole or something?"

"All the time. How else can we get to the dirt? In fact, it's quite often the case that the person recruited to act as an informant has committed crimes. That way the Bureau can put the screws to the person to get them to cooperate. You go after the low-hanging fruit and pressure them with prison time to make them flip against the top folks. That's a classic technique."

Nash took a sip of his wine to steady his nerves. "I'm not sure the writer has really put that in there, either."

"Give him that suggestion, too. Hell, maybe I can get a partial screenwriter credit."

The two men laughed, Rankin genuinely and Nash just for effect.

"One other question I had was, why should the potential inside guy take the FBI's word that his company is engaged in criminal activity? I mean, couldn't they lie about that? Wouldn't the man need more proof before agreeing to help? I mean, if he wasn't a criminal himself, like you were saying."

Rankin turned serious. "In my experience the Bureau does not approach a potential target unless they have evidence of potential wrongdoing, Walt. It would be a waste of time and resources, and there are laws against fishing expeditions and defamation and the like. It might not be enough to execute arrest warrants and take to trial, but they have to have a compelling basis to initiate something like that. Hey, if the writer wants to put in that the guy is snooping around on his own to find out the dirt before making a decision to help, that would be plausible. I actually had that happen on a case I handled. And it could add some excitement. You know, will he or won't he get caught, that sort of thing? And maybe while he's doing that the gal agent saves his butt at the last second and they fall into bed earlier than the third act." Rankin guffawed over that one while Nash could only manage a smile.

As they walked back to the house Nash said, "I guess the last question I have is motivation—for the spy, I mean."

"Like I said, Walt, most of the people who do this sort of thing are criminals themselves. So they really don't have a choice."

"You said you had worked some cases like this?"

"Quite a few. Organized crime. South American drug cartels. Some white-collar stuff right here. Household-name firms up to their armpits in shit you wouldn't believe. Environmental polluters, fake or faulty parts for aircraft or cars. I can tell you stories about Big Pharma that would curl your hair. I swear to God it's like corporate folks sit around all day thinking of ways to poison, maim, and cheat us, all in the name of the almighty dollar."

"So how did you nail folks like that?"

"Corralled some high-level executive types and squeezed them, hard. They cried like babies, but they went along with it. Then they went into WITSEC. And they kissed all their money and big homes bye-bye." He chuckled. "They had to live like the rank-and-file for once. I remember the cases I'd work with the U.S. marshals. We'd ship most of these former rich assholes off to the wilds of Oregon or Bumfuck, Idaho. They'd end up working for minimum wage at a Dollar General, but they should've gone to prison."

"Uh-huh, wow, that is amazing," said Nash, trying to keep from hyperventilating.

"We always approached the target in secret, of course. We didn't want to give away the game from the start."

"And how did things go for the most part?" Nash asked.

"A slew of really big victories and a few defeats."

"You don't often hear of the big victories."

Rankin shrugged. "That's because the company's lawyers would often negotiate secret big-dollar settlements and no admitting of a criminal act by the corporation, but they still paid a big price and some folks went to prison."

"And the inside people working with the FBI?"

"I have to admit, going into WITSEC did cause a great deal of problems in the families. As you can imagine spouses and children living an upscale life don't appreciate having to get by on scraps. Broke up a lot of families. But you may not want that in the movie. End the film with the sex. Everyone will be happier."

"And the few defeats?" Nash said, his voice a bit raspy with anxiety.

"The moles got caught and didn't make it through still breathing. Nature of the game, unfortunately. But like I said, most of them were crooks, too. Bad acts catch up to you. I never cried over any of that. Sleep with the devil, you know."

Rankin slapped Nash on the shoulder, startling him so badly he nearly spilled his wine. "So stick to fiction, Walt. Lot safer."

Rankin's laughter and words rang in Nash's head all the way home.

CHAPTER

13

NASH CAME IN THROUGH THE garage and noted that his daughter's BMW was not there.

Oh boy.

His wife was in the kitchen and she marched toward him, the look on her features a warning light blinking brightly in Nash's face.

"What did you say to her?" Judith demanded, her usually lovely eyes now seeming like twin electrical circuits misfiring.

Nash sighed. "She gave me a proposal for her influencer business. She asked for my honest opinion. I gave it."

"She ran out of here crying and drove off in a terrible state. I hope to God she doesn't get into an accident."

"Look, Maggie basically wanted to *blow* her college fund plus three hundred thousand more of *our* money on traveling around the world in high style to concerts and Cannes and expensive restaurants with no prospect of making any actual money. Nice job if you can get it," he added. "But she won't be getting it from me."

"You must have been very harsh for Maggie to storm out of here like that."

"She asked me to be brutal and I was *candid*, like I would be with anyone else."

This comment did not smooth over matters. Judith fingered the locket at the end of her necklace and snapped, "She's not anyone else. She's your daughter!"

"Do you really want her wasting a half million dollars of our money?"

"I'm simply saying that there are different ways to convey your opinion and feelings on the subject. Don't you offer constructive criticism at work?"

"There was nothing I could say constructively about her proposal. And you were the one to tell me not to get suckered in by Rosie Parker."

"How dare you compare our daughter to a woman we don't even know?"

"I didn't mean it that way," protested Nash.

But Judith had already stalked off.

* * *

Nash heard Maggie come home at two in the morning because he stayed up listening for her. He had dreaded getting a visit from the police saying that his daughter had wrapped her BMW around a tree. He had texted her numerous times, but they had all gone unanswered. He had even attempted to call, a blasphemous thing to do to a Gen Z, apparently. It had gone straight to voice mail.

She had stomped up the stairs and slammed the door to her room.

Nineteen going on four, thought Nash. *What did we do wrong? What did I do wrong?*

Later, unable to sleep, Nash went downstairs to his study. He poured out a scotch from his private stock and took it to the back patio. He stood in the exact spot where he'd been when Reed Morris had appeared and torpedoed his life.

He had slipped the man's card into the pocket of his robe, and now he took it out and looked at it. There was an address for an office in town, a main number, and then Morris's extension. Nash had looked up the FBI field office number online, and it matched the number on the card. So it all seemed legit.

And if it is? I have a decision to make. Please let it be a huge prank, Shock crapping on me one last time in my dad's honor. That I can handle.

Two floors above were women he loved dearly and who were

both angry with him. As he then stared out into the darkness it seemed to him that there was something, or someone, out there, watching him.

Okay, Nash, paranoia is not going to help you, but logic and fact-finding will.

Rankin had suggested that a potential target do a little snooping on their own. Thus, Nash sat down in a chair and thought about what Morris had told him. Rhett Temple working with dangerous people. But what exactly was he doing with them? He began to look at this through both his general business prism and his specific knowledge of how Sybaritic Investments operated.

The firm had both working capital and investment funds. The former mostly paid for the salaries, rents, and light bill, and the latter was deployed into other companies as investments. Some of the firm's funds were maintained in accounts at leading financial institutions around the world. All secure, all aboveboard. The invested funds were obviously held and used by the myriad companies in which Sybaritic invested. Nash was head of the division that found, vetted, and closed the deals with the companies they decided to invest in. Sometimes Sybaritic bought specific assets. Occasionally they negotiated a majority stock interest. But they most often purchased the firm outright, everything from rolled-up chains of car washes to real estate to AI enterprises and windmill and solar farms.

The key was picking exactly which companies and sectors to invest in, and Nash was meticulous about that: reading all the available information, going over the numbers with a fine-tooth comb, asking probing questions of both management and rank-and-file employees. Traveling to their places of business; seeing things for himself on the ground; researching competitors, intellectual property strengths and weaknesses; the full business terrain. Sometimes it was the seemingly unimportant facts that turned out to be the most critical.

Sybaritic's bond department was the staid, boring part of the business, but that was the intent. There was nothing champagne-popping about getting a few dozen basis points of return, but they were vital for consistent, dependable cash flow.

The third division at the firm dealt with special deals, which Rhett ran personally. If the FBI was looking for a place where criminal actions were taking place, it would be there. This division was not doing well. They needed grand slams and hadn't registered one in almost two years, while the losses had piled up to nearly unsustainable levels.

So what is Rhett doing on his end that has the FBI interested? And if he's losing his ass on these investments, how is he running a successful criminal enterprise?

He went to bed remaining unconvinced by the FBI's claim about criminal activity. But mostly he wanted his wife and daughter to still love him no matter how all of this played out. Right now Nash didn't see how that was remotely possible.

CHAPTER

14

RHETT TEMPLE STARED DOWN AT the corpse—a fatherly type in his fifties.

The man kneeling next to him with a slim black-matte-finished semiautomatic pistol in hand was John Burr. He was thirty, muscled and tough looking, with the sort of permanent calm in his manner that would never acknowledge being surprised or remotely scared by anything or anyone.

"What are you going to do with the body?" asked Rhett as he studied the bullet hole in the corpse's forehead. "Same as usual?"

Burr shook his head. "Cops eventually catch on to 'same as usual.' So my call is cinderblocks, chains, and deep water. But slit the gut and lungs first."

"Why?"

"Gases build up in the lungs and gut like air in a balloon. And chains and concrete can fail. But if you cut the organs open, it can't float."

"Okay. But we can't keep doing this, either," said Rhett. "The odds against us go up and not down with this sort of stuff."

"You have to take that up with people above my pay grade, Mr. Temple."

"Your cleaning crew on call?"

"They're always on call," Burr replied tersely.

Rhett forced himself to stare down once more at Peter Lombard, until recently a respected member of his local business community. His curiosity had unfortunately propelled him down a path that would now end in deep water, with slit organs and cement booties.

Rhett rose and took in the small space. Concrete floor with plastic laid over, one door in and out, and no windows. All in the middle of nowhere. There was minimal blood and brain matter. Yet he had learned that DNA was like smoke, it got into every nook and cranny. But he also knew that Burr's cleaning crew did a true blitzkrieg on forensic evidence.

"I want you handling the body dump personally."

Burr nodded. "I like to finish what I start."

Rhett knew that he had been forced to travel a long way both to see the dead man and to park himself right in the middle of a murder. Skin in the game, his partner in crime would call it. Only this was the third time now, in the last two years. And he still wasn't used to it.

God help me if I ever get used to this.

"They want you to check in, Mr. Temple, after you…witnessed it."

He looked at Burr. "I got the message and the address."

"And I understand that 'she' will be there tonight."

Something seized up in Rhett's chest. "*She* will?"

"Yes."

"Let me know when it's done."

Rhett left the death room, now thinking only about…*her.*

CHAPTER

15

RHETT REACHED THE ISOLATED HOUSE thirty minutes later and was met out front by the security team. He knew that each of them could shred an NFL lineman or a WWE warrior with their pinky. They scared the piss out of Rhett just by existing.

They checked his ID, though they well knew who he was, and they expertly searched him for weapons, though they knew he never carried any. However, they were part of a world where you did these things routinely, because if you didn't and someone under your protection died, then so would you.

He was escorted inside and up to a room on the second floor. She made him wait for ten minutes before making an appearance, because she could.

Victoria Steers was a few years shy of forty and the product of an Asian mother and a Caucasian father. She stood five nine and was whipcord slender with black hair. She possessed delicate, porcelain-like features that were, in contrast to the hair, as pale as cream. Her voice was nearly as low as a man's, and her manner was understated and sometimes stilted, if somehow still imperious.

Steers was battle hardened in tactics, superbly schooled in ruthless backstabbing, and had absolutely no compunction about killing anyone who might challenge her interests. Rhett had once listened to her unemotionally order the execution of someone, who, up until then, had been one of her closest allies. The message spun off this had been clear and intentional: *No one is safe.*

She appeared dressed in black slacks, an untucked, long-sleeved black shirt, and white tennis shoes with three-inch platforms that brought her up nearly to Rhett's height. She smiled at him, but it was a smile without genuineness. Her small affectation completed, she sat cross-legged on the floor, and motioned for him to join her. More inflexible than the limber Steers, Rhett still managed to get down there with only a bit of a struggle.

"The problem?" she said.

"Solved. Burr is handling disposal."

"And?"

"Deep water, diced organs, and heavy footwear." Rhett hesitated for a moment, drawing up his nerve. "It's the third in two years. That is unsustainable."

"I disagree," said Steers.

"I'm looking at the long game and—"

"That is the only game there is, Mr. Temple. But if you allow yourself to appear weak? Then there is no long game possible because you will not be around to execute it."

"So, if we appear so strong, why does this keep happening?"

"I summoned you here for that very answer," she replied, neatly turning the tables on him.

He leaned back and reconfigured his pretzeled legs to allow him a moment's reflection, better circulation, and a chance to think of a response now that he had lost the advantage.

She beat him to it. "I feel compelled to also ask whether you are feeling out of your depth."

"No," Rhett said instantly because he sensed if he did not, he was dead.

"So explain," Steers ordered.

"I believe this keeps happening because we have a leak somewhere."

"Obviously, and just as obviously that is *your* responsibility," she replied.

"But it seems that every time I close one hole another one pops up. That can't be a coincidence." He glanced at Steers to see the woman's reaction.

"My response to that is exactly the same as my previous one."

"I'm not afraid to ask for advice from someone far more experienced than I am."

He knew that she either bit on this and showed some mercy, or he might suffer the exact same treatment as Peter Lombard had.

"It is not a weakness to seek help from others better established to make decisions of importance," she remarked. "It is a strength. Up to a certain point."

Steers had this awkward way of speaking that he had noted before. But her words were true enough, and even more important, they agreed with his.

"What do you suggest?" he asked.

"That you use the intelligence gained from each 'problem' to make sure there is not an additional 'problem' with which to contend. I sense a pattern here. The government is looking for a pathway in. They have not succeeded yet because we have been too quick for them." She paused. "You have done well on the reaction time, Mr. Temple. But reaction is eventually a losing tactic. So *proactive* is the method we must adopt here."

"And to accomplish that?" he said.

"Observation: The other targets of FBI complicity were all mid-level people who had access to financial information the authorities would find useful. This is correct?"

"Yes," replied Rhett.

"And you and others were able to discover their betrayal and prevent them from reaching the level where any damaging information could be transferred?"

"Also correct." He looked at her expectantly and she gazed back at him with a disappointed expression that froze his blood. He scrambled to think of...

He blurted out, "Then the feds would next look for *highly placed* people, to change things up on us."

"That is how I would perceive the situation, yes."

"Then I just need a way to drill down on who they might target next. And then either eliminate them or convince the person that partnering with the authorities is a bad idea."

"And why not just kill them?"

Rhett was ready for that one. "First, if people keep dying or disappearing, then that will raise suspicion in and of itself. And every death is another opportunity to make a mistake and leave a trail leading right back to us. And second, if I can turn a potential informant into an ally, ensuring their loyalty? That is a good outcome for us."

She allowed him a smile and Rhett realized this had been a test.

"You are required to think at that *heightened* level at all times, Mr. Temple, not simply in rare instances where you are desperate and thus panicked. Panic brings with it a diminishment of judgment that quite often leads to catastrophic results."

He nodded. "I understand."

When she leaned forward Steers was no longer smiling. "Do you really *perceive* exactly what I am attempting to convey to you, Mr. Temple?"

Rhett held her gaze. "I...perceive, Ms. Steers."

She kept eye contact for a few moments before sitting back. "Then my trip here has been worthwhile, and my return journey will be joyful." She dismissed him with a curt wave.

As he rose to leave she said, "One more thing."

"Yes?"

Three men appeared out of the darkness. One pinned Rhett's arms while the other slid his jacket down and ripped open his left shirtsleeve. And though he was young and strong, Rhett was helpless against them.

The third man laid out a large sheet of plastic on the floor. The two other men effortlessly lifted Rhett so that the plastic could be placed under him. Then Rhett felt a blade cut into the flesh of his left arm near his wrist. The cutter casually walked the blade up his arm, neatly missing all veins, arteries, and muscle with a hand well practiced in this form of human carving.

Even restrained as he was, Rhett writhed around a bit, his teeth grinding as he tried desperately not to scream out. He feared that would result in his immediate execution.

When the man reached nearly to Rhett's shoulder capsule, he pulled the knife free. The other men let go their steel grips and Rhett sank to his knees in his own blood on the plastic, and threw up.

Steers nodded at another man who had appeared. He administered an injection to Rhett's arm, causing him to slump unconscious on the plastic.

The men carried Rhett and the plastic, and his blood, out of the room, while Steers sat there with her eyes closed and her breathing subdued.

She appeared to be meditating.

Meanwhile, Rhett was laid on a table in an adjacent space where the bleeding was halted, and his wound thoroughly cleaned, sutured, and bandaged.

When Rhett came to, he was sitting in his Porsche wearing a fresh set of clothes.

Taped to the steering wheel was a piece of paper with words typed on it.

FOR EVERY WRONG THERE MUST BE THE RIGHT PUNISHMENT. FOR EVERY PUNISHMENT THERE IS THE POTENTIAL FOR EVEN MORE. ACT WISELY.

A groggy and still nauseous Rhett rolled up his shirtsleeve, eased back the bandage, and looked at the long, stitched wound. It weaved its way up his arm like a snake, and it ached like he'd been shot. He then noted the bottle on his console.

It was Oxycodone. The dosage and other instructions were on the label.

One pill daily as needed for pain. If you cannot otherwise stand it. And if you cannot otherwise stand it, perhaps you are in the wrong business.

He drove off to catch his private jet ride back home. Despite all that had happened, and now with a permanent scar on his body, Rhett Temple exhaled in relief.

I'm alive.

CHAPTER

16

THE FOLLOWING MORNING JUDITH WAS gone from the bedroom before Nash woke. He imagined he could hear the treadmill in the lower-level gym whirring away. After getting ready for work he passed by Maggie's room and thought he might tap on her door and say some conciliatory words that would soften what he had said before. But he doubted she was even awake, and he doubted he could find the necessary phrases.

He bought a cup of coffee on his way to see Mort Dickey. The man's office was in a strip mall about a mile from his father's home. Dickey and Associates was sandwiched in between a vape shop and a dry cleaner. A forty-year-old pale yellow Mercedes convertible was parked out front. Its vanity plate read THE LAW.

He had to buzz to be let in, and a woman in her sixties greeted him. "Mr. Dickey is expecting you, Mr. Nash. If you'll wait out here, I'll just go and get him."

"Thanks," said Nash as he looked around at an office space that clearly had not seen a serious refreshing in decades.

He sat and spied a *Sports Illustrated* magazine lying on a table. Nash did a double take because Michael Jordan in a Bulls uniform was on the cover. He thought it might have been some sort of recent commemorative edition until he saw the date of the publication on the cover.

Nineteen ninety-six?

He hoped Dickey's legal skills had been kept more updated than his waiting room reading selections.

A minute later the man himself appeared in the doorway and beckoned him back.

The brown three-piece suit hung heavy on the man, and Nash noted the large, blackened mole on his neck as he followed Dickey to his office. Nash didn't see any other people around and wondered if the "and Associates" in the name of the firm still was or had ever been true.

Dickey led him into a cluttered office smelling of cigarettes. It had an oppressive mustiness that Nash would never have tolerated. But then again, Dickey might not have a choice. The lawyer pointed to a stained, upholstered chair. Nash sat and waited as the man pulled out some documents from an estate box labeled TIBERIUS Q. NASH.

Nash knew that the Q stood for Quarles, though his father had never told him where his given names had come from. In fact, while he had met his maternal grandparents, Nash had never met the paternal side of that equation, nor did his father ever speak of his parents. He had learned from his mother that his father's first wife's suicide had occurred while Ty Nash had been deployed in Vietnam. He had no idea why she had taken her own life. But then again that might not be something a husband would divulge to his second wife.

"Not quite the official digs you're used to, I'm sure," said Dickey, with defiance stitched over his grizzled features. That made Nash think that his unspoken opinion of Dickey's office environment had been betrayed in his expression, and the lawyer was calling him out over it.

Dickey added, "I've driven past your building. One of the biggest skyscrapers in town, and you right at the top. In lots of things, so to speak. Symbolic."

Nash made a point of looking around. "But as with any office, the address, size, drapes, carpet, and furniture matter for little. It's the work product that counts, isn't it?"

Dickey's defiant look vanished and was replaced with a more sober expression.

Nash continued. "And the quality of that comes from what's up here." He tapped his forehead. "And since my father entrusted his last wishes to you, Mr. Dickey, you must be decidedly more than competent, because he never suffered fools gladly or any other way."

Nash did not have time to indulge in pointless games with the man. He just needed information so he could make decisions and move forward. That, in essence, had been Nash's entire life: data, consideration, decision, and then move the chess pieces.

A chastened Dickey coughed to clear his throat. "Your father was a good, if demanding, client."

"He could be very demanding, in many ways," remarked Nash.

Dickey spread out some papers, then picked up one set with a blue backing and unfolded it.

"First things first. As I alluded to before, you *are* named as the executor of his estate. He owned the house free and clear. Your father wanted his companion, Rosalyn Parker, to have a life interest in it. But she would be liable for all the payments, taxes, insurance, utilities, and so on. However..."

"However what?"

"He left it to your discretion whether she would get the life interest or not."

"And why would he leave that decision up to me?"

Dickey shrugged. "He didn't confide in me on that point."

"Do you know anything about his and Parker's relationship?"

"She took wonderful care of him. And your father expressed feelings for her to the extent he could for anyone other than your mother."

With this comment, Nash thought that Dickey was more than simply his father's lawyer.

"I know she's employed at the VA, but do you know if she has the financial ability to keep up the property, pay the taxes?"

"She will."

"Meaning my father left her some money?"

"Yes. Now, after Parker's death the house is to be sold and the proceeds donated to the American Cancer Society, in your mother's memory."

Nash sat back. "That was good of him."

"I don't have to tell you that your mother walked on water in your father's eyes."

Nash decided to go there. "You two were not just client and attorney, I take it?"

"We were drinking buddies, you could call us. And I fought in Nam as well, though not with your father. But we had that in common, and it's a lot—more than a lot, actually."

"I'm sure."

"He had savings and checking accounts and a small life insurance policy. Half the money is to go to Isaiah York."

"Shock," noted Nash with a frown.

"By the way, he really unloaded on you at the church service."

"Did you expect otherwise? Which also leads me to ask why my father named me as executor. You said you would fill me in on that?"

Dickey seemed to be working to hold back a smile. "To quote him, your father said you were 'good with stupid shit like that.'"

"Right," replied Nash. "Well, let's get on with the stupid shit, shall we?"

"The rest of the funds go equally to the other members of the, um, motorcycle club. All told those equal around $75,000."

"But I thought you said he had left some monies to Rosie Parker?"

"I'll get to that. He sold the Ford Bronco, and his Harley was left to Shock. I think he may have already picked it up. And his mementos from Vietnam also go to Shock, with the proviso that you can select any you may want beforehand. That includes medals, military papers, weapons, that sort of thing. Shock has been informed of this and is waiting his turn."

Nash was surprised about this testamentary disposition, but didn't remark on it.

"You also have first dibs on your mother's possessions. I'm not sure what they all are, but they may be the usual things—letters, photos, keepsakes, perhaps things from your childhood. There is a small safe and they may be in there." He handed Nash a card. "The code for the safe."

Nash pocketed it. "So he kept my mother's effects?"

"From what I understand, Mr. Nash, he never got rid of anything belonging to her."

Except for me, thought Nash.

"Burial and related expenses have all been paid for, as has my legal fee. And now we get to the remaining item." He picked up some other papers and ran his gaze down them. "You may be aware that back in the 1980s, veterans exposed to Agent Orange settled a class action lawsuit against a number of manufacturers of the chemical herbicide that had been dropped into Vietnam to kill crops and cover foliage being utilized by the North Vietnamese. It was $180 million spread over more than two million veterans—so not that much, actually. But due to some unique conditions pertaining to his individual case, your father also reached a separate settlement with the Army over his Agent Orange exposure."

Nash sat up straighter. "I wasn't aware of that."

"No one was, really. Not even Shock. In 1991 a bill was signed into law designating injuries suffered from exposure to Agent Orange and other herbicides as wartime injuries so that the VA would be responsible for taking care of the medical issues associated with that exposure. That was why your father was able to receive treatment there."

"What unique conditions pertained to my father's case?"

"Again, something I was not privy to. He received the funds shortly after your mother's death. The total amount was $550,000."

Nash sat up even straighter. "My God. That's quite a sum to get out of the military. But I understood that such payments were typically done on a monthly basis and were based on a complicated calculation of the veteran being married or not, how many dependents, the exact harm caused by the Agent Orange exposure, and the like."

"You seem to have done some research into this," observed Dickey.

"When she was alive my mother had some questions, so I tried to find some answers for her."

"Well, you're right, monthly disability payments *are* the norm based on calculations and the elements you just outlined. However, your father argued, successfully, for a lump-sum payment due to some particular circumstances of his case."

"The unique conditions?"

"Yes."

"He did tend to keep things close to the vest."

"I actually initially represented him as I have other veterans in similar situations. For the most part the Army routinely stonewalled them until they either died or gave up or sought payments from the likes of Monsanto and the other manufacturers of Agent Orange. But Ty persisted even after I had told him there was no hope, and he apparently made a forceful case to get such a payout."

"It was in his nature. But if he did so without benefit of legal representation, that was a Herculean feat."

Dickey smiled and his eyes danced as a result. "Didn't you know, Mr. Nash?"

"Know what?"

"Your father *was* Hercules." Dickey looked down at the papers. "The amount was not taxable under the prevailing law. So he immediately invested all the money in a portfolio of good stocks and also some high-quality bonds. And he reinvested all the bond interest, dividends, after tax, etc. The total amount now is $850,000 and change."

"An excellent return over five years," noted Nash, who could hardly believe his father had been sitting on this much money.

"Yes. He actually said you had rubbed off on him."

"We were long since estranged by the time I entered the business world."

"I think he was referring to your logical mind for business and the discipline to invest long-term."

"I went by the house yesterday. It looked fixed up. Did he use some of the Agent Orange money to do that?"

"He did, yes. I believe the amount spent was around eighty thousand dollars."

"So his return was even better than I originally thought. So where do those funds go? Some to Ms. Parker surely, as you mentioned?"

"Yes, $250,000 to her. The same amount to Shock."

"And the residual?"

Dickey read off one page in front of him: "$350,000 to his grand-daughter, Margaret Nash, to be invested and held in trust for her benefit until she is twenty-five years old, when half the amount will be disbursed outright, and at age twenty-eight, when the other half will be released to her."

Nash just stared wide-eyed at the man for a moment. "He never even met my daughter."

"That may well be, but his testamentary wishes were clear. And you are also appointed as the trustee and, despite the trust distribution instructions, you have the discretion to release some or all of the money to your daughter at any time in your reasonable judgment upon a request by her for said funds."

Well, this complicates the hell out of things with her influencer dream.

"I guess my father thought I was 'good at that stupid shit,' too," he pointed out.

"Apparently, yes," said Dickey, without looking at him.

"So am I bound to tell Maggie of the trust and the amounts in it?"

"The document does not explicitly say so, but—"

"Understood. I will set up accounts in which all the funds can be deposited prior to disbursement in the case of Shock, the motorcy-cle buddies, and Ms. Parker. Has a trust account been set up for my daughter?"

"A temporary one. Your father was of the mind that you would know best how to deal with the investments, market conditions, dividends, tax returns, and the like."

"Fine. I'll handle all of that. I will also visit the house and look over the items to which I am entitled. Now, the titling of the house?"

"If you so choose, a legal vehicle can be set up showing Ms. Parker's life interest. When the time comes, you, as trustee, will have the authority to sell the property, with the proceeds going to the Cancer Society. And there is no estate tax, since the exemption amount did not come close to being exceeded in your father's case. Only the super wealthy are affected by it in any case. Any documents needed to implement the sale of the house can be done at that time." He paused and glanced at Nash. "Are you leaning toward letting Ms. Parker stay in the house?"

"I will take all of my father's wishes into consideration," Nash said guardedly.

"Well, if you do let her stay, so long as Ms. Parker pays the taxes and insurance, and maintains the property, we should be good to go. Now, I have applied at the courthouse for twenty copies of the death certificate. You will have to provide them to various persons and institutions, of course."

"My wife's parents both died a few years back in an accident, and I was their executor. So I'm familiar with the routine."

"Fine. If you need any other assistance I am here to help. For no additional fee."

Nash held up a hand in protest. "That's not necessary. If you do additional work, you should be paid."

"I was your father's *friend*, Mr. Nash. This is my final parting gift to him."

Nash nodded. "All right. Thank you, Mr. Dickey."

Dickey's secretary put together a packet of the necessary documents and Nash left with them safely tucked into his briefcase.

He went to his Range Rover, but didn't start the vehicle.

Instead, the up-to-now all-business and logically minded Walter Nash lay his head down on the steering wheel and quietly wept.

17

A HALF HOUR LATER NASH LIFTED his head and wiped his eyes with a tissue pulled from a pack in the console. Then he applied eye drops so he wouldn't go into the office looking like a total wreck.

Before he started the SUV he phoned the main number for the local FBI office. A woman answered and Nash asked to speak to Agent Reed Morris.

The woman put him on hold and then came back on the line. "He is not available right now, but I can put you through to his voice mail."

"That would be fine, thanks."

The voice that came on was an automated one, so Nash couldn't compare it to the man's actual voice.

"This is Walter Nash, please call me back on this number as soon as possible." He then left his phone number.

He started the engine and pulled off. He hadn't left the parking lot before his phone rang. It was Morris.

"Why didn't you call my direct line?" the agent said. "It was on my card."

"I had my reasons. I want to meet with you and your superior."

"Excuse me?"

"Your superior, as high up as possible."

"And why is that?" Morris demanded.

"To confirm that all of this is on the up-and-up."

"You've been talking to your neighbor Hal Rankin, haven't you?"

Nash involuntarily glanced over his shoulder to see if he was being tailed. "And how do you know about Hal Rankin?" he asked.

"He told you to trust but verify?"

"More verify than trust, actually."

"That's right. He made the big bucks, which is why he's your neighbor. He's not getting into that gated community with Uncle Sam paying the freight."

"And how did *you* get into my gated community that night?" asked Nash.

"Not at liberty to discuss."

"So, your superior?" said Nash.

"You're traveling to Washington, DC, tomorrow, correct?"

"How did you hack into my calendar?"

"That would require a search warrant, Mr. Nash. We have other ways."

"*Illegal* other ways?"

"Will you have time in DC to meet for, say, a half hour with someone?"

"Yes. Where?" said Nash.

"Your hotel. Text me with the place and a time. We'll take care of the rest."

"Oh, so you don't know what hotel I'm staying at?"

"If it makes you feel better, no, we don't," replied Morris.

That did not make Nash feel better. "Who will you be bringing?"

"I'll leave it as a surprise."

"I'm sorry if you think this is overkill on my part, but there is a lot of crime going on out there, committed by some really scary people."

Morris said in feigned surprise, "Oh really? I had no idea."

"No, I meant that I just need to be careful, that's all."

"Look, truth is, if I were you, I'd be doing the same thing, too."

That was the first time that one of the agent's comments had not pissed Nash off. "I'll text you," he said, and clicked off.

He reached his office twenty minutes later and rode the elevator up.

Ellen Douglas, the prim receptionist, pointed to a tray of cookies set on the counter.

"Fresh this morning, Walter. Almond and chocolate chip. Two of your favorites."

Nash, who hadn't eaten breakfast, snagged two and thanked her. He strode quickly to his office to find that someone was waiting for him.

Rhett Temple was sitting on the small couch in the meeting area off to the left of Nash's desk. Rhett looked pale, and he carried one arm stiffly as he rose to greet Nash.

"You okay, Rhett? You look like you're coming down with something. And what's up with your arm?"

"Late-night flight back to town. And en route I fell and banged the crap out of my arm," he added, lifting his limb up a few inches. "Feel like an idiot."

"You probably need to rest and put your feet—and arm—up for a few days."

"I'm fine," said Rhett distractedly. "And I've got meetings this afternoon."

"So what's up?"

"You're out tomorrow, right?"

"Yes, DC. Those regulations in the hopper we want to push back on. Our lobbying folks thought if the key legislators heard my take, it might change some minds."

"Right, right, good," said Rhett absently. "Look, I got a call right when I landed. You know Peter Lombard?"

"He's the comptroller of Nano-BioLogics, a company we purchased two years ago."

"What's your take on him?"

"He's a good guy. And Nano's been an outstanding performer for us." Nash then picked up on Rhett's obvious distress. "But what about Lombard? Is he leaving the company? I should have heard if that was the case."

"No, it's a lot worse. They just found Lombard's car abandoned in a mountainous area near his home."

"What?" said Nash sharply.

"And there was a suicide note found inside the car."

"Oh my God! Did they...did they find his body?"

"They're searching, but from what I heard, it's pretty treacherous terrain."

"Why would he kill himself?"

"I was just wondering if you had some idea. You obviously led the acquisition."

"I met him a half dozen times. And there's been lots of emails and Zooms as he's reported in with his team. He seemed a normal, stand-up kind of guy. He was a good resource during the deal and afterwards from an operational sense. I recall that he was happily married with grown kids. I never saw anything that would point to a suicide."

Rhett nodded thoughtfully. "It just doesn't add up at all."

"Could you keep me in the loop if you hear anything?"

"Sure."

Nash regarded him and said, "You really should look after yourself better."

Rhett glanced up at him with a weary expression. "Yeah, I'll get right on that."

After he left, Nash sat at his desk and recalled two other tragic deaths connected to Sybaritic: Alexandra Singer and Danielle Cho.

Singer had been an accountant at Wheelhouse, Inc., a company that had been purchased by Sybaritic four years before. Wheelhouse was a niche business that helped other businesses get their operations going full bore in as short a period of time as possible. While on vacation with her boyfriend nearly two years ago, she had fallen off a cliff at the Grand Canyon and died.

Danielle Cho had been a midlevel contracts person at PLA Corp., a company that looked for undervalued industrial assets in the Pacific Rim region. Cho had been shot and killed in a home invasion in San Francisco that was still unsolved a year later.

And now Peter Lombard, the comptroller at Nano-BioLogics, had abandoned his car and left a suicide note.

Each case was starkly different: supposed accident, perhaps a burglary gone wrong, and now an alleged suicide. But three people connected to three different acquisitions by Sybaritic were now dead in just under two years.

A possibility hit him like a freight train.

The FBI had recruited a mole connected to Sybaritic three times before, but they've been discovered and killed.

And now I'm number four.

CHAPTER

18

You're going to have to do something," said Judith when Nash arrived home. "She's been in her room all day."

"She's *always* in her room," countered Nash. He still had to pack. His flight was early in the morning and it was already past nine. He'd had to work late and had grabbed a burger and fries for dinner, then ate it on the way home.

"Not like this she's not. She was going to play tennis with friends and then lunch at the club, but she cancelled."

Nash wanted to tell his wife that at nineteen years of age neither of them had had the opportunity to *cancel* tennis and lunch at the country club, because they had never belonged to a country club at that tender age. And if *that* was having a bad day then bring it on, he also thought.

Instead, he said, "I'll see if she'll talk to me."

He trudged upstairs and knocked on her door. "It's Dad."

"Go away! I'm mad at you."

Okay, that was a grown-up response. Why not drop hundreds of thousands of dollars on a wacky business idea with an immature person at the helm?

He was about to "go away" when the meeting with Dickey reentered his mind. "I met with my father's lawyer."

"So?" she called out.

He gritted his teeth and said, "He left you something."

"What? His 'Fuck Off' jacket?" she shot back through the door. Nash had told her and Judith about his father's profanely named motorcycle club. "You can keep it," she added.

"No, he left you some money, actually."

He heard her feet hit the floor and the door opened two seconds later.

Her hair was disheveled, and she wore baggy shorts and a T-shirt with a silkscreen of Lenny Kravitz. "How much money?" she said.

"You want to come down and we can discuss it?"

She followed him to his study like a puppy looking for treats, and curled up in a seat opposite him.

"So what money?" she said. "FYI, I drove past his house one time when I was in high school, and it didn't seem like he had much money."

"Why did you do that?"

"I was thinking of Grandma, and, I don't know. I just wanted to see where she lived. And I missed her even though we didn't see her all that much when she was alive."

Nash looked at his daughter and suddenly realized that he was not the only one affected by his father's bizarre behavior. "He didn't really have many assets. But he left you some of his Agent Orange settlement money."

She looked confused. "His what?"

"Agent Orange. It was a toxic chemical the U.S. military used in Vietnam against the enemy. Only they often doused their own troops with it. It causes a host of bad things, including many forms of cancer. Your grandfather fought the government and won a settlement."

"Wow, cool."

"It wasn't cool for him. Agent Orange destroyed his body and then killed him."

Nash knew that his daughter, while entitled and self-absorbed, was also kind and empathetic. Her happy look vanished. "Oh, I didn't know. That's . . . terrible, Dad."

"Many former soldiers and their families got nothing because the military wouldn't do the right thing. You're lucky that your grandfather never gave up."

Except maybe with me.

"I'm really sorry, Dad," she said sincerely. "Stuff like that shouldn't be allowed. I mean, they all fought for their country and we should take care of them."

"Very true. So, anyway, he left you the money in trust. You can access the first tranche at age twenty-five and the second half at age twenty-eight."

Her face fell. "But that's years away. I'll be nearly thirty by the time I get it all."

"But as trustee I can distribute funds out before that time, if I deem it to be sensible."

She looked at him warily. "But you made it clear that you don't think my influencer idea is *sensible*. I believe you thought it was crap."

"That was your *first* proposal. You can always do another one where there is less emphasis on flying around the world attending concerts and eating at five-star restaurants."

She sat back, deflated, but also anxious. "So what do you think I should do?"

"Basic Business 101: Find a need and fill it. Your generation seems to want more of a life balance than people my age or older, and not pointlessly lusting after the lifestyles of the rich and famous. Build a business that speaks to that and you may have something. And then keep in mind that consumers are fickle as hell. But if you frame it right and continue to evolve your offerings you can be a game changer in that space."

"I never thought of that," she said, sounding deeply chagrined.

"Business is not easy at any age, Maggie. But if you keep a few principles in mind, your chances of success can be enhanced. Some of them are: keep it simple, know your audience, and never grow complacent."

"So back to the drawing board." She hesitated and glanced at him.

He knew what she was going to ask. "It's six figures," he said. "The money he left you."

Stunned, she said, "But he didn't even know me."

"You're his flesh and blood. I guess that was enough."

"But why did he treat you so poorly then? You were his son!"

"He was complicated. And now I have to get ready for my trip tomorrow."

She rose. "Thanks, Dad. For the business lesson. Even if it did piss me off initially."

"Just initially?" he said.

"Okay, I'm still kind of mad at you, but...you did give me some great business advice."

"It's one of the very few things I'm reasonably good at."

At the door she turned back. "And...I'm sorry for how I acted before. I guess since I didn't go to college I was feeling sort of inadequate and that life was...passing me by."

"Social media sells the lie that if you're not rich with a billion followers by the time you're fourteen, then you're a failure. But life is long, and it's no fun going through it either in a neutral gear or facing absurd expectations. I just want you to find your passion. Once you do, I know you will excel."

"But how do you know my generation wants different things?"

"Well, different generations often do."

"Oh, okay," she said, looking a little disappointed.

"But I've also been looking into the things that are important to people your age."

"What, for some business deal?"

"No."

"Then what was your incentive to spend time on that?"

"You're my daughter, Maggie. *That* was my incentive. I thought the more I know about what's important to you, the better advisor I can be to you. And a better...father."

She looked surprised.

"I know I wasn't always around when you were growing up. That my job took me away a lot. But that didn't mean I wasn't thinking about you. That...that I didn't care. Because I do. And I have since the day you were born."

She stared at him for an intense moment, perhaps seeing

something in him that she hadn't before. "Thanks, Dad. I'll…I'll get back to you."

Nash felt awful doing this to her, knowing full well that whatever decision he made with respect to the FBI's proposal would probably mean his daughter's dreams of building a business online would never happen.

I doubt she will think me father-of-the-year material after that bomb drops.

Nash sent a few emails and then loaded his briefcase with documents he would need for his meetings on Capitol Hill. He then went upstairs to pack. Judith poked her head into his closet. She already had her PJs on, and a purple sleep mask rested on her forehead.

"I see you smoothed things over with the princess," she said.

"She's doing some more homework." He folded up a tie and put it into his roller bag. "By the way, my father left her three hundred and fifty thousand dollars in trust."

Judith gaped. "What! Where did he get that sort of money?"

"Agent Orange settlement with the Army. The trust funds are paid out half at age twenty-five and the remainder at twenty-eight. But the trustee can give her money before that if it's deemed suitable."

"Who's the trustee?"

"Me."

Judith's expression turned somber. "He left his Agent Orange settlement to Maggie?"

"Part of it. Some went to his best friend, Isaiah York, and the rest to Rosie Parker. My father wanted Parker to have a life interest in the house, and the money will help her keep it up. I'm working with the lawyer to get things in order."

"Well, no one's better at that than you."

"I just told Maggie it was six figures. Don't tell her the exact amount, okay?"

"Mum's the word. Are you going to let her have some of it?"

"If she comes up with a decent mousetrap, probably."

Judith hugged him. "You really are a good father, whether you think you are or not."

She left him to his packing. After that he texted Agent Morris with his hotel information and a time to meet.

Judith was asleep by the time he climbed into bed. The private flight was wheels up at six fifty a.m. on the trip to the nation's capital.

And sometime after that Nash would be meeting with the FBI to see how spectacularly he could blow up his life. *And* the lives of the two people he cared most about.

CHAPTER

19

HIS OFFICIAL WORK IN WASHINGTON done, Nash had dinner and drinks at Café Milano in Georgetown with two of the firm's lobbyists, cabbed back to his hotel, and sat staring blankly at a wall, waiting.

The politicians he'd met with had been uniform in their enthusiasm for truth, justice, and the American way, and they seemed amenable to Nash's arguments that the regulations in question would cost jobs and stifle both competition and innovation. These were the standard excuses every time businesses wanted to run wild and the government sought to rein them in, however reasonably. It almost always worked because the business community had all the money and made sure theirs was the only message that resonated with people who would never share in that wealth. Indeed, Nash knew it was often the poorest folks who were injured the most by corporate malfeasance. But regardless, this was America and that was just how it was. Nash didn't necessarily like it, but his job was to work within that reality.

However, he noted that the politicians' staffs had hovered over them, waiting to pounce if anything said seemed like it might require their guy to actually *do* anything.

He stopped thinking about all that when he received a text from Agent Morris.

He left his hotel room, rode the elevator three floors up, and knocked on the door to Room 506. He was admitted into a large suite by a burly man with a comm line in his ear and a transponder snapped into his belt. The man patted Nash down for weapons, and Nash glimpsed the holstered pistol when the man turned to let him pass.

From another room Agent Morris appeared with a woman by his side. He said, "This is Special Agent Amy Braxton, Mr. Nash."

"This way," said Braxton tersely.

They led Nash into a small living area. A tall, suited man with sandy hair and a beefy build stood and held out his hand.

"Mr. Nash, I'm Bernard Duvall, deputy attorney general of the United States."

The men shook hands, and then Nash glanced in surprise at Morris. He had not been expecting anyone this high-level.

"I was told you wanted to meet?" began Duvall, indicating a chair. Both men sat.

"Yes. I've been *told* a criminal enterprise is ongoing at my firm, but I've been given very few details and no proof. Without that, I'm not sure how or why I should sign on."

Duvall cleared his throat. "You can appreciate that our level of disclosure at this juncture must be limited."

"And I'm sure you can appreciate that I'm being asked to give up my entire life and that of my family. What would you do if confronted with that same situation?"

Duvall glanced at the two agents and then edged forward, his hands braced on his thighs. "We understand that this is a personal sacrifice. But we believe that you are uniquely placed to help us bring down an organization that has a chance to upend our entire country."

Nash decided to fire the first salvo right across the government's bow. "Just like Danielle Cho, Alexandra Singer, and now Peter Lombard were uniquely placed to do?"

He would not break the silence until one of them did. This was like the phase in a negotiation where one side had to blink. Well, Walter Nash was a world-class nonblinker.

I'll wait it out until we all die of old age in this damn hotel room.

As it turned out, it only took Agent Morris ten seconds to blink. "And how did you come to know about that?"

Nash took his time turning his gaze to the man. "When someone approaches me with any offer of significance, I take it upon myself to perform some due diligence."

"I'm not sure we can get into any of that with you," said Braxton, while Duvall remained silent. "And your conclusions could well be incorrect."

Nash said, "Well, if I am wrong, you won't mind my asking Rhett Temple about the three of them then? I'm sure he'll have a perfectly reasonable explanation."

He watched as Morris and Duvall exchanged a nervous glance.

Duvall said, "Seldom do these sorts of endeavors work out the first time."

"Or the second or third," observed Nash, who was having none of this. "So you intend to make me the fourth? And when they punch my ticket, what will you tell the fifth sucker? Because they're going to have questions, and the EVP of acquisitions going down along with three other affiliated company members in a fairly short period of time would be tops on my discussion list."

Duvall chuckled feebly. "I believe we overlooked the fact that you are a highly experienced negotiator, Mr. Nash."

Nash gave the deputy AG a slow burn of a look before leveling an even more withering gaze on Morris. "And the fact that I wasn't told about the three other people beforehand but had to find out for myself? Well, I think we can all agree that trust just got tossed out the window."

"We need your help, Mr. Nash. Desperately," said Duvall, now sweating a little despite the coolness of the room.

"If you are that desperate and there is personal danger involved, that should be reflected in the offer you make, don't you think? But I don't really see what I get in return except spending the rest of my life stocking shelves at a dollar store in Idaho."

"Excuse me, a dollar store in Idaho?" said a confused-looking Duvall.

"I think he's talking about WITSEC," explained Morris.

"Ah, right."

"Yes, 'ah, right,'" parroted Nash. "And threatening me with criminal prosecution if I don't cooperate doesn't move the needle for me, either. Quite the opposite."

"We do not engage in those tactics, Mr. Nash," said Duvall huffily.

Looking directly at Morris once more, Nash replied, "Then you need to circulate a memo, because I don't think everyone on your team has gotten that message."

Duvall shot Morris a stern glance, but the FBI agent wouldn't look his way.

"So are you saying you have chosen *not* to work with us?" said Duvall.

"I'm saying that I believe there is a reasonable likelihood that three people who worked at companies affiliated with Sybaritic may have been murdered. So perhaps my doubts about there really being criminal activity are probably now less than they were. However, I can't make a decision to work with you unless you tell me what this is all about. It's like you want me to argue a case before the Supreme Court without my having gone to law school first."

Duvall sat back and let his arms dangle freely off the sides of the chair. To Nash, he looked like a chubby marionette whose puppet master had cut all its support lines.

"An apt analogy," Duvall replied. He nodded at Morris.

The FBI agent promptly said, "The org we're targeting is run by Victoria Steers."

"Never heard of her."

Morris snarled, "You wanted to get briefed on what this is about? Well, I'm telling you, so listen up."

Nash, sensing the man needed to save some face with his boss, said, "Go ahead."

"Her father, Joseph Steers, was in the British navy, but then got out and settled in Japan. There, he married Steers's mother, and they had quite a brood. Victoria was the youngest. She's also the only surviving sibling."

"What happened to the others?" asked Nash.

"We believe that Victoria killed them, or had them killed," said Morris.

"Excuse me?" exclaimed a shocked Nash.

"Joseph Steers was pretty much a nothing burger who seemed to lead a quiet life. However, his wife, Masuyo, had very different plans."

"*Masuyo*, translated from Japanese, can mean 'to make the world your own,'" noted Duvall. "And Masuyo Steers did just that, and taught her youngest to do the same."

"Is Masuyo still alive?" asked Nash. "And her husband?"

"We don't know the answers to that," conceded Morris. "They have not been seen in public for years. But we know that the empire the Steers family built up over the last five-plus decades is now run solely by Victoria. She is smart, nimble, tough, cruel as they come, and a master manipulator. She came up through the school of hard knocks and survived." He gave Nash a probing look. "Sort of like you did."

"But I never killed anyone to get to where I am," pointed out Nash. "Tell me more about her operation."

Duvall said, "She controls dozens of carefully constructed companies with subsidiaries and interlocking corporate relationships and partnerships, labyrinths of legalese spread all over the world that the lawyers at Justice have not even made a dent in despite grinding away for years. It's all seemingly legitimate."

Morris said, "The important point to understand is that we have recently come to learn that Steers's mother is not Japanese. She is actually *Chinese*. And as a young woman she was planted in Japan as a Communist Party agent to undermine democracy in that country. Her subsequent marriage to Joseph Steers was apparently part of that cover. But then Masuyo went rogue and began creating the behemoth that their daughter Victoria now runs. And Victoria, we believe, has thrown in her lot with Beijing."

"Thrown in her lot to do what, exactly?" said Nash.

"To bring this country to its knees," answered Duvall.

CHAPTER

20

"How?" NASH ASKED. "HOW WILL they bring us to our knees?"

Morris picked up the story after another nod from Duvall. "We're averaging nearly a hundred thousand opioid deaths a year. This country has no real strategy to fix that problem, and it is seeding civic unrest, Mr. Nash. We at the FBI see that clearly every day in innumerable ways as people feel they have been forgotten."

"But China?" prompted Nash.

Morris said, "Steers's drug operations alone are responsible, we believe, for a huge percentage of those overdose deaths, because they are lacing every pill out there with fatal doses of not just fentanyl but other, more recently created, synthetic opioids. Mexican and other cartels have tried pushing back against this because they, reasonably enough, don't want to kill off their customer base. But the Chinese want to do exactly that."

Agent Braxton interjected, "And it's incredibly profitable. Currently a kilo of fentanyl costs around three grand wholesale. You can make a half million pills from it and sell them at thirty dollars a pill. You can see the profit margins, Mr. Nash."

"A five thousand percent return on investment. They must be rolling in cash."

Duvall said, "Illicit drug trafficking revenue is estimated at around forty billion dollars annually, and control of that is closely held in the hands of a few, like Steers."

Braxton added, "The street dealers market the pills online, mostly on Snapchat, because the communications automatically disappear within twenty-four hours. Still, I've had friends in local law enforcement rushing to break the passcode of a dead kid's iPhone to get their Snapchat screens before they disappear. And Snapchat has unique features like My Eyes Only, which lets them hide and store client info, as well as a back-end deletion function."

"China has the largest chemical industry in the world," said Morris. "And the regional base for that is the Hebei province. Companies there sell everything from air fresheners to lethal drugs. When fentanyl started hitting our shores you could buy it online and the postal service would deliver it right to your door, a fact Chinese firms advertised. Overdose deaths soared."

Braxton added, "If you sell fentanyl in China, they'll execute you, but no problem shipping it here. And they openly advertise that they'll get the product safely through customs."

Duvall said, "We've tried to cooperate with Beijing, sending teams over there with proof of the problem. They either stonewall, deny, or do superficial crackdowns that amount to nothing."

Morris interjected, "Hell, some of the fentanyl producers are state-owned, so it's not like they don't know what's going on."

Braxton said, "When President Xi moved to cut fentanyl exports, Chinese sellers simply moved the precursors to Mexico. And China is a hub for groups like Steers's to launder billions for traffickers. Beijing's fingerprints are all over the process, from raw materials to laundering the profits."

Duvall said, "And at the macro level it also means children here grow up without their parents, and grandparents can't enjoy their retirement because they are raising their grandkids. Unemployment soars along with health care costs for everyone, tax bases dry up, businesses go bankrupt, home prices plummet, whole towns are wiped out, and public services are cut when folks need them the most. People become more and more desperate and isolated, ready to believe any rabbit hole conspiracy theory presented to them. And the Chinese are all over social media conspiracy platforms promoting crap that would truly boggle your mind. Hell, people in our own Congress are parroting Chinese political messaging probably because they're being blackmailed."

"And they've been promoting Russian talking points, too," interjected Morris. "Because we believe the dragon and the bear have teamed up on this. They can't beat us economically, or militarily, but they can surreptitiously provide us the tools to defeat ourselves."

Duvall said, "Their overall messaging is clear: The government is failing their people. So why should you be loyal to it?"

Nash asked, "But how does that really help China? Or Russia?"

Duvall said, "Geopolitically, we will become absorbed with our internal problems and withdraw our presence and with it our influence from the rest of the globe, creating a power vacuum. And then Beijing and Moscow will fill that vacuum and run rampant. I can tell you that they are champing at the bit to do exactly that. Putin's bloody foray into Ukraine, China's bullhorn broadsides over Taiwan, and manufacturing prowess are only the beginnings of a strategic plan for a completely new world order."

"And they really see a 'drug dealer' as a viable partner in all this?" asked Nash.

Duvall said, "China has had a rocky relationship with wealthy Chinese families. They routinely set them up as partners, but then invariably something happens and the families fall out of favor, as occurred to the Wei, Bai, and Liu families in the Kokang region. But Steers has made herself invaluable to Beijing in a hundred meaningful ways. She is a superb dealmaker and has the skill set to play and win at geopolitics with the best of them. And in return, Beijing gives her resources and protection."

"I assume you know what she looks like?"

Duvall motioned to Braxton, who produced a photo on her phone screen.

"We don't circulate it for obvious reasons," she said.

Nash gazed at the woman on the screen. He was surprised because she was young and attractive, and *normal* looking. But he then focused on the eyes: sharp, resolute, intimidating.

"She looks…tough," he noted.

The agent nodded and put her phone away.

"So what's going on with my firm and Rhett Temple, money laundering?" asked Nash.

"Not only that." Duvall hesitated. "You see that we are taking you into our confidence now, Mr. Nash. At a very high level. If you choose not to participate at this point—we can't force you, of course. But…"

"If you think I would ever disclose what you have told me to anyone at Sybaritic or anyone else? Well, I am *not* a criminal. I have never had any ambition to go outside the law. I've never even had a traffic ticket. I have my faults as we all do, but I am scrupulously honest, Mr. Duvall. And I would never do anything to harm my country. I am a proud and patriotic citizen. I pay my taxes. My late father was a veteran." He abruptly stopped because Nash could sense he was losing his advantage by rambling.

Duvall sat back, appeased, for now. "We think they are grafting on to each of the companies that Sybaritic invests in or purchases a…separate unit of varying degrees and elements, like a parasite. It has a legit cover being connected to a well-known company like yours. But the business they conduct is only for her and the Chinese government's benefit. Different books, different agendas, with an endgame that is totally in line with Steers's overall mission. More than that we can't say, unless you agree to help us."

"What's the deadline for my answer?"

Duvall replied, "I hesitate to give you an expiration date on our offer, but you can surely understand that time is of the essence."

"And the others, Singer, Cho and Lombard? If they were killed, how will you ensure that a similar fate doesn't happen to me or my family?"

Duvall chose his words with the due care of a lawyer finding himself in the uncomfortable position of being a witness of sorts. "Without casting blame on the departed, Mr. Nash, it seems that indiscretions on their part led to their unfortunate outcomes, not anything that we did on our end. We provide every conceivable resource, but we can't control other people and what they may say or do. I will note that what is needed here is absolute discipline, rigorous attention to detail. The playing of a role, if you will. No mistakes, no—"

"—indiscretions?" broke in a stone-faced Nash.

Morris interjected, "But by recruiting you, a high-level source within the company, we are doing two things: We will get better information because of your position, and we will completely throw the other side off, because up till now we have only focused on lower-level bean counters, if you will. Thus, they will never suspect your involvement, Mr. Nash, because it does not fit the pattern."

This only made Nash feel slightly better about things.

Duvall added, "And come hell or high water, we are going to bring these people down, Mr. Nash. But keep in mind that in doing so, the destruction of the organization you work for may well occur, and that will have a deleterious effect on your financial well-being. That cannot be helped. But better to be part of the solution than a piece of the problem."

Nash sat back, relaxed his position, and opened the negotiations.

"I'm actually glad you brought up the topic of my financial well-being. Because if I do decide to help you, these are my terms."

"Excuse me, your *terms*?" snapped Morris.

Duvall put up a restraining hand. "Let's hear the man out, Reed."

Nash said, "When we first met, Agent Morris told me I could be deemed a whistleblower."

Duvall shot Morris a brutal look that actually made the FBI agent wince.

Nash continued, "And whistleblowers, I've come to learn, are entitled to reap a percentage of the spoils that they assist the authorities in acquiring. Now, if I help take down Steers and her vast organization, I will be ensuring that Beijing and/or Moscow does not supplant America as the leading force in the world, both politically and economically. The value of those outcomes *must* be measured in the trillions. Therefore, as a relatively small percentage, my compensation for aiding in all that will be one point five billion dollars."

"One and a half billion dollars!" barked Morris. "You must be nuts."

"Well, if I am, you probably don't want to use me as your spy. In which case this meeting can end now." He started to stand.

Duvall said, "Look, let's just calm down everyone and discuss this *rationally*."

Nash sat back down and said, "I *am* calm. And what I just said is completely rational. And since I'm risking my life and the lives of my family in order to do this, let's add another twenty percent for that." He glanced at Morris. "That makes one point eight billion dollars. It will be tax free. Plus new identities, which you were already committed to doing through WITSEC. However, with that much wealth I can take care of my own living arrangements and security. Although I will expect regular threat assessments from your experts to ensure my family's continued well-being."

"You really are unbelievable," muttered Morris.

Nash plowed right on. "And all of this will have to be put in writing. I will leave the agreement in a safe place with instructions to my executor, in case the government tries to pull a fast one. Oh, and one more thing."

"Please tell us, Mr. Nash," snapped Morris. "We can hardly wait."

"If I'm killed as part of this…mission, my wife and daughter will still receive the money and they will be accorded full security protection for as long as they so desire. Those are my terms. Take them or leave them."

When Morris started to say something, Duvall beat him to it. "We will take all of this under consideration, Mr. Nash, *serious* consideration, and get back to you ASAP."

"Then have a pleasant rest of your evening," said Nash. He rose and walked out.

CHAPTER

21

AFTER A FITFUL NIGHT AT his hotel in DC, a weary Nash looked out the window of the corporate jet the following morning as they soared along. The flight attendant provided him with breakfast; he could manage only the coffee.

He put his seat back, took off his shoes, let his long legs straighten in front of him, and closed his eyes. He had already googled Duvall. There was the man's pudgy face beaming out at him from the official DOJ website. The number two government lawyer in the country was putting his faith in Nash to help bring down an international criminal scheme headed up by what sounded like a woman so purely evil as to be beyond belief. And if that was not enough, she was being fueled and supported by the Chinese government with its limitless resources and cagey leadership. Oh, and maybe the Russians were in the mix, too.

I'm not Tom Cruise or James Bond, for God's sake. I wield a briefcase, not a gun.

It truly seemed laughable.

I will end up dead. My family will end up dead. There is no way in hell I can do this. Even if they paid me ten billion dollars. The dead can't spend money.

Then, a simple solution occurred to him. Of course it would mean some personal disruption, but it was also a clear exit from this nightmare. Surprised he hadn't thought of it before, Nash took out his phone and sent off some emails.

That done, he breathed a sigh of relief, closed his eyes, and quickly fell into a deep sleep. He awoke to the attendant gently tapping on his shoulder.

"We've arrived, Mr. Nash. Your Range Rover is on the tarmac and your bag is loaded in."

Rousing, and in better spirits, he said, "Great, thank you."

He got into his Rover and left the airport. Nash wasn't going straight to the office. He had decided to take care of some other pressing business.

He drove to his boyhood home, and Rosie Parker answered the door.

"Mr. Nash?" she said. Parker looked frightened, and gave a quick glance behind her.

"Hello, Rosie, and it's just Walter, okay?"

She kneaded her fists into her thighs and jerkily nodded. "Right, okay, W-Walter."

"I came to pick up some things, and also to tell you that my father left you a life interest in the house. You'll also inherit a substantial amount of money from him."

"Money?" she said cautiously.

"Yes, a quarter of a million dollars."

She slumped against the wall. "Where did Ty get *that* kind of money?"

"He didn't tell you about his Agent Orange settlement?"

Open-mouthed, she shook her head. "No, nothing."

"Well, that's where it came from. I will have those funds placed into your account. You will be responsible for the property taxes and utilities and such, but the house is yours for as long as you are alive."

The decision to give her the life interest had been made on the plane ride back. He had also decided to let Parker believe that his father had left her the life estate outright. He had a pretty good idea why his father had given him the right to make that decision.

Nash saw tears trickle down her cheeks and he diplomatically glanced away.

She wiped her eyes with the back of her hand. "Well, that...that was so awfully, awfully kind of him."

Now Nash looked at her. "He obviously thought a lot of you."

"Well, I thought a lot of him, Mr. N—Walter."

"I'm just here to go over some of my parents' effects."

"Um, Walter, can I...show you something first?"

"Okay," he said, looking puzzled.

The house was spic-and-span clean, and many of the furnishings looked relatively new, while a very few he recalled from his childhood. His mother had been a disorganized person, with odd things ending up in odder places. But his father's military background had lent itself to a neatness approaching compulsivity. Nash had also always kept his personal and business spaces meticulous.

Like my father, he thought soberly.

"Just up the stairs here," said Parker.

It was an enclosed staircase. Nash remembered the various times he had jumped from the top step to the bottom to land on some pillows and blankets he had piled there. Once he had crashed into the wall, sending his mother into hysterics, but prompting a show of blunt appreciation from his father.

"That's how you take on life, sonny boy, with both feet and damn the consequences."

Yes, damn the consequences. Nash touched his forearm where he'd broken both the radius and the ulna when he'd collided with the wall. He felt himself smiling at the memory but then quickly became all business again as they reached the top landing and Rosie led him to Nash's old bedroom. She opened the door slightly and peeked through the gap.

"Okay, she's awake."

A startled Nash said, "I'm sorry, *who* is awake?"

In answer she pushed the door fully open and led him inside. "My mother."

22

THE WOMAN LYING IN THE bed looked to be well into her eighties, thought Nash as he drew a bit closer. The twin-size bed seemed to dwarf her emaciated frame, although he noted that her legs were long with bony knees propping up the covers.

"This is my mother, Alice," said Parker.

The woman stared up at her daughter and then at Nash. She gummed her lips for a few moments before saying in a low, croaking voice, "Thirsty, Rose."

"Yes, of course, Momma."

Parker rushed to the little nightstand next to the bed and poured out water from a pitcher, then got her mother to sit up and gently helped her to drink. As she did so, Nash looked around the confines of his old room and fixed on the spot where he'd had his desk and his first computer, a Bondi blue Apple G3 that he'd bought with money earned from his paper route and mowing lawns.

Standing there now were a portable toilet and a rolling table with some prescription bottles carefully arranged. An oxygen tank was set next to the bed. Its tubing was attached to a canula in Alice's nostrils.

Nash turned back to Parker with an inquisitive look. When she rejoined him he said quietly, "How long has your mother been here?"

"She...I brought her the day after your father passed."

"I see. And where was she before?"

"At a facility. But they said she needed to go somewhere else. Only I had nowhere else." She glanced at her mother as the woman closed her eyes and slowly drifted off to sleep. "They told me to put her in hospice, but her benefits are limited and the ones that would take her, well, the level of care there I knew was not…not what my mother deserved. Not that anyone does. Particularly at this stage in life."

"I understand."

"I did talk to your father about it before he passed. He knew my mother and liked her. He said it would be okay."

"But how will you manage this while you're working? She looks like she needs constant attention."

"I got a month's time off to care for her. Under FMLA."

"Right, the Family Medical Leave Act. But isn't that leave unpaid?"

"Yes, Mr. Nash, but I had no other options. I had already used up all my sick and vacation time. I wasn't sure what I was going to do. And my salary doesn't go far. But with the money your father left me." Her eyes again filled with tears. "Well, it makes things a lot easier, that's for sure."

"Very timely," he said gently. "I'm glad this has worked out for you, I really am."

She lowered her voice. "She doesn't have long."

"What's wrong with her?"

"Old age, mostly. Things are pretty much worn out. And she was a smoker for fifty years and has COPD as a result. That's why she's on oxygen."

"When you followed me to the deli and met up with me after, who stayed with your mother?"

"A friend of mine from the VA. I just had to talk to you. That's why I…followed you. Things were getting…desperate."

"I understand perfectly, and I'm sorry." He looked at her mother. "This must be incredibly difficult for you, Rosie."

"I look after people like this every day, Walter. I don't mind it. I…like to feel useful. And people who are sick and scared and… well…they shouldn't be alone to look after themselves, should they? They should have someone to help them."

"Yes, they should. And she's lucky to have someone like you." He paused and added awkwardly, "Well, as I said, I came to look over some of my parents' things and to open the safe and review the contents."

"That's all in the bedroom closet downstairs. The safe is also in the closet."

He left her there and went downstairs, through the living room, past the minuscule dining room where he had eaten every meal with his parents, and down the short hall with the varnished floors to his parents' bedroom. He opened the door and surveyed the space. It hadn't changed much since his childhood. The bedcovers, of course, were newer, and there was a chair he didn't recognize. When he looked at it more closely, he saw that it was one of those assisted-lift models. In his mind's eye he imagined his father using it to get to his feet. He would have hated that vulnerability, Nash understood quite well. That *weakness*, as his father would see it. He opened the closet and saw his mother's clothes still hanging there. She had been petite, but his father had been six four and chiseled out of granite. Nash had taken after him in the height if not the musculature department.

On a shelf in the closet were two plastic boxes with lids. He pulled them out and placed them on the bed. Inside one were letters that he'd written to his mother while he'd been in college and through his first few years of marriage, before everyone started corresponding mostly via emails and texts. He read through several of them, each bringing back important memories. He found himself forgetting about his present dilemma and allowed himself to be whisked back in time to the simpler existence of a little boy, then a teenager, then a young adult. He pulled out his Eagle Scout sash with all the earned merit badges. He had felt proud wearing the uniform and working toward that elite status. He had thought his father would be proud of him, too, but he'd been pretty much indifferent about the whole thing.

There were also presents that Nash had made his mother for her birthdays, simple things crafted from popsicle sticks and plastic, and lots of Elmer's glue. And Hallmark cards, which his mother loved. Then there was his high school diploma and senior yearbook. He couldn't even look at the gawky, nerdy youth he'd been at eighteen.

There was an old bottle of pain pills that his mother had taken for her cancer. He would dispose of it properly.

He decided to take the whole box with him.

The second box contained mementos of his father's military career. One of his Army hats, his medals and ribbons, his discharge papers, letters of commendation, and one old photo.

Nash sat on the bed and looked at the picture.

There was his young father and a youthful Shock, both bare-chested, and looking more like armored trucks than human beings, in the middle of a jungle. His father had a can of beer in one hand and his M16 in the other.

Shock had let his dog tags dangle from the muzzle of his rifle and held a machete in the other. Behind them was a chopper with its long blades hovering over them like the long limbs of a metal tree.

He turned the photo over and saw written in pen there: *My life in the worst damn war in history.*

And under that line in writing he recognized as his father's was: *I'd rather be at fucking Woodstock.*

I bet, thought Nash with a smile.

As he dug into the box he found two other things: his father's Army Ka-bar knife with the initials TQN carved into the handle. As a young boy Nash had imagined blood on the knife blade and had felt chills down his spine with the thought.

There was also his father's Colt .45, also known as the M1911A1. Ty Nash had schooled his son about the weapon: It was a single-action, recoil-operated, semiautomatic chambered in the forty-five caliber ACP.

Saved my life more times than I can count after my M16 piece of shit jammed for the millionth time, he'd told his son.

Nash set the knife and gun aside after checking to make sure the latter was unloaded. He put his father's box next to his mother's and stared at them for a long moment. It didn't seem substantial enough to represent the lives of two people who had mattered to him greatly. The boxes should have held more, a lot more.

But what will my box hold when I'm gone? Maggie and Judith will be set financially, but what else did I really contribute to either of them?

Depressed by these thoughts, Nash pulled out the paper with the code to the safe, and located it at the rear of the closet.

Inside were the deed to the house, what looked to be Ty Nash's settlement papers with the Army over his Agent Orange claim, a copy of his will, three spare mags for the Colt, and an envelope, sealed and with Nash's name written on the outside along with: *To be opened only after I'm dead and buried.*

Nash's fingers trembled as they held the envelope. He put it inside his father's box along with the other papers, then carried everything out to the Range Rover.

On coming back in, he met Parker in the foyer.

"Did you get everything you wanted?" she asked anxiously.

"I think so, yes. My mother's clothes can be donated, along with my father's, unless you want anything?"

"Well, I have been wearing some of your father's shirts. He…he got thin before he passed. And I can roll his pantlegs up and wear his jeans."

"Rosie, you will have the money in your account shortly. You can buy some new clothes all your own."

"But I don't want to waste anything and I'm used to being… frugal."

"I think the best thing you can do is make a fresh start. Purchase some things of your own, clothes, furniture, I don't know, pillows, whatever. Take your time, select what you want. You will have the money to pay for it. And if you like, I can invest the settlement funds for you so that it will generate interest and dividend income. I'll be glad to do that free of charge."

"I…I was just thinking of putting it in my savings account."

"That pays next to nothing, which is why banks have all the money. Please let me set that up for you. It won't be a huge amount, but I believe I can get it to generate over ten thousand a year, and some of it is tax free."

"Ten thousand!" she exclaimed. "Dollars? A year?"

He was a bit taken aback but nodded and said, "Yes. The interest will go in each month for the bonds and with the dividends when they are declared and distributed."

"Thank you so much, Mr. Nash."

"It's Walter, remember?"

"Yes, but with this business stuff and all, I really think you're *Mr.* Nash."

He smiled at the compliment. "How is your mother?"

"She's awake again, if you'd like to say goodbye."

She led him upstairs where Alice was now propped up in bed. The woman watched Nash like a hawk as he approached.

"Momma, this is Walter Nash, Ty's son. And we get to stay here. Momma, do you understand me? Walter is helping us, so that this is our house for now."

Alice continued to eye Nash with an unfriendly look. "You really Ty's son?" she said in a voice raspy and faint.

"I am, yes."

"You sure don't look the part."

Nash glanced down at his suit and tie and polished shoes. "No, I suppose I don't."

He gazed back up at her. And in that look, there seemed, at least to Nash, to be a bit of a bonding moment.

Alice said, "Sons ought to be different from their fathers. Otherwise, what's the point?"

"I think so, too," said Nash with a smile.

"But," began Alice.

"But what?" said Nash pleasantly.

"But I see some of Ty in you."

"Your eyes are better than mine then," joked Nash.

However, Alice didn't crack a smile. "I been around a long time, son. Seen a lot. And I *see* Ty in you."

Nash looked at her awkwardly until Parker, sensing his discomfort, quickly said, "Walter was just leaving. He wanted to say goodbye."

"Goodbye, Walter. Thanks for the house."

"Well, you can thank my father for that, Alice. But on that point he and I are in complete agreement."

She then gave him an endearing smile and it hurt his heart, because Nash thought it quite likely that this would be the last time he would see the woman. And he also thought about what she had said.

She can see some of my father in me?

No one had ever said *that* before. Quite the opposite, in fact. He had heard some of the dads of his few friends growing up discussing in quiet tones how a combat warrior like Ty Nash—a man's man, as Shock had said at the funeral service—could have a son like him. And even as a youngster, the precocious Nash understood it was not meant to be a compliment.

He started to walk out to the Range Rover but then changed direction and ventured into the backyard. Miraculously, the house next door still had the old doghouse from his younger days. He leaned on the chain-link fence, closed his eyes, and imagined himself a little boy again sneaking over there to play with his furry chum, Rusty. When he opened his eyes he saw a little boy emerge from the back of the house followed by a yapping and bouncy terrier puppy.

He saw Nash and waved. Nash waved back and asked, "What's your dog's name?"

"Sup."

"Sup?"

"Like, 'what's up?' You know."

"Yes. Right." He pointed to the doghouse. "Does Sup stay in there?"

"No way, mister. He sleeps with me."

"Very smart," said Nash. When the boy's mother came out of the house and gave Nash a suspicious look, he turned and left.

CHAPTER

23

As NASH ENTERED HIS OFFICE his phone dinged. He set his briefcase down, sat behind his desk, and looked at the text.

Nash had reached out on the plane ride back to a firm that had been hot to grab him up for years. It had started nearly a decade before, after Nash had outfoxed them on a deal that had netted Sybaritic an unexpected $200 million. This was because Nash, then a midlevel exec, had discovered a drastically undervalued asset buried in a list of inventory during due diligence that everyone else had missed. And then Nash had found a buyer willing to pay top dollar for that asset after the purchase of the company was completed. Because of that feat Barton Temple, then the CEO of Sybaritic, had sent him, Judith, and Maggie off on an all-expenses-paid vacation to Australia and New Zealand as a reward, and he had also promoted Nash to his current position as head of acquisitions.

The president of the rival firm had had dinner with Nash shortly after the deal had closed to congratulate him. And then he had made a very hard pitch to get Nash to jump to his company. They would even match his salary and full benefits and bonuses for the length of his one-year noncompete. Nash had politely declined the offer, but every year the man reached out to Nash to see if he would accept the offer, the last time barely four months ago.

So it was with deep perplexity that Nash now read in the text that the company had no interest in him working for them. No reason was given.

Nash's plan had been to leave Sybaritic and his FBI problem behind. He could not be recruited to work for the government if he no longer was at Sybaritic. He had thought it a workable solution. But apparently not.

He texted another firm, one even more anxious to poach him as recently as two months ago. He had barely sent the text to the firm's head of recruitment, a friend of his, before the reply came back. No interest. But at least he had tacked on, *Sorry, Walt.*

He immediately called the man on his personal phone. It went right to voice mail.

I have been outplayed by the FBI, it seems. They're engaging in an advanced version of chess, and I'm stuck on tiddlywinks.

His anxiety, repressed ever since he had come up with what he had thought was a brilliant solution, now came roaring back. He used his personal phone to text Morris and ask for a conversation that night.

Morris had written back that a face-to-face was not possible, explaining that they could not be seen together in public. He would instead call Nash at nine that night.

Nine o'clock sharp, replied Nash, in an attempt to assert a little control. After he sent the message, he put his face in his hands and let out a light moan.

"Walter, are you all right?"

He glanced up to see one of his team members, Elaine Fixx, standing in his doorway. He quickly straightened and said, "Early morning. And visiting Capitol Hill is a sure recipe for frustration."

She smiled. Fixx was hardworking, disciplined, and smart as a whip, and he felt she would be ruling this place in no time, if there was a place left to be ruled.

"I hope it was a productive trip anyway."

"Crossing t's and dotting i's, so yes, it was. Anything up?"

"The OxiControls acquisition? I had a question about some of the metrics?"

"Email me and we'll go over it this afternoon in the daily summary meeting."

"Will do, thanks."

After she left he closed his door and settled his face in his hands once more.

Four seconds in, hold for four, four-count exhale, hold for four. Repeat.

He had left everything he'd taken from his father's home in the Range Rover except for the letter addressed to him. He had placed that precisely in the center of his desk and now stared down at it. The writing on the envelope was in his father's hand, clearly, but a weakened one, a sick one. He had obviously done this shortly before the end.

However, instead of opening the letter Nash slipped it inside his briefcase.

Better to read it at home, he told himself. *Procrastination isn't always a vice.*

He had his meetings and answered the metric questions Fixx had.

Rhett stopped him right as he was leaving for the day. "Hey, Walt, I heard DC went okay."

"Nothing more and nothing less than usual," Nash replied, trying to remain calm and controlled around his boss. The problem was every time he looked at the man he saw Victoria Steers's intimidating visage along with the images of three dead people.

"Anything new on Lombard?" he asked before he could catch himself. But it was a perfectly appropriate query. Indeed it would have seemed unusual if he hadn't asked.

Rhett shook his head. "I don't know if they'll even find the poor guy's body."

You know they won't, thought Nash. "Well, it's quite a tragedy. His poor family."

"We've already taken steps to see that they're taken care of."

How? thought Nash. *Bullets to the head and body bags dumped in a landfill?* "That's very good of the firm," he said, now nervous that Rhett might find out he'd been shopping himself at other firms. But maybe they had been told to say nothing by the FBI unless they wanted an IRS audit for the next ten years.

When Nash drove through the gate to his community, the guard, a pudgy man in his forties named Rolf, stepped out and said, "Mr. Nash, a guy came here saying he was your father's friend and that you asked him to meet you at your house. I let him through."

"I gave no such permission."

Rolf took a step back. "Oh, um…"

"What was his name?" Nash asked sharply.

Rolf said nervously, "He didn't give a name."

Nash was more than a little put out. Why bother having a damn gate and paying a guard if anyone could just bullshit their way in? "What did he look like?"

Rolf told him and said, "Do you know him, sir?"

Through clenched teeth Nash said, "I know him."

"So it's okay?"

"Oh, we'll have to see about that."

24

SHOCK WAS ASTRIDE HIS HARLEY in the driveway of Nash's home.

Nash parked by the motorcycle and got out of the Rover.

Shock eyed him calmly. The man had been a frequent guest in the Nash home while Nash was growing up, and he had found Shock impossible to read. His father had told him that Shock was the best poker player he'd ever seen.

He was the same way in combat, Ty Nash had told his son. *I joined up but he got his ass drafted over to Nam, though if he'd been white he would have gotten a deferment because he was married and attending college.*

His father had also told Nash that Shock had adapted quickly to the toils and dangers of the war. *The man could go from cracking jokes one second to cracking necks the next, and calm just as quick,* his father had said.

Nash had known that his father was not easily impressed and feared no one. But Shock was the only man he knew who had captured his father's full respect. His unpredictable nature had also sometimes made his father anxious.

Normally, the Army doesn't like that feature in its soldiers, his father had once told a thirteen-year-old Nash after Shock had visited them. *But our second lieutenants were getting killed so fast we had to lead ourselves. And be unpredictable, because nobody had our backs.*

Nash said, "Come looking for the world's biggest prick? Sorry, he doesn't live here."

"Nice what you did with Rosie and her ma," rumbled Shock. "I saw her after you did."

"It was a test from my father."

Shock got off the bike and approached. Nash took a step back. It just seemed the smart thing to do when confronted by a man the size of Isaiah York.

Shock came to a stop a couple of feet from him and said, "And you passed."

"Why wouldn't my father just tell me what to do? That was more like him."

"Maybe you read him wrong."

"Don't think so. He wasn't subtle in that way."

Shock looked up at the imposing house. "Can a workin' man get a beer in a place like this, or do you only serve *Chardonnay*?"

Judith and Maggie were out, so it was only Nash and his visitor in the house. Nash led Shock to the lower level and poured them out beers from a tap set up at the bar.

They sat on the covered rear patio with views of the lovely and sculpted grounds that seemed to shimmer in the diminishing light—more illusion than reality, or so it suddenly seemed to Nash.

Shock took a sip of his beer and eyed the backyard vistas. "Nice setup. Real nice."

"But I'm sure you hate this *setup* with every fiber of your being, correct?" said Nash.

Shock cocked his head at him. "Why would I? Man works hard, earns money, you can do what you damn well want with it, is my opinion."

"It wasn't my father's perspective."

"Maybe, maybe not."

"He left you money."

"I know he did. Mort Dickey told me. I had the same in my will, if I'd gone first. Kinda wished I had. Strange as shit without Ty 'round."

"Nice to see he kicked the Army's ass on the Agent Orange."

"Yep. I got diddly-squat. Not sure they hold a Black man in the

same esteem as they do that 'other' race. Back then and today, too."
Then he surprised Nash by belly-laughing.

"You find racial injustice funny?" Nash asked.

Shock slapped his log of a thigh and said, "Racial injustice? Now
I find *that* funny comin' from you."

"I don't support any sort of discrimination."

"Oh, yeah? How many Black folks you got at your business?"

"We have people of color at my firm."

"How many? I mean in the top jobs? Not the secretaries and
mail room dudes."

"Well, not enough, certainly."

"Uh-huh. I wonder why that is. Got any suggestions? Come on,
help a bro' out."

"Okay, I guess I stand corrected."

"Yeah, that makes it all better. You stand corrected. Let's go
on the TV news and tell everybody it's all over now, go 'bout your
business. Racism is no more. Walter Nash stands fucken corrected."
Shock seemed to be enjoying this and grinned wickedly.

Nash, remembering what his father had told him, said, "You
were in college and married. How come you didn't fight the draft?
You could have gotten a deferment or gone into the National Guard.
That's what a lot of guys did."

"You mean a lot of *white* guys. And I *did* fight it. But they were
so horny for fresh Black meat that they pulled up an old police arrest
I had when I was sixteen and threw it in my face. They said if I didn't
go to Nam, I was goin' to prison. So's I went to war."

"I'm sorry that happened to you."

"Your daddy had joined up right outta high school, while I went
on to Gramblin' State. We played high school ball together. I was
pretty much the entire left side of both the O and D lines. Your
daddy was our smashmouth quarterback who could fling it sixty
yards on a rope, and then run over you if nobody was open for the
ball. He also played linebacker and would put your teeth right in
your balls when he hit you."

And joy, joy, I chose tennis, thought Nash. "So you hooked back up in Nam?"

"Got off the chopper and there he was. Couldn't believe that shit, man. But later I found out that he had pulled some strings and got me assigned to his platoon. Guess he wanted to make sure I didn't die the first week in the jungle." Shock took a swallow of beer. "He got three Purples and pretty much every other medal twice over."

"You got your share, too, including two Purples, a Bronze, and Silver Stars."

"Your daddy tell you that? 'Cause I don't talk 'bout that shit. Never have."

"He was proud of you."

"Went both ways. He did the full ride, mustered out as a sergeant major. I did my time and come back home. But we always kept in touch no matter what. When he got transferred here to finish out his stint, I moved here, too. So did a bunch of the old guys from the war."

"You must have really bonded for all of you to do that."

"Hell, he saved all our butts over there. Your daddy was a professional soldier. We were all just tryin' to survive. None of us would be here 'cept for Ty." He took another swig of beer and eyed Nash with interest. "You read the letter yet?"

"How do you even know about it?" demanded Nash. "Have *you* read it?"

Shock shook his head. "Ty told me he was gonna do it. Man say he gonna do somethin', he do it."

"I haven't read it yet. I just got it today."

Shock burrowed down in the comfortable chair. It was actually a chair and a half, which was why Nash had directed him to it. Even so, with Shock seated there, it was difficult to glimpse very much of the chair.

"You think Ty hated you, right?"

"No, I didn't think it. I *knew* he did."

"Based on?" asked Shock.

"My life." Nash set his beer down. "Look, is there a point to you coming here? If so, I'd like to get to it. I do have some things to do before an appointment I have tonight."

"Oh, right, I forgot, you a big shot. Not much time for us plebes."

"Come on, I know you can do better than that in the insult department if you really try. I mean, you set such a high bar at the church. You can't bring your B-game now. It makes you look downright *small*."

Shock smiled broadly and it added creases and dimples to the man's face that both relaxed and enhanced it, Nash thought. It was suddenly a nice face, a kind one. And that thought confused Nash because he had always believed that Shock was neither nice nor kind.

At least to me. He obviously worshipped my father. Like everyone else.

Shock said admiringly, "A fine stinger. You good all right. On fire with your barbs."

Nash decided to throw him a bit of a curve, and he was also interested in the answer. "What were you studying in college?"

"Finance."

Nash looked surprised, but Shock didn't look the least bit surprised at Nash being surprised.

"You thinkin' I was a football jock, right? How else a brother gettin' into college back then, right? Especially one my size."

"No, I was…"

"I'm just pullin' your chain, Walter. I *did* play football. Started my freshman year. But back then it ain't like it is today. Army didn't give a crap that maybe I had a shot at the pros. And back then the pros didn't pay shit anyways. No, I was lookin' at a job on maybe Wall Street. Be one of the first Black men to make his mark there. But I got shot up in Nam, so there went my football scholarship. Got back to the States and found out my GI Bill benefits were basically squat. So bye-bye college. I went to work at crap jobs so my family wouldn't starve, and then took control of my life and ended up doin' what I did."

"Which was what, exactly? Dad never said."

"Private security. Ty was the one who encouraged me to do it. When he was home on leave he helped me with the paperwork, gettin' my company set up. Even made some calls to his friends in the defense sector who'd done really well. My first clients came from there, in fact. I guess when it comes to savin' your own ass and bein' tough they think Black dudes know their shit. Only time my skin color helped me, come to think."

"Private security meaning what exactly?"

"Seventies were some crazy times, man. Patty Hearst gettin' snatched by the Symbionese Liberation Army and then robbin' banks. Oil Getty's grandson gettin' grabbed in Italy and losin' an ear. So rich people were on edge 'bout that stuff. And lots of American executives were gettin' kidnapped and held for ransom, especially down in Latin and South America. That shit happened all through the eighties and on. So they and their companies hired me to show them how to stay safe. Self-defense. How to break free from restraints, talkin' their way out of bad situations. Threat assessments so you don't get in those situations in the first place and also by practicin' hypervigilance for yourself and your family. Basic and then advanced weapons trainin'. Martial arts, hand-to-hand, whatever it took to stay alive and out of harm's way."

"So using your skills from the Army?"

"Me and your father was Green Berets. Delta Force didn't come into being until after the war was over. If Delta had been a thing, me and Ty woulda been part of it. We were just cut out for the crazy shit."

"They talked about your Green Beret experience at his retirement party. The places you went to and the things you did while you were there? You were both lucky to get out of southeast Asia alive."

"Nearly sixty thousand of us didn't," retorted Shock.

"I'd like to ask you a question about a *recent* event."

"Okay, shoot."

"Why the episode in the church?" Nash asked.

"Your old man told me to do it, so I did. No hard feelin's?"

"No hard feelings?" Nash said incredulously. "What you did was public humiliation of the worst sort at my *father's funeral*."

Shock rubbed his bald head and then shrugged. "You still standin'. Right? No permanent wounds that I can see."

"That you can *see*."

"Maybe he made you stronger with his shit, only you didn't realize it. Maybe what I said in that church was another test for you, too. What do you think?"

"What I think is I stopped having a father at age fourteen, right when having a father was actually really important."

"I got me four kids. Half would say I sucked, the other two think I'm Jesus. And they both right."

"So you just pick your battles *and* your kids?"

"Or they pick you."

"Didn't know it was a choice. Good thing I only have the one."

Shock finished his beer. "So you a perfect daddy? Good for you, Walter, baby."

"At least I made an effort. My father cut me off because I chose tennis over football. Who knew the choice of one's high school sport was such an important thing in a father-son relationship?"

"Is that what you really believe?"

"He made it pretty clear."

"Then you best read the letter. Might *enlighten* you more than I already have."

"If you think whatever he could put in a letter will change anything, well, you are as wrong as wrong can be."

"Read the letter, then we can talk."

"So you *have* read the letter then?"

"I told you I haven't, and I haven't. But your father didn't talk 'bout much else the last six months of his life, so I got a pretty good understandin' of what he was tryin' to say."

"Wait, are you telling me he worked six months on the letter?"

"After the VA docs gave him that much time to live, yeah. It was important to him."

Nash, who was clearly having none of this, shook his head. "Couldn't have been. Otherwise, he would have picked up the goddamn phone and called me."

"And you coulda done the same."

"Don't try and lay a guilt trip on *me*, Shock. I tried to talk to him. I tried to reconcile."

"Okay. But you gonna read the letter tonight?"

"Probably."

Shock pulled out a card and handed it to him. "Call me when you do. My private number's on the back."

Nash looked down at the front of the card. "SCIF?"

"That's government-speak for Sensitive Compartmented Information Facility. I took the acronym as my company name. Sounded cool, I thought, for my training academy."

"Your training academy?"

"Yeah. I got a condo in town not too far from Ty's. But my trainin' center's in another state. Remote. Nobody around to bother me, or my trainees."

The business side of Nash kicked in. "How many trainees do you typically handle at a time?"

"Depends. Somebody gets kidnapped or killed, my phone's ringin' off the hook. Things calm down then so do my numbers. 'Course I been windin' things down. I'm gettin' up there in age, semiretired."

"So you cheer for chaos then?"

"What do you cheer for?" asked Shock.

"Stability, predictability."

Shock rose. "Yeah, borin' as hell. Figures."

"Well, as you can see, boring worked out *great* for me."

"Guess it depends on how you define *great*," Shock retorted.

When Nash stood, too, Shock said, "Don't worry yourself, Walter. I can find my way outta here. It's big but I seen way bigger. Some of my clients fly me out on their private wings to their own fucken island. They don't have no houses, see, they got *compounds*. Or some own a whole street of big-ass places, so's they can sleep in a different mansion every day for a whole week, for some fucked-up rich dude's reason. And they also got people to tell 'em how great they are and other people to wipe their ass. Way I see it, those jobs are the same. They both dealin' with shit. So long, *prick*."

As Shock trudged off, Nash sat back down in his chair and stared out at his lovely backyard, but no longer really seeing it or pretty much anything else.

CHAPTER

25

Maggie had not come home; she was probably holed up in a Starbucks redoing her pitch, Nash figured. He had tried Judith's phone, but it had gone to voicemail. Then he recalled that she was having drinks and dinner with a girlfriend.

He'd changed into khaki shorts and a Polo shirt and tennis shoes, then made a tuna sandwich and added a bag of baked chips, and ate it standing up in the kitchen with a glass of iced tea. It felt like his college days, when breakfast, lunch, and dinner might all be rolled into one meal, depending on how much or how little he had in his wallet.

He drove off in his Range Rover, and a few minutes later pulled into a parking space at the park where he would bring Maggie as a child for soccer practice and matches. It was hopping on a fine, warm night. There were people playing tennis under the lights. He could hear the cries from the adjacent baseball field where a rollicking game was clearly going on. A number of people strolled along the paths through the trees. A nice, early-summer's evening, and here he was waiting for a call from the FBI.

He put his AirPods in and started down a path that he knew led to the soccer field.

The phone rang at precisely nine o'clock.

"Where are you?" asked Morris.

"I'm at the park near my house. Just going for a nice walk like lots of other people."

"Yeah, well, just keep your defenses up. Strange stuff happens all the time."

Nash said pointedly, "Really? I had no idea."

"Touché."

"Have they found Lombard's remains?" asked Nash.

"No."

"What indiscretions?"

"Excuse me?" said Morris.

"Duvall said Lombard and the others had made indiscretions that led to their being found out and killed. What sorts of indiscretions? I need details."

"You're going to work with us then?"

"I'm still going through my due diligence. So, indiscretions?"

"Danielle Cho, we think, divulged some information to a coworker she trusted. That coworker let it slip to someone who could not be trusted. In Alexandra Singer's case, we believe it was her boyfriend."

"Her boyfriend? Did he betray her?"

"Not exactly. We believe that Steers's group already suspected Singer. Piecing things together, we think they set up her boyfriend with a woman. She probably got him drunk, they had a one-night stand, and he more than likely spilled things he shouldn't have. Singer died shortly thereafter."

"Yes, from a fall at the Grand Canyon. And the boyfriend?"

"He was on the trip with her to the canyon. He vanished right after she fell."

"Dead?"

"I would bet my house on it," said Morris. "He was a distinct loose end. And the way the media reported it, if there was foul play, they blamed the disappearing boyfriend. The local police are in full agreement with that assessment. Very neatly done on Steers's end."

"And Lombard's indiscretion?"

"We think he divulged something to his wife or one of his adult children. They might have let it slip. Anything else?"

Wife and adult children—good to know. "Yes. Black Cliffs Investments."

"Never heard of them."

"Really? I contacted Roland Zuckerman, the CEO, who has been trying to get me to jump there for years. I made noises about wanting to do just that. I got turned down flat. A similar result happened with another such firm. I would assume the same would occur with the seven other investment outfits who wanted to hire me."

"What can I tell you, Mr. Nash? It's national security."

"Won't it look suspicious to, say, Rhett Temple that firms that lusted after me now won't touch me with a ten-foot pole?"

"It's pretty simple. You can be part of the solution or the problem."

"And my demands? The money, the personal security, all the rest?"

"Working on it. But I can tell you that you're valuable to us."

"The normal way to show you value someone is by giving them what they've asked for, or at least close to it."

"Like I said, working on it."

"Then work faster," said Nash curtly.

He ended the call and walked to the soccer field, where a group of teenagers were playing a match. They were fit and active and energetic and most of all free of … shit, he thought.

I have a wonderful wife and daughter. Plenty of money. Beautiful home. A job that is challenging and has taken me around the world. And now?

Nash sat on the bleachers and watched kids simply being kids, and right now wished more than anything that he could be one of them, too.

CHAPTER

26

"So, HAS WALT BEEN ACTING funny lately?"

Rhett climbed off Judith Nash and lay beside her, breathing hard while pulling the sheet over both their sweat-frothed, naked bodies. She had noted his heavily bandaged left arm when they had undressed. Rhett had told her he had injured himself while doing some rock-climbing.

"Ripped the crap out of it. Got stitches all the way up. Lucky I didn't kill myself."

"Oh my God, you poor thing."

She had been extra gentle with the injured arm.

Now he lit up a cigarette and offered her a puff, but she firmly declined and then just as firmly told him to put it out.

"I can't go home smelling like smoke, Rhett. I'm supposed to be out with a girlfriend who's a *triathlete.*"

"Sorry. Force of habit. I should quit. I hear it's bad for your health," he quipped. He stubbed out the smoke in an ashtray on his nightstand.

They were in the master bedroom of his penthouse. As usual, Judith had come up in the service elevator wearing a floppy hat, sunglasses, and a long coat, despite the warmth of the evening. She would leave the same way, walk two blocks to a parking lot where she had left her car, and then drive home with a cover story to tell her husband.

"So, about Walt?"

"We just had amazing sex and you want to talk about my *husband*?" Judith asked. She turned to look at him, her brow furrowed and her features tight. "I remember not that long ago when we'd do it, and you'd be ready to go again in five minutes."

"I'm not in my twenties anymore."

He cracked a grin that made Rhett actually seem ten years younger.

She kissed him on the lips. "I actually like you just the way you are."

He sat up and took a sip of scotch from the glass next to the ashtray. "Okay, here's my offer: Answer my question about Walt, then seduce me all over again with that gorgeous body of yours and we'll go for round two. Orgasm guaranteed."

"Why are you worried about Walter? He's the rock of frigging Gibraltar."

"You make that sound like a bad thing."

"Rocks are boring, Rhett."

"If we go for round two, it won't be boring."

She slipped her hand to his crotch. "To sweeten the deal, I'll start it off with something I know you really, really like and which I don't even do for Walter."

"I love things you do for me that you won't do for him."

"You had no intention of going to the funeral, did you?" she said abruptly, letting go of him.

He eyed her curiously. "Forgot all about it, actually."

Judith made a pouty face that was reminiscent of her daughter. "Although the flowers were a nice comeback."

"Walt said it went okay."

"Actually there was a man there who publicly humiliated him."

Rhett glanced sharply at her. "At his dad's funeral? What was that about?"

"Walter's dad was one mean son of a bitch. Completely cut Walter out of his life. He was in Vietnam. I think it made him nuts. And his friends, too, including the jerk that was talking crap about Walter from the church pulpit."

"Damn," said Rhett.

"And that Agent Orange stuff? Walter's father got sprayed over and over with it. He got a big financial settlement from the Army. He left some of it in trust for Maggie. Walter is the trustee. We just found all that out."

"Is he going to let Maggie use the dollars for her influencer business you've been telling me about?"

"I'm sure Walter will analyze everything and then arrive at a decision that is fair and equitable."

"Fair and equitable. Rock of Gibraltar. And boring as shit."

She smiled weakly. "Let's not talk about him anymore. I really do care for Walter. A lot. He's a good husband and father. He works really hard. He's just…I don't know. Too damn predictable." She let out a sigh.

"Well, to answer your question about why I'm concerned about Walt, I found out that your *predictable* hubby phoned a competitor and asked about taking an executive position there."

Judith sat upright so fast the sheet slipped off her. "He never told me about that."

"Which is why I'm worried."

She took Rhett's scotch from him and took a sip before handing it back and covering herself with the sheet.

"He's always seemed perfectly happy working for you."

"He really works for my father, not me. Walt is a superstar in my old man's eyes. I'm just the nepo hire."

"Well, he *is* great at what he does."

"And yet here you are."

She gave him a sharp glance. "I didn't say he was great at *everything*."

"You married the Eagle Scout, but you really like the badass boys like yours truly."

She giggled. "Did you know? He *was* an Eagle Scout."

They both laughed hard, holding on to each other and shaking with mingled amusement.

"So, no clue what's going on in the man's head?" said Rhett when they'd both calmed and lay back against the pillows. He fingered the groove along her collarbone while he admired the soft, ample breasts just below.

"No. He and Maggie *did* have a falling-out. She really wants to build her influencer career and he told her that her proposal was bullshit, which, knowing Maggie, it probably was. She's smart and quick on her feet, but attention to detail and work discipline are not in her wheelhouse. She definitely did not take after her father in that department."

"Few people know business better or work harder than your hubby. He is scorched-earth when it comes to that. Never misses anything."

"But he talked to her again and she's all right now. But I don't see how that would make him want to change jobs."

"Me either." He finished his scotch.

"How did you find out about the other firm?"

"We have spies everywhere." Something in his response seemed to pulse in Rhett's eyes.

Judith, who was looking at him, apparently noticed. "You okay?"

"Yeah, just thinking of stuff. Luckily Walt is Superman again, coming to save the day with a real earnings blowout for his division. Let me survive another year in my dad's eyes."

"Then make sure he gets a great bonus. I want to go to Thailand, Hong Kong, Vietnam, and Malaysia in the fall and shop to my heart's content."

"With or without Walt?"

"He has no interest. I'll probably go solo." She gave him a significant look and hiked her lovely eyebrows enticingly. "Maybe you and I could hook up there. I won't have to sneak up the service elevator. We could actually go out in public as a couple."

"I'm always up for sex and shopping with hot chicks in new lands."

"You should be a greeting card writer for Hallmark," she said sarcastically.

He slid the sheet off them. "I'd actually much rather be a lover."

She looked down at him there. "Well, Rhett, you clearly don't need my help."

He pulled her toward him. "Sorry, Judith, you promised and can't renege on the deal now. And keep your eyes and ears open about Walt. Don't want to see that bonus go away."

Later, as he labored on top of a loudly moaning and writhing Judith, he was thinking far more about her husband than he was about her.

CHAPTER

27

NASH WAS IN HIS STUDY when Judith returned home late that night. He appeared in the doorway as she was heading up the stairs.

"Did you have a good time?"

She was startled. "Walter? I thought you'd already be asleep."

"Just finishing up some work."

"Yes, it was nice. Jean is doing another triathlon in September in Thailand."

"Better her than me."

"I was actually thinking about going out there, to cheer her on, do some shopping, see the sights. I might even venture to some other places. Hong Kong, Malaysia, Vietnam."

"Sounds exciting."

"You wouldn't care to come, I'm sure, right?"

"You know that's my busiest month."

"Oh, I forgot." Judith had picked September for that very reason.

"Maybe Maggie would like to go."

"Oh, I doubt that," Judith said quickly.

"It might be good for her influencer business."

"I thought you didn't want her jetting around the world."

"You're right, I don't. By the way, she got home about twenty minutes ago."

"I'm glad you patched things up with her." She stared at Nash for perhaps a beat too long.

"Everything okay?" he asked.

"It's fine. I'm just tired. Did you eat?"

"Yes, I did, plenty."

"You never eat plenty, Walter."

"Am I that predictable?"

Her face fell but just for a moment. "I like predictable. It's reassuring. You're my rock. My...Eagle Scout."

"Thanks, babe."

She slipped off her high heels, and headed up the stairs as he returned to his desk.

On the blotter was the letter from his father.

Come on, just read it. How bad can it be? Surely no worse than what you already imagined.

He took a deep breath, slit open the envelope, took out the letter, and unfolded the pages.

Here goes.

> *Dear Walter Nash:*

Nash said out loud, "Okay, that opening doesn't bode well."

> *We had a fine time together you and me sonny boy*
> *right up until you betrayed and destroyed the one*
> *person I held above all others.*

Here, Nash stopped and his mind started whirling as to what in the hell his father was talking about. Had Agent Orange eaten his brain as well as his body? He read on.

> *You were fourteen just starting high school. I drove*
> *you and your mother to play tennis because you*
> *wanted to try out for the team and your mother*
> *was really good. I wanted you to play a sport which*
> *one didn't matter. I hung around to watch. Do you*
> *remember that day as clearly as I do?*

Nash slowly leaned back in his chair. He *did* remember it quite clearly. The girl's name was Lisbeth Stamatis; she went by Liz. She was an incoming freshman like himself, and he'd had a hopeless crush on her. She had long, straight dark hair, huge brown eyes, and lovely olive skin. He had heard that her grandparents had come from Mykonos. She was the most beautiful girl he'd ever seen.

His stiff-limbed mother had been dressed in baggy sweatpants and an oversized shirt, with a bandanna around her head. She'd been under the weather for a while now. After several years of tests with no answers and lots of ineffective treatments and medications, she would finally be diagnosed with lupus. But despite her pain and lack of energy, she had been happy to play tennis with her son when he'd asked her to. And Nash was eager for his mother to show him some of the skills she had learned in her youth, when she'd been captain of her high school tennis team and had also won the state singles championship.

However, as soon as he and his mother had stepped out on the court, Nash had seen Stamatis and two of her girlfriends heading their way, rackets in hand. The real reason Nash had wanted to play tennis was because he knew Stamatis was trying out for the girls' team. And he also knew that the girls' and boys' teams practiced together and also traveled to matches and tournaments together.

But that day Nash had freaked out.

He had rushed across the court and told his mother to please leave. He would walk home. She didn't know what was going on and didn't want to go, but he kept on and on until she became angry and stalked off. Nash had then gone over to Stamatis and her friends and suggested that they play doubles, since there were four of them now.

Nash returned to the letter.

> As your mother walked away crying by the way
> because she couldn't understand what was happen-
> ing I drew closer. You were so absorbed with your
> pretty "friend" that you never saw me. But I heard
> the girl ask you who the woman was you had been
> there with. And you said just some sort of crazy per-
> son wandering around. And then all of you laughed.
> Only I didn't think it was funny. I thought it was
> the opposite of funny. I thought it cruel and dirty

*and a betrayal of the woman who smothered you
with love her entire life. Did you know she took pain
pills before going out with you that day? And that I
rubbed her arms and legs to get the stiffness out and
the circulation going? I told her to just tell you no,
that she couldn't play with you that day. But she said
she would never disappoint you.*

*I never told your mother what I heard from
you that day because it would have broken her heart.
That night I held her as tightly as I could but she
wouldn't stop crying. Now I know you were only
fourteen sonny boy but you damn sure should have
known better. So when you came over that night
with the food and beer when your mom was in the
hospital you seemed shocked when I knocked your
ass off my porch. But all I saw that night was your
fourteen year old self being embarrassed by your
poor sick mother. And my heart turned to flint and I
forgot about the good husband and father that you
grew up to be. I know I should have just let bygones
be bygones. And for just about anything else I would
have.*

*Your mother died loving you. And despite every-
thing I've written in this letter I died loving you too.
We all have regrets Walter and that one is mine. If I
could do it over again I would have patched things
up. But I am a proud old bastard set in my ways and
more than capable of carrying a life-long grudge. I
just never intended to do it with my only child. But
I picked that hill of all hills to die on. I should have
known better because I spent years of my life taking
back and losing hills in Nam for no reason whatsoever.
But sometimes people are so full of anger they can't see
straight and I guess that was me.*

*Thank you for doing right by your mother as
I know you will do right by Rosie. Tell Judith and
Maggie that I love them and to not think too harshly
of an old foolish man. If you ever need help of any
kind seek out the one person that I hold above all
others with the sole exception of your mother. Shock
will be there for you no matter what. Because I have
asked him to be. I hope the rest of your life is everything you want it to be.*

Love
For better or worse
Your Old Man

*P.S. I've told Shock to kick your ass at the funeral
service and I know that he will. It won't be done to
humiliate you Walter though I'm sure it will in a certain way. My father was neither kind nor good to me.
But him raining hell down on me every day didn't just
make me rebellious and angry it made me tougher
smarter and cagier. I know most shrinks wouldn't agree
with that approach and I never earned a sheepskin but
who the hell knows? What I know is if I didn't care
about you I would have had Shock ignore you to show
that you weren't important to me at the end. But you
are important to me Walter. You're my son.*

Nash slowly folded the paper after carefully blotting away all
the teardrops and slid it back into the envelope. He placed it in a
drawer of his desk.

He rose, turned out the light in his office, sat back down in his
chair, and never really moved until he heard Judith come down the
stairs the next morning.

28

"WALTER, HAVE YOU BEEN UP all night?" Judith exclaimed as she poked her head into the study after seeing him sitting there.

He glanced at his wife, who was outfitted in her workout gear. "No. I just came down a little bit ago."

"But you're still wearing the clothes you had on from last night?"

He stretched. "I slept in them, in the sitting room. Didn't want to disturb you."

"It's impossible—"

"—yes, I know, to wake you. How about some coffee? I was going to make some."

"I'm going to hit the gym. I'm a little…um, sore this morning and want to stretch."

"Okay. Have a good workout."

She left him there, shaking her head and wondering what was going on with her Rock of Gibraltar Eagle Scout looking to change jobs and staying up all night.

As she headed down to stretch, run on the treadmill, and pump some weights, Judith suddenly thought, *Wait, does he suspect? Is that why he wants a new job? Rhett and I probably need to cool things for a while. But maybe we can still make the Asian trip work.*

* * *

Nash made his coffee and fried an egg and burned some toast, and ate and drank it all fast.

He had reread the letter once more and his emotional response had been even fiercer.

Dad was right. What I did was unforgivable.

He trudged upstairs to begin a new day when all he felt like doing was crawling into bed and assuming the fetal position.

He showered, suited up, and passed Maggie on the way downstairs as she was coming back up with a bagel and a cup of Starbucks.

"Working hard, Father dearest," she said. "I'll have something to show you soon."

He drove to work thinking of nothing but the letter from his father. When he got to the parking garage he remembered. He pulled out the business card and made the call.

Shock answered and said, "You read the letter?"

"How did you know it was me? You don't have my phone number."

"Your mom did and she told Ty, and he told me. It's in my contacts."

"I read the letter."

"And?"

"And now I understand better why...things were as they were. And also why you said what you did at the funeral service."

"But keep in mind that your daddy was sorry for all the shit, Walter, he really was."

"But he was also right. I should have known better."

"Guys' brains don't finish formin' till they 'bout twenty-six. Yours was basically mush and you had the girl thing goin' on and that is some serious shit to a young buck."

"I see he told you a lot."

"I helped him with some phrasin'. But know that I didn't agree with him 'bout all of it. I told him I woulda done the same thing if I wanted to get in a girl's pants."

"I just wanted her to *like* me. I was only fourteen."

"Some boys start later than others. Had my first kid at seventeen. Did he mention regrets?"

"He did. I take it that was your influence?"

"If he hadn't felt it, he never would have written it. Ty was his own man."

"He also said that if I ever needed help that you were the one I should turn to."

"Yes, I am."

"But you really don't even know me, Shock. I don't think you even *like* me."

"I knew and loved your father. That's enough."

"He never told me how you got your nickname. He said I hadn't earned the right to know."

"Guess you didn't then" was all Shock had to say about that.

"I . . . I have regrets too. If I had made more of an effort. If maybe he and I could have talked it out, because—"

"—because before that things were good between you two?"

"I feel like I pissed away over a quarter century's worth of father-son adventures."

"But your old man died lovin' you, Walter."

"That's what he wrote, so I believe it."

"Damn right," said Shock. "Man's word was his bond."

"Still hard to believe I'm his son."

"Why?"

"Because he was right. I *am* a prick."

"No, you Ty Nash's boy. And Ty Nash was the best friend I ever had. So I will always have your back, Walter. And you can take that to the fucken bank."

29

RHETT HAD BEEN SUMMONED AGAIN by his father, so he made the trek out to the splendid estate nestled in the privacy of the hills. To him, the place looked moderately different in the daylight, like a forlorn castle instead of an angry prison.

On the drive out he thought about Nash looking to jump to another firm and wondered why he would want to. The man was making a great deal of money at Sybaritic. He was master of his own ship. But maybe not really, corrected Rhett. It could be the man wanted to be the top guy, not just a division leader. It could be as simple as that.

And maybe he is tired of carrying my water.

He was admitted to the mansion by the butler.

Rhett said, "What's your name again? Hubert or Herbert?"

"It's Colin, sir."

"Right. How's the old man? Good mood?"

"I wouldn't begin to know, sir. He is as he always is."

"And Mindy?"

"It's not yet noon, so madam will not be up. She arrived back, I believe from France, last night."

"Cannes, I heard."

"If you say so. Your father is in his office. Shall I show you up, sir?"

"No, go back to polishing the silver. I know the way."

Rhett jogged up the stairs and turned right, not left, because he wanted to see someone else first.

He knocked on the door. "Angie, it's Et."

The door was whisked open, and Angie stood there dressed in purple pajamas with pink bunny slippers.

"Et!"

She motioned him into the room and over to a table set up with teacups and a large pot. There were four chairs around the table, and three of them were occupied by large stuffed animals, including a zebra.

She had him sit down in the fourth chair and poured Rhett out a cup of cold tea, tapping the pot four times in front of him and mouthing words that he knew were part of her ritualistic incanting. He drank the cold tea and bit into a cookie from a plate offered him. Then he watched as she poured out cups of cold tea for her friends and fed the zebra a cookie.

"Why you here?" she asked her stepbrother.

"To see Dad."

Her smile faded.

"What's wrong?" he said.

She pointed to the door and shook her head fiercely. The expression on her face was so bitter and potentially explosive that Rhett thought she might be about to have a traumatic episode.

Didn't they give Angie her meds today?

"What is it?"

She pointed and shook her head again.

Then it hit him. "Are you saying Dad doesn't come to see you?"

She nodded and said, "And I hate Indy too. She a *bitch*. Bitch, bitch, bitch."

"Yeah, Mindy is a piece of work."

Angie put the plate of cookies down, picked up a sketch pad and pencil, and began drawing stick figures on it. Her features relaxed and she hummed away, seemingly forgetting that he was even there.

Rhett slowly got up and left. Outside Angie's room he watched as his stepmother sauntered down the hall. She was wearing the tiniest of string bikinis and carried a beach bag in one hand and a magazine in the other. Her body was long and lean and fit and quite tanned.

"What are you doing here?" Mindy Temple said in an unfriendly tone.

"The commander ordered me up. Heading to the pool to get over the jet lag?"

"No, I'm going to go mow the grass."

He glanced at her small bits of clothing. "Lucky grounds crew."

Mindy passed so close by him that her scent cascaded over him.

"In your dreams, Rhett. In your *wet* dreams."

"I don't actually dream much anymore. How was Cannes? Win anything?"

"I won your daddy's affections. And who knows, you might have competition in the heir department soon." She made a rounding motion over her flat belly.

"I always enjoy a good game," he replied. "Keeps me on my toes."

She drew closer. "I bet you'd like to keep me on *my* toes, wouldn't you?"

"You're off the market, Mindy. Even by my standards."

Her expression became far less flippant and far more strategic. "The thing is, I don't want to have a kid. It screws up your body and I don't want to blimp up. It's why I'm on the pill. But that's not the point."

"Not following."

She glanced around to make sure no one was nearby. "Look Rhett, I'm sure you know I'm locked into a shitty prenup. Barton's lawyers screwed me but good. But if I forego the kid, what can you do for me when you get the grand prize? It'll have to be in writing, of course. Otherwise, I'll let him get me pregnant and all bets are off for you."

"You're very transactional."

"Hell, you Temples swear by that philosophy. So why not me? I have to look out for myself."

"Well, what I can do is think about it."

"Think *hard*. None of us are getting any younger, especially your father. And who knows, there might be some added perks in it for you if we can make a deal."

She bumped him with her hip and headed on, slowly walking catlike down the hall and giving him a view from behind. She turned to look back once, smiled at his riveted attention, and kept going.

If my dad does manage to impregnate you, Min, I know a urologist who's going to get his ass sued off.

CHAPTER

30

Rhett headed to his father's office on the top floor, knocked, and was told to enter.

Barton Temple was sitting behind a whale of a desk that Rhett had been told had come from one of the Chanel chateaus in France. His father was dressed in dark slacks and a white shirt, open at the collar. He was puffing on a cigar, and a glass of bourbon was next to his elbow.

His father pointed to a chair opposite and Rhett plunked himself down.

Barton took a few moments to peck on his keyboard, then took off his trifocals and studied his son, who had slouched in the chair and was gazing at the ceiling.

His father barked, "Sit like a goddamn CEO! Not like some jock in eighth-grade math class!"

Rhett slowly sat up straight and stared across at his father. "I had to cancel some meetings to come out here. What's up?"

"What's up is your company, which I gave you, is in danger of going right into the shitter."

"My numbers are not that bad," said Rhett. "And Walt—"

"And Walt is looking to jump ship."

"So you heard?"

"I guarantee I heard before you, boy," snapped his father.

"Nothing happened."

"No, something *did* happen. What happened was he got turned down."

Rhett sat up even straighter. "Every one of our competitors would sacrifice a child to get Nash. So what happened?"

His father smashed his fist down so hard on the desk's surface that his bourbon glass moved an inch. "It's your job to know the answer to that question."

"I can make some inquiries."

"You should have already made them."

"Okay, why do *you* think they turned him down?"

His father gave him an incredulous look. "I would imagine they turned him down because they are scared shitless of yours truly, boy."

"O-kay."

"And at some point I won't be here, so then it won't be *o-kay* if you keep your head buried in your ass."

"I hear you."

His father didn't even appear to be listening. "Nash is tired of cleaning up your messes. Who wouldn't be?"

"What do you want me to do about it?"

"You do whatever you have to do to keep him happy because there are shops out there that don't give a shit about taking away one of my top people, and sooner or later they will make a play for Nash. So more salary, more bonus, more everything."

"How much more?" asked Rhett sharply.

"Just make sure it's more than you make, boy. And I will check. Now, get out of here."

"That's it? Really? Again, you never heard of a freaking text?"

Barton smirked. "What, and not spend quality face-to-face time with my only son?"

Rhett rose and turned to the door.

"One more thing," said his father.

Rhett turned back.

"You keep screwing the man's wife, you are going to get burned." Barton shook his head. "I can understand your interest. I've wanted to jump Judith's bones for years. But I'm far too smart to go down *that* road. There's a lot of other ass out there, boy. Go after that and steer clear of her."

"And who's going to burn me? Walt? Highly doubtful."

"Not Walt."

"Who then?" Rhett sneered. "You? And give me a break. Like you never screwed the help's wives."

His father studied him for a long moment. "Okay, I guess you finally need to know. Not exactly my favored choice of timing, but I'm old, tired, and sick of your shit."

"Need to know what?"

He looked his son over. "How's the arm where they sliced and diced you? Still hurt? See, they thought you needed a lesson taught. Forcefully. They actually wanted to kill you, but I talked them out of that. So they cut up your arm instead. But you keep doing what you're doing, your ass is done, and I'll have no say in it. Understand me?"

Rhett felt as though every nerve in his body had just been set aflame.

His father picked up on this and smiled but there was nothing behind it this time except resignation. "Yeah, boy. If you ever think you know more than I do, think again. Now get out of here. As I said, I'm busy, with matters of importance, which obviously rules you out."

Rhett left the room, rushed down the stairs, and then plopped into a chair set against a wall in the long hall.

This can't be happening. He knows. He more than knows. He's... all part of it. Which means he...got me into this...nightmare.

He got up, struggling to catch his breath, desperate for some...help.

Rhett hurried downstairs to the wing where there was an indoor gym and spa area that his father had built out for Mindy. It had a large fitness space, a hot tub, a lap pool, a steam shower, a sauna, a massage room, a hair and nail salon, and an immersion tank. He rushed into one of the bathrooms and did his line of coke, snorting it with a velocity powered by a burst of anxiety he had never felt before in his entire pampered existence.

I am so screwed. And my own father screwed me.

He turned and walked out of the bathroom only to see Mindy staring at him. She had stepped out of the adjacent sauna, lightly perspiring and with a towel wrapped around her.

"You look a little out of sorts, Rhett," she observed.

Regaining his composure he answered, "And you look a little out of clothes, *Mom*."

"Oh come on, I'm wearing more than when you were watching me all the way down the hall. And if you have complaints I can always put my itty-bitty bikini back on."

"I don't have time for this, Mindy."

"Did 'Daddy' drop a bombshell on you or something?"

"What do you know about it?" he said sharply.

"Just taking a guess based on your pale face and that smear of coke on your nostril, and the fact that you're not looking like you want to screw me right now."

"That was then, this is now."

"'That was then' was the night before my wedding, Rhett. We had a nice time before I said my vows to your father." She dropped the towel, drew close, and ran her fingers over his chest. "I can act the supportive stepmom and help you through what must be a crisis and let you get back at Barton for whatever he did."

He gave her a searching look, but in his heart of hearts Rhett knew that his father never would have disclosed anything about Victoria Steers and his involvement with her to this woman.

She said, "And then you can help me with the little matter we discussed earlier."

As she nudged herself against him, Rhett's faint defenses fell away. He knew he shouldn't. But it might have been the coke pop, the stunning revelation that his father was in business with Victoria Steers, or the fact that when it came to women, he had no willpower. They headed for the massage room, where there was an adequately sturdy bed.

Thirty minutes later he walked out, leaving a contented Mindy still lying under the sheets.

As he drove away from his father's home he had problems to solve.

And Walter Nash was right at the very top of his list.

CHAPTER

31

IN HIS HOME STUDY, NASH stared at his personal laptop screen. He had connected to the internet using a burner phone hot spot and a VPN address. He had full access to all records and databases having to do with his division. And as a member of the board of directors he also had access to the records and financial performance of the rest of the company. He was diligent about reviewing this information, so his delving into these materials would raise no suspicions. But he had chosen to be overly cautious by conducting this search via his personal devices and the use of a VPN wall because all computer keystrokes on company computers were monitored and the search history captured for certain eyes to see. And there would be a record of who had accessed the site. Fortunately, the password was the same for all board members, so the company wouldn't be able tell the identity of the user solely through that.

Nash didn't know much about money laundering, but he had done some quick research. He had found that the money had to be placed, layered, and then integrated or extracted. And there were myriad ways to do that, but it basically came down to mingling ill-gotten gains into the legitimate financial world in a way that would evade scrutiny.

Deputy AG Duvall had said that the government believed Sybaritic used parasitic elements presumably as the placement stage of the laundering. He wasn't sure what "parasitic elements" meant, exactly, but it could be the use of shell companies, staged transactions, and doctored or duplicate sets of business and transaction records.

Cho, Singer, and Lombard had worked at three different companies, all acquired by Sybaritic.

All really acquired by me, thought Nash uncomfortably.

He had pulled up the financial records for the trio of companies and had already spent the better part of a day going over them. He was about to give up when something odd caught his attention.

On the surface it was innocuous enough: an asset purchase by Danielle Cho's company, PLA Corp., with the seller being a firm based in Hong Kong. The purchase price had been $100 million. The amount had been paid partly in cash and partly by promissory note. There was nothing strange in that, but what *was* unusual was the promissory note had been issued not to the selling party, but to another company with a very similar name. In fact, the names were identical except one was "LLC" and one was "LLP."

So thirty million dollars in the form of a note went to LLP instead of LLC. And who was behind LLC?

When Nash looked up LLP online, he found that it had been sold six months ago for exactly $34.5 million. It appeared that the only asset the company had was the promissory note issued by Cho's company, PLA. When he did a calculation Nash found the additional $4.5 million represented the total interest payments due. But when he checked the financial records for PLA, he could find no interest payments being made at all. When he looked at LLP he found that it had been incorporated apparently for the sole purpose of acquiring the note. When he researched LLC—the actual selling company that had been paid the rest of the purchase price by Cho's company in cash—Nash found that it had quickly wound up operations and dissolved, taking the $70 million along with it.

And what exactly had PLA purchased with the $70 million? Because it was clear that the $30 million note and interest thereon would never be paid.

The answer—which aligned with PLA's business of acquiring

Pacific Rim assets—was a food-processing plant in Vietnam that had been closed down by the government six months later for numerous building code and health violations. So the entire investment had been written off as a loss by PLA. The $30 million note should have continued to be listed as a liability of PLA, but it had mysteriously disappeared from the company's balance sheet.

Nash sat back and closed his eyes. This fulfilled the trio of elements of money laundering: placement, layering, and integration/extraction. Seventy million dollars had been funneled from PLA to a company based in Vietnam. That company no longer existed. The asset purchased, namely the processing plant, no longer operated. PLA had dropped a $30 million liability from its balance sheet, but otherwise had, on paper, lost seventy million on the deal.

But there was one remaining detail. Where had the $70 million in cash that PLA used to buy the processing plant originated from?

Nash got incredibly lucky by happening on a password that had apparently been recycled. What was revealed was, in essence, a second set of electronic books.

As he hunkered down and went through the screens, the financial happenings started trickling out. PLA had borrowed $104.5 million—which represented the cash and note portion of the purchase price plus interest payments—from two firms, one based in Chad and the other in Haiti. Those countries did not have the best reputations when it came to anti-money-laundering regulations, Nash knew. For that reason he avoided doing business with anyone who used either country for anything.

So presumably Victoria Steers had laundered nine figures' worth of illegal proceeds and walked away with $70 million of clean money. Not a bad price to be paid, particularly when one's profit margins on the fentanyl side were thousands of percentage points.

But now came the obvious difficulty. PLA had suffered a $70 million loss on paper, plus it still owed the repayment of the loan.

That would place it squarely on the acquisition division's P&L statement, meaning that the purchase of PLA would have been a terrible deal for Sybaritic and seriously impacted the returns of Nash's division. But that had not happened, Nash knew, because he monitored all acquired companies' performances closely. In fact, looking at PLA's financials, the loss due to the processing plant's closure had been more than made up by a $150 million profit from the sale of... Nash couldn't quite believe it. Another processing plant in Vietnam. Acquired the previous year for $50 million, PLA had then sold it for $200 million.

They just cleaned another chunk of change in that deal. And PLA can offset nearly half of the gain on that sale by the loss they'll take on the processing plant's being shut down.

Nash exited out of the accounts and thought about all of this.

So Cho must have discovered these bogus transactions, just like Lombard and Singer no doubt ferreted out financial misdeeds at their own respective companies. And Steers's involvement in the companies that I acquired has actually helped their performance, which means I'm not as smart as I thought I was. But then why was Rhett's division racking up all those losses?

The answer hit him immediately.

They're losses on paper only, and by using two sets of books, they're able to shield actual, legitimate income from taxation, which means illicit funds are flowing right through my company and taxes that should be paid aren't being paid.

Both Steers and Rhett Temple are walking away with record profits free from taxation and hidden behind false sets of electronic books. To his father, Rhett's a loser, but in reality, he's probably a bigger winner than I am.

Which means my boss really is up to his neck in crime.

Then something struck him.

Were our accountants and auditors also in on it? Some of them must be. Hell, am I the only one at the company not in on it? Bernie

Madoff, the king of the Ponzi players, had always claimed that he acted alone. But that was impossible.

But then an obvious point occurred to Nash.

Cho, Singer, and Lombard clearly weren't in on it, which is why they're all dead.

And now there's me right in the crosshairs.

CHAPTER

32

THE GULFSTREAM G800 TOUCHED DOWN and slowly
rolled to a stop. Victoria Steers didn't look out the window at the
cloudy, windless day in one of the most unstable countries on earth.
The most recent coup several years earlier had left a military junta in
charge, though its grip on the country was now slipping badly. Here,
corruption, human trafficking, and drug smuggling were rampant,
and they had been exploited by certain forces within China.

Steers did not like to be summoned by anyone and there were
few in the world who could command her to do anything. But one
of them was about to come aboard her jet.

She now glanced out the window to see the arrival of the impressive motorcade.

Steers eyed her five immensely capable bodyguards. There were
traces of anxiety in all of their features. They knew as she did that
the power represented by the man she was about to meet dwarfed
anything they could muster.

She rose when the man appeared in the front galley. He wore a
dark suit, a white shirt with a matching pocket square, and a light
blue tie. There was nothing particularly remarkable about him, for
he was not tall or handsome or physically impressive in any way. But
one only needed to look into his eyes to see his confidence, intelligence, and ruthlessness. Even Steers, no slouch in the field of intimi-
dation herself, could feel it.

She moved forward to greet him, and then led him back to the
private room just forward of her sleeping quarters.

They sat at the conference table. Hot tea and bottled waters were distributed by the plane's attendant, then Steers and the man were left alone to discuss what needed to be discussed.

Steers wore a long robe of equal parts red and green. In her heels she was taller than he was. Sitting down, they were of roughly equal height. In all other perspectives, she was dwarfed by him. And he also had a trump card, which she knew he would not hesitate to play if the need arose.

The man smiled and said, "This is a nice plane, Ms. Steers. Very new, I see." He rubbed his fingers along the fine wood of the table top. "Business must be very good."

"This is the longest trip I have taken on it. I was in the United States before."

The man's gaze rose to meet hers, his expression an unusual mix of humor and quiet gamesmanship. "We always know where in the world you are."

"You flatter me with your attention."

He glanced out the window. "I remember well the families of Kokang," he said. "Wei, Bai, and Liu." He looked at her. "And *Steers*. British among the Han Chinese. Think of that!" His words and tone carried a lightheartedness that did not carry over into his features.

"My mother is Chinese. A faithful communist, as you know."

He nodded. "But *you* are a capitalist, as everyone needs to be. There is no greater need than one's own well-being. The philosophy of survival of the fittest weeds out the weak and unambitious."

"I am what I need to be. And my gratitude is endless for our partnership."

The man's congenial look faded. "The word *partnership* implies an element of *equality* that is not present between us, Ms. Steers."

"If I misspoke, my sincerest apologies. I have no doubt as to the structure of our arrangement or its relative hierarchy."

"Your eloquence does you justice, as does your diplomacy."

She nodded but had nothing to add. The fewer words said the better with this man. He neither forgot nor forgave, and she had already stumbled.

He glanced out the window, where in the distance sat a towering range of mountains. "There are those who believe that another coup will take place in Myanmar in the very near future. Only they are at odds over who will be behind it."

Steers had thoughts that this man might be behind it because control of an entire country could be valuable. But she said, "Is the current junta not to your liking? The economic engine is beginning to purr, I understand."

"Coups are for many reasons, not all tied to money. And the junta is weak. Large parts of the country, particularly to the north, are out of its control."

"And how do you see such playing out?"

"What I foresee is not for dissemination at present, nor is it the reason for this meeting."

Steers took a sip of her tea and waited. She knew that this man would choose his words with calculated care and she needed to do the same.

"We have given you a long leash on the Temple family. They started well initially, but conditions have recently deteriorated. Cleaning up problems creates other problems. The FBI is engaged and cannot be easily shut down. To be frank, they know of your involvement. They also know about Rhett Temple. They suspect the two recent deaths and one disappearance at the various companies are related to what you are doing. They may suspect the motive. Or at least one of them," he amended.

He stopped talking and looked at her.

Steers began, "I have met with Temple and expressed these same concerns. I have been assured that in the future different practices will be deployed to head off any other unfortunate outcomes."

"You rely on him to accomplish this?"

"To a certain extent, which is not the same as trusting him." She looked at him but was unable to read his features. He was as good at this game as she was.

No, he is better at it than I am. But knowing that may be an advantage.

He said, "Let me venture into the weeds. Walter Nash? You know of him?"

"Yes. He is truly excellent at his job and unwittingly aids us."

"That is irrelevant now. Walter Nash has been approached by the FBI. I must admit being disturbed that you did not know this."

This is my second stumble in fewer than five minutes.

She said, "They obviously moved from low to middle level to the upper executive ranks. I also spoke to Rhett Temple about this very possibility."

She glanced at him to find the man watching her closely. "Your answer is inherently unsatisfactory," he said.

"I understand that it is. I must do better."

"Whether *that* response is satisfactory or not will be tabled for now. Nash must be dealt with. But not in the usual way. Death here is not enough of a deterrent, as has been shown from past results. *Living* people can be dissuaded."

"Blackmail?" asked Steers.

"Actually, something more than that is needed." He paused, but it seemed only for dramatic emphasis, because she could tell he knew exactly what else he wanted to say.

"What is needed is personal devastation, which will leave no possibility of reliance on anything that the man says or does. That will pull all the teeth from the FBI. They may well abandon him and, indeed, rethink their entire strategy, with the result that our *problem* may go away. That is the forceful tactic needed here." He looked at her. "Do you not agree?"

Steers thought for a few moments. "There are ways that such can be done."

"You will see to the formulation of a plan. If sufficient I will approve it."

She nodded and took another sip of her tea, fortifying herself. Steers had noted that the man had touched neither the tea nor the water. A careful person.

As he started to rise she discovered the courage to ask the question. "And my mother?"

He sat back down. "Yes?"

"Is she . . . well?"

"As well as the last time you asked. But future responses may differ from past ones. It all depends on you, Ms. Steers. All on you. You recognize this, do you not?"

She nodded. "Is there the possibility of me speaking with her?"

"You bring the Walter Nash matter to a successful conclusion and I will do better than that. You will be able to *see* her. At my discretion and on my timeline, of course."

Steers's eyes widened slightly at this offered treasure. "I will have an excellent plan to you in one week for your approval."

"You will have it to me in twenty-four hours."

She nodded.

"And this is *not* for distribution to the Temples."

She nodded once more and watched him stroll out like he owned her and her plane.

And in all significant ways, he did.

After he and his motorcade were gone, her jet turned around and taxied to the runway. A few minutes later Steers was soaring upward toward an altitude of forty-one thousand feet, where she would sail along, with a vigorous tailwind, at nearly seven hundred miles an hour.

The woman closed her eyes, and as the jet hit pockets of turbulence during its ascent, her fingers closed around the sturdy arms of her chair. Though she routinely flew all over the world, Steers did not enjoy air travel and for a very simple reason. She had been on a plane that had crashed, killing her father and four other people, including the pilots. The fact of the crash and her father's death had been kept completely secret.

The stench of spilled jet fuel and smoke, the screams of the dying, and the bite of the flames invading her body would never leave Steers. She had seen her father perish right in front of her, his head crushed to pulp by the violent propulsion of a section of the plane's interior, a fate that had narrowly missed her.

She lifted the sleeve of her robe and studied the damaged skin there from burns suffered during the crash and its aftermath. The marks were not simply on one arm.

She had refused all entreaties to have the burned flesh surgically repaired using skin grafts and other plastic surgery measures. Instead, she had done the minimum required to avoid infections and restricted movement. Steers wanted it as a reminder that every day could be her last.

As the air smoothed out, she looked out the window. In her mind's eye she saw her father's image, and then her mother's. And after she erased both from her brain, she saw the image of a man who looked like millions of other men.

She did not know Walter Nash personally. Steers knew if she did she would find him distinctly uninteresting. However, to destroy a man you needed to know what he held important.

Steers had endured misery and physical agony at the hands of her siblings. She now stood alone, towering over their vanquished bodies where they rested in fragments in unknown and forgotten graves. She had not asked to be placed into such a life-and-death struggle, but she had been. And, to her, survival was a goal above all others.

I count on myself.

Ten hours later, after receiving some intel from various sources, she settled upon her plan, beating the twenty-four-hour deadline by an impressive margin. She instinctively knew it would be acceptable to the man who had walked off her jet and traveled back to a world where he reigned head and shoulders above almost all others.

And I will be able to see my mother. If he keeps his word.

She closed her eyes, squeezing the lids tight and thereby seeing only blackness. "Goodbye, Walter Nash."

33

H EY, WALT, GOT A MINUTE, my office?"

Nash looked up from his desk to see Rhett staring at him from the width of the doorway. It bothered Nash that Rhett could sneak up on him with such ease.

"Sure, Rhett, what's up?"

"Just some things to go over. Won't take long."

He disappeared and Nash slowly rose, taking a few moments to process this.

One question burned in his head: *He can't know of the research I did on Cho's company, can he?*

The fact that he didn't have a firm answer to this question made his heart sink right into his gut.

He crossed the hall and entered Rhett's office. The man was sitting behind his desk squeezing a stress ball and looking distracted; Nash did not take that as a good sign. He perched in a chair and looked at his boss expectantly.

When Rhett didn't seem inclined to immediately engage, Nash took a few moments to look around the space. Dozens of framed photos covered a large part of one wall: Warren Buffett and his late partner, Charlie Munger, looking very humble and Midwestern in their boxy suits, and Peter Lynch, Ray Dalio, Jim Simons, and Mark Cuban, among a dozen other legendary investor types. Rhett was smiling and shaking hands with all of them. Nash wondered if most of them even knew who Rhett was.

Rhett also had another photo section of celebrity meets: Brad Pitt, Mariah Carey, and Steve Carrell, and figures from the worlds of professional tennis, baseball, football, and soccer. And there Rhett was again, beaming and looking ultra pleased with himself.

Nash caught sight of one picture he had never seen before. "You met Lionel Messi?"

Rhett glanced at him. "Yeah, just last month in Miami. Little dude, but the things he can do on a soccer field? He's worth the billion or so they're paying him. I got my pic with him and got out of there. See, I had a date later with the most beautiful Brazilian woman you have ever met."

"Well, I haven't, to my knowledge, met any Brazilian women, beautiful or otherwise, so that would be a low bar—"

Rhett sat forward and interjected, "Are you happy here, Walt? Anything I can do to make you...happier?"

Okay, he knows I made the outreach to the other firms. So tap-dance, Nash.

"I guess you heard that I contacted a couple of companies, including Black Cliffs?"

Rhett sat back and waited.

"I'm not sure why I did. No, I am. It's, well, it's Maggie."

A clearly surprised Rhett said, "Maggie? What's the issue there?"

"I think she would prefer living in New York or on the West Coast. Black Cliffs has substantial offices in both."

Nash felt bad about throwing his daughter under the bus, but his tap dancing had produced nothing else of a useful nature.

"Well, have you considered allowing the little bird to fly from the coop?" said Rhett.

Nash's eyes widened. "Letting a nineteen-year-old who has not figured out what she wants in life loose in the Big Apple or LA?"

"Best lessons are from mistakes."

"I'm not entirely opposed to that philosophy, but letting her screw up so far away does not seem to me to be a good practice from a parental perspective."

"What does Judith say about all this?"

"I haven't addressed it with her yet. I'm sure she'll have her own opinion."

Rhett nodded his head so quickly and accepted this statement so readily that Nash's always nimble radar turned on.

He added, "And I'm not certain that's what Maggie wants. It's just an assumption of mine."

"Well, regardless of your reasons for looking for a new shop, the thing is, Walt, you are a highly valued *partner* in our business. And I can tell you that we will move heaven and earth to keep you on here. You know that, right?"

Nash sat back to give himself a few extra moments to process this now that he knew more details about the schemes they were involved in. But another thought occurred to him. *If he knew of my reaching out to Black Cliffs, he probably would also be aware that I was turned down. So why this sudden generosity?*

"I appreciate that, Rhett, I really do. And I've decided that that move was not a good one on my part. I'm relatively happy here."

"I want you *more* than relatively happy. So what extras can I give you?"

Nash was about to say no extras were required, but then it occurred to him that the zero-sum-minded Rhett would find that inherently suspicious.

"If you want to sweeten my options deal by another couple percentage points and bump my salary, say, fifteen percent? And the fiscal year-end bonus? Judith mentioned wanting to go to Asia in the fall. So an extra half mill there would be good. My production this year certainly justifies it."

"Done, done, and done. I didn't know Judith was into Asia."

"She has a friend who's doing a triathlon there. And she also mentioned shopping."

"Shopping? Where exactly?"

"Malaysia, Hong Kong, Thailand, among others. Oh, and Vietnam. Maggie actually wants to go there, too."

"Shopping in Vietnam? We've come a long way from the war there."

"Yes, we have."

Rhett grinned. "My father did the medical disability route. Got a doctor to lie and say he had flat feet or some shit."

"My father didn't," Nash said tersely.

Rhett instantly assumed a somber look. "Right, a real hero, that man. Damn shame. But he got his Agent Orange money. He got his pound of flesh from them."

Nash looked at him pensively. "Yes he did. He never gave up."

"Like father like son, right?"

This comment startled Nash but he masked his reaction.

"Well, that's all. Glad you're staying aboard, Walt."

Nash rose and walked back to his office.

CHAPTER

34

LATER THAT WEEK, NASH FINISHED setting up the necessary accounts to administer the trusts for the funds his father had left his daughter, and also an investment account for Rosie Parker. He met with Parker at his father's house and gave her a checkbook and the other necessary details about the account. He also provided her a new smartphone and set up an email account for her.

As they sat at the kitchen table she said, "Thank you so much, Mr.... I mean Walter. All of this is so nice of you. And your father was beyond generous to do this. I mean, I'm not family or anything."

"Well, he thought you were family to him, and that's what counts. If you have questions, you have my contact information. How is your mother, by the way?"

"The same. I mean, she's not any worse. And she won't be getting any better. But she's comfortable."

"Well, let me know if you need anything."

He rose to leave when she said, "Walter?"

"Yes?"

"Your father said something about you right before he died. I don't believe he would want me to tell you, but I think you ought to know. It's only right."

Nash sat down again. "What was it?"

"He was in hospice by then. He was in and out of consciousness. He slept a lot, which was natural. He was on enough pain meds to be...comfortable."

"Yes?" prompted Nash.

"Well, his eyes suddenly opened. He didn't look at me. I'm not even sure he knew I was there. He just looked up at the ceiling and said, 'Nikki, tell sonny boy I love him. Just tell him, okay? Don't let him think I didn't, Nikki.'" Parker looked at Nash. "I know your mother had long since passed, but what he said was clear enough, Walter. He never spoke another word before he passed that night."

"Wait, those were his last words?"

"Yes. I was with him right up until the end. No one deserves to die alone."

"I would have been there, if I had known he was dying," Nash said stiffly.

Parker reached out and gripped his hand with her strong fingers. "He made me swear not to tell anyone. But you have to keep in your heart that at the end you were on his mind. And he wanted you to know. *You.* His son that he loved."

Nash turned away and rubbed at his eyes. Standing, he said, "Thank you for sharing that with me. And thank you for all you did for him."

"That's what people do, Walter. They help others in need, or at least that's what we're all supposed to do."

"Some certainly do it better than others," he replied.

On his drive home he received a text from Agent Morris instructing him on how to download a particular secure messaging app on his phone. It was probably some invention of the CIA or NSA, he assumed. Morris had left an email address where Nash could send a message once he had gotten on the app.

Parked in his garage, he downloaded the app, created an account, and messaged Morris. A few seconds later he received a reply that read: FOLLOWING TERMS AGREED TO BY UNITED STATES GOVERNMENT.

Nash read down the list and was astonished to learn that the amount of money they were offering him was double what he had reasonably been expecting. And his demands for security, for his wife and daughter to be taken care of if he were killed, had also been agreed to.

Morris had ended the message by saying that they would set up a private secure account with 10 percent of the funds deposited right away and that he could withdraw or do with them what he pleased. But first he had to agree to help. A formal executed document memorializing the terms in the message would follow immediately.

Nash slowly typed out his response and then his finger hovered over the send key.

He drew a breath and lightly touched the key and the message was gone.

And maybe my life along with it.

The agreement reached his inbox seconds later. He read every word, and then electronically signed the attachment and sent it off. A minute later the details for the account and how to access it had been delivered. He went on the account and set it up with a new password. He checked the sums deposited and confirmed that they matched the 10 percent of the total amount the government had agreed to pay.

"Walter?"

He looked up to see Judith staring at him from the door leading into the kitchen.

He opened the Range Rover's door. "Yes?"

"Are you going to come into the house or sit out there all night?"

"Be there in a minute."

He finished up and walked into the house. Judith was at the stove stirring something in a pan.

"How was your day?" she asked.

"Fine. Rhett met with me."

"Really, what about?"

"He found out I had inquired about a position at another firm."

"What?"

"It was just an inquiry. I told him it was because I think Maggie might want to live in LA or New York, and the firm I contacted has offices in both."

Judith said angrily, "You never talked to me about any of this.

And I can't believe you would reach out to someone about a new job without discussing it with me first."

"I never would have made any *decision* without talking it over with you."

"Well, I would hope not. And why do you think Maggie wants to live in those places? Did she say anything to you about it?"

"No, it was my assumption, I guess. Two very exciting places, where lots of cool things are happening."

"Well, I'm not sure she wants to live there, though she does like to visit them."

"But you'll be happy to know that I got a raise and a big bump in my bonus. I told Rhett it would help fund your Asian shopping trip."

She smiled. "Well, it's not just shopping. I am going to cheer Jean on, too."

"You know I might just take some time off and go with you."

She forcefully stirred the contents of the pan. "But you said it was your busy time."

"I can afford to take some time off. What are the exact dates?"

"I'll…have to check with Jean and get back to you."

"I don't have to be there for the triathlon, of course. Just the fun part."

"It's a long way to go," she pointed out. "And knowing how demanding your job is, you'll probably be on the phone or computer nonstop."

"If I didn't know better, I'd start to think you didn't want me to go."

She turned and hugged him. "Don't be stupid. If you can make it work, awesome. I'll find out the dates from Jean."

"Sounds good."

She turned back to the stove and added some salt and pepper to a pan, then got a bottle of extra-virgin olive oil from an upper cabinet.

"Now, any other secrets you're hiding from me?" she asked in a jovial tone.

When he didn't reply, she turned around.

Nash was gone.

Judith leaned against the counter and closed her eyes. She loved her husband, but she also loved being with Rhett. And she knew at some point she would have to make a choice. And she was not looking forward to that at all.

35

WHEN THE WEEKEND CAME NASH got up early, put on shorts and a T-shirt, and went for a walk around the neighborhood to just think about things without interruption. By the time he got back to his house he had not resolved many issues. While he had some coffee and ate a granola bar, Nash thought he could hear his wife downstairs in the gym. He was just about to go upstairs and shower when Maggie came into the kitchen.

"How goes the revised proposal?" he asked.

She yawned and stretched. "More difficult than I thought, but I'm making progress."

"Good. Um, did you know your mother was thinking of going to Asia in the fall? To watch her friend Jean in a triathlon?"

Maggie poured out a cup of coffee before settling on a barstool and looking at him. "No, she never mentioned it to me."

"She wants to hit a few countries, including Vietnam. I told her I might go, too. And you wanted to see Vietnam and other places in that part of the world."

"But you said that was a bad idea."

"I don't mean for your influencer business. I just mean for your general education, broadening your horizons. And we don't have to just go to the cool, hip places. I'd, well, I'd like to see some of the places where my father was located during the war."

Maggie eyed him with deliberate care. "You...miss him, don't you? Even though he was so mean to you?"

He sat down on a stool next to her. "He left me a letter that I read recently. It explained why he pushed me out of his life. And the fact is, I did something really stupid, hell, even cruel, having to do with my mother. That was the cause of the estrangement."

"I can't believe that, Dad. You're like the most sensitive person I know. You, well, sometimes you care too deeply. I know you love me and Mom even though sometimes you can be really aloof. But I think part of that was your relationship with your father. Or the lack of one. And you've always been so supportive of me." She smiled and playfully punched him on the arm. "Even when I come up with stupid business proposals that I haven't thought through."

He shook his head, still feeling miserable despite her complimentary words. "I was fourteen when I did what I did, and it was because I wanted to impress a girl."

"Fourteen! Dad, do you remember all the stupid things I did when I was that age? I know I did some things that drove you and Mom nuts. And I know that boys are even worse, by a lot."

"But my father loved my mother more than anything. And he valued loyalty, having someone's back, more than anything. I had a recent talk with Shock about it."

"Who?"

"The man who dissed me at the funeral."

"He was a jerk."

"No, he was my father's best friend. And Shock told me that if I ever needed anything that he would be there for me, because I was Ty Nash's son."

"Then why did he say those awful things at the church?"

"It's complicated, Maggie. But life often is, especially when you're dealing with people and their emotions. Anyway, before my father died he told Rosie Parker, the woman he was with at the end, that he loved me. And in the letter he told me the same thing. And that he was sorry he had cut me out of his life. That he regretted it. And he wished he could take it back."

Tears formed in Nash's eyes and he looked away from his daughter and covered up his vulnerability by taking a quick sip of coffee.

"And I feel regrets, too, about a lot of things. I feel like I wasted all those years when I could have been close to my father, if I had tried harder. Now it's too late."

She put a hand on his shoulder. "Dad, I think the important thing to remember is that at the end your father loved you. His last thought was about you, his son. You need to forget everything else and remember that." She touched his chest. "Hold it right there, okay? Never let that go. It'll get you through a lot. I know it does with me. I always feel like you and Mom are my rocks. That you'll support me no matter what stupid stuff I do. And even when I act like a spoiled brat, I know how lucky I am. Not just for living in a place like this and having it pretty easy, but knowing that you guys really care about me. You work really hard, travel all over the world and while you missed some dance recitals and school plays, you always were there when I really needed you to be. That stuff counts. It really does. I will never forget that you did all that for me."

He hugged her tightly and said, "I think maybe you've missed your vocation. Your influencer business might be tied to counseling and mental health."

"Well, I've actually thought something similar."

"Really?"

"You told me to find a need and then try and fill it. Well, so many of my friends are addicted to stuff online and it's not just doom-scrolling. There are so many online sites and chatrooms that put up impossible standards, of beauty and wealth and achievement and fitness and, well, everything. Sort of like you said before. No one can live up to that, and it's really causing a lot of problems, especially with my generation. It's like we all need an intervention."

"You could be part of that intervention."

"But I don't have any special training or anything."

"You have the funds to earn that training, if you want to. And then build something off that. Something that would actually help people."

She smiled weakly. "No Taylor Swift concerts?"

"You can always go to Taylor Swift concerts, but they don't have to be how you earn your living. And if you want real satisfaction from what you do, then helping others is a great way to get that." He paused. "Sounds sort of hypocritical coming from me, though. My job is just to make money for people who already have too much of it."

"But you provide a great living for me and Mom."

"But I'm not out there actually helping my fellow human beings who really need it."

"You build successful businesses that employ lots of people and give them a good living. And their families."

"Yeah, I guess."

"And you can always do something else, if you want. You're still a young guy. You can have a second, third, and fourth act in life."

He smiled. "I think this might be the most meaningful conversation we've ever had. I wonder why."

"I think both of us needed to get to the point where we could actually have it."

After this truly eye-opening discussion with his daughter, Nash wanted to tell her all that was going on with the FBI. But he knew he couldn't. It might get them all killed.

"Dad, you okay?"

Nash looked at her, saw the worry in her features.

He gripped her hand. "I'm just enjoying the moment, sweetie. That's all. Moments like this you need to hold on to. Because tomorrow is guaranteed to no one."

CHAPTER

36

Nash knew how to move money around. The U.S. government had deposited the funds into a special account. Before he left for the office the following Monday he transferred those funds into another account that he had set up and to which only he had access. And then, to be sure he left no trace of the funds, he moved it to yet another account he had also set up because, for him, the philosophy of belts and suspenders was a way of life.

With that done, he contacted Agent Morris on the secure messaging app.

He told the agent that he had business meetings in New York the following week that would require an overnight stay. He gave him his travel info and requested that a meeting with the FBI take place.

Nash then drove to his office and ran into Barton Temple in the hallway outside his son's office.

"Walt, long time no see, how the hell are you?" said Barton, extending a hand.

The men shook and Nash said, "Fine. It's good to see you. I...I suppose Rhett has filled you in about...things?"

"Come on, Walt, I don't know how we've kept you this long. A man has to look out for himself. And he told me about your daughter. Hard to believe she's an adult. And as pretty as her mother."

"Thank you. Are you here to see Rhett?"

"Yeah, it's my time to kick him in the ass on his numbers. Don't let me keep you. Just go on and keep making me money." He added a laugh and a hard slap on Nash's arm.

Nash went to his office and closed the door. He suddenly

loathed this place and everyone in it. And although the FBI had not mentioned Barton Temple's involvement in criminal activity, Nash instinctively knew that if Rhett was working with Victoria Steers he was not doing so without his father's knowledge. Rhett was not that smart, tactical, or strategic, while Barton was all of those things. He was also not above bending rules or breaking laws if it served him.

If Barton got himself and his son into business with Steers, the question was why.

Firmly ensconced on the *Forbes* list, Barton Temple was one of the four hundred wealthiest people in the world.

Or was he?

The issue was that Temple had legions of companies, spread across the world. Only he really knew the status and fortunes of each, and how it all came together—the intricacies, the entanglements, the shared debt loads, the source and flexibility of cash flow, the strength of various markets, the under- and overexposure to certain asset classes, the labyrinth of accounts, blank walls, and shell companies pretty much immune to any official scrutiny or oversight. Nash's access was limited to planet Sybaritic. The rest of this financial universe belonged solely to Barton Temple.

But you could do some sleuthing on that, Nash.

He got to work.

* * *

Barton eyed his son over the width of the desk for so long that Rhett finally exclaimed, "What?"

"Saw Walt out in the hall. He looks happy."

"He should be. I just off-loaded a bunch of money to the guy. Just like you told me to."

"Best investment you'll ever make, trust me."

"Come on, granted he's good, but you make it sound like he's Warren Buffett 2.0."

"In my mind he's better."

"You're not serious," sputtered Rhett.

"Taking nothing away from the Oracle of Omaha, but he mostly sticks to the tried-and-true companies and just sits on them. What Nash does is find the new crown jewels before anyone's heard of them. In the last fifteen years over seventy percent of the companies he invested in or acquired outright have either gone public or were sold for a ten-bagger," Barton said, referring to a thousand percent return. "His clear misses?" Barton held up one hand and bent down two fingers. "This many. Name me anyone else who's done that in our industry where the failures far outweigh the wins."

"If he's such a genius, why did Black Cliffs turn him down?"

"I told you. If Zuckerman steals my star talent, he knows I will make his life so miserable he'll jump off the top of his skyscraper, or else I'll push the bastard myself."

"Nice guy that you are."

"Nice guys don't only just finish last in our business, they die."

"Don't get melodramatic, Dad."

Barton leaned forward. "Now that you know what I know, I hope you understand, boy, that I am conveying the literal truth to you."

"What I know now is that *you've* been shoveling all the losses into my division to launder all the dirty money coming through your companies. What, just determined to make me look bad, Dad?"

"You'd look bad regardless of what I did or didn't do. And those *losses* are making us rich."

"We already were rich. And *you* got me hooked into Victoria Steers. Why?"

"Because you can't run a business to save your ass, laundering money or not. I was actually doing you a favor."

"Come on, if that were really the case you would have just canned my ass and put Nash in my place."

"Think what you want."

Rhett assumed a more confident look. "You *needed* Steers." He paused. "Not as rich as you say you are, Dad?"

"You're talking out of your butt. My wealth is unassailable. Not even Mindy can spend it fast enough."

"Which begs the question of why you're in business with a woman who employs people who put bullets into other peoples' heads."

His father held up his hands. "Okay, I concede it was a mistake on my part to let you know of my involvement. I lost my temper with you, which is what you do to me because of your incompetency. But now that I have, let me just make things real clear to you."

The big man leaned forward and put his elbows on his son's desk. "You toe the line like your life depends on it. Because it does." He glanced at his son's arm. "If you think that was bad, you have no idea."

"Well, Dad, let me tell *you* something."

"What?" said his father with a sneering look. "I'm all attention."

"*You* better watch *your* step with her. Because you're not used to playing second fiddle to anybody, especially a woman. You live to issue the orders, not take them. And from what I've seen of her, she'd gut you for looking at her wrong and feed you to the fish." He looked over his father's bloated physique. "And what a smorgasbord you'd make."

Rhett stood. "Now, I've got some important business to attend to. Which, of course, doesn't include you."

He walked out, leaving his father sitting there staring at a wall.

CHAPTER

37

"YOU MOVED THE MONEY," Agent Morris said accusingly to Nash as he opened the hotel room door.

"You said I could do whatever I wanted with it. Now, I have some things for you."

Nash passed by him and entered the room. Agent Braxton appeared from around a corner and greeted him.

"Where's your boss?" asked Nash.

Morris said, "Back in DC with a full plate. So what do you have for us?"

Nash set up his laptop on the desk, inserted a thumb drive, and went through in great detail what he'd discovered about Cho's company, the two food processing plants, and the second set of electronic books.

"Clearly money laundering on an impressive scale," said Nash. "And Steers obviously has other partners she's working with."

Morris looked impressed. "That's good, Mr. Nash, really good. This is far more than we've ever gotten from anyone."

"That's not all. Have you ever considered that in addition to Rhett, *Barton* Temple is also involved with Victoria Steers?"

Braxton said, "We had obviously considered that, but couldn't find a connection, or any proof."

Morris added, "What makes you think otherwise?"

"Quite frankly, having known and worked with him for a long time, I know that while Rhett is smarter than people give him credit for and can think fast on his feet, especially when cornered, he's not focused, disciplined, or savvy enough to have pulled this off alone.

Nor do I think someone as intelligent as you say Victoria Steers is would approach him to do business. He's just too reckless. I believe that foundation had to be laid through the father who then passed off the daily grind work to the son. For all I know Rhett doesn't even know his father is involved. It could all be backroom dealing. And Rhett *is* the sort of person who could be manipulated into something like this. And while Rhett plays tough, a woman like I think Steers is could easily manipulate him."

Braxton said, "Remember, Reed, I mentioned that possibility a while ago."

Morris said, "But Barton Temple is a billionaire. Why would he partner with Steers?"

Nash said, "Well, Rhett is rich, too. So why would *he*? And it's easier to appear to be a billionaire than it used to be. And while I'm not denying that Barton was wealthy in the past, there was no guarantee that he still was when he ran into Steers."

"How so?" said Morris. "He was on all the 'most wealthy' lists. I know those are subjective to a certain extent, but you can't fudge everything. You have to have some big bucks somewhere to qualify."

Nash nodded and said, "People inflate the value of their assets, particularly when you get away from those whose wealth is tied to publicly traded stock that is easily verifiable, like Bill Gates, Larry Ellison, Warren Buffett, and the like. Barring that, people make assumptions. They often let past wealth levels dictate future assessments of riches."

Braxton interjected, "And Barton Temple has hundreds of legitimate companies for Steers to work through, while his son just has Sybaritic."

"Do you have any *proof* that Barton is involved?" asked Morris.

Nash brought up another screen on the laptop. "Because Sybaritic is one of his companies, profits and losses flow from it into Barton's other orgs, which have blended ownership interests in Sybaritic. For that reason I had a slightly open doorway into the financial goings-on of his other businesses. From that I was able to wrangle data on him from as far back as nearly twenty years ago."

"Okay, what did that data tell you?" asked Morris.

"In 2008 he was legitimately worth at least six billion dollars. But 2009 was a catastrophic year for the markets and most businesses in general. The world was in a recession, and the U.S. markets plummeted. The Dow slumped to around 6,000. To give you some context, it started out this year at around 44,000."

"And how did Barton Temple fare with the 2009 recession?" asked Braxton.

"Terribly. At the time I was in a junior role at Sybaritic. I remember losses taken on assets, assets entirely written off, some severe cost-cutting measures, job layoffs, reduced salaries and bonuses. I thought nothing more of it until *you* came into my life."

"Glad I could prompt you to expand your horizons," said Morris sarcastically.

"Barton's company structure is very hierarchical. At the top of the pyramid is the mother ship, BT Holdings. Stands for 'Barton Temple,' of course, because he has to have his name on everything. Now between 2009 and 2011, BT's cash flow went fully into negative territory. By the tune of well over a billion dollars. Commercial real estate also took a huge hit, and he had enormous, leveraged positions in that sector, many with personal guarantees attached. Dozens of his companies declared bankruptcy. His profits vanished and along with it his free cash flow so he could no longer service his debts. Subsequently, loans were called in, he couldn't find new lenders to take out the old debt, and, most ominously, his personal guarantees were triggered. The result was his entire empire was imploding."

"How the hell did you find out all that so fast?" Morris wanted to know. "We did some digging and our guys couldn't make a dent. It was just too complicated, they said, and there were parts of his business they couldn't get into at all."

"When I became a board member at Sybaritic I was given access to a lot of financial records. I'm sure it was unintended, or maybe unknown to the IT folks at Temple's other companies, but certain passwords to review records at affiliated companies were either the same or close enough for a simple decryption program I used to figure them out. It took me the better part of three days, and I had to run down a dozen rabbit holes and break through a few firewalls and gain entry to second and third sets of digital financial books, but I was able to piece certain things together and come up with the analysis I just provided you."

Braxton said, "So the hammer was about to come down on Barton Temple?"

Nash brought up another screen. "Yes. And as a result Barton, over the next year or so, started off-loading assets in fire sales for pennies on the dollar to raise cash. He was so desperate he bought a bunch of layered derivatives and got hosed when they became worthless. Then he ended up selling his most valuable remaining properties, a portfolio of BT-owned buildings in New York City, to a PE firm based in Singapore."

"But you said commercial real estate had gone into the shitter. Didn't he lose money on the deal?" replied Braxton.

"It *was* at the very bottom of the market, so the buildings should have *only* sold for around three hundred million dollars total, leaving Barton on the hook with his personal guarantees for over seven hundred million to the banks. That would have wiped him out, and he would have been on the streets looking for a job along with everyone else. I'm sure he was desperate to avoid that fate."

"But that's not what happened," said Morris. "He made it out the other end."

"Right, because the Singapore PE firm paid *three billion* for the collection of BT properties. That allowed Barton to pay off his debts and walk away a billionaire again. His wealth has grown exponentially since then."

Morris looked stunned. "Three billion! That's ten times what you said the market rate was for the buildings. How is that possible?"

"If you have a buyer willing to pay, who's going to complain? And no banks were involved. PE dollars are not regulated. Those firms make their own rules."

"But that smacks of money laundering right there," said Braxton, looking at Morris.

"Right, but who's going to go after a foreign-based PE firm with hundreds of billions in assets, *and* someone who had long been on the *Forbes* list, and their collective army of lawyers and accountants? The IRS?" Nash added skeptically. "That would truly be David and Goliath. That's why rich people never get audited, or if they do they just run out the clock until the government gives up."

"That all stinks to high heaven," said Morris.

"And Barton had enormous loss carryforwards to lay against his profits, so he didn't pay one dime of capital gains on his windfall. You see, the tax laws were written to benefit commercial real estate developers above all others. But the bottom line is that cash infusion saved him and his empire."

"So is the Singapore money in bed with the Steers org?" asked Braxton.

Nash said, "Why else would they overpay so dramatically? And you said the Chinese are backing Steers, and China has enormous leverage in the Asian financial markets and local governments over there. They could have been the ones to really come up with the purchase price, which would have been chump change for them. What I can tell you for certain is that the quid always comes with a pro quo. So if the Steers org saved Barton's ass, they own him lock, stock, and barrel."

Morris sat back and wiped his brow. "This is even more complicated than we thought." He eyed Nash. "I know our relationship didn't get off to the best of starts, but you are the real deal, Mr. Nash."

"I had the advantage of being able to get into certain financial records and understand what I was seeing. And it's Walter, Agent Morris."

"And I'm Reed."

The two men shared a smile over this sudden change in their working relationship.

Morris said, "I don't think Victoria was running the empire back then, so it might have been her parents, more likely her mother, who put this all together with Barton Temple."

Braxton added, "But Victoria would have known about it. She was right at her mother's shoulder before the woman vanished. So the daughter now owns the Temples."

"I need to make a call," said Morris. "I'll be back in a couple minutes."

He went into the next room.

Nash took out the thumb drive and handed it to Braxton. "I have no idea if this is any good from an evidentiary point of view considering how I came by it. But I think it will be a valuable launch pad for the collection of more information."

"Like Reed said, amazing work, Mr. Nash."

"It's Walter for you, too."

"And I'm Amy."

He noted her wedding band. "I've heard an FBI career is hard on a marriage, which isn't easy under any circumstances."

"You heard right. It's not easy."

"I got married early. We had our daughter while still in college. But my business is a meat grinder, too. Sometimes I wonder if it's worth it. Like right now."

"Well, if this all plays out the way we want, Walter, you can start over and find out."

Nash smiled. "From your lips to God's ears, Amy. Oh, there is one more thing." He told her about Rhett's injured arm and his explanation of falling on his jet.

Braxton nodded. "I think I can fill in that part for you, but I'm not sure it will make you feel better."

"I'm data driven, so I think I need to know."

"We've been tracking the comings and goings of Rhett Temple's private jet. On the night Lombard disappeared, it landed about a hundred miles from where Lombard's car was found the next day."

"You think he was there when Lombard was taken and presumably killed?"

"We know that Steers likes her associates to have skin in the game, so him being forced to witness the murder would make sense. Legally it would make him an accomplice. We also have been tracking Steers's various aircraft. One of them was in the same vicinity that night as Rhett Temple. They may very well have met up afterward."

"And his injury?"

"If you had looked under his shirtsleeve you might have seen a cut starting here." Braxton touched a spot near her wrist and then ran it up just above her bicep. "And ending there. No permanent injury, but it will leave a scar. A bad one."

"And the point?" said Nash.

"In Steers's world, a cut from wrist to shoulder that scars over is like a form of ownership of another human being."

"Like how plantation owners would brand slaves?" Nash was appalled.

"And it's also meant to be both a form of punishment and a warning. If he did suffer that sort of cut, Rhett must have done something to displease Steers."

"I wonder if his father has the same *brand*."

"I guess the only way to find out is to nail the son of a bitch and strip-search him during his intro to prison."

Nash was looking down at his own arm and thinking that if Steers did that to people who worked with her, what would she do to people who were working against her?

Like me?

CHAPTER

38

"M<small>OM</small>, WHERE HAVE YOU BEEN?"

A startled Judith Nash looked around at her daughter, who was standing in the second-floor hall of their home.

"Maggie, what are you still doing up?" said Judith, who was not looking pleased with this unexpected encounter.

"It's one in the morning. Where have you been? I texted and called."

"I..." Judith looked at her purse. "I guess I turned my phone off."

"So where have you been?" Maggie persisted.

"Not that I need to account for my whereabouts with you, but I had dinner with a friend and we went back to her house and had a few drinks."

"You had a few drinks and you *drove* home?"

Judith tensed. "You are not my mother, okay, Maggie? And I was not under the influence. I was fine. I had dinner and the drinks were spread over several hours."

Maggie folded her arms over her chest. "What friend?"

"Excuse me?"

"What friend were you out with?"

"That is none of your business."

"Was it Sally? Or Jean? Or Katherine Tucker?"

"I...I don't have to answer that."

"You don't have to because I called *all* your friends looking for you. No one had heard from you. I thought you'd been in an accident."

"Please don't tell me you called your father in New York? He's due back tomorrow."

"I didn't, because he would have probably run all the way home." Maggie looked her mother over. "That's a pretty clingy, low-cut dress for a night out with a *girlfriend*." She took a whiff. "And *that* perfume? Really?"

Judith's expression turned ugly. "I resent the hell out of what you're implying."

"Who said I'm implying?"

"Go to your room."

"I'm not a child. You can't make me."

"Then I'm going to bed. I'm exhausted."

Maggie stepped closer to her mother and drew in a fuller breath. "You might want to grab a shower first. To get the men's cologne off. And the sweat."

"Watch your mouth!" She pointed a finger at her daughter. "And if you're even thinking of mentioning this…this *nonsense* to your father, well, you better think again."

"What happened to you?" said Maggie, now looking like she might cry. "Don't you love Dad anymore?"

"Of course I love him!" exclaimed a now-stricken Judith.

"Then what is all this about?"

"This is all a product of your overactive imagination," her mother barked. "And I don't want to hear another word about it."

Maggie shouted, "He loves you. He dotes on you. He gives you everything you want and you do *this* to him! You don't fucking deserve him!"

Judith slapped her daughter so hard on the cheek that it hurt her hand.

Maggie's eyes filled with tears and she gasped, holding her injured face where the skin was already reddening.

"I…I," said Judith, wavering. "Mag—"

She staggered off to her room, leaving Maggie staring after her.

A minute later Maggie heard the shower come on in her parents' bathroom. She hurried back to her bedroom, slipped under the covers, pulled them over her head, and began to weep and shake.

In the shower a naked Judith slumped to the floor and let the water run over her. And she, too, started to cry.

I'm sorry, Maggie. I'm so sorry... Walter. So...

She turned to the side and threw up. Then Judith lay on the shower floor, her body curled tightly into a ball as she moaned and shook while the hot water streamed over her.

39

THE NEXT MORNING WHEN HE arrived back in town Nash went straight from the airport to the office. He had phoned home and spoken to his wife, who sounded like she was coming down with a cold. When he asked about Maggie, Judith said that she was in her room working away, probably on the new proposal.

"I love you," Judith had said before clicking off.

Nash sat at his desk working on his day job. He had given the FBI a great deal of information, and he had decided to let them toil away on it before he started sifting for more incriminating material. He also knew that he would soon have to sit down and have a talk with his family about what he was engaged in. But then the warnings the FBI had given him about *indiscretions* leading to the deaths of Cho, Singer, and possibly Lombard came back to him.

He closed his eyes and thought about what his father would do. He suddenly wished he could pick up the phone and ask for advice from the former soldier.

But maybe I can do the next best thing.

He took the card from his pocket and made the call.

"Walter?" said Shock. "You all right?"

"I'm calling in the request my dad made to you to help me if I needed it. See, I'm in a bit of a mess and I need your advice. And it's better to do it in person. And maybe not in town, if you can manage it."

To his credit Shock asked no questions, but simply gave Nash precise instructions on where to meet him in two hours.

Nash left his office and took an Uber to the train station. There he hopped on a commuter rail to the next town over. From there he took not the first or second available taxi, but the third.

Shock was driving it.

"How'd you manage the taxi?" asked Nash.

"Buddy of mine owns the company. I actually have my chauffeur's license. Long story not worth telling."

As they left the station, Shock looked in the mirror and said, "So talk to me."

Forty-five minutes later, Nash finished. During the whole of that time Shock had driven in an ever-widening circle around the area, and had asked no questions. He simply listened to Nash's extraordinary recap of all that had transpired from the moment the FBI had walked into his life on the night of his father's funeral right up until the events in New York the previous evening with Agents Morris and Braxton.

"Damn, Walter. I thought it was some stupid business shit you were involved in. I have to say, in a way—a significant way, in fact—that I'm proud of you. And Ty would be, too. Your country needed you and you stepped up to the plate."

"But what do I do, Shock? This is not my world."

"From how you've already helped the FBI, I'd say it's very much your world."

"The business stuff I can handle. It's everything else. The violence. My family..."

Nash could not help himself. He started to weep. His heart was suddenly pulsing so fast he thought he might be having a heart attack.

Shock slowed the car's speed, observed this, and said, "Okay, four in, hold for four, four out, hold for four, Walter. Like I know your daddy taught you. Panic attack, nothin' else. I know it, you know it. Take back control. Your heart does what your brain tells it to. Do it, son. Now."

One minute later Nash's pulse was normal and he was no longer crying. He wiped his eyes and face clear and looked at Shock's reflection in the mirror. "If I don't tell my family what's going on, well, it will be a huge and disruptive event when the truth does come out. But if I do tell them, it might endanger all of us."

"What I would do if I were you, is get all the stuff the Bureau needs. Then, if you're still livin', you lay it all out for Judith and Maggie. Everythin'. Then you guys disappear with a shitload of money and start a new life somewhere else. Why worry them now if you don't have to? And maybe have somethin' leak?"

"I...I suppose you're right."

"It don't matter a damn if *I* think it's right, Walter. *You* have to believe that the decision you make is the right one. You got one helluva logical mind, so use it."

More miles passed in silence and Nash finally nodded. "Once I've fulfilled my mission for the government, I'll tell them. Right before we get on a private flight to a destination unknown. And with the money we'll be fine. Far better than most people. I shouldn't complain."

"The hell you shouldn't. Them boys are messin' up your life big-time. Now, the government gonna do right by you with the money? After Nam and Agent Orange I don't trust them muthers one lick."

"They've already paid some of it. It's only ten percent so far, but it was actually more than I thought they were going to give me in total." He looked out the window. "We can head on back now."

As they returned to the train station Nash said, "Have you ever heard of Victoria Steers?"

Shock glanced at him in the mirror. "Shit, *she's* involved?"

"So you know of her?"

"I've only heard her name *once*, Walter. It was in connection with a client of mine. He had business in the Far East, maybe not so legit if you know what I mean. Shady kind 'a guy tryin' to play legit. He crossed her path. He told me a little about her before he headed back there."

"What happened with her and him?"

"Don't know. Man never made it back to tell me."

Nash slowly nodded. "Look, just to face facts and using my logical mind, it's doubtful that I will survive this, Shock. But the government has agreed to protect Judith and Maggie for as long as needed."

"You think they gonna keep their word?"

"I hope so. I have no real way to force them."

"I can look after them, Walter."

"I've endangered you just by this meeting. I...I simply wanted some advice from a person I could trust. And with my parents gone, well, you were the only one I could think of."

"I appreciate that. But just so you know, my whole life has basically been one long shitstorm after another. And I'm still standin'."

They reached the station and Nash opened the car door to get out.

Before he did, Shock reached over and put a big hand on his shoulder.

"You're not alone, Walter. Remember that, all right? Sure, you got the FBI. And you got your family. But now you got *me*, too."

"Thank you. That really...means a lot."

Shock watched him all the way into the station before driving off.

CHAPTER

40

AFTER WORK NASH CAME INTO the kitchen from the garage to find Judith in sweatpants and a rumpled T-shirt sitting on a barstool with a cocktail in front of her.

"Judith, you okay?"

She glanced up at him. Her eyes were bloodshot, her hair messy, and her face absent of her usual makeup. "I'm fine, Walter. Per-fect-ly fine."

"How did your day go?" he asked tentatively, wondering what was going on with her.

"It was great. I worked out, I had lunch. I had a drink. I took a walk. I worked out. I…no, that was yesterday. Or the day before. I…I forget." She giggled.

He drew closer and was struck by the smell of alcohol wafting off her. "And Maggie?"

She shrugged. "I haven't seen or heard *her* all day."

"Nothing? She hasn't eaten or shown herself?"

"I thought I just said that, Walter," Judith said, now slurring her words. "I'm sure she's in her room working on that thing for you."

He slid the remains of her glass away and said, "You might want to hold off and maybe get some food and coffee into you."

She jerked the drink back. "Or I might not."

Concerned about Maggie, he left the kitchen and hurried up the stairs.

He knocked on his daughter's door. "Maggie? It's Dad. Are you all right? Your mother said you haven't been out of your room all day. Maggie?" He knocked again and then started to panic. He had seen her car in the garage. Granted, she could have taken an Uber or gone for a walk. "Maggie? I'm…I'm coming in."

He tried the door but it was locked.

"What's going on up there?"

Nash edged to the top of the stairs and saw Judith down below looking up at him. Her drink was in one hand.

"She's not answering, and her door is locked."

"She might be soaking in the tub."

"She could still hear me."

He went back and pounded on the door again. "Maggie, open the door."

He waited, praying with all his might that he would hear her footsteps coming to the door. And that it would open and his daughter would be there smiling at him. He had always been a worst-case-scenario sort of parent, always thinking about potential disasters if anyone was late or wouldn't answer their phone. He felt sick to his stomach when he heard no one approaching the door.

He stepped away from the door and then rushed forward, slamming himself against the thick wood. The only thing damaged was his bony shoulder.

He heard Judith coming up the stairs. "Walter, what the hell are you doing?"

"Trying to find my daughter!" he called back, rubbing his shoulder.

She walked down the hall, looked at him, and deduced what he had attempted. Then she took a bobby pin from the top ledge of the door frame. She inserted one end in the door lock and pushed hard.

They heard a click. She turned the knob and opened the door.

"Voilà," she said, smiling stupidly. "I used that when she was a kid and wouldn't let me in to change her clothes or make her take a bath—while you were out globe-trotting."

An agitated Nash pushed past her and into Maggie's room. He looked everywhere, but it was evident that his daughter was not there.

Judith came in and sat on the bed. "She probably slipped out when I wasn't looking."

"Her car's in the garage."

"So she went out with friends. It's no big deal. She's a grown woman. When I was in college my parents wouldn't hear from me for weeks."

"Yeah, well, it's different when you live in your parents' home." He stopped and looked down at the floor.

"What? Did you find a condom?" she asked jokingly.

He stooped and picked up one of Maggie's purses, and pulled out her wallet. "Money and credit cards."

"She has Apple Pay," said Judith.

"No, she doesn't, not without this." He pulled out her phone from the purse.

Now Judith looked concerned. "That's not like Maggie to leave her phone."

"I can't access it. She's got the facial recognition thing. Look, when was the last time you actually saw Maggie?"

Judith had grown instantly serious. "I...um, last night."

"What time?"

"Around...midnight."

"Why so late?"

"She...she came downstairs and we talked."

"About what?"

"Nothing important."

"How about before that? Did you two eat dinner together?"

"I...uh, no we didn't. She was up in her room. She might have made herself dinner. I...was in my room all last night."

"But you just said she came downstairs and talked to you."

Judith set her drink down on the nightstand and sat rigidly. "That's...that's right. I...came down to get some tea. I couldn't sleep. She must have heard me."

"And then what?"

"I assumed she went back to her room."

"And you really haven't seen her all day?" he said in disbelief.

"No. I mean." She stopped and looked guiltily at him. "I wasn't feeling great. I just chilled out today."

"My God, Judith, she could have been sick or…" He eyed the phone and then glanced around the space. "Is it my imagination, or is her room messier than usual?"

Judith suddenly rushed to the closet and flung the door open. "Her luggage is still in there. I thought…I thought she might have…"

"Might have what?" asked a confused Nash.

"She, she just seemed upset last night."

"But you said you talked and it was nothing important."

"Maybe the influencer thing? The way you ticked her off?"

"Things were good between me and her with that. Judith, you *know* that."

"Right, yes, that's right. I…I don't know, Walter, okay? She's a nineteen-year-old woman. Who knows what's going on behind the scenes."

"She hasn't been seeing anyone, has she?"

"Not that she mentioned, but again, who knows?"

Nash noted that his wife would not look him in the eye when she said this.

"Well, there's no way to contact her if she left her phone here," said Judith.

"What about her laptop?" said Nash. He hurried over to his daughter's messy desk set against one corner and said, "No, it's here." He turned it on but, like the phone, couldn't access it. "I'm going down to the security gate to see if they saw her leaving last night or any time today."

"I'm sure it's nothing. She probably just went for a walk."

"Without her phone?" said Nash. "It's usually glued to her hand." He hurried down the stairs and into the garage.

41

NOTHING IN THE ROOM HAS been touched?" said the policeman as he looked around Maggie's room. His tone was firm but also contained an element of delicate understanding in a situation where a family member might be missing.

Nash said, "I picked up her purse and phone and checked her laptop. Other than that, no, nothing has been touched."

The security guard at the gate had seen nothing of Maggie since he'd come on duty. He had checked with his colleague from the previous shift, who said the same thing. That was when Nash had called the police. Judith had retreated to her bedroom to lie down because of a sudden migraine.

The officer opened up his notebook. "Okay, the last time anyone saw her was around midnight last night?"

"Yes," said Nash. "My wife talked to her. I was traveling, in New York. I got back this morning and went straight to the office."

"Technically, since she's of age, we really can't take a missing person report until the person's been gone twenty-four hours."

"She didn't take her phone or her laptop. You look like you might have older children. Would they leave their electronics behind?"

"I don't know. Was she into all that?"

"If the ship was sinking she'd leave everything else behind except her phone."

"Do you have a picture of her?"

Nash took one from his wallet and passed it to him.

The cop looked at it and said, "Any boyfriends?"

"No one steady."

"You've checked with her friends?"

"Yes, no one has seen her since earlier yesterday."

"Young people do run away, all the time."

"Look, Officer, I know you don't know Maggie, but this is not like her. She would not have just vanished without a word. She's never given us trouble."

The cop looked around. "Most runaways have different economic situations than this one, but rich kids run away, too."

"Not Maggie. And her car is still in the garage. And leaving home without money and credit cards and ID?"

"Okay, any signs of forced entry into your home?"

Nash had not thought of that and said so.

The cop said, "Let me look around, sir."

He walked off and Nash immediately went to his bedroom to check on Judith. He was stunned to find her lying nearly naked on the bed with a wet compress over her eyes, her clothes strewn across the floor.

Nash was about to rouse her when she let out a soft snore. He looked at the bottle of Ambien on the nightstand and a half-empty bottle of water, covered her with a sheet, and quietly retreated.

He was sitting on the stairs when the cop came back into the foyer.

"Come with me, sir."

He led Nash to a room where there was a large washer and dryer, and pullout bins for laundry. An ironing board was housed behind a panel on the wall, and an iron sat on a shelf next to it. There was also a long counter for folding clothes and a mud sink. On the shelves were bottles of detergent and bleach.

The cop pointed at the lock and doorjamb on the rear door here. "Forced."

The blood drained from Nash's face. "Oh my God."

"You didn't notice this?"

"No, I always come in through the garage. This is obviously the laundry room."

"Do you have an alarm system?"

"Yes, but I'm not sure if my wife turned it on last night."

"Cameras?"

"Just on the front door."

"Can you see if your wife had the alarm on last night?"

"She...took a sleeping aid."

"She took a sleeping aid?" said the cop incredulously.

Nash said, "I'll ask her as soon as she's.... No, wait, I can check the alarm record. I have it on my phone app."

He checked. "The alarm was not turned on last night."

"Okay. With this development I'm going to have a forensics team out along with the detectives. And we're putting an alert out on her."

"You...you think she's been kidnapped?"

"Well, sir, a forced entry and a person potentially missing? What would you conclude?" He looked Nash over and said, "Please don't touch anything, and don't go into your daughter's room. In fact..." He went up the stairs. When he came back down he said, "The detectives will need to speak with you and your wife. So do whatever you can to wake her up. The first twenty-four hours are critical in matters like this."

"Of course. Thank you."

The officer walked off. Nash hurried upstairs and saw that he had sealed off Maggie's door with yellow crime scene tape. He stood there for a few moments, his mind unable to deal with what was going on. His life had been anything but normal recently, but this... this was just too much.

He hurried to his bedroom and sat next to his sleeping wife. Nash pushed a strand of hair out of her face and then gripped her shoulder.

He said gently, "Judith? Judith, you need to wake up, honey. Can you hear me?"

She made no sound or movement. He rose with an idea that he would make some coffee for her. He made a detour into the bathroom to wash his face. When he passed by the shower he saw something on the tile-and-pebble floor.

It was vomit. Revulsed, he used the handheld shower head to hose it down the drain and then used some cleaner to get rid of the smell. Curious, he looked into Judith's closet. It was always a mess, but piled in one corner were the clothes she had apparently worn the previous night: a very short, clingy skirt, a low-cut blouse, a thong, push-up bra, and stilettos.

She said she didn't go out last night, but this says differently. Where was she when I was out of town?

He bent down, picked up the blouse, and took a whiff. Alcohol— wine, most likely. And the aroma of her perfume. And...something else.

He dropped the blouse and headed downstairs to make coffee.

CHAPTER

42

BY ONE IN THE MORNING the forensic team had finished their examination, and shiny fingerprint dust lingered on many surfaces around the house like glittery remnants from a birthday party.

Judith, wearing a terry cloth robe and sitting on the couch in the living room, stared at her bare, tanned feet.

Nash was perched beside her, his mind racing with mingled thoughts of his missing daughter and where his wife had been the night before, and whether there was a connection between the two.

The pair of detectives seated across from them looked like they had seen things most human beings would never encounter. John Ramos was tall and stocky, and Nash had noted that he was methodical and deliberate in his movements and line of questioning. The other, Carroll Summers, was small, wiry, and nimble. Dressed in rumpled suits, with ties loosened, they now stared across the heft of a $2,000 coffee table at the devastated couple. Summers had his notebook out and had been industriously scribbling in it, while Ramos leaned back, one thick leg crossed over the other, and apparently committed what he needed to memory.

Summers said, "So, Mrs. Nash, you saw your daughter last around midnight. How was she, her mood, attitude?"

Judith took a moment to clear her throat, draped the fold of her robe over her dimpled knees, and said, "Maggie seemed fine. Nothing out of the ordinary."

"So she wasn't upset about anything?"

This came from Ramos, whose eyes had been closed while Summers spoke but now they were open and staring fixedly at her.

"No," said Judith. She glanced at Nash, as though for support. "It was just...normal."

"You two were home together all evening?" asked Summers.

Judith broke off looking at her husband and said, "Yes."

"Dinner together?"

"I, uh, wasn't that hungry. I snacked. Maggie probably made something for herself."

"What did you two talk about?" asked Ramos.

"I said it was just normal stuff," said Judith, her voice raised.

"Be that as it may, sometimes a small detail becomes important," noted Ramos, his voice low and calm. "We're doing all we can to find your daughter. But we need your help."

Nash said gently, "Whatever you can remember, honey, please."

Judith closed her eyes and drew a deep breath. Then she took a sip of water from the glass in front of her and said, "She was talking about her influencer proposal."

"Her what?" said Ramos.

"Our daughter wanted to be a social media influencer," explained Nash. "She wanted funding from us and was working up a proposal."

Summers looked around the room and said, "O-kay. What else?"

"She was asking me some questions about what she should put in it. You know, what would persuade you to fund her, Walter," she added, speaking directly to him.

Summers said, "Did she mention any plans to travel somewhere? To meet some friends that night?"

"No," Judith said forcefully. "She just went to her room. Okay? She went to her room and now she's not there anymore." She stared at the two policemen. "Find my daughter."

Then Judith burst into tears and rushed from the room. The flap of her robe knocked over the glass, and water streamed out over the granite top of the coffee table.

Nash had risen to go after her but then decided that would be counterproductive. He sat down and watched the water pool on the granite after righting the glass.

"She's upset," he said unnecessarily.

"We understand, Mr. Nash," said Summers. "So you were in New York?"

"Yes, on business. My plane landed at eight this morning. I went right to my office. I got home at seven, and that's when we realized Maggie wasn't here."

"You hadn't talked to her by phone during the day?"

"No. I don't usually call her."

"Text?"

"No. I had a busy day. And she didn't text me, which is not unusual."

"So you came home from work and what?"

"My wife was in the kitchen. I asked her about Maggie. She mentioned she hadn't seen or talked to her. I went up to her room and got no response. Her car was in the garage. We got into her room and found it empty. But she'd left her wallet, phone, and computer. We called the police, and that's when the officer found the back door had been forced."

"The alarm system had not been turned on. Is that usual?" asked Ramos.

"When I'm home I always turn it on. My wife is sometimes not as diligent."

"I thought it would be the reverse. Women at home alone would want it on."

"Well, Judith usually does, but I guess she must have forgotten."

The detectives exchanged a glance that Nash tried and failed to read.

"You can think of no reason why your daughter might have gone off on her own?" asked Summers.

"No, none."

"Were your relations with her good?"

"Yes. The same with her mother. We're a happy family."

"She's nineteen, you said. Is she in college and off for the summer?"

"No, she...decided to take a gap year."

"And is thinking of doing this influencer thing?" Ramos reminded him.

"Yes. I was helping her with it."

"And you said you work at Sybaritic Investments?"

"Yes, I'm in charge of acquisitions."

"Considering your…heightened financial position, it's not out of the realm of possibility that you might receive a ransom demand," said Summers.

Nash looked perplexed. "Kidnapping and ransom? Does that even happen anymore?"

Summers said, "Unfortunately, it does. Fortunately, not nearly as often. Although with electronic funds, crypto, whatnot, the kidnapper no longer has to worry about plucking a bag of cash out of a trash can or it being embedded with explosive dye."

"Well, I've gotten no ransom demand."

"Make sure you let us know if you do. If it is a kidnapping we'll want to call in the FBI."

At the mention of the Bureau's name Nash felt his gut tighten.

"You okay, Mr. Nash?" asked Ramos, who, Nash had observed, did not miss much.

"I'm just trying to process this nightmare."

"We understand, sir. We know it's not easy and we're doing all we can to get her back safe and sound. So if you receive any communication from anyone about your daughter let us know immediately."

"What will you do now?"

"We'll go over the forensics. We have officers canvassing the neighborhood, and we'll speak to the list of her friends you provided."

"Good, good," Nash said absently.

"We'd like to get into her social media accounts."

"She's on Instagram, Snapchat, and TikTok."

"You wouldn't happen to know her account info and passwords?" asked Ramos.

"No. She might have them on her phone but I can't get into that, either."

"We'll need to get a warrant."

"You do whatever you need to do to find my daughter."

43

AFTER THE DETECTIVES LEFT, NASH went to his study and texted Agent Morris. He couldn't tell the police this, but it had instantly occurred to Nash that his daughter's disappearance might be tied to what he was doing with the FBI.

Remarkably, at this hour of the night, Morris texted right back: I will call in two minutes.

The phone buzzed 120 seconds later.

"Tell me everything," said Morris.

Nash did and then waited.

"You're sure she wouldn't have gone on her own?"

"And breaking in the back door on her way out?" said an incredulous Nash. "And leaving her car, phone, wallet, and laptop behind?"

"Okay, let me look into this and I'll get back to you. Keep your eyes and ears open. Anyone contacts you, let me know." He clicked off before Nash could say anything else.

Upstairs Nash found his wife lying on the sofa in their bedroom sitting room.

He sat across from her.

"The detectives have left," he said.

She nodded absently, her gaze on the wall, her eyes vacant.

"Can you tell me the truth now, Judith?"

"What are you talking about?" she said dully, glancing at him.

"You told me that Maggie was upset last night. But you told the detectives that she was normal, no problems."

"I...I was confused. And when I said she was upset, it was just the normal stuff. Nothing that would explain...*this*," she added with a sharp wave of her hand.

"Okay, I have another question."

"Walter, do we really have to do this right now?"

"Where were you last night?"

Her features became so still it was like she was in rigor. "I...was...here. Like I told you."

"I found the vomit in the shower. I saw the clothes on your closet floor."

She leapt up and hurried into the bedroom.

He called after her, "Running away is not doing Maggie any good, Judith. Right now, I really need the truth."

She slowly walked back into the sitting area. "Look, Walter, I just think that—"

He stood. His furious features and his towering presence made her shrink back.

"You were with another man last night. Your *clothes* said as much. Maybe you and Maggie got into an argument about that. Maybe it made you throw up in the shower and you were too out of it to clean it up. Or hide your clothes from me."

She wavered and then plopped down on the couch.

He sat across from her in the chair, the distance between them far greater than that right now. "So...how long has Rhett been screwing you?"

Judith shuddered, but then looked defiant. "Rhett? Temple? Are you insane?"

"He knew about my dad's Agent Orange settlement. I never mentioned that to him, or anyone else, except you and Maggie. Now, I highly doubt Maggie would have anything to do with a guy like Rhett. So the only way he could have found out was through you." He stood and started to pace. "And the other night when you came home late and found me still awake? You looked...guilty. You had clothes on that were, well, not the sort that one would wear to a dinner with a girlfriend. I always knew you were attracted to Rhett.

Over the years I've seen how flirty and handsy you are around him, and he around you. And I think we can both agree that Rhett will screw anything in a skirt. And I'm sure the thrill of doing it with other men's wives was just the cherry on top. And, as a final clue, his cologne, which is very expensive and distinctive, is all over the clothes on your closet floor."

"Walter, please stop." She was shaking now, her head dangling, her arms limp.

"I guess the Asian trip was another way to be with Rhett. I mentioned it to him. He tried to hide it, but I could tell he already knew all about it. And then you did your best to dissuade me from going."

"Walter, I—"

He sat back down. "But that is not something I want to think about right now. The only thing I care about is finding Maggie."

"I...I don't know where she is."

"Did she confront you last night when you got home? About being with another man?"

Judith slowly nodded. "Y-yes."

"And what happened?"

"She was angry. I was angry. I stormed off. I...I didn't see her after that. And I didn't check on her because I thought she would be...I just didn't."

"Did she threaten to tell me the truth?"

"No, no, she never said that." She shot him a glance. "Wait, what are you implying?"

Nash said, "I'm implying nothing. But I need you to answer the next question truthfully. Did you call Rhett and tell him that Maggie knew about you two?"

"No, never. I...hold on. You think Rhett might have done this?"

"I have no idea. That's why I asked."

"What would be his motive to...to take Maggie?"

"Rhett wants to keep me happy and at the firm. If I found out he was bedding my wife? That might disrupt our business relationship just a tad, don't you think?"

"Rhett is not like that. You don't know him like I do," replied Judith.

He said stonily, "Well, granted I've never slept with the man, but there are things about him that you don't know."

"Like what?"

Nash came close to answering her but, in the end, couldn't bring himself to do it. His trust in his wife was shattered, perhaps irreversibly. And he couldn't be certain that whatever he told her would not end up known to Rhett. And then to Victoria Steers.

He rose. "Do you need anything?"

"Just my daughter back."

"Right. Me too." Nash walked out of the room and slammed the door behind him.

44

NASH SLEPT FITFULLY FOR AN hour and then awoke. He checked his watch, had a sudden idea, and left the house in his Range Rover.

"Hey, Billy?" said Nash as he drove up to the little guardhouse.

Billy Adams was a stout young man in his early twenties who dearly wanted to be a real police officer or at least a mall cop, or so he had once confided to Nash. He covered the graveyard shift at the neighborhood's security gate.

Adams came out of the guardhouse and said, "Mr. Nash, I talked to the cops. I'm so sorry. Have they found out anything about Maggie?"

"No, not yet."

"She's gotta be okay. I mean, she's so beautiful and everything. And nice. When she'd come in late she'd bring me a burger and fries or a Red Bull, stuff like that. And sit here in her car and talk to me. She didn't have to do that. Nice, like I said."

"Look, Billy, I wanted to ask you some questions."

"Sure, Mr. Nash. What do you want to know?"

"Well, the previous night, did anything unusual happen?"

Adams squinted at him. "Unusual like what?"

"Out of the ordinary. People coming and going? If someone came and took Maggie, I would imagine they probably came through this gate."

"Do you know what time we're talking?"

"Say around one to around five, when it would start getting light. So you would have been on duty, right?"

"Yeah, my shift goes eight to eight. It was pretty quiet, not much going on. Only a few cars. Some folks are away on vacation and all. They let us know so we can check on their homes." He glanced at a Smart Car emblazoned with the name of the community on its sides parked in a space by the guardhouse. Next to it was a small Ford compact, which Nash knew was Adams's personal vehicle.

Adams pointed to the Smart Car and said, "I patrol in that for fifteen minutes on the hour."

Nash knew that residents had RF strips on their windshield that automatically opened the gate. And visitors were given a special code by the homeowner that they could input in the call box, so if there was no guard at the gate they could still gain access.

Feeling a little out of his depth, Nash looked around and tried to piece together questions that would lead to answers that he needed to know. "So, um, any visitors last night? Or anyone waiting here when you came back from patrol?"

"There were only three visitors. They weren't on the list, so I called the homes they were going to and received confirmation. I let them in." He ducked back inside the guardhouse and came back out with some papers on a clipboard. He leafed through them. "The last one was at ten fifteen, so outside the time window you asked about."

Nash studied the long metal bar that stopped traffic from freely entering. "Could someone, say, push the gate open while you're gone on patrol?"

"They could, but it won't go back into position. It locks. That way it shows that there's been an intrusion. There was nothing like that last night. The only time that's happened to my knowledge is when old Mrs. Brunson hit the gas instead of the brakes and bam. She was really embarrassed. Quit driving for good the next day. Safer all around."

"And that was it? You didn't see anyone else?"

"Well, except for the nine-one-one call."

"The what?" Nash said sharply.

"Cops showed up around two fifteen in a squad car. Said there was a nine-one-one at the Perkins residence over on Falkirk. Turned out it was just a swatting attempt."

Nash looked blankly at him.

Adams said, "Swatting. You know, when someone calls the cops and says something bad is happening somewhere just to get the cops there, hoping something bad *will* happen. It happens a lot to politicians. It's a really shitty thing to do."

"Is that what the cops told you? That it was this *swatting* thing?"

"Yeah. They stopped on the way back out and told me."

"Why would someone *swat* the Perkinses? They're in their seventies and retired. And neither of them was ever in politics."

"No clue. But that's what the cops said."

Nash mulled this over for a few moments. "Did you tell the cops that questioned you regarding Maggie about this?"

"Well, no. I just assumed they'd know what the other cops were doing. And the cops last night said it was no big deal, just to forget about it, and so I did. It could have nothing to do with Maggie disappearing."

"And you're sure it *was* the cops?" asked Nash.

Adams looked at him funny. "They were in a police car and had on uniforms with badges and guns, Mr. Nash. Look, I know this has been a real shock and all," he added with a sympathetic expression.

"What did the cops look like?"

"Um, they were a guy and a gal."

"Can you describe them? Did they give you their names? Did they have name tags?"

"No, they didn't mention their names and I couldn't see their name tags. The guy was big and broad shouldered. The girl was slender. Both had dark hair. I'd say they were in their late thirties, something like that."

"What else?"

"Uh, the guy was white, and the gal was Asian."

"Can you go down to the police station and tell them what you just told me?"

"Well, I can after my shift is over. But they probably already know."

"Just in case, I'd appreciate it."

"Sure thing, Mr. Nash. Anything to help find Maggie. I'll go right after my shift ends."

Nash next drove to the Perkinses' home. He knew them from some HOA meetings and neighborhood barbeques. He had learned that Phil Perkins had been a banker and his wife a Realtor.

A sleepy-looking Phil answered the door in his pajamas and robe. After Nash explained about Maggie being kidnapped and what Adams had told Nash, Phil said that no one, certainly not the police, had come to his house the previous night.

Phil said, "What the hell is going on?"

Nash had an idea about that, and it scared the crap out of him.

CHAPTER

45

NASH LEFT A MESSAGE AT the number Detective Ramos had left with him asking the detective to call him as soon as possible. He then drove back to his house. Judith was locked in their bathroom and he could hear her weeping. He walked to Maggie's room and stood looking at the police tape strung across it like some visible virus overtaking his world.

He texted Morris for an update and received a terse reply: Working it.

He was exhausted and not thinking clearly. He knew he really should get some sleep, but how can you rest when your child is missing? And he really wasn't sure what he felt about Judith right now. The fact of her affair with Rhett, which would have crushed him under any other circumstances, seemed pushed to the far recesses of his emotional universe. All that mattered was Maggie.

Is this how quickly one's life falls apart? Before my father's funeral my world was perfect. Now, it's been shattered into pieces so small I can't recognize a single bit of it.

Hours later, his phone buzzed, waking him from where he had finally fallen deeply asleep on the family room couch. Morning light was coming in through the window.

Shock said, "Is it true? Maggie's gone? I saw the news this morning."

A groggy Nash said, "Yes. Someone broke into our house and took her."

"You think it's connected to your stuff?"

"It has to be."

"Does Judith know about all that?"

"No. I haven't told her. And there was something weird."

"What?"

He told Shock about the fake cops and the so-called swatting attempt.

"That would make sense," said Shock. "A way in through the gate, nobody would question them. She might have been drugged or dead and in the trunk on the way out."

This comment made Nash collapse forward and a sob escaped his lips. He tried to cover the phone, but didn't quite make it.

"Damn, I'm sorry, Walter. I shouldn't have been that blunt. I was thinkin' with my pro hat on, not my human one."

"It's nothing I haven't been thinking myself," replied Nash as he straightened and slumped back on the sofa.

"Let me dig around. I'll get back to you."

Nash stumbled to the kitchen, where sunlight was streaming in all the windows, and made some coffee. He sucked down the cup greedily, as though the caffeine would give him some superpower to aid him in locating Maggie.

Twenty minutes later Judith came down the stairs. She was dressed to the nines with full makeup, hair teased out and frothy, and a half-dozen jangling bracelets on each wrist. She stopped on the bottom riser and eyed the unkempt and bloodshot-eyed Nash as he sat at the kitchen island in the clothes he'd slept in.

The only thing he could think of to say was "Going somewhere?"

She didn't answer, but stepped into the kitchen, crossed the space, snagged a cup, and poured herself coffee. She leaned against a counter and drank it down.

Nash eyed her for a bit and then retreated into his own thoughts.

"Have the police called?" she finally asked.

He looked up to see her pouring out another cup of coffee. She was unemotional, calm, robotic even. It was starting to freak him out. *Was she on drugs?*

"No, they haven't."

She nodded, pursed her lips, and took a sip of the coffee. "Have you eaten?"

"I'm not hungry."

"You need to eat, Walter. You're too thin as it is. It won't do Maggie any good if you collapse from hunger."

Nash grabbed a banana from a bowl, stripped it, and ate it.

"There. Happy?" he said.

She started rummaging in the fridge. "I'll make you a proper breakfast."

"Judith, I'm not hungry, okay?"

"You say that now, but I know you. You'll be fussing in no time. 'Where's my damn dinner? Why isn't the house clean, woman?'"

"I don't believe I've *ever* said that, in over two decades of marriage."

"Maybe not in actual words, but with your eyes, with your manner. Men do that, you know. Women talk, men just emote, badly."

He shook his head in bewilderment at this ridiculous conversation. Was this her guilt coming through? Or was it something more? He felt inclined to find out.

"Did you take some meds that are doing a number on you?" he asked.

"Eggs, bacon, toast, avocado, and fruit. Protein, carbs, fiber, and some healthy fats. In a jiffy, Walter. You can always count on me. You know that."

He watched her pull skillets and bowls out of cupboards and food from the fridge. She put things together, and soon the kitchen was filled with the comingled smells of eggs, sizzling bacon, and bread toasting. She tossed blackberries, blueberries, and raspberries in a bowl with some yogurt, and sliced up an avocado after depitting it and scooping it out of its skin. She set out a plate at the table along with utensils and a cloth napkin pulled from a credenza drawer.

When the meal was ready she plated it, took his empty cup,

refilled it, poured out a glass of orange juice, and set it down next to his plate.

"All ready to go. Eat up."

He was oscillating between telling her to go to hell and sitting down to the meal. For reasons not readily apparent to him, Nash chose the latter. Perhaps it was because he could imagine the brittle fragility of his wife's psyche right now and he did not want her to fully collapse.

As he took up his napkin and started eating she hovered next to him and said, "Everything to your liking?"

"It's fine, Judith. Thank you."

"I'm so glad." She squeezed his shoulders, kissed him on the cheek, and walked back up the stairs.

He swallowed some eggs, had a piece of bacon, spooned two mouthfuls of fruit and yogurt into his mouth, took a couple bites of toast, and ate one slice of the avocado. Then Nash stood and went upstairs.

He saw Judith's shoes lying outside of Maggie's room. Next, he saw that the police tape had been ripped down. He peeked through the opening and saw his wife lying on her daughter's bed, curled into a fetal position. She was saying something over and over but he couldn't make out the words.

As he drew closer he finally heard it.

"I'm sorry, I'm sorry, I'm sorry, I'm sorry."

He quietly withdrew and went to his room, showered, and changed into slacks and a polo shirt.

He walked to the guardhouse. Billy Adams was already off duty, and Nash hoped he was at the station telling the police what had happened. He was concerned because Ramos had not called him back.

Rolf was now on duty. He did not look good at all, Nash thought, as the man came out of the guardhouse.

"Rolf, you okay?"

"No, I'm not."

"What's wrong?"

"It's Billy Adams."

"Billy? What about him? I talked to him late last night. He was fine."

"Not anymore. He's dead."

Nash staggered back. "What! How?"

"Apparently he lost control of his car and it went off the road and flipped. He died instantly, they said."

"Where?"

"About three miles west of here. Funny, because that's not on his way home."

But it is on the way to the nearest police station, Nash thought.

Rolf looked like he might cry. "So pointless, right?"

"Yes," said Nash. He was actually thinking that Billy Adams's death had no doubt contained several elements, but being *pointless* was not one of them.

46

"YOU NEED TO GO TO the police with that info, Walter," said
Shock.

Nash was back at his home and had called Shock about Adams's
death.

"If the cops were fake, and it looks like they were, the killers were
tyin' up loose ends by takin' out the one dude who could ID them."

"Okay, Shock, I called the detective last night and left a message
but he never called back. I'll try again." Then he blurted out, "I wish
to God I'd told Billy to go straight to the police yesterday."

Nash clicked off and phoned Ramos, leaving another message
for the man. He then went upstairs to check on Judith.

She was no longer in Maggie's room. Nash heard the water running and poked his head in to see Judith in the shower. She glanced
up at him, embarrassed.

"I'm ... sorry, Walter. I know I was ... this morning. I ... "

"Just shower, you'll feel better. And you must be hungry. Can I
make you something?"

"No, I'm ... I'll eat later. I'm going to go for a walk. I need
some ... air."

"Okay."

"Walter, if Maggie has been kidnapped, we can pay to get her
home safe, right?"

"I'll sell everything we have to get her back, Judith."

Nash left her and was halfway downstairs when Ramos called
him back.

"Sorry I missed you last night and this morning, Mr. Nash. I've been running around on a bunch of things and time got away from me."

Nash explained what Billy Adams had told him about the 911 call.

"I checked with the Perkinses. The police never came by. And they told Billy not to mention it to anyone, which is why he didn't tell you. And now he's dead, allegedly in an accident. Only he wasn't going in the direction of his home when he died, he was going in the direction of the police station, where I told him to file a report on what he'd seen."

"So a man and a woman posing as police officers got through the gate and then took your daughter? And this Adams had to die because he knew about them?"

"Yes."

Nash could almost see the detective shaking his head.

"We've got to prove that connection, Mr. Nash."

"Then prove it. I just told you what I found out."

"Why would you go and talk to the security guard in the first place?"

"To see if he knew anything."

"But we had already talked to him and the other guard," pointed out Ramos.

"Right, but he didn't tell you about the fake police, did he?"

"Well, we need to corroborate that story."

"*I* just corroborated it. Adams told me and I told you. And there're the Perkinses."

"No, the Perkinses never saw these two people, according to you."

"Yes, that's right, they didn't," conceded Nash.

"So right now, with Adams dead, we only have *your* word for it."

"I'm not lying. Why the hell would I lie?"

"I'm not saying you're lying, Mr. Nash. But in a criminal investigation, every fact, every statement, must be verified. I can't accept anything at face value."

"Then...then verify it." A fuming Nash clicked off.

Nash was a control person and he had never felt more out of control in his life. Nothing seemed to make sense. But there was one obvious fact that stood out: His daughter was gone. That, for him, *was* verified. And if the people connected to Steers were behind her kidnapping, then Rhett and Barton would know all about it. The problem was, how could Nash find out what they knew without guaranteeing that Maggie would indeed be killed? If she hadn't already been.

The thought of his daughter being dead, which had been floating just below the surface of his conscious being, now exploded out of its depths, and Nash felt the urge to throw up. He ran to the bathroom, but when he hovered over the toilet, his gut calmed and he straightened.

You running around like an idiot is not going to help Maggie. You've got brains and some bit of nerve. Use them, for God's sake.

And then an idea hit him. He put on a suit, saw Judith off on her walk, and drove to work.

47

Walt, what in the hell are you doing here?"

Rhett stood in the open doorway of Nash's office staring in disbelief at him. "Shouldn't you be home with Judith?" he added.

"I didn't come in here to work. I came in here to think, and I can't do it in a house where my daughter was taken from."

Rhett shut the door and sat across from him. "I'm so sorry about all this, Walt. Has there been any word about Maggie?"

Nash studied him closely while trying hard not to appear to be doing so. "No, nothing."

"You know, when I was a kid someone tried to snatch me."

Nash looked at him in astonishment. "What?"

"Yeah, I was out playing in the rear grounds of Dad's old estate. A guy jumped the fence and grabbed me."

"What happened?"

"My mother saw what was going on. Luckily she'd been skeet shooting and still had her gun. She ran toward us and fired her weapon over our heads. That freaked out the guy who had me. He dropped me and ran for it. When he reached the fence my mother fired at him and winged him. He dropped over the fence where another guy helped him get away. My mom called the cops but they never turned up anything. After that, we always had a security guard with us."

"Damn, Rhett, that was close."

"To tell you the truth, I'm not sure my father would have paid the ransom, if I had been taken. But Mom would have made him."

Seemingly embarrassed by this admission, Rhett glanced away.

As Nash looked him over, it occurred to him what a damaged man Rhett Temple probably was. It did not make him necessarily feel sorry for him, because no one's life was perfect and everyone was accountable for their choices. But still, he felt *something* for the guy.

Nash said, "The kidnappers might have been seen."

"Really? Well, that's good, right?"

Nash shot Rhett a glance to see his expression. The man seemed truly sincere.

So he might not be in the loop on this. Had Steers acted alone?

If so, his plan about coming to the office today might not work. But he had to try.

"Yes. Um, they might have been posing as cops to get through the gate on a phony nine-one-one call."

Nash believed he saw a hint of panic in the other man's eyes at learning about the possibly fake police officers. Maybe at least Rhett suspected what might have happened.

"Damn, I wonder what that's about?" said Rhett.

"I don't know. But I'd do anything to have Maggie back safe." He looked squarely at Rhett. "Anything. It doesn't matter what they ask for, I'll do it."

Come on, Rhett, I'm being pretty damn obvious here. Give me Maggie back and I won't do anything to hurt you or your father.

Rhett slowly nodded. "Well, I hope the cops find her, and fast." He paused. "How is Judith doing? I'm sure she's beside herself."

Nash closed his eyes for a moment because Rhett's comment had brought back the fact of this man's having an ongoing affair with his wife.

Apparently Judith didn't give him a heads-up about her confession.

"She is very upset, obviously. She, uh, blames herself."

"What, why?"

"She was out that night, late. And she and Maggie had an argument about something when Judith returned home from wherever she was."

Rhett paled, quickly rose, and said, "Well, give her my best. Look, keep me in the loop and if there's anything you need, just say the word, okay?"

When the door closed behind the man, Nash said quietly, "If my daughter doesn't come back safe, I will fucking kill you."

48

TWO DAYS LATER NASH RECEIVED a text from Morris on their secure link. The FBI agent had nothing to report, but insisted he was still working diligently on the matter. Despite that, Nash did not like the tone underlying the man's words. Something was off, he could feel it.

Later, Shock phoned him.

"I've got some calls in to folks I trust and who are in the know, Walter. Anythin' pops, I will get right back to you."

"Thanks, Shock. I...I went to the office the other day and subtly suggested to Rhett that I would do anything to get Maggie back safe."

"You think he bit?"

"I'm not sure, but he nearly ran out of my office. I haven't heard anything, though."

"But looks like he wasn't aware that folks workin' with him had taken Maggie?"

"I don't think he knew, no. Shock, if Steers took Maggie, what will she do? Will...will she let Maggie go if I—"

Nash broke off because he had no idea what to say next.

"I don't know, Walter. But I'm not goin' to sugarcoat this. Steers is very dangerous."

"I'll leave my job. I'll never call the FBI back, if...if they agree to let her go."

"Right," said Shock, but with not much behind it.

Nash clicked off, his spirits even lower now, if that was possible.

Judith was sleeping in their bed. He made sure her breathing was normal and then he stepped into his closet to change. Every normal routine he performed now seemed ridiculous in the face of losing Maggie.

I should be out there searching for her. But where do I even begin to look?

As he was taking off his clothes he noticed something.

A pair of gray khaki pants was missing, as was one of his beige shirts. When he slipped off his shoes and put them away in the shoe rack he noted that a pair of his sneakers was also gone.

What in the hell?

He later drove up to the guardhouse and asked Rolf if he knew exactly where Adams's car had gone off the road. Rolf gave him the location and Nash headed to the spot.

It was a winding double lane stretch of asphalt with mature trees boasting large canopies lining both sides. He parked and got out and noted the marks on the road and then the gouged dirt where Adams's car had left the pavement. There was a huge, dislodged chunk of earth where presumably the car had rolled. The damage to the ground continued on until it ended at a massive oak that showed signs of a violent collision.

The car and body had obviously been removed, but there was police tape strung up, though Nash could see no marked car or sentry around. Although he knew virtually nothing about these types of situations, it didn't take a forensics genius to observe that there were the marks of another vehicle's tread paralleling Adams's. He stooped to see if he could find any metal fragments that would show the two vehicles had actually collided. But there was nothing; the asphalt looked as though it had been swept. The police had probably collected whatever evidence there was from the scene.

"Looking for something?"

Nash turned and saw John Ramos sitting in a car across the road. How could he have not heard the man drive up? However, when he glanced at the car, he noted it was an EV.

He walked over to the detective. "There are two sets of tire tracks there. Did someone run him off the road?"

Ramos got out of the car and stood eye to eye with him. "Mr. Nash, you really need to leave this to the professionals. You've already potentially contaminated what might indeed be a crime scene."

"That was not my intent," retorted Nash. "I'm just trying—"

Ramos did not let him finish. "I know what you're trying to do, and it's not helpful. So I would appreciate if you would get back in your vehicle and leave."

Nash held up his hands in mock surrender. He walked back to the Range Rover, climbed in, and turned the SUV around. He was about to pull off when Ramos ran into the road with his hands up for Nash to stop.

"What is it?" called out a perturbed Nash. "I'm trying to leave like you *ordered* me to."

"When did that happen, sir?" asked Ramos, pointing.

"When did what happen?"

"That!" Ramos was indicating something on the passenger's side front fender.

Nash put the SUV in park, got out, and walked around to that side. He felt his gut tighten when he saw the large dent and jagged strip where the paint had been ripped away.

"Did you hit something?" asked Ramos in a tone that Nash did not like at all.

"No, I certainly would have noticed."

Ramos bent down and examined the smears of paint. "Your Rover is burgundy, but there's some blue in here."

"Blue?"

"From whatever you hit. Maybe another car?" Ramos looked at where Adams's car had gone off the road. "The deceased drove a blue Ford."

"What?" snapped Nash.

Ramos stood. "I'm afraid I'm going to have to impound your car, Mr. Nash. I'll call in a squad car to take you back home."

"Impound my car? Why?"

"To see what you hit, sir. I'm sure you can understand the possible significance."

"I...Look, I didn't hit anything. I would have known. It would have been evident."

"Yes sir, I'm sure you would have." He gave another significant look at the torn-up earth where Adams's car had flipped and then slammed into an oak.

"Wait, you're not implying...I didn't hit Billy's car. I didn't cause...this." He waved his hand at all the destruction.

"Then you won't mind us checking your car. Paint doesn't match, you are good to go."

"Look, if it does match, someone obviously took my car and did this."

Ramos said incredulously, "Took your car? From your garage? And you wouldn't know about it?"

"If Billy was killed shortly after he got off work, I was dead asleep at the time. But they could have taken it, done this, and then driven it back to my garage. My security strip would have gotten them back in the gate if the guard wasn't there. And the garage remote is on the visor."

"And you didn't notice the damage?"

"Obviously not. It's on the *passenger* side."

"And no one else noticed it, while you were out driving?"

"Apparently not."

"Nevertheless, the car is staying here. Your keys, please." Ramos held out his hand.

Nash stared at the man's open palm. "Don't you need a search warrant or something?"

"There is more than enough probable cause for me to impound this vehicle. But if you want to engage a lawyer, feel free to do so. However, I am not going to let you take the vehicle, because you could then attempt to remove vital evidence."

A weary and out-of-his-depth Nash rubbed his eyes and said,

"Take it, if it'll help you find out what happened." He handed the keys to Ramos.

"Oh, I'm sure it will, sir."

He looked at the detective and, in addition to everything else he was confronted with, Nash was now certain that he had just become the number one suspect both in his daughter's disappearance *and* in Billy Adams's death.

CHAPTER

49

BEFORE THE TWO OFFICERS DROVE Nash home they had conferred with Ramos. And the grim expressions the cops gave him told Nash that Ramos had conveyed his suspicions about Nash to the pair.

He went into the house to find Judith in the kitchen making a cup of tea.

"Where have you been?" she asked.

"I went for a drive."

"I didn't hear the garage door open."

"I...Look, are you feeling...better?"

She confronted him with a harsh look. "No, Walter, I'm *not* feeling better, okay? Our daughter is gone. My God, what is wrong with you?"

"With me!"

She stormed from the room without answering him.

He called Shock and told him about the latest development.

"Okay, Walter, they are obviously settin' you up for all this."

"I know, but how did I not notice the damage to my car?"

"I don't know. But you didn't, and that played into their hands. They took a risk, though, since you called Ramos *before* Billy was killed. If he'd answered you back right away he could have talked to Billy before they had a chance to silence him. But he didn't, and then Steers made sure he never could tell the police anythin'. They might have assumed that given what the fake cops told him the kid wouldn't have mentioned it to the real cops. But Steers's people might have had you or him or both of you under surveillance and seen or heard your exchange with Billy where he told you about the fake cops."

"So I might have been the reason he was killed?" said an anguished Nash.

"This is the fault of nobody other than the people who actually did it, Walter."

"But Ramos must know I wouldn't have been driving the damn SUV around if I had known it had evidence all over it."

Shock barked, "Look, get one goddamn thing straight right now in your head. This ain't TV, Walter. The real cops always look for the easy and obvious. They don't have an episode's worth of time or resources to go over every nook and cranny or think outside the box. They care 'bout makin' an arrest and then makin' it stick. The question of actual guilt or innocence does not weigh as heavily as you may think. And you drivin' it 'round? They think all criminals are stupid and make mistakes just like that. Or the bad guys think they're smarter than the cops, and still do stupid shit that gets 'em caught. I think this Ramos dude saw how you live and what you got and that's the path he's takin'. He'd love nothin' more than deep-sixin' your ass in prison for life regardless whether you actually did anythin' wrong."

A shaken Nash exclaimed, "I might be screwed."

"You might be. But let me see what I can do. Now, Walter?"

"Yeah?"

"Guaranteed this sucker is gonna get worse before it gets better. And there's a chance it ain't never gonna get better."

Shock clicked off, leaving Nash paralyzed.

Later, he made himself an egg and toast for dinner and then retreated to his home office with a cup of coffee. He placed his phone in front of him and waited for either Shock or Agent Morris to get back to him.

By midnight neither one had.

He went upstairs. As he was brushing his teeth and then washing his face he glanced at the hairbrush he used every morning. He picked it up and pulled out the hairs stuck among the bristles of the brush. He threw them away in the trash can.

It's a miracle I'm not all gray.

He walked into his closet and looked around, something gnawing at him intensely, although he wasn't sure what it was exactly.

A sense of impending doom, perhaps?

On sudden impulse he grabbed a small carry-on bag and put some clothes, shoes, and toiletries inside, along with cash that he took from the wall safe behind a panel in his closet. Inside the safe were his father's .45 and Army Ka-bar knife. He loaded both into his bag along with extra ammo mags. Zipping it closed, he set it on top of one of his shelves and walked out.

The motto of the Boy Scouts: Be prepared.

Judith was now in the bedroom's sitting area. She had the locket that she wore in her hands. It was open and she was looking down at the picture there. She sat up when Nash called out to her.

"Did you eat?" he asked.

"I had something," she replied abruptly. "Where is your Range Rover? It's not in the garage."

"I...I took it in for service."

She said incredulously, "Your daughter has been kidnapped and you took your Range Rover in for service?"

"Judith, I need to tell you something."

"What?"

"It might be the reason Maggie's gone."

She sat up and said stiffly, "What are you talking about?"

Nash was about to tell her everything when her phone buzzed. For a moment he thought it might be Rhett calling.

Judith looked down. "It's Linda Marshall, Debbie's mom. Deb's one of Maggie's closest friends. Do you think she knows something and told her mother? It must be important if she's calling at this hour."

She answered. "Hello, Linda, what's wrong?" She listened for a few moments. "What? I don't under...Online? Maggie? My God. What are...? Okay, yes, okay."

She clicked off, jumped up, and grabbed her laptop from the nightstand. She sat back down on the sofa and started clicking keys.

Nash sat next to her. "What is it? What did she say?"

Judith didn't answer right away as she focused on what she was doing. "She said Maggie posted something online."

"Maggie! When?"

"Just now, apparently. Deb was online and saw it and told her mom."

"Did she say what it was?"

Judith gave her husband a strange look. "Some of it, yes."

"What? What did she say?" barked Nash.

Judith didn't answer. She turned back to the screen as an image came on.

It was Maggie looking distraught with tears running down her face.

"Oh my God," said Nash. "The kidnappers are having her communicate online."

"Shut up so we can hear her," snapped Judith.

Maggie was looking directly into the camera. She was wearing the same rose-colored velour warmup suit that Nash had previously seen her in.

She said in a halting tone, "My name is Maggie Nash. I...I faked being kidnapped."

"What!" exclaimed Nash.

"Shut up!" shouted Judith.

Maggie continued, "I had to get away from him. He...was horrible to me."

Nash said, "Who is she talking about? I thought you said she wasn't seeing anyone."

Judith gave him a cold stare, a look that made a deeply puzzled Nash fall silent. What he heard next froze every liter of blood in his body.

Maggie said, "My father, Walter Nash, has been abusing me for years. He would come into my bedroom late at night when my mother was asleep. He would—" she sobbed for a moment before continuing "—he would do things to me, terrible things. And then he told me he'd kill me and my mother if I ever told the truth."

Nash just stared at the screen, open-mouthed. He could not feel his body, it was like all he had left was his overwrought mind along with a heart that had just been rent in half.

"He pretends to be this hardworking, nose-to-the-grindstone businessman, but he's a monster. I couldn't take it anymore. I had to get away. But I'm so worried that he might find me. And that he'll hurt my mom. I only told one person, my friend Billy Adams. He's the night security guard at the entrance to my neighborhood. I hope he's okay. I have to go now. Please don't try and find me. And make sure my mom is okay."

Her image faded from the screen.

Judith, who was breathing hard with tears covering her cheeks, slowly closed the laptop. She turned to Nash.

"Is that what you were going to tell me?" she demanded in a quiet voice.

Nash shook his head, still trying to process what had just happened. "What?"

"Were you going to confess before Linda called me?"

"Confess to what? I never touched Maggie."

"You're actually calling her a liar? After all she's been through?"

In his withering anxiety, Nash stood and backed away. "Look, I don't know what the hell is going on. But I never did anything to Maggie. I swear."

Judith started to shake. "I...don't want to believe any of this, Walter. And...Maggie never mentioned...anything...to me."

"And she would, Judith. She would have told you. You two never kept secrets from each other."

Judith looked up at him and her expression was not a sympathetic one. "You sound like you're trying to convince me."

"I'm trying to tell you the truth."

Judith pointed at the laptop. "Then why in God's name would our daughter tell everyone that you...you *abused* her?"

"I...I don't know, Judith," said Nash in a trembling voice. He could barely speak. He could barely think. The image of his daughter saying these terrible things dominated everything in his life at the moment. "I just don't know."

Judith shook her head. "I..." She swallowed, hard and with difficulty. It was clear she, too, could barely speak or think clearly.

"My God, Judith. Do you really think I'm capable of that? I love Maggie. I would never do anything to hurt her."

"You're asking me to believe you over her, Walter."

"I'm asking you to just look at this logically."

"Fuck logic," she suddenly screamed. In a lower, far more menacing tone she said, "Fuck logic. This isn't about logic, Walter. This is about our daughter saying you have molested her for years."

"But you said she would have told you."

She looked at him sharply, something appearing in her features that was cagey, guarded, possibly triumphant, like a decision had been made. As he looked at her Nash felt tendrils of icy dread wash over him.

"No, Walter, *you* were the one who said that. Not me."

"Judith, please. Think this through clearly."

"You're trying to manipulate me. That's what you do so well. I'm not another business negotiation, Walter. I'm your wife. And Maggie's mother."

"And I love you and it hurts me that you think I could do something like that."

She now looked at him with revulsion. "There you go, trying to swing the blame onto me. My Eagle Scout? My perfectly predictable gentleman of a husband. You've played me for a fool. You tried to make me believe you with this *logic* crap. You tried to manipulate me into believing you. And now our daughter has run away, because of you. You!"

She picked up the laptop and chucked it at Nash, striking him on the shoulder.

"Judith! I'm telling you the truth."

"No, Walter. I believe my daughter, not you." She lunged at him. "You monster! I will fucking kill you." She struck him across the face.

He grabbed her arms. "Judith, please stop. This is insane. I didn't do anything to her."

A breathless Judith pushed him away and pulled out her phone.

"Who are you calling?" he cried out.

"Who do you think, you piece of shit? The police."

"Judith, don't. I did nothing. They...they must have forced Maggie to say all that."

"Who? Why would anyone do that?"

"Because I'm—"

"You're what?"

"I...I can't tell you."

In disgust Judith turned back to the phone. "Hello, police? I need you to come out to my home. There is a child molester in the house and it's my husband."

"Judith!"

"Don't touch me. Hurry, please hurry," she screamed into the phone. She gave them the address.

Nash turned and ran to his closet, grabbed his bag, and raced down the stairs. On the way he called Shock. He answered by the time Nash was out the front door and running down the street, his pulse increasing with every stride.

Before he could say anything Shock said, "I saw Maggie, online."

"It's all a lie."

"This is their way of takin' you out without pullin' the trigger and causin' themselves more trouble. Where are you?"

Nash told him. "Judith has called the police. They'll be on their way."

"Just get out of your neighborhood. Can you do that without the guard seein' you?"

Nash looked up ahead. There was a way around the gate. "Yes."

"Throw your phone away right after you click off this call. They can track you."

"But I can turn it off."

"Don't matter. They can track you even if the phone's off. I'll meet you in fifteen minutes." He gave him a pickup location.

Nash clicked off, tossed the phone into a storm drain, and ran for his life.

50

A TERRIFIED NASH HID BEHIND A tree along a lonely road that was nearly a mile from his neighborhood. Two cars had passed, but neither housed Shock. He had heard sirens in the distance as he was running, and knew it would be the police coming in response to Judith's call.

My daughter called me a monster? How did they force her to do that? Now everyone believes I'm...my own wife...

He tensed as a van drove slowly down the road and then stopped across from where he was hiding.

A voice called out, "Walter?"

Nash ran out from behind the tree, climbed into the passenger seat, and looked at Shock.

"You tossed your phone, right?" said Shock.

"Down a storm drain."

Shock drove off at a sedate pace and then glanced at the bag Nash had set on the floorboard.

"When did you pack that?"

"Right before we saw Maggie online. I had this feeling of doom." He unzipped the bag and pulled out the gun and knife. "My dad's."

"Smart move."

"Where are we going?"

"Someplace safe."

"Shock, you said you saw the video? How so fast?"

"I set a tickler on Maggie's Instagram, TikTok, and Snapchat pages for any activity."

"Why would you think to do that?"

"I'm in the security business, Walter. A kid disappears, you always check their social media platforms."

"They must have forced her to say those things. But at least this shows she's still alive."

Shock gave him a funny look. "Maybe."

"What do you mean, *maybe*?"

"You said Judith called the cops?"

"She believed Maggie," Nash said simply. "I was starting to tell her about my working with the FBI and that being the reason that Maggie was taken. But before I could tell her we got a call from a neighbor whose daughter is one of Maggie's best friends. She told her mom about the video, and her mother phoned Judith. Judith then thought I was about to confess to her that Maggie fled because I molested her." Nash shook his head. "She's known me for over twenty years. I've never done anything remotely like that, always been the calm, good guy, and she just believes that of me."

"Well, in Judith's defense, it was her daughter sayin' it, Walter."

"I know, I know," Nash said miserably. He stared out the windshield with a hopeless expression. "How the hell do I get out of this, Shock?"

"We'll think of a way. But for now I want you to get in the back of the van and pull that blanket over you, just in case the police stop me."

"Why would they stop you?"

"Because this here is America and I'm a big, scary Black dude drivin' around in the middle of the night in a van, Walter. Trust me, that's enough."

Nash climbed into the back and covered himself with the blanket. Shock drove on into an ever deepening darkness.

* * *

The next evening Judith answered the knock at her front door to see Rhett standing there.

Tears streaming down her face, she hugged him. "Oh, God, Rhett, my whole life has just...disintegrated."

"I know, I know, babe. I wanted to come last night when you called, but I figured what with the police and all I should give you all some space."

She nodded and led him inside. They sat in the family room.

"So what did the police say?" asked Rhett.

"They searched all over the area for him, but as of thirty minutes ago they hadn't found him."

"Weird that he could just vanish like that." He put his arm around her quaking shoulders. "Anything you need, just let me know, okay?"

"Okay, Rhett, thank you."

"Can I make you some tea, coffee?"

"No, I'm fine."

"I watched the video, Judith. The things Maggie said about Walter. Did you ever suspect?"

She said angrily, "Do you think if I had I wouldn't have put a stop to it?"

"Right, right, sorry, I didn't mean that," Rhett said quickly. "It's just all so...messed up. Walt just seemed so...normal."

"I...didn't believe it, at first. I didn't *want* to believe it."

"What made you change your mind?" asked Rhett.

"I don't know. Maybe it's because I'm a woman. And a mother. And I could not believe that my daughter would ever say those things unless they were true."

"And Maggie mentioned a Billy Adams. Didn't I read about him dying?"

Judith dabbed at her eyes with a tissue. "Detective Ramos came by early this morning. He's working on Maggie's disappearance."

"What did he say?"

Judith shuddered. "It's just unbelievable."

"What is?"

"Walt's Range Rover."

"What about it?"

"Walt told me he had taken it in for service. But the police impounded it."

"What! Why?"

She looked at him. "It was damaged. And it had paint on it. Paint they matched to Billy Adams's car. They think Walter ran Billy off the road and killed him because Maggie had told him about what Walt had done to her."

"Jesus. This is truly unbelievable. Walt a child molester *and* murderer."

Judith let out a sob and bent her chest to her thighs.

"Oh, God, I'm so sorry, babe. Let me get you some coffee. Only take a minute."

Rhett left her there and walked quickly into the kitchen. He had been to the Nashes' for dinners and parties, so he knew where everything was. While the coffee was brewing he popped a pill to calm his nerves. He opened the door to the garage and saw Judith's Benz and Maggie's BMW and then the empty bay where Nash's Rover would usually be. He shook his head, closed the door, made the coffees, and returned to the family room. Judith was sitting with her head pitched back against the sofa and her eyes closed.

"Drink some of the coffee, babe, it'll be good for you."

She opened her eyes, thanked him, and took a few sips.

"So, any idea where Walt could have gone?"

"No. I didn't even know that he *had* gone until I got off the phone with the police. I looked through the whole house for him. He had to have left on foot. My car and Maggie's are still here. And the police said they checked Uber and Lyft and the taxi services. He didn't call any of them."

"Can they track his phone?"

"They tried. But no luck."

"On the phone you said you were sitting with him when you watched the video. What did he say?"

"He denied everything, of course. But I think he was about to admit his guilt even before we saw the video."

"What do you mean?" Rhett asked quickly.

Judith explained about what Nash had been saying before she'd gotten the call from her friend about Maggie's posting.

"That's so...weird. He was about to confess but then he denied it all."

Judith shot him a look. "R-right. I didn't think about it like that."

"Well, probably the sudden shock of Maggie exposing him made him defensive."

"Yes, I guess...that makes sense," she said uncertainly.

A moment later there was a knock at the door. It was John Ramos and his partner, Carroll Summers. They both looked depressed and angry.

Judith introduced Rhett, and Ramos eyed him curiously.

"So you're Nash's boss?" Ramos asked him.

"I am, yes."

"Any light you can shed on any of this?" asked Summers.

"None. I'm as stunned as everyone else."

"No signs, no slips of the tongue?" asked Ramos. "No rumors?"

"No, everyone would describe Nash as a consummate professional above suspicion," replied Rhett. "Including me."

"It's often the case," said Summers. He turned to Judith. "So nothing with any of your daughter's girlfriends? Any of them ever feel uncomfortable around him?"

"No, never," said Judith. Her lips trembled. "I feel like a complete idiot."

Rhett swept an arm around her. "It's not your fault, Judith, he fooled everyone." He looked at Ramos. "So he's also suspected in the death of this other person?"

"Billy Adams," answered Ramos. "Maggie mentioned him in her video."

"So you think Nash killed him because she had told him about her father?"

"Seems pretty obvious," said Summers. "And the paint on Nash's Range Rover matched Adams's car."

"I guess that's conclusive," said Rhett.

Ramos said, "He was trying to tell me some cock-and-bull story about fake cops coming into the neighborhood on the night your daughter went missing. He said Adams told him about them. He was trying to convince me that these 'cops' had something to do with it. But I think your daughter might have let it slip that she'd told Adams about the molestation, so he had to get rid of him. He invented this story about the fake cops to cover his tracks."

Rhett, who had been told by Nash about the fake cops, paled and said nothing.

Judith said, "Is there any way to track Maggie now that we know she hasn't been kidnapped?"

"We're working on it. She filmed the video even though she didn't have her phone or laptop. She could have purchased another phone or laptop. Did she have her own credit card?"

"Yes, but it's tied to our account."

"Can you check and see if a purchase like that occurred?" asked Ramos.

Judith left them for a minute. When she came back she said, "No, no charges on any of the cards she has access to."

"That is strange," said Ramos. "I mean, she has to be staying somewhere. And you're sure none of her friends have seen her?"

"Not the ones who live in the neighborhood. But she has several who are at college over the summer, or who live in different places."

"We'll need a list of them with their contact info. She might be with one of them. She could have used their laptop or phone to do the filming and posting."

Judith looked on her phone and provided that information to them.

Ramos said, "As you know, we searched through your husband's things last night. And we did a thorough scrub of your daughter's room."

"What did you find?" said Judith fearfully.

Summers said, "In a bottom drawer in his closet were a pair of pants, a shirt, and a pair of sneakers. We matched fibers from the clothing to fibers found in your daughter's *bed*."

Judith shuddered and let out a low moan.

"We also found hair fibers there that matched ones we took from your husband's hairbrush."

"Damn," exclaimed Rhett.

Ramos said, "And the imprints from the sneakers were matched to a set we found near where Adams died. Nash probably got out to see that he was dead and left the sole impressions in the dirt."

Judith dumbly nodded.

"I'm sorry, Mrs. Nash," said Ramos. "But we'll get him, I promise."

"I just want my daughter back."

The detectives curtly nodded and left.

Rhett said, "Look, I have to run an errand real quick, but I'll bring back dinner. I don't want you to be alone right now."

He hugged her, and she gave him a tender kiss on the cheek. "That would be nice, Rhett, thank you."

"Anything for you, Judith."

"My rock. My *new* rock."

Once outside he sat in his Porsche, took an elongated breath to calm himself, and then called his father.

"I think we have a big fucking problem," he said.

51

AFTER AN ALL-NIGHT DRIVE THAT had crossed state lines, Shock finally pulled to a stop in the late afternoon of the next day.

"Okay, we're finally here."

Nash slipped into the passenger seat from the back, and looked out at the metal security gate that looked like it could withstand the charge of an Abrams tank. "Where are we?"

"At my trainin' center."

Shock hit a button on a remote attached to the sun visor, and the big gate slid back with a whisper of hydraulics. He pulled through the opening, and the gate automatically closed behind them.

Nash looked up at twin two-story buildings connected by a long enclosed passage on the upper floor. "How long have you had this?"

"Nearly thirty years. Been addin' to it as needed."

"Really impressive, Shock."

"Your dad would come up here and help me train the folks in hand-to-hand combat and weaponry. He could still hit the bullseye nine times out of ten well into his sixties. Natural marksman."

"No surprise there."

They climbed out of the van. Shock unlocked the main door, and they went inside.

"But is it secure? I mean, might they be able to find out about this place?" Nash asked.

"All anybody knows is you and your daddy weren't close. And why would anybody think I'd be helpin' your ass out after the church crap? But if shit does happen I got cameras all 'round here and some special surprises for folks just *droppin'* in."

"Okay. But I called you on your phone. They can get the phone logs."

"That phone number ain't in my name. It's untraceable, in fact. In my business, you got to take precautions. It's why I gave you that number in the first place. Never know how things will shake out."

"Right. I'm sure."

"Now, livin' quarters are in this wing. Sort of college dorm setups, but you got your own bath. There's a big kitchen, TV room, pool, ping pong, relaxation stuff, even hot and ice tubs because the work here gets people pretty sore. The other buildin' is all the trainin' facility."

"You have other people here now?" Nash said anxiously.

"Wouldn't have brought you if there were, Walter. And like I said before, I'm windin' things down. I've made enough money to retire comfortably."

"Then you don't need me blowing those plans up, Shock."

"I've made my decision."

"Okay, if you're sure. And I have about ten thousand in cash I brought with me."

Shock cracked a smile. "Good man. Still have places that take the green."

"I can check my emails and texts and phone messages if you've got a phone I can use. I've got all my account info and passwords memorized."

Shock was already shaking his head. "I can get you a burner phone, but the technology they got these days? You access any of your accounts even from a burner they can use that as a toehold to find you."

"What about my contact at the FBI? He gave me a secure app to use. I can download it on the burner. That should be safe."

"Let me think on that. Right now *all* the badges are potential enemies for us, okay?"

"I defer to your expertise, certainly."

He led Nash to his quarters, where Nash dropped off his personal items. He took out the gun and knife and placed them in a secure receptacle that Shock showed him how to access.

"So what's going to happen now?" asked Nash.

"We lie low. We see what the landscape looks like. We gather intel and then base our decisions and actions on that."

"Sounds like your Army training talking."

"It's applicable to a lot of things in *civilian* life, too."

"I suppose they have some APB out on me."

"Hell, Walter, don't sell yourself short, son. You are one of the most wanted fucken dudes in America right now."

"I don't really care what happens to me. I just want to get Maggie back."

Shock wouldn't look him in the eye and it slowly dawned on Nash.

"They…they can't let her go now, because she would tell everyone that what she said was a lie. She's probably already—"

"Look, I can't tell you one way or another for certain, but the probabilities do lie there. I will never sugarcoat things, Walter, I told you that before. It wouldn't be fair to you."

Nash slumped back against the wall. "This is all my fault."

"No, this is Victoria Steers's fault and the dudes you work for. You and Maggie were just collateral damage."

"If they hurt Maggie, or…" He glanced up at Shock. "I will kill them. All of them. Can you…teach me…how to do that?"

"Whoa, now, I think you gettin' way ahead of yourself."

Nash persisted. "Will you, if it comes to it, Shock? Because I've got nobody else to turn to. Nobody."

"Walter, you're a good man with all the best intentions. But you are a normal man who ain't never seen the part of the world you're askin' me to dump you in. It's not a good place, for nobody. Even dudes who got all the skills in the world, mean and cruel as shit, belly fire that never goes out? They get eaten alive there every minute of every day by people like Victoria Steers, just how it is."

Nash just stood there and stared at him. "Please, *Isaiah*."

Shock's large brown eyes gleamed. "Okay, Walter, if it comes to it, I will teach you how."

CHAPTER

52

"THERE HAS TO BE ANOTHER way," said Rhett to his father as they sat in the latter's office at Barton's mansion in the hills. It was well after midnight. Paranoid beyond belief right now, Rhett had left his car parked down the street and scaled the back wall. He didn't want anyone to know he was here, and there were security cameras posted everywhere and men on duty around the clock to watch them. But he knew where the gaps were. Rhett had quietly let himself in through a side door, roused his father from his room, and they were now meeting over Maggie Nash's disappearance.

"She's totally innocent of anything. Not even twenty years old, smart and beautiful with her whole damn life ahead of her. I mean, come on, Dad!"

His father shrugged. "The police think it's Nash. I saw the video. He molested his daughter? This probably has nothing to do with Steers."

"Have you asked her?"

"I'm not in a position to ask her anything."

"You must have been pretty damn desperate to hitch your wagon to her. And then drag me into it."

"If I hadn't you wouldn't have had a pot to piss in, boy. The gravy train had no more gravy in it. And my competitors were just fine with seeing me go right down the crapper. And Maggie looked okay in the video, so what's the problem?"

"Do you really think that video was legit?" said Rhett. "Do you actually think Nash molested his daughter and then killed the guy Maggie said she told about the abuse?"

"Look, maybe Walt was too good to be true. You've had teachers and preachers and people beyond reproach who later turn out to be scum. Maybe he's one of those."

Rhett shook his head. "Judith told me that Maggie and Nash were discussing him financing her influencer business. And yet he was screwing her? I just don't see it."

"So why would Steers have taken his daughter?"

"Walt tried to jump ship."

Barton exclaimed, "I know that, boy, stop wasting my time."

"Only the firm he wanted to jump to turned him down. You said it was because of you. Did you call Zuckerman at Black Cliffs and tell him to back off?"

"No, I told you that. I didn't have to. They know to fear me."

"You think that highly of yourself?"

"What other reason could there have been?"

"When I met with Steers last we discussed a potential change in tactics by the FBI. Instead of going after low- and middle-level fruit, the FBI might be aiming higher."

His father now looked uncertain. "You mean Walt? No, I don't believe it."

"He was at the office after Maggie was taken. I met with him. He told me he would do anything to get Maggie back. Anything."

"So?"

"I think he was being literal, Dad. I think he was telling me that he knew the people I'm working with took her and he would stop working with the FBI if Maggie got returned."

Barton scoffed, "You're extrapolating what is just a cockamamie theory to absurdity, boy."

"You weren't there. And why else would he come into the office right after his daughter was taken and say that to me?"

"You really think Steers took Maggie? And had her record that video?"

"Yeah, I do."

"But Nash ran for it."

"What would you have done?"

"So what do you want me to do about it?"

"It's Maggie," snapped Rhett.

"I *know* it's Maggie—who I've known since she was a toddler, by the way."

"So we just let her die?"

"There's still no proof Steers took her. And without that…" Barton's voice trailed off and he looked out the window.

"And if I bring you proof will you do anything?"

"Look, I feel badly for the gal, I really do, but I'm not getting killed over her. Are you?" Barton's features hardened. "Hell, I can't believe even you're that stupid, *boy.*"

Rhett flung himself over the desk with such force that he knocked his father out of the chair. His hands were around the man's throat and squeezing hard. His father was old and obese but still had some strength. He cranked his arm back and slammed his fist multiple times into Rhett's gut and ribs. Rhett retaliated by punching his father in the face and knocking him out.

Wincing, he touched his bruised ribs.

"Rhett!"

He turned to see Mindy standing in the open doorway. "What the hell is going on?" She stepped forward and saw her husband lying on the floor. "Oh my God. What did you do?"

"We had an argument. He attacked me and I defended myself."

"He's an old man."

"He outweighs me by over a hundred pounds, and though you can't see it he got his licks in on me."

She knelt down and checked Barton's pulse. "We need to call an ambulance."

Rhett sat back on his haunches. "Who's in the house?"

"Colin is in his quarters. Angie's asleep. The security team's in their cottage and the house staff are in theirs. Now call a damn ambulance."

Rhett made no move to do so.

"Okay, fine, you asshole, I will." She started to rise but he grabbed her arm.

"Rhett! Let me go."

"He will destroy me."

"Well, you should have thought about that before you did what you did."

"He's a tough guy. He'll probably come around without going to the hospital."

"No, he won't!" she said so emphatically that he stared at her curiously.

"How do you know that?" he asked.

"Because Barton is…ill."

"How ill?"

"He…he has pancreatic cancer. He'd been in a lot of pain. Tons of tests and misdiagnoses. It was found a few months ago. Advanced stage four. They gave him eight months at most."

"Shit. Why didn't anyone tell me?" asked Rhett.

"He just told me two days ago and then ordered me to keep it secret."

"So that's why he was talking to me a while ago about how things would be after he died."

"I didn't know about that, but I guess it makes sense," she said.

Rhett eyed the set of French doors that opened out to a balcony. "Mindy, you're always complaining about your shitty prenup, right?"

She stared at him in confusion. "What in the hell does that—"

"Right?"

"Yes. Frankly, I was hoping that a child might change things. But you knew that. And we talked about if I *didn't* have a kid with him and set up a competing heir, that you might help me on the prenup."

"FYI, you were never going to have a kid with him."

"Well, not now, not with the cancer and everything. The medications he's on mean that—"

He interjected, "No, I mean he got snipped, years ago."

"What!"

"He had a vasectomy. He's got no bullets in the gun."

"That...that can't be possible."

"I can get you the medical records. We talked about it. He told me he was going to blame it on you that you couldn't conceive. He didn't want any more heirs, you see."

She stared down at her unconscious husband. "You son of a bitch."

"Oh, and when you were at Cannes he was screwing a hooker right here."

Mindy blanched. "A hooker?"

"A nineteen-year-old named Laurel Burke. Set Dad back two grand for about ten minutes' pleasure."

"How do you know that?"

"I drove her home. She had no idea who I was and she laid it all out for me. And it was unprotected sex, just so you know," he lied. He knew his father and Burke hadn't had intercourse. She had simply *serviced* him. But he needed to change Mindy's perspective on her husband, and the more disgusting Rhett could make him out to be, the faster that perspective would transform. And Rhett didn't have much time to pull all this together.

Mindy once more looked down at her unconscious husband. "I...I could have caught some disease!"

"So he really didn't give a shit about you. But if you help me, I'll help you."

"How?"

He eyed the French doors again. "That balcony is right over the rear patio. Four stories up."

"W-what exactly are you getting at?" she said tremulously, her eyes bulging.

"In business parlance this is known as seizing an opportunity. Old man's terminal, didn't want to suffer through the agony. Clean up a bit in here. Get him out there. He'll never feel a thing. All good."

Mindy said, "Oh my God, are you insane?"

"Okay, then call the ambulance. I claim self-defense, my injuries will back me up, he croaks, and you get financially hosed by a guy who lied and cheated on you. Your call, Min."

She sat back on her haunches and processed all this. "How… how would you get him out there?"

"Just help me carry him to the balcony. I'm strong enough to get him over the railing. He goes face-first into the pavers, which will coincide with the injuries I caused. I was never here, and you'll back me up on that when his body is found tomorrow."

"And the prenup?"

"You challenge it on the grounds of him lying about his ability to procreate and I'll be your star witness regarding that *and* his infidelity. I imagine the prenup has enough ambiguous language on moral turpitude for your lawyers to use. And I won't fight it, nor will my sisters."

"So how much do I get?"

"I know roughly the terms of your prenup. Let's say ten times."

"Twenty."

"Fifteen."

She nodded. "Deal. Now, let's get this done. I think I'm going to be sick."

A half hour later, a bloody Barton Temple lay dead face down on the stone pavers, and Rhett was whizzing down the road in his Porsche. His adrenaline was running even faster than the car. No need for lines of coke. A simple murder apparently did just fine as a potent narcotic.

Part of him felt liberated. Part of him felt like he was a dead man walking.

He had no idea which feeling, if any, would turn out to be right.

But he needed to take an additional, obvious step. He stopped by the red door marked number twelve and knocked. A sleepy Laurel Burke opened the door dressed only in a T-shirt.

"Do you remember me, Laurel?" he said.

Burke smiled. "I recognize your voice." She looked him up and down. "And the rest of you ain't half bad. What do you want?"

He slipped his arms around her waist and pulled her close. "I think you know."

"Same rate?"

"Double."

He closed the door and Burke led him into her bedroom.

CHAPTER

53

NASH SAT IN HIS ROOM and studied the video of his daughter saying that he had molested her. Shock had provided him with a burner phone along with a laptop.

He was looking for telltale signs in her voice, facial tics, anything that could help him understand the situation better. When nothing readily popped out he closed the laptop and slumped back against the wall of the small room. As he looked around the Spartan surroundings, his thoughts ventured back to his beautiful home and how not all that long ago his life had been pretty wonderful. And predictable. Yes there were problems, but everyone had problems. At least he had the financial ability to weather things better than a lot of families who were living paycheck to paycheck. But in the end, the money couldn't really get you what you wanted.

It can't get me out of this.

There was a knock on the door, and Shock opened it a moment later. "This is your guy, right?"

"Who?"

Shock perched next to him on Nash's bunk. He passed Nash his phone, where there was a news article loaded. Nash quickly read through it. "Barton Temple was found dead at his estate, in what looks to be a suicide? He jumped off a balcony and fell four stories to the ground?"

"They quoted his wife. Said Temple was terminal with pancreatic cancer. His son confirmed that and so did the man's doctor. He had months to live and it wasn't going to be pretty. Might make sense."

Nash shook his head. "Maybe for someone who doesn't know

the man. Barton Temple lived life to the fullest. He would have partied right up until the casket closed."

"So you think Steers?"

"She seems to be the likeliest suspect."

"Maybe she and Barton had a falling-out."

"If so, that confirms that he was working with her, and that also now leaves Rhett as the primary contact with her."

"You mentioned a secure messagin' app the Bureau gave you? Think you can still access it?"

"Yes, but you told me not to download it onto the burner."

"Let's take a ride."

"Where?"

"Cell towers ping burner phone calls, too, which is why I didn't want you usin' it at the trainin' center. Now, just accessin' emails or text messages makes it a lot harder to track your location if the cops are just lookin' at that sort of data. Then you're just talkin' IP addresses. Cops do that to see who sent or received somethin', not where they physically are. But someone who knows what they're doin' can still use message data to drill down to what city you're in, etc. So I'm gonna let you access that communications app, but let's not make it any easier for them."

Hours later, when they were hundreds of miles from the training center, Shock called to Nash in the back of the van. "Okay, we're far enough away. Download the app and see if you have any messages."

Nash did so and then his finger trembled a bit as it hovered over the key. He hit it and a list of messages came up.

He read through the first ones quickly.

"What does the Bureau say?" asked Shock.

"Agent Morris says they think the video might be fake," Nash said excitedly.

"Why?"

"They had their experts look at it and found it very well done, but there were just enough anomalies that they concluded it might be AI generated. But they can't prove it," he added in a less hopeful tone.

"Wait, so maybe it wasn't actually your daughter at all?"

Nash kept reading and then looked miserable. "They said that they may have taken Maggie to scan her body and record her voice, and then used that to create an AI version of her for the video so they could control exactly what she said and how she said it. But he was clear that they can't prove it. Which means he and the FBI don't one hundred percent believe I didn't do it."

Shock glanced in the mirror at Nash. "Okay," he said slowly.

Nash said, "If he's right, that means they don't need Maggie anymore."

"Anythin' else from the Bureau?" asked Shock, looking away from Nash.

"They have a leak. That's how they believe Steers might have been made aware of my involvement with the Bureau, and why she would have taken Maggie to discredit me."

"Do they have any idea where the leak is?"

"Yes. An Agent Amy Braxton, who I met with. She's not the leak, at least not directly. Her husband, Frank, had a gambling problem. Frank got into bed with a loan shark. Steers maybe became aware of this vulnerability, bought out the loan, and exploited the connection. Braxton apparently left some documents lying around at home that she shouldn't have. Frank saw them and ratted me out to repay the loan."

"How do they know all this?"

"Frank confessed. He never met Steers, of course, and doesn't have a shred of proof. He's now in custody, but that really doesn't help me."

"At least the Bureau doesn't necessarily believe you're guilty."

"But Morris was clear that in the current climate they can do nothing to help me without jeopardizing their entire operation."

"So you're basically SOL?"

"Not that surprising, really." Nash paused and said, "She's dead, isn't she?"

Shock took a few moments to answer. "We can't be sure of that. Yet."

"I thought you said you'd never sugarcoat things."

"Unless we see her remains for ourselves, she's still alive. Are the percentages good that she is? No, they're terrible. Are they more than one percent? Yeah. But not by much."

Nash exited out of the app and leaned against the side wall of the van. "Why would they kill Barton Temple?"

"He pissed off Steers, like we discussed."

"I could see Rhett pissing her off, but not Barton. He was too smart."

"Who else had a reason to kill him then?"

"Well, Rhett, and Barton's widow, for starters. They'll inherit a lot of wealth."

Shock nodded. "One of the oldest of motives to kill someone: greed."

"Oh, and did I mention that Rhett was screwing my wife?"

Shock swerved the van before regaining control. "No, you left that one the fuck out, man."

"Maggie found out about it right before she disappeared."

"Right before? You don't think—?"

"No. Judith would never be party to that. And, honestly, neither would Rhett. And when Judith saw that video I was with her. She was as shocked as I was."

"But maybe Barton jumped off that balcony with some help?"

"Maybe he did."

"So what do we do with that information?"

"I think it's time that you teach me what I need to know and then let me go and take care of this, like we talked about before."

Shock eyed him again, this time with the scrutiny of a man appraising human potential. "It won't be easy. In fact it'll be the toughest thing you'll ever do in your life. You will beg me to quit. But I won't let you. I may end up killin' you, in fact. You ready for that?"

"I've got nothing else to do with my life," replied Nash. "Nothing."

"We have to change your appearance, I mean, really change it."

"How?"

"Well, musclin' you up will go part of the way. You got the right frame to pack it on, you just never did shit with it. But I see your daddy's genes in you, so there's that. And the hair's got to go. Grow a beard maybe. And somethin' else that will help."

"What?"

"You'll see. And also *feel* it."

Shock paused and seemed to be deliberating something, something important, for both of them. "Look, Walter, this shit ain't gonna be quick, okay? I'm talkin' many, many months, probably over a year even."

"A year! Shock, if Maggie is alive I can't waste a year—"

"The odds of Maggie being alive are pretty much nil, okay? You're right, I was sugarcoatin' things before. Now, we need to get real. Real, real. We can't do this half-ass. The whole fucken country is lookin' for you. And I'm harborin' you, so that means you go down, I go down."

"It was a mistake calling you to help. Just drive me—"

"Shut the fuck up, Walter, and listen 'cause I'm only gonna say this one time."

Nash sat back and looked at him apprehensively.

Shock said, "This is a risk, a big risk for us *both*. You don't want to go down and I sure as hell don't want to spend what years I got left in prison. But it is what it is. Now, you either take the time and make the commitment to do this right, or you might as well just go turn yourself in to the cops right now, 'cause you shortchange this, they gonna catch your ass no problem. Slow and methodical, put the hard work in, wins the day. Bet you conducted your business the same way, right?"

"I did," conceded Nash.

"So whatever time it takes that's what it takes. And at the end of the day you won't look, act, or *be* Walter Nash no more. Ain't no other way to slice this sucker." He paused again. "You really ready for all that? 'Cause I'm all in. I'm all in 'cause I promised your daddy. Now when I made that promise to him I didn't know it would turn into this shitshow, that is for fuck sure. But a promise to that man is a promise that I cannot break. Just so's you understand. I'm with you all the way. Now, how 'bout you? 'Cause half-ass don't cut it. Not now, Walter. We partners on this or we ain't. Your choice."

Nash didn't answer right away. Going through his mind at hyper speed were all the pros and cons of his situation. The latter easily overwhelmed the former. But then his mind stopped racing and settled onto one image. Maggie, online saying those things, none of them true. Maggie, being taken. Maggie, being coerced.

Maggie, being almost surely dead.

"I'm ready," said Nash.

Shock scrutinized him for a long, uncomfortable moment. "I believe you."

Nash said, "I believe me, too."

54

M<small>Y GOD, RHETT, YOUR FATHER,</small>" said Judith as they sat in the dining room together at her home.

"It *was* a shock. I'd only just found out he was ill," he added. He'd brought them dinner and they'd just finished eating. She poured them each out another glass of cab.

"What will happen now?"

"You mean to the business? I don't know. I presume I'll take over, but it will have to wait until the lawyers disclose the contents of the will."

"You said one of the staff discovered the body?"

"Yes. Dad...he'd been dead for a while."

"How awful."

He gripped her hand. "But I didn't come over here to talk about that. You have your own worries. Do the police know anything more?"

"No, they've been by several times, but they still have no idea where Maggie might be. But at least she's alive. And there's been no sign of Walter."

"Amazing that he made such a clean getaway. Almost like he had help."

"When he ran out of here I think he had a bag with him. It was like he had prepared for something like this. Just like an Eagle Scout," she added derisively.

"Any idea where he would go?"

"None. I mean, all of this is really unthinkable."

They both turned their heads when someone rang the doorbell.

Judith opened the door to reveal Detective Ramos standing there.

"Have you found out anything?" she asked.

He shook his head. "Is Mr. Temple here?"

"Rhett? Yes. He brought dinner. Please come in."

She showed Ramos into the dining room, where he sat down opposite Rhett.

"Would you mind if I had a few minutes alone with Mr. Temple? I'm also handling the matter of his father's death."

"Of course not. I'll just take things through to the kitchen."

After she left Rhett said, "What is it, Detective?"

"We've just gotten the preliminary pathology report back. The bottom line is there are some issues with your father's death."

"I'm afraid I don't understand."

"The medical examiner would not rule it a suicide."

"Excuse me?" said Rhett. "Why not?"

"I'm not at liberty to say. But for right now we're treating it as a homicide."

Rhett pretended incredulity. "Someone *killed* my father? But why?"

"I don't know, sir. That's why we're investigating."

"How did you even know I was here?"

"Your office, they told us you were coming here," answered Ramos.

"What do you need from me?"

"Well, for starters, and this is just routine, where were you when your father died?"

"What time are we talking about?" asked the quick-thinking Rhett.

"Between midnight and two the night before he was found."

Rhett said, "Well, the fact is I was with a woman, downtown. I was there all night."

"Do you have her contact information?"

"I do, yes. Her name is Laurel Burke." He provided the information to the detective.

"Thank you, Mr. Temple. This is just routine stuff, I hope you can understand. We checked the video footage at your father's estate. No cars came in during that time, so someone must have gained access another way. Unfortunately, the road is isolated and there are no cameras."

"If my father was killed I want to know who did it, Detective. That's all that matters."

"Understood." He looked around. "And how is Mrs. Nash doing?"

"Daughter missing, husband on the run? I'm surprised she can function at all." Rhett shook his head and then an idea came to him. He thought it through for a few beats and said, "I have to tell you, I would have trusted Walter Nash with my life. I never saw any of this coming. Now Walter's disappeared and you think someone might have killed my father? It seems weird, you know? So close together."

Ramos stiffened and said, "Would Nash have any reason to wish your father harm?"

"Walter? My father? No, I...I can't believe that." But Rhett made certain not to sound too sure of that.

"Well, you couldn't believe he would do what he did to his daughter and the security guard, correct?"

Rhett slowly nodded as he thought through the next phase of his plan with the detective. "But there is something, I don't know if it's connected, but it was odd."

"What was odd?" asked a clearly interested Ramos.

Rhett leaned forward, and, though they were alone, spoke in a low voice. "My father approached me a while back and told me to give Nash a raise and more bonus money."

"He *was* an employee. Wasn't that the sort of thing your father would do?"

"No, not at all. I run Sybaritic, not my father, and compensation decisions go through me. Now, Nash was already being richly rewarded. A little too much, if you want my honest opinion. And my father was acting a little funny when he asked me. Like he didn't really want to do it. But I did what he asked because he was *my* boss, not because Nash deserved the extra money. I can get you the paperwork. It's all there."

"I'd appreciate that, thank you. Any idea as to why your father did that?"

"I do know that Nash had spoken with one of our rivals about joining them. Now, Nash has a lot of institutional knowledge about how we operate. It would not be good if he jumped ship."

"Did your father know about that?"

"He was the one who told me."

"So the extra comp could have just been to keep Nash at your company?"

Rhett shook his head. "To tell the truth, there was just something fishy about the whole thing, Detective. My father had never done that before. Nash was a good man, but he was no superstar. I don't know why my father would have treated him special. Unless…"

"Unless what?"

Rhett looked embarrassed. "My father has had an eventful life. Three marriages, some scandals, some shady business partners. If someone had gotten ahold of something… well, really bad, and held it over him?"

Ramos tensed. "You think Walter Nash was blackmailing him?"

"I can't say for certain, of course. But since my father just found out he was dying? Maybe he told Nash to screw off. Or maybe my dad told Nash that he was going to expose him as a blackmailer."

"That definitely could be a motive for murder," noted Ramos. "Could he have gotten into your father's home?"

"He's been there many times over the years. For all I know my father gave him the gate code and a key to the house. He'd been an employee for nearly two decades. And he could have left his car down the road and maybe gotten in over the back wall, since you found the video footage on the gate was clear."

"I see."

"I'm just speculating. I have no proof, you understand," added

Rhett quickly, even as he evaluated the impact his words had had on the detective.

"Thank you nonetheless, sir. I will follow up."

After Ramos left, Judith rejoined him.

"What was that all about?" she asked anxiously.

"Nothing important," replied Rhett.

He left her and immediately phoned Laurel Burke to finalize his ironclad alibi.

Please God, don't let there be any cameras around Burke's place showing me arriving after my father was dead.

55

Nash's door slammed open at five a.m.

He jerked up, still groggy with sleep. "What the hell?"

Shock stood in the open doorway.

"Get up! It's way past time you got your ass in gear."

Shock lurched into the room, grabbed Nash by the arm, hauled him off the cot, and dumped him on the floor. A moment later a set of workout clothes and shoes hit Nash in the face.

"Meet me in the training facility, first floor, in five minutes. Piss or poop and do what you got to do but be there!"

Shock marched out.

Nash sat there stunned for a few moments but then he got to his feet, stripped off his T-shirt and underwear, tugged on the clothes and shoes, emptied his bladder in the bathroom, and hustled to the other building.

The training facility's first floor was dominated by a vast weight room, what looked like a cardio fitness complex from hell, and a large boxing ring.

Shock looked up as Nash raced in. "Hope you did your business before you got here 'cause we ain't stoppin'."

"I did, but keep in mind I'm forty, not twenty-one, and if I have a heart attack I'm not going to be good for anyone or anything."

"Most dudes I train are older'n you, so no damn excuses. Okay, let's get to it."

Shock led him to an old-fashioned scale, where his height and weight were measured.

"Six three and one-half inch, one hundred and sixty-five pounds.

Okay, *string bean*, we got our work cut out on that. You're gettin' a gram of protein a day for each pound, a wedge of complex carbs, a ton of fiber, and just the right mix of fats. And water, plus electrolytes."

"With what endgame?"

"I got to strengthen you up, and you need muscle to do that, and muscle burns more than fat, so you need extra fuel. Forty-five hundred calories a day for you should do the trick."

"I'm never *that* hungry."

"You will be after I work your ass out. Six meals a day. But I'll wean you on to that. Gut and intestines are delicate things. You can kill a starvin' man by feedin' him too much of the wrong food and doin' it too fast. You'll work your way up to all those meals and calories."

"Who's prepping all that food?"

"I got a commercial freezer full of premade meals, all measured out to the last healthy gram. Most people can gain anywhere from a half pound to two pounds of muscle a month. We gonna do better than that with you. You need targeted trainin', and the right nutrition, includin' surplus calories. And as you gain muscle mass, you also add fat, water, and carbo storage, so you can put on muscle pounds, but your overall weight gain will be far higher'n that. And I got a few tricks of the trade to accelerate the process."

"I'm not taking steroids like the Hollywood actors do to muscle up."

"Not to worry, Walter baby. I'm a natural herb sort of dude."

"This just seems impossible."

Shock's expression turned serious. "We take it step by step. You get ahead of yourself, you'll freeze up like a deer in the headlights. And I don't want you to bulk up. We want lean, strong muscle, and you got the perfect frame to build it. I'm not sayin' it won't be hard, because it will be, trust me."

"Any alcohol allowed? I think I'll need it."

"I'm not a monster. A glass here and there. Okay, I'm done gabbin'."

Surprisingly, Shock had him stretch for half an hour and then tested Nash's range of motion, flexibility, and grip strength.

"You got a pliable body, man," Shock said.

"That's good?"

"It sure as hell ain't bad. 'Cause I intend to *pliable* the shit out of it."

The next hour was weight training. Nash had never pumped iron, and he could feel what little muscle he had straining as the sets and time wore on.

Cardio came next, and he was dreading it until he got on the treadmill and ran for thirty minutes without too much problem, though he was left breathless and felt his heart rate popping uncomfortably high.

"That wasn't so bad," gasped Nash.

"No fat on you, and long limbs mean you got a lot of torque and leverage and can eat up the ground," said Shock knowingly. "That helps, but this is just the tip 'a the iceberg."

After a meal of several eggs, raw nuts, tomatoes, an avocado, wheat toast, fruit, and several glasses of water, one of which was mixed with protein powder, Nash was led over by Shock to a boxing dummy with the shoulders and torso of a Hercules mounted on a black stem with a weighted base.

Nash noted the X's on the dummy's torso fashioned from yellow and black tape strips.

"What are those for?" he asked.

"Yellow are incapacitation points. Black are where you strike most effectively to kill."

Shock stepped up to the boxing dummy and proceeded to use his forearm, elbow, fist, knee, and crown of his head to efficiently hit all the yellow spots.

"With any one of those strikes, dude goes down," he said. "In hand-to-hand I'll show you how to get the advantage on your opponent's arms, neck, and legs and take 'em out. And I have another dummy here with limbs. They have the same taped X's on 'em. Branchial and femoral artery and the like. Cut 'em, dude is dead."

Nash's anxiety spiked as Shock picked up a serrated knife.

"Is that your Army Ka-bar knife?" he asked.

"Served me well for a long time."

He then proceeded to hit each black X with the knife blade.

He pointed to the dummy's gut. "Now on this strike you go into the belly right here, pull the knife hilt straight up, and when you get two inches below the sternum you twist the blade sideways and then cut from left to right to make sure you pop the aorta." Shock made the motions with his knife. "Dude'll bleed out in about thirty seconds. Okay, your turn. Take your time. Speed will come later. What I want right now is accuracy and appropriate weapon positionin'."

He demonstrated to Nash how to hold the blade, correcting him numerous times until Nash, who had always had an eye for detail, readily picked up the grips and stabbing and slicing motions. Shock nodded approvingly as the session wore on.

"Okay, let's do some push-ups, pull-ups, core work, and then you hit the stairs for some more blood pumpin'."

"Remember the heart attack warning I gave you," said Nash.

"Like I said, Walter, I might end up killin' you. But better me than some scum you run up against out there."

Nash struggled mightily through the rest of the workout and at the end he lay on the floor drenched in sweat and fighting to regain his breath.

"You ain't in as bad 'a shape as I thought you'd be. You been workin' out and not tellin' nobody?"

Nash sat up and said, "If sitting in a chair was an Olympic event I might medal."

"Let's hit the gun range."

"I can't even feel my arms."

"Best time to do it. 'Cause when it comes down to it, out there, you probably ain't gonna be in good shape, but you still got to hit your target. Otherwise, you dead."

The gun range was in a long, narrow room with mechanized targets running on long cables at one end. Behind the targets were stacks of large hay bales as backstop and sloped cinderblock walls behind them designed to drive any stray round to the floor and prevent back splatter.

Arrayed across a long table was a line of weapons: revolvers, semi- and autopistols, and assault rifles.

"When was the last time you fired a gun?"

"When I was fourteen and went to the range with my father."

"I take it that was pre-*tennis*?"

Nash didn't bother to answer.

Shock picked up a Smith & Wesson .45 revolver, gauging the weight and balance. He then put on ear protection and a pair of safety glasses, took aim, and fired the full six-shot load. When he hit the button to bring the target to him on the cable, Nash saw that four shots had hit the bullseye, one was right outside it, and another had struck the third concentric ring.

"That third ring strike was actually my first shot. I was calibratin'. After that, bullseye or second ring is acceptable."

He reloaded the .45 and handed it to Nash. "You right-handed, like your daddy?"

"Yes."

"The target has grids that will tell you what you're doin' wrong dependin' where on the target you hit. Breakin' wrist up, jerkin', heelin', anticipatin' recoil, etc. It's instructive. But clear your head, step up, and do what your daddy taught you to do all those years ago. You'll be rusty but that's okay. Just don't shoot yourself. Or me!"

Nash stepped to the line and donned the ear protection and safety goggles. "Do I have to calibrate, or can I aim for the bullseye on the first shot?"

"You do you, Walter, and then we'll see what's what."

Nash assumed the firing stance his father had drilled into him as a young teen, weight equally distributed to each leg and hip, knees and elbows slightly bent to eat the recoil, a two-handed grip, shoulders square. He eased out a breath, steadied his arms and hands, took careful aim, and banged off six measured shots.

As Shock drew the target to them, Nash opened the .45's cylinder gate and dumped the spent, heated shells into a trash receptacle.

When he saw the targets he would have smiled under any other circumstance save the one he was in.

Five shots dead in the center and one on the line between the bullseye and the closest ring to it.

"Your daddy taught you well."

"What's next?" asked Nash.

"Shit, you think one round of shootin' with one gun is enough?"

The next two hours were spent firing every weapon on the table multiple times. Nash's accuracy deteriorated with every session as the fired rounds added up.

"Damn it," he exclaimed when he didn't bag one bullseye at the end.

"You got high expectations for yourself. I respect that. But don't be stupid, either. This is day one of I don't know how many."

"So we're done for today?"

"Hell, no. You're gonna take apart each of those weapons and put 'em back together again. You gonna get to the point where you'll be able to do it blindfolded in a tenth of the time it'll take you today. And then you got more meals to eat and we got the mental side of this shit to start. And let me tell you, that be a whole lot harder than what you just done."

"I don't see how that's possible," said an exhausted Nash.

"Oh, you will, baby, you will. And today I went easy on you. From now on, it gets fucken serious."

56

LATER THAT WEEK NASH AND Shock sat at a small conference table in a windowless room. The place smelled of sweat and other body fug and maybe desperate feelings, if such things had an odor. The walls were bare, the floor concrete. It was cold in here and Nash, after another long day of physical labor, his sweaty clothes clinging to him, shivered. He would have showered and changed, but Shock said they didn't have time to waste.

Binders were piled on top of each other and Nash was doing his best to concentrate despite being exhausted. And he could feel the soreness creeping into every muscle he had. He examined some of the binder spines. "Surveillance, communications, intel drops, internal security precautions, field tradecraft, detecting danger, room lockdown. I suppose you're going to test me on all this?"

"You bet your ass I am," said Shock.

Nash looked at another binder. "Making low-grade explosives from everyday items?" He gazed at Shock in confusion.

"You never know when a little boom will save your ass. But we need to discuss somethin' else first." Shock eased forward and said, "Besides your daddy, do you know who was the most lethal dude I ever met in my life?"

Nash shook his head.

"Little guy name 'a Peanut. 'Bout five three, one twenty. Hell, girls were stronger'n him."

"Then what made him so dangerous?" said Nash.

"He wouldn't waste a second of his time thinkin' 'bout whether to end your life. Man just do it and then he *walk* away like nothin' happened, 'cause for him nothin' of importance *did* happen. No real way to defend 'gainst that."

Nash sat up straighter. "And your point?"

Shock tapped his head. "Your body ain't never gonna go where your mind ain't been, Walter. Street soldiers like Peanut? Their whole lives are wrapped up in two things: dodgin' death and causin' it. Not only do you get real good at both, there ain't no place on this earth your mind ain't been. So that way your body won't hesitate when the brain say, 'Do it, just fucken do it.'" He looked at Nash. "You ain't never killed nothin', right?"

"A cricket with my BB gun when I was nine."

"How'd that make you feel?"

"I cried," Nash replied candidly.

"Right, you cried. Your mind did somethin' your conscience don't agree with and then your body carried out the mission, and you cried. Peanut ain't never cried, guaranteed, Walter, and that man ain't killin' no crickets."

"So you're saying I need to think like a killer?"

"No, I'm sayin' you need to be able to kill without hesitation. Sounds straightforward but it ain't. It's hard as shit less you like a serial killer. See, the two seconds arguin' in your head 'bout whether to do it or not, one of Steers's muthers will cut you in half. Now, I can tell you that you need to do it, and I can demonstrate how to do it, and why it's important, but I can't really make you pull the trigger when you need to pull the trigger 'cause I ain't gonna be there. That between you and whoever you got in front 'a you." He touched his temple again. "The answer to all that shit's up here. Sounds weird, but thing is you got to make peace with yourself so you can inflict violence on others."

"How did my father do it?"

Shock's mouth eased to a grin. "I was hopin' you'd get there." He leaned back in his chair, interlaced his fingers, and cracked them. "Ty tell me one time over in Nam, 'Shock, in this war we got us and we got them. Now, I don't know them. I ain't got no particular beef 'gainst these folks. We in their country and we fightin' 'em and maybe we shouldn't be here fightin' 'em, but here we are doin' just that. So this is how it needs to play out. Every time one of them tries to kill me, every time I get one of 'em in my scope, every time I see one of 'em try to take out one of my boys, here's what goes through my mind: They ain't people no more to me, Shock. They are obstacles. They are like the shit the Army makes us slough through in boot camp while the man is breakin' us down, erasin' everythin' we brought to the Army and then the man rebuilds us into the machines he needs to do his war business. Walls, trenches, ropes, water: *obstacles*. And it's all 'bout goin' from here to there. But in our case *there* is livin' and the journey through is 'bout dyin', for the other guy. So an obstacle to me or my boys livin' or dyin' is somethin' I can take on without one shred of personal dilemma.'"

Shock paused and studied Nash, ostensibly to see if he was getting the point being made here.

"*Personal dilemma*, that is the term your daddy said to me while we're in this fucken jungle gettin' et up by mosquitoes and dodgin' snakes and poison frogs and then the dudes with the guns, machetes, and grenades and their own version of no *personal dilemmas*, while they seein' us as only obstacles, too. What Ty meant was he takes his gun, or his knife, or his bare hands, and he removes not a livin', breathin' person, but an *obstacle*. And then the next obstacle and then the next one, till they ain't no more in front of him."

Nash let out the breath he was holding. "Can I learn to do that, really? I'm not a professional soldier. I'm not Peanut growing up having to dodge death every minute of his life. There is no way to really simulate that. You have to have lived it."

"You the only one who can answer that, Walter. I can make you strong. I can teach you to whip ass. I can train you to shoot even better than you can now. I can build you up to haul butt all day and night without collapsin'. But obstacles and personal dilemmas?" He touched his head again. "That shit lives up here, son. That's a *wall* in your mind you got to obliterate. You gotta knock that right out your conscious self. Ain't no other way. That why I tell you this is way harder'n liftin' weights, runnin' your tail off, and shootin' till you can't lift your arms above your damn waist."

"Does the wall have a name, Shock? That might help me."

Shock sat forward even more, placed his elbows firmly on the table, and leaned into the other man.

"Sure it do, Walter. It's called your *humanity*."

CHAPTER

57

Laurel Burke provided Rhett an alibi from ten o'clock at night to six in the morning, which was well within the forensic window of when his father pitched over the balcony to the stone pavers below. And it only cost him another ten grand. And he had confirmed there were no cameras between his father's estate and Burke's home that could definitively prove otherwise.

Thank God I didn't drive through the gate, so no one other than Mindy saw me.

"And maybe you can come by and take me out to some nice places," Burke had told him.

"Maybe I can, yeah," he'd told her with no intention of ever doing so.

Barton's funeral had been attended by VIPs from all over the world, and Rhett had accepted condolences from people he barely knew. The accolades bestowed upon his dead father by a litany of innocent-eyed celebrities, politicians paid off by Barton for decades to do his bidding, and fellow business titans who would have slit the dead man's throat if they thought they could get away with it nearly made Rhett retch. But now, with the grieving period over, he was headed to the lawyer's office to see what his father's will said and what his piece of the empire would be.

If you screwed me over, old man, I will dig you up and feed you to the coyotes.

Mindy would be there too. Angie, of course, would not be, and DeeDee was still in Paris and only cared about her outrageous bills being paid. Rhett's sister, Beth, was also not in the country currently.

She had told her brother to let her know the terms. Though she had felt no need to hurry back in the wake of her father's death, she apparently was sure she would be taken care of.

You have more faith than I do, sis.

The law firm of Hobart, Selkirk and Robins, LLC was in a downtown office building not that far from Sybaritic Investments. As Rhett walked in, he saw the fruits of client billings on the walls in the form of expensive artwork, and the luxurious finishes throughout the space. He also knew there was a fitness center and on-site massage therapist. He'd also seen the expensive cars in the part of the garage reserved for the law firm.

Harvey Robins was his father's lawyer, a bloated, pompous man of sixty-five, who drew most of his professional self-esteem as well as his wealth from having repped the late billionaire for nearly three decades.

Rhett and Mindy met in the anteroom of Robins's office and were led to a private conference room adjacent to the lawyer's corner office suite. Robins also brought along a lovely young woman and introduced her as Lindsey Cole. He proudly told them she was a second-year attorney who'd graduated from Stanford.

"Only the best and the brightest here," he added.

They all sat at the table, and Robins conveyed to them in succinct sentences the last earthly wishes of Barton Temple and his billions.

At the end of it Rhett looked at Mindy and Mindy looked at Rhett. She was dressed as conservatively as she probably ever did, meaning her butt was fully covered, her cleavage was not visible, she wore nylons, and her heels were a mere three inches high and not open-toed.

Rhett said, "So Mindy gets a quarter of the estate outright despite her prenup, my sister gets fifteen percent, DeeDee gets fifteen percent, and Angie gets forty-five percent to be held in trust?"

"That is correct," said Robins.

"And when Angie dies?"

"The residual goes to the Barton S. Temple Foundation to fund good works around the world."

"Like what sort of good works?" asked Rhett.

"That will be up to the committee."

"What committee?"

"The one appointed by your father's executor," answered Robins.

"Who is?"

"Me, actually."

"And I get what exactly?" said Rhett.

Robins appeared to struggle to hold back his sneer. "Well, I'm no math whiz, but after those distributions your share would naturally be *zero*."

"And his homes?"

"The main one goes to Mrs. Temple. The other homes are to be held in trust for the benefit of his daughters."

"So no roof for me?" said Rhett.

Robins's sneer deepened. "You have your penthouse, Mr. Temple. Our records show it is valued at fourteen million dollars. So you have a very nice *roof* indeed."

Rhett's fingers curled to fists and he cleared his throat. "And my position at Sybaritic?"

"In the will Walter Nash was designated to take over as CEO of Sybaritic, but that, of course, will not be possible now. As a backup your father named Elaine Fixx. His other companies will continue on with current management in place."

"But Elaine Fixx is a junior exec with no experience at the CEO level."

"Nevertheless, those were your father's wishes," said Robins, as though that would explain all.

Rhett looked at Mindy. "He was clearly screwing her, too."

"Excuse me?" said Robins with an indignant harrumph added on.

Rhett looked at him. "I said he was *screwing* Elaine, too, Harv. She was apparently good in bed, so why not give her my job?"

"I have no knowledge of—"

"Yeah, just stop right there because you said all that needs to be said in the way of your knowledge or lack thereof," snapped Rhett.

He eyed Lindsey Cole, who looked enough like Margot Robbie to arouse Rhett's baser instincts. She had managed a tiny smile at his retort to her boss.

Mindy said, "Well, if he was sleeping with her, she's been handsomely paid for it." She was obviously over the moon at her good fortune, since her side deal with Rhett was no longer needed.

"Any other questions?" asked Robins, who looked highly offended by Rhett's comments and none too happy with Mindy's words, either.

"Not unless you can find a few billion for me," replied Rhett. He rose. "So when am I getting kicked out of my office?"

"Close of business today. The will is clear on that."

"I'll be sure to give Elaine the old Temple rah-rah speech and wish her luck." Under his breath he said, "All bad." He eyed the young lawyer. "You have a card, Ms. Cole?"

She hesitated, glanced at Robins, but then handed him one.

"I'll be in touch," he said. He turned to Robins. "I guess I'll have to make do with my personal fortune and my locked-in percentage of the firm's ownership and profits, which is, thankfully, beyond the reach of my old man. So I'm going to leave here and have my own little party since the asshole's no longer around to jack me just because he wants to."

"Sir, really," exclaimed Robins.

"Oh, and just FYI, I will be advising Elaine Fixx and the CEOs at all my father's other companies to drop your firm as corporate counsel. I'm tired of overpaying for below-par performance."

Robins looked like he had bitten his tongue off. "Mr. Temple, I can assure you—"

"Oh you have, Harv, you've assured me so much it's taking all my willpower not to beat your fucking face in." He stalked out.

"Wait!" exclaimed Robins. "We're not done!"

But Rhett was already gone.

Mindy looked at Robins and Cole, and smiled. "I miss Barton so very dearly, but it's so heartening to know that he thought so much

of me as to make sure I was taken care of after his *tragic* passing."
She produced a tissue and rubbed her eyes with it.

"Um, there is one more thing, Mrs. Temple, as I just indicated,"
said Robins in a delicate tone.

Mindy said eagerly, "Yes? Did he leave me something else? I am
partial to the Gulfstream jet. It's so roomy."

"Actually, the entire distribution to you is premised on your
being pregnant with Mr. Temple's child. Naturally, you will have to
be tested for this."

Mindy's smile dimmed. "And if I'm not?"

"Then your prenup will kick in."

"But that only provides for twenty million."

"*Only* twenty million?" said a wide-eyed Cole.

"What happens to the money if I'm not pregnant?" asked Mindy,
ignoring the other woman's comment.

Robins said indignantly, "I'm afraid your share then goes to
Rhett along with the house and the Gulfstream. I would have told
him so if he hadn't…if he hadn't walked out…prematurely."

"*Are* you pregnant?" asked Cole.

Mindy swiveled her gaze to the woman. "Yes I am, actually."

"I'm sorry I have to ask this, but *is* the child Mr. Temple's?" said
Robins.

"Yes, it most certainly is," answered Mindy quite truthfully.

CHAPTER

58

I DON'T KNOW WHAT TO TELL you," Rhett said to Victoria Steers. He was on a specially encrypted phone with the woman. "I'm no longer the CEO of Sybaritic. They took my security key, my ID card. I have no way to get into the building or access records, and I no longer get to ride on the company jet."

Steers said, "This is most unfortunate, all of it."

"Well, blame my dead father, not me. But if you had told me before this phone call that Nash was working with the FBI, I could have helped you plan this better. When you set him up and he ran for it, it might have actually prompted my dad to do what he did."

"I see no connection there."

"I spoke with my father shortly before his death. He didn't believe that Nash was a child molester," Rhett lied. "My father believed that you had set Nash up, and he was terrified that Nash would somehow bring the house of cards tumbling down. So he left you and me to hold the bag and took the easy way out by jumping off that balcony."

"On the contrary, the plan with Walter Nash has worked to perfection."

"And me no longer being in control at Sybaritic? And my father having left me nothing? How is that perfection?"

"The latter is your problem. Not mine."

"Well, you still have a problem, because I'm out. You'll have to find someone else."

This was actually the exit that Rhett had been praying for. He could spend the rest of his life having fun with the substantial money he still had.

"You do not ever leave these sorts of partnerships, Mr. Temple."

"But what can I do for you? I have no more position in the firm."

"I will find things for you to do. Beginning with you locating Walter Nash."

A shocked Rhett exclaimed, "What? Why?"

"I need to discern what he has told the FBI."

"I thought you had already *discerned* that."

"I need details, Mr. Temple, not generalities."

"I have no idea where he is."

"But you will locate him and bring him to me," said Steers.

"When you pulled the thing with his daughter, why didn't you take him then?"

Part of Rhett couldn't believe he was challenging her like this. If they had been in the same room, her men would have already hacked him to pieces. But it wasn't only him not being physically close to the woman that had provided this newfound courage.

I killed somebody. That changes you. It makes you stronger, or at least less afraid of people who kill other people routinely. Because now I'm part of that group. I'm a killer. I could kill her one day.

"He moved a bit too fast for us, unfortunately. He must have had help. You can find out what that help was and then use that intelligence to find him."

"After you framed him with his daughter, the FBI won't touch him. I assumed that was your plan?"

"Depending on what he already disclosed to them, they may not need him anymore in order to get to me. And *you*."

"Okay, what's in it for me, other than the FBI staying off my back?"

"You will get to live."

"Frankly, Ms. Steers, with the shitstorm I'm in, I need more than that."

"There will be money—a lot of it."

"Okay, but will I ever get a chance to spend it?"

"That is somewhat up to you and somewhat up to me."

"Great. And what about Maggie Nash? Is she alive?"

The line went dead and so did all his hope that Maggie might still be among the living. Rhett had very little of his humanity left. But what had happened to the young woman had hit him hard in the part he had retained.

His other phone buzzed and he looked at the caller ID. *Just what I need.*

"Hey, Mindy. What's up with the world's newest billionairess?"

"Can we meet? Like now?"

"No we can't. I'll pencil you in for a month from now."

"A month! You can't do it earlier?" she asked.

"I already left town and I'm not coming back early. I needed some R and R. I'm lying on a beach right now sucking down a margarita. Where do you want to meet? Your place?"

"No, your place. Okay, a month from this Sunday. At seven?"

"I'll even order dinner and open a nice bottle."

"See you then."

He clicked off, dumped his phone on the couch, and looked out the window of his fourteen-million-dollar bachelor pad.

I have everything in the world to make me happy. And yet I'm the unhappiest man in the world, except maybe for Walter Nash. And I know it's only gonna get worse from here on. Unless I figure out a way to make it better. And maybe I can. I'm not stupid, like Dad told everyone I was. So now's my chance to prove it.

CHAPTER

59

NASH LAY ON HIS BUNK. Every molecule in his body was in pain. And he had never felt such exhaustion. And in three hours' time it would all start again. He wasn't even sure how long he'd been doing this. Isolated like this, he'd lost all track of time. Every day was the same.

Work out until he felt like he'd died, with perfect nutritional meals interspersed. Cram and practice sessions on all subjects necessary to observe and assess foes, and how to find people, hide from people, kill people. He'd learned how to make improvised explosive devices from fairly ordinary items and set them off in the inner courtyard of the training facility. He had gotten so good at hitting the black tape X's with knife strikes that Shock had allowed him a beer one night as a reward.

The first time he'd gotten into the boxing ring with Shock for close-quarter-combat training he had been a little cocky because of Shock's age and bulk. That feeling had disappeared the first time Shock had knocked him out of the ring. And the second and third times had done nothing except reinforce the reality that a very large, but still nearly eighty-year-old man had kicked his ass with ease.

He rubbed his arm where one of Shock's massive hands had clocked him with a classic blocking maneuver. The bruise there was so purple and large it was like an eggplant had sprouted on Nash's limb. Next, Shock had swept Nash's leg out from under him, dumping him right on his ass. Then the big man had knelt down and in a real fight would have killed Nash with an elbow strike to his throat, crushing his windpipe.

Shock had told him, "We don't have time for me to train you up as a black belt in any particular martial arts, Walter, but what I can do is teach you key moves in each that are fairly straightforward. You learn to do those in your sleep, you can beat pretty much anybody out there."

Nash subsequently practiced kicks, blocks, arm strikes, and attacking nerve pressure points until he could barely lift his limbs or bend his fingers. It was not all physical, Shock had said. "Ninety-nine percent of the folks are oblivious to what's going on around them. Got their eyes stuck on their stupid phones. The one percent that have situational awareness could rob, rape, or kill any of them. The one-tenth of one percent of those folks could rob, rape, or kill the other ninety-nine and nine-tenths."

He had taught Nash in detail how to look for tendencies of his opponents and then use those against them.

"Some folks are dominant leg or arm strike happy. That gives you an openin'. Others like distance between them and whoever they're goin' up against. With a weapon in hand, that can be an advantage. The close-in dudes who like to control your hands? They often forget about the legs."

One day Shock had led him over to a swimming pool that was situated in its own room. The space reeked of chlorine.

"Can you swim?" he'd asked Nash.

"Not all that well, no."

Shock had pushed him in and Nash had gone under, fully clothed as he was, with weights on his ankles, because he'd been running on the treadmill.

He struggled to the surface, spitting out water. "Are you trying to kill me!" he shouted.

"Not necessarily. But they sure as hell will be only it won't be by drownin'. You'll be a fish by the time I'm done with your ass."

Nash had gone through dozens of close-quarter-battle drill techniques, with Shock being alternately patient and then losing his shit when Nash messed up. And when he did, Shock would lay him out, hard.

"Is that really necessary?" said Nash after struggling to get up one time after being knocked down. "It's not like you praise me when I get it right."

"You mess up here, I whack you in the head 'cause I want you to remember it. You mess up out there? You not just whacked around. You dead."

Nash had considered that to be one of the most compelling explanations he'd ever been given on any subject.

He got to the point where, especially with the mental side of the game, he would reference his experience in the business world. Summing up an opponent, viewing the lay of the land, deciding which techniques would work best with which opponent. When he did that, Nash found, he was far more successful than not.

He had still thought of quitting every day, but he hadn't. And he knew the reason.

He slid the photo from his wallet. In it Maggie was eighteen and the senior prom queen. Her smile had filled the high school football stadium. Nash had jumped on a red-eye in order to be there for it. He'd later had jet lag from hell, but not on that night. That night had been as magical for him as it had been for Maggie.

And now? I have no idea where she is. I have no idea if she's still alive. No, I have a pretty good idea that she is…not. And everyone thinks that I…

Nash felt his eyes tear up and he ran his finger along the photo and tried to remember how good that day had felt. He and Judith both so proud, and Maggie so radiant.

He put the photo away and wondered if all of the work he was doing would end up having even a speck of value or make any difference whatsoever.

Shock is making me strong, capable of going into situations and surviving, able to track people down while avoiding being tracked down myself. I can now kill someone in a dozen different ways. I can make an IED out of kitchen products and blow shit and people up.

He paused in these thoughts.

But I've never had to kill someone for real. I still have no idea if I can.

He brought the image of Maggie into his mind's eye and turned it this way and that. She was worth everything to him. When she'd been born, he had felt this overwhelming sense of wanting to protect his daughter from all harm, all worry. No parent can do that, Nash understood. But then you taught the child to take care of herself. You taught her to be strong and independent. And Maggie had been getting there, she really had been. Their last conversation had been...wonderful. He still remembered the feel of her hug, the fatherly pride he had felt in her mature thoughts and supportive words. And, still, *this* had happened to her.

Because of me.

He so wanted to hold her now. To quiet her fears, to keep her safe. And the only shot he had at that was to push his body well past all points of endurance and pain.

And, more important, to take his mind to places it had never gone before, perhaps never contemplated before. He had told himself that if Maggie was not returned safe he would kill Rhett Temple. He had never felt such hatred before.

But when it comes down to it, can you do it, or is that just cheap talk, Nash? Can you be a Peanut who kills without even thinking about it? Leave a human being dead and go on with your life as though nothing important happened? Can you see your human opponents as mere obstacles like Dad did? Can you go there, Nash? More critical, do you want *to go there?*

He closed his eyes, and when he opened them, he no longer felt tired. He got up and went into the training facility. He turned on the lights and proceeded to work on hitting all the pressure and kill points on the boxing dummy until he could do it with his eyes closed.

Exhausted, he spent another hour doing pull-ups, push-ups, squats, lunges, and core work. He got back to his bed and fell asleep for two hours of rest until he took up the task once more.

* * *

Nash was surprised because there was another man waiting with Shock when he showed up to begin his workout two weeks later.

"Walter, this here is Byron Jackson."

Nash shook Jackson's hand; the latter's grip was like steel pincers. Jackson was around six feet, in his sixties, with deep brown skin, a furrowed brow, and thick, dark eyelashes. A ruler-straight set of lips rode above a lantern jaw. Jackson looked like a former NFL player who had never gotten out of shape.

When Nash shot Shock a curious look, Shock said, "Byron is my partner."

"Your business partner?"

Shock draped a big arm around Jackson's broad shoulders and said, "No, I don't got no business partner. Byron is my *life* partner."

Nash looked from Jackson to Shock.

"Guess you finally earned the right to know where my nickname come from," said Shock. "Like your daddy said."

"When did he find out?" asked Nash.

"Long time ago."

"And *he* came up with the name?" When Shock nodded, he asked, "How did he take it?"

"He said, if I could find a man dumb enough to have me, to go for it. See, I was married at seventeen and had my first child right after. Got three more, bang, bang, bang. Then years later, my wife Libby died in a car accident. We still had some of our kids at home at the time. Your daddy had helped me set up my business, like I told you before. He come and helped me with the kids when he could. My folks were back in Mississippi and so were Libby's. So it was hard. But we got by. I wasn't the best father in the world, but I did what I could. Then, when the last child was grown and gone?"

He turned and looked at Jackson. "Well, I called your daddy and he come to see me. We talked. Well, mostly I talked and I told him... who I was. Who I really was. And that's when he hugged me and said, 'You just give me the biggest shock of my life. But in a good way, so's from now on I'm gonna call you Shock, in a good way.' And that was that." He hugged Jackson tighter. "And me and Byron been together a long time now. And it's been good. Real good," he added with a smile. But his smile faded. "Your daddy's first wife, Gloria, killed herself. You knew that, right?"

"But I don't know anything else about it. He was in Vietnam at the time."

"I was with him in Nam when he got word that she was dead."

"Do you know any of the details, or why?"

Shock shook his head. "No. Your daddy never shared anythin' with me 'bout it, really, but the man was in pain. We grew up with Gloria in Mississippi. She and Ty were tight in high school, but nothing serious. Then he went home on leave, and came back married. Surprised me, all right. Then a year later, she was dead."

"My God," said Nash.

Shock patted Jackson on the shoulder. "Now, I asked Byron up here to help with your trainin'. Take it to another level, so to speak. He played college ball, too, former Special Forces. Saw combat in Desert Storm, and the Second Gulf War; man can do it all."

Jackson appraised Nash. "Isaiah said you're working hard. You ready to work harder?"

Part of Nash wanted to say no, he wasn't. He actually wanted to leave and give himself up, hire a good lawyer, and fight it in court. But the image of his daughter's picture on senior prom night came back to him with the impact of a streak of lightning colliding with a tree.

So he said, "I'll do whatever I have to do, Byron, to get to where I need to go."

CHAPTER

60

RHETT POURED OUT ONE MORE glass of wine and looked across the dining room table in his penthouse at his widowed stepmother.

"So, Min, you want to finally tell me what's on your mind?"

"I might have a problem that you could help with."

"Okay. What's in it for me?"

"Ten percent of my inheritance."

"Make it a quarter and I'm listening," replied Rhett.

"You shit, you haven't even heard what I need."

"So tell me. And it's still a quarter."

"Your father put a provision in the will that conditions my inheritance on a certain event occurring."

"What event?"

"That I'm pregnant."

"That's not possible. I told you that, Min."

"But I *am* pregnant, Rhett."

"Come on, don't bullshit me."

She touched her stomach. "I've already seen my ob-gyn. She confirmed it. I gave that information to the lawyers, which meets one of the criteria. And the child's father is a Temple. I told the lawyers that, too. And it was the truth."

"It's obviously not my father's, so who are—" Rhett stopped and gaped. "Wait a minute. Are you saying…"

She nodded. "When we did it in the massage room. You're the only man I've slept with in the last six months, and that includes your father."

His face turned red and he said furiously, "Shit, you're pregnant with *my* kid? You said you were on the fucking pill!"

"Please, Rhett, don't be that way."

"What way do you expect me to be? You wanted to get pregnant, so you *seduced* me."

"It wasn't hard. It never is with you. You jumped me the night before my wedding just because I let you feel me up and French-kiss me when we were alone back at the hotel. You were like an animal. I loved it. But I have to look out for myself."

"Right, you're just as selfish as everybody else."

"I acted surprised when you told me Barton had gotten a vasectomy, but the thing is I already knew."

"How?"

"Barton got drunk one night and said some things that made me suspicious. I got the code to his wall safe. Some papers were in there that told me. So he couldn't provide the baby that I needed."

"You said you didn't want to get pregnant," he reminded her.

"I lied. Just like all you Temples lie. A kid was the only protection I was going to have. Absent that, I was going to be stuck with the puny prenup."

"Puny? Twenty mill was more than you would ever earn in your entire life slopping on makeup and hair spray."

Her features grew hard. "True, but my expectations changed when I married a *billionaire*!"

"Have to hand it to you, Min, you're a sneaky little shit," remarked a still clearly angry Rhett.

"Come on, this could be a happy occasion."

He barked. "You're my stepmother, for God's sake. And you're having my baby! What the hell is happy about that?"

"You're going to be a father."

"Right, uh-huh. Father by deception, always on my top five things to experience in life. So why do you need me?" Rhett demanded. "It seems I've already performed the *service* you required."

"Because of the *other* condition."

He shot her a glance. "Wait, of course. You need to prove it's my *father's* baby, right? And Dad knew that would be impossible. He screwed you over, Min, without actually *screwing* you."

"But since you're his son, the DNA shouldn't be a problem, right? I mean, it'll show that the father is a Temple. And you can back me up on that, right? You know he couldn't be the father but you can take care of that part, can't you? Pay off the doc who did the vasectomy? *That's* why I need your help."

Rhett looked at her in disbelief. "Mindy, I'm not a scientist, okay? But I think the only people who have the exact same DNA are *identical* twins. They'll know it's not my father's baby, but they will be able to show that the actual father is related to my old man. And for all I know they may be able to tell that it's his *son* who fathered the baby. And my father only has one son. Me!"

"Okay, then maybe you can help me give them a DNA sample that is actually yours, but you can say it's your dad's."

Rhett shook his head while rubbing his temples, his expression weary. "Okay, I don't want to say that you're as dumb as a fucking rock, Min, but the lawyers are not going to take any DNA evidence from *us*. I'm sure they already have a sample of my dad's DNA, since that was a condition of the inheritance provision."

Mindy collapsed back in her chair. "Shit, so I'm screwed?"

"Where does the money go if you can't meet the conditions?"

"To that stupid foundation your father set up," Mindy lied.

"Great! Thanks, Pops!"

"So there's nothing we can do?" she said.

"I don't know. Let me think about it."

"You can come up with something, right? Your father didn't think much of you, but I've always known how devious you can be."

"If I do come up with something, it'll cost you half," replied Rhett.

"Half? But you said a quarter!"

"Just chalk it up to my natural *deviousness*. And I said a quarter before you dropped a baby in my lap, sweetheart. Half or you can kiss the billions bye-bye and live off the twenty mill on your pre-nup. Knowing you, you'll burn through that in a year."

"Okay, half."

"In writing."

"You don't trust me?"

"I trust you as much as you trust me," he countered.

She rose. "Let me know as soon as you think of something. And just so you know, I already told them I'm not doing anything to jeopardize my pregnancy by having them take a DNA sample from my amniotic fluid. They have to wait the full nine months with everything in limbo. They said they'd get back to me on that, but I don't think it'll be a problem."

"I promise I will do whatever I can to cut those billions loose. The old man owed me that."

She bent down and kissed him on the lips. "I really appreciate this, Rhett. And I'll show my gratitude lots of different ways."

She left, and Rhett sat there thinking. Then he pulled out a business card from his wallet, picked up the phone, and made a call.

"Hey, Lindsey Cole, it's Rhett Temple."

"Hi, Mr. Temple," said the young Stanford lawyer who had sat in on the will reading with Harvey Robins.

"Got a question for you. An important one."

"Okay, I hope I have the answer."

"I think you will. How about I ask and you answer over a drink?"

61

RHETT PICKED A BAR NEAR his penthouse and met Cole there an hour later, right when the place was starting to hop. He knew the manager, the head bartender, and the comely twentysomething hostess, all of whom lavished attention and praise on him as the hostess led them to a private table in a back room.

"Wow, you're a popular guy here," noted Cole.

"All it takes is money."

He ordered a dirty martini while she selected a glass of Riesling.

"I'm very interested in your question," she said.

"Probably not as interested as I will be in your answer."

"Okay, let it fly."

"A little birdie told me that there were conditions attached to my stepmother's inheritance of a quarter of my father's estate."

Cole grinned. "I thought that might be it. If you had hung around, you would have been fascinated."

Their drinks came and they clinked glasses. He said, "I'm prepared to be fascinated now. Maybe for more than one reason."

She said brightly, "Well, since you're part of the family there's no reason I can't tell you. In fact, Mr. Robins would have if you hadn't walked out that day at his office."

As she filled him in, Rhett nodded approvingly. When she came to the part about him inheriting Mindy's share if she were not pregnant with his father's child, he chuckled.

"And here I was bad-mouthing my father."

"But I suppose Mrs. Temple *could* be pregnant with his child?" Cole said hesitantly.

"It would have been the *second* immaculate conception."

She laughed. "You obviously know more than I do."

"So how will the process work? I mean, she might be pregnant, for all I know. But you have to determine whether my father is the one, even though he couldn't be."

"With her permission we spoke to her ob-gyn and were provided with definitive test results that show she's pregnant. The question of paternity can be determined by a simple blood draw from the mother and DNA from the father, usually by a cheek swab."

"My father is dead. How are you getting his DNA?"

"Your father had provided the firm a DNA sample, but since his death has been ruled a possible homicide, a postmortem was done and tissue samples taken. I suggested to Mr. Robins that DNA should be extracted from those official samples to use in our situation, so no one can challenge them later."

"Meaning Mindy?" When she nodded, he said, "That was smart of you. And you sound well read on the subject of forensics."

"I actually want to be a criminal defense attorney. However, I got roped into working trusts and estates with Robins for the next year. But my time will come."

"And does Mindy have to agree to provide her baby's DNA?"

"If she refuses, her share of the estate goes to you. The will wasn't clear on when she had to provide the proof. You can do a DNA draw from the amniotic fluid starting at seven weeks and then up to the first trimester. But she's asked for us to wait until the baby is born. Mr. Robins hasn't agreed to that but he probably will. I mean, the money will be there months from now regardless—the pie will have just grown larger because of bond interest and dividends and capital appreciation." She took a sip of her wine. "I take it your father was concerned with...infidelity?"

"Since Mindy's pregnant, he was right to be." When she looked at him curiously, he added, "My father had a vasectomy years ago. Irreversible. It's in his medical records. So no way the baby could be his. Hence my 'immaculate conception' comment."

"Then I wonder why she was so confident," said Cole thoughtfully.

"When the stakes are high enough some people will try anything, no matter how ridiculous, Ms. Cole."

She drew a bit closer. "Please call me Lindsey."

"And I'm Rhett. Lindsey? Beautiful name, so it matches you well."

"Is that a standard line of yours?" she said coyly.

"I don't think you'd find a man to disagree with me."

"Wow, you are good."

"Well, maybe you can find out just how good I am." He touched her hand. "I appreciate the information, Lindsey. And you will find me grateful in many ways. I think you'll make a terrific defense attorney. Maybe I can finance your practice if you go out on your own."

"Now that is worth discussing. Are you free now?"

"No, but I will be tomorrow."

He paid the bill and saw her into an Uber. She waved from the car window and then vanished into the darkness of a city winding down for the night.

As Rhett walked to his penthouse, he assumed that he might be needing a criminal defense attorney one day. And why not retain one lovely enough to sleep with?

Then he, too, disappeared into the darkness, finally feeling good about things.

62

MONTHS LATER RHETT SAT UP in bed and eyed the person sleeping next to him. Judith Nash's body had grown doughy, robbing the woman of her sexiness, at least in his estimation.

Judith had constantly pestered him for his help in locating her daughter—who must be somewhere safe, she told him. Rhett gave her platitudes in return, told her he was dispensing resources, making progress, a tantalizing tidbit here and there, when he was actually doing nothing. But her constant neediness was getting on his nerves.

They'd had sex regularly since Maggie had vanished, always at his place, as her home was deemed too risky. All blame for everything that had happened was solidly on Walter Nash, and Rhett wanted to do nothing to change that impression, especially with the cops.

His father had been right. While he hated that Maggie had been taken and almost certainly killed, he was not going to risk his life to avenge her. He had his own problems. And sacrificing his life for another, who was most likely dead anyway, was just not on his bingo card.

His alibi, Laurel Burke, had never bothered to find out when his father had died. If she had she might have put two and two together and tried to put the screws to Rhett for more money. And then Rhett had headed that off by buying her a luxurious condo in Las Vegas and getting her a cushy job at a casino there that his father had partly owned. She'd met a nice guy, which Rhett had actually arranged, and they were enjoying each other's company. But the guy was there to keep watch over the woman. If Burke started disclosing things she shouldn't be, Rhett would know about it. And then he would have to take action. Before he'd killed his father he would never have contemplated doing the same to Burke. But now?

I'm pretty much capable of anything. And it feels good.

And on top of all that, Steers was still expecting him to hunt down Nash and bring him to her. She constantly hounded him about that, even threatening to send some of her agents to help him. So far he had managed to hold her off, but he wasn't sure how much longer that would work. Plus, he had an idea that the woman was searching for Nash herself. And, with her resources, she might find him. But Rhett wouldn't necessarily bet against Nash. The man was strategic and tactically brilliant, and never missed even the smallest detail. His still being a fugitive after all this time despite the worldwide hunt for him was a testament to the man's resourcefulness.

Rhett rose and poured out a drink from the bar in the other room. A G & T at six in the morning, it went down as crisp and smooth as the breaking dawn appearing through his penthouse floor-to-ceiling tinted windows. It warmly lit Rhett's face like he was on a film set.

He smoked down a cigarette as he thought things through. He had a meeting with Mindy tonight, and then a rendezvous with attorney Lindsey Cole to discuss legal strategy, but also something else. He had bedded her numerous times now, and he had pleasantly found the seemingly reserved lawyer was a wildcat between the sheets. He would use her for what he could, get some great sex in the bargain, and leave her in the dust like he did every other woman who crossed his path with a few dollars thrown her way to keep the woman in line. He no longer found fault with himself for doing this.

Look at my gene pool. I come by it honestly.

To be fair, his mother had taught him to be respectful to women. But his father had, mostly by example, counseled him to screw them, abuse them, and then deep-six them. He knew that if Barton had lived, Mindy would have been kicked to the curb right before her prenup auto-ratcheted to a higher number. And still the woman had the audacity to want a chunk of his old man's wealth when she'd done nothing for it.

Even cheating on him with me. But she *came on to* me. *What was I supposed to do?*

He had put Mindy off for months now, resisting her pleas to meet, making excuses by telling her that he was working on a plan and that she had to be patient. Cole had finessed it so the lawyers weren't demanding the DNA sample until Mindy gave birth. He had used that to keep Mindy hanging, telling her, truthfully, that he had orchestrated that. But he'd really just wanted to string her along, make her desperate, while he had some fun. And along with that, he hadn't had to work his ass off at Sybaritic or deal all that much with Steers other than her complaining to him about finding Nash. But now with his batteries recharged, he was going to put his plan into motion. And what an interesting meeting he and his stepmother were going to have.

He snorted a fine line of coke right off the rim of his claw-foot bathtub and looked up to see Judith standing naked in the doorway.

She had had such a rocking body, he thought, but despair had ruined the vibe of it, like a film of gritty varnish on a fine piece of artwork. Compared to Lindsey Cole, or Mindy, Judith Nash was well past her prime. He wasn't sure why he was sleeping with her anymore.

Well, I do feel sorry for her. I'm not a total prick.

"Do you have any more?" she asked, eying the razor on the countertop and then the short chrome straw he had used to snort it, a few white grains still clinging to the metal hide.

"My, my are we getting wild again?" he said, rising from the floor with a smile.

"Do you?" she asked again, without a corresponding smile.

"For you, anything."

He expertly cut it for her, lined it up enticingly on the bathtub's rim, and handed her the chrome straw.

She dropped to her knees, a move that managed to instantly arouse him, and did the line like a pro, taking a deep breath, seemingly savoring the toxin she had just downloaded into her bloodstream.

Rhett looked down and eyed his sudden erection. "I did you. Care to reciprocate?"

Judith did not look so inclined, she looked the polar opposite of so inclined. But still, she crawled over on her hands and knees.

And reciprocated.

When she was done, he bent down and kissed the top of her head. "I've got to go. Stay as long as you want."

She crawled back to his bed and fell between the sheets.

He showered, dressed, and left her there, probably in a drug-induced dream of lost daughters and fugitive husbands.

* * *

That night Rhett sat next to Mindy on the spa level of his father's mansion. He eyed the room where they'd had sex, while Mindy nervously intertwined her fingers.

"I was wondering when the hell you were going to get back to me, Rhett. It's been forever. You *said* you were going to take care of things," she added in a pouty tone. She rubbed her now large, protruding belly. "I'm not that far away from dropping this baby."

"Well, I got the DNA deadline extended, so I had some time to work on things. And I have."

"And I appreciate that. I really do. But now I need to know where I stand financially. And don't *you* want to work something out?"

"Before I make important decisions I have to collect the facts, Min, which takes time. And in that vein, I had an interesting discussion with the estate lawyers. So now, like you just said, it's time to move forward."

Mindy looked relieved, he thought. That was certainly not going to last.

She said, "Okay. How?"

He gave her a patronizing look. "They filled me in on what I missed when I walked out of the will reading, Min. I was surprised, to say the least. You lied about where your share would go if you couldn't prove the baby was my dad's. It's not going to the trust, it comes to me."

Her face flushed and she wouldn't meet his eye. "I...felt bad about lying to you, Rhett. I really did. But I...I was so scared. And I was going to tell you the truth. I swear."

"Oh, I'm sure of it. Now if the kid really is mine—and you'll have to take the test to prove that—what are your expectations?"

"I don't *expect* marriage, of course, but I would like you to be in our lives. And then there's the matter of support."

"But is that really a good idea? I mean, if people find out I'm the father of my stepmother's child? And my dad took a dive off the balcony? Not a great look unless you want the kid to come visit Mommy and Daddy in prison."

"I can move away from here if you don't want me to stay in the house. Then maybe people wouldn't talk."

"Right, so just to clarify, the house comes to me, along with billions of bucks because that baby is not my dad's."

She assumed an aggrieved look. "So you're just going to leave me with my prenup money? That hardly seems fair."

His expression grew darker. "You were only married to him for about a year. I had to deal with the monster my whole fucking life. And twenty mill is nothing to sneeze at."

"Not compared to billions. And you *did* murder him."

"Correction, *we* killed him, Min, me and you. So you going to the cops would not be a smart idea. He said, she said. I turn state's witness, you do the slow burn in a cell for the rest of your life, while I get probation and a new life with the billions."

"Come on, Rhett, let's not fight. Let's work together. You couldn't even spend a tenth of all that money if you tried."

Rhett felt the time was right to cut the deal he needed to get done. "Okay, then let's do something about that. When you married

Dad I know that he had you named as Angie's backup guardian, and that now, with him dead, you have a power of attorney for her."

"That's right. I was actually surprised when he made me the backup for her."

"I'm not. It was a chip he used against me."

"I don't understand."

"He never gave a shit about Angie. He hated the idea that any child of his would be like that. But he knew that I actually loved Angie, and I believe he figured that you wouldn't care for her half as much as I would. And there would be nothing I could do about it. He would have loved that, screwing me over from the grave."

Mindy looked stunned by his words. "My God, you two really had one fucked-up relationship." She paused, watching him guardedly. "Look, Rhett, it's not like I know Angie all that well. But I would always take care of her. I'm not heartless. She can't help who she is."

"That's great, Mindy, and I am touched by that, I really am. But here's the thing—you won't have to take care of her. You appoint me as her guardian and you give me the power of attorney. I've seen the documents and you have the ability to do that. Then I'll have the lawyers do their two-step legal dance, and increase your payout to a quarter of a billion dollars. And you walk away with it all—no tax, since you were his legal spouse. Well, it's actually a little more complicated than that. But I'll take care of it."

She looked at him suspiciously. "Why would you do that?"

"Because I want to take care of Angie, like I said, and I need those powers to do that."

"I don't understand stuff like this. What's the process? How will it all work?"

"It's simple. You first have to certify to the lawyers that you are not pregnant with my father's child and thus are not entitled to anything other than the prenup settlement. Then, to pay you the quarter billion, I have to liquidate some holdings from my inheritance, an inheritance I will now receive because you failed the condition in the will of carrying Dad's child. But we're only talking a couple of weeks' delay. How would *you* like the payout, by the way? I assume by wire transfer?"

"Yes," she said quickly.

"Okay, I'll have the lawyers draw it all up. You sign what you need to sign for the estate lawyers and Angie's guardianship and power of attorney, the wire goes off, and you'll be set for life. You can raise our kid like a king. Or queen."

"And will you ever visit?"

"You know what, Min? You can stay at Dad's place. Well, *my* place now."

"But you just said—"

"Forget that. People will assume the kid is Dad's. And it's not like anyone will have the right to check because you won't have to give DNA now. Dad told me about the vasectomy, but I doubt he told anyone else. And his doctor is bound by HIPPA, so he can't reveal it without getting his ass sued off. And the same for the lawyers," he added, thinking of how he had revealed that fact to Lindsey Cole. "When the time comes you list Dad on the birth certificate as the father, okay?"

"Okay, but I don't get you, Rhett. You can be a real shit. Dump your dad off the balcony one minute and then worrying about your disabled sister the next."

"That's what makes a complex man, Min." He kissed her on the cheek. "And I'm glad I could give you something my old man couldn't. But if it's a boy, for God's sake, don't name him Rhett Jr."

He walked out, leaving Mindy sitting there and absently rubbing her swollen belly and thinking that Rhett had subtly outmaneuvered her.

But a quarter of a billion bucks was certainly worth it, she concluded.

63

A FEW WEEKS LATER, ALL TRANSACTIONS completed, and all documents signed, sealed, and delivered, and Mindy Temple $250 million richer, Rhett marched into the offices of Sybaritic Investments with a dweeby, irrelevant looking sixty-year-old man named Hugh Prentiss, who had become chairman of the board of Sybaritic at Barton's death. Dressed in a tailored two-piece gray suit with a blue polka-dot tie and matching pocket kerchief, Rhett looked on top of the world. For his part, Prentiss appeared like he was being forced off a cliff.

They knocked on the office door of Elaine Fixx, the CEO, and were told to enter.

She glanced up at them in surprise. "Rhett, Hugh? What are you two doing here? You're not on my calendar."

"Well, that doesn't really matter, does it?" said Rhett. "Not now."

"I'm not sure what—"

Rhett turned to Prentiss, "Hugh, deliver her the 411."

Prentiss, without meeting Fixx's eye, said, "Um, it appears that Mr. Temple is once again the CEO of this company."

"There's no 'appears' about it, Hugh," snapped Rhett.

Fixx stood. "I don't understand. I was named in Barton's will as the CEO."

"Yes, but, there were, um, complications that, I mean today, well, it seems that—" stammered Prentiss.

Rhett interjected, "Jesus, just shut up, Hugh. Here's the deal, Elaine. I own sixteen percent of the voting shares in this company."

"Right. Not nearly enough to remove me as—"

"And I have been named guardian of my sister Angelina's trust, and I also have her power of attorney. Her trust owns fifty-one percent of the shares of Sybaritic Investments, meaning that I control *sixty-seven percent* of the voting stock, a supermajority. That means that I can name me as your replacement, and I have." He turned to Prentiss. "And by the way, you're fired, dumbass. Get out. I already canned the rest of the board this morning, but I saved you for last because I wanted to tell it to your ugly face."

Prentiss blanched. "But—"

"Leave now or security will give you the heave-ho."

Prentiss hurried from the room, leaving Rhett and Fixx staring at each other.

Fixx said, "You got control of your disabled sister's trust and you're using it to take back control of the company? That is beyond... brilliant, Rhett."

He appraised her in a new light. "That response might have just saved your ass, Elaine. But I need to know one thing first."

"What?"

"Did you sleep with my father?"

Fixx looked at him nervously. "I'm smart and I work hard, and I really want to stay at the company."

"Then tell me the truth."

"Yes, I did. Your father made it, um, clear..."

"Fine. That is the perfect answer. You're now executive VP in charge of acquisitions."

"Walter Nash's old job?"

"If you want it."

She came around the desk and hugged him. "Rhett, I don't know how to thank you."

He cupped her firm butt with his hand, startling her. "I already have some ways for you to thank me *properly*. Now, move across the hall to Nash's old office. Oh, and dinner tonight, just the two of us."

She looked at him nervously. "Oh, I'm so sorry, my *husband* and I have—"

"It wasn't a question, Elaine. And hubby or not, you let my dad bed you, so get with the program, my new senior executive VP." He kissed her on the lips and left with a spring in his step.

64

Normally, nash would not look at himself in the mirror, but he did after another exhausting day of training. And he was impressed with what he saw.

Damn, I'm ripped.

He'd always had a flat belly, but now he also had an eight-pack and his core was strong as iron. The muscles in his arms, back, shoulders, chest, glutes, and legs rippled. He felt taller, looser, infinitely more powerful and physically confident.

He flexed his triceps and his quads, and was pleasantly surprised to see hardened domes of veiny muscle emerge all over. He could now run on the treadmill nonstop for an hour. He had done thousands of miles, mostly up mountains, on a stationary bike, until his thighs, hammies, and calves swelled with sinewy brawn. He had learned dozens of ways to fight, and incapacitate an opponent, from small, precise motions to more complex maneuvers that would be devastating to any combatant.

And he had been taught how to kill with a pen, a finger, a coin, a foot, a fist, an elbow, a knife, a gun, or anything else he could manage to get his hands on. It was like Nash had learned a difficult foreign language, one that he never knew even existed, like Russian and Chinese marbled together into a comprehensible hash, only with lethal outcomes.

His body was black and blue from the beatings he had taken from Shock and now Byron Jackson, who had revealed himself to be a cagey and skilled close-combat warrior. At first, he had knocked

Nash down multiple times with simple leg and arm taps against strategic body parts.

Jackson had lectured, "There are about a dozen spots on the human body where a bit of targeted, concentrated force will take an opponent down. Remember that torque against joints is the key. Muscle man, ninja warrior, dude on the street, we are all built structurally the same. You move a limb in the opposite direction it was designed to go, your man is going down, in pain. And in the seconds after that, he is vulnerable to whatever you want to do to him: knock out or kill."

Then Jackson had demonstrated methods of seizing control of Nash's arms, neck, shoulders, legs, loading them up and then driving them in the opposite direction the bones, tendons, and ligaments were designed to go. Nash then trained relentlessly to do the same until even Jackson praised him.

"Now, untrained people always try the wrong thing when someone has them in a neck lock," Jackson had said. "They struggle trying to pull the dude's arm forward and off. That's always a loser because you're going against his strength and using only your weakness. But this?"

He had Nash encircle his neck from behind with both arms as tightly as he could. Jackson didn't struggle trying to pull the arm free, or turn to the left or right. He merely ducked under the lead arm holding him, torqued that limb against the structural grain, jacked it up Nash's back to a painful degree, and while Nash was dealing with that and teetering to maintain his balance, Jackson easily kicked his left leg out from under Nash and he went down hard.

"Finish with an elbow strike to the cervical spine, and the dude is toast. Then you move on," said Jackson.

To another obstacle, thought Nash, echoing Shock's story about Ty Nash.

He'd then had Nash hold a knife against his throat before again effortlessly ducking under, controlling the limb, and "stabbing" Nash a dozen times with his own knife, while Nash was still holding it!

Despite the relentless training on close-quarter combat, it was really about early observation, Nash had discovered, seeing enough before the confrontation began so that you were never really surprised. And then using your opponent's tells, mistakes, bravado, and momentum against him. Without breaking much of a sweat, or using very little muscle, you could beat men two or three times your size.

His proficiency on the gun range had grown by leaps and bounds. He could break down and then rebuild blindfolded every weapon Shock had in his armory. Nash would never be a world-class sniper, but he didn't have to be to accomplish what he needed to.

He ate his sixth and final meal of the day and then was free to go to his quarters, where, after a shower, he did what he always did at night: He scoured the internet looking for news of Maggie. He had hoped that her kidnappers might post another video of her, but nothing ever appeared, and his hope that one would show up had faded to almost nothing.

The alerts were still out on him everywhere. He was considered armed and dangerous after it was determined he had taken his father's old gun and Army knife. He had shown them to Judith, who obviously had told the police.

He was also a cuckolded husband, and his wife had done it with his boss. Talk about poor judgment of character on her part. But what Nash feared was that Rhett would provide a shoulder for his wife to cry on, and that would put Judith in danger of stumbling onto what Rhett was involved in. Because despite everything, Nash still cared for his wife, and he wanted no harm to come to her.

He rose, went to the doorway where Shock had placed a pull-up bar, and did as many as he could until his strength failed.

You have to get stronger, Nash. As strong as you can. It's the only shot you have.

Because you have to find her. Please don't be dead, Maggie. Please God don't let her be dead.

He did another pull-up and then another, even as the tears trickled down his cheeks.

* * *

"Come on, Isaiah, what are you really doing with that man?"

It was a month later. Shock and Jackson were in their bedroom having a nightcap, Shock a bourbon neat, and Jackson a cup of peppermint tea.

Shock sipped his drink before answering. "Exactly what I said."

Jackson shook his head. "Sure he's getting some muscle. He can run faster and longer. He can shoot fine, and in a fight he could hold his own with ninety percent of the dudes out there, maybe ninety-nine percent because most guys don't know shit about defending themselves or really hurting somebody else. But the dudes he'll be going up against, according to you, are in that one percent he can't overcome."

"More like the one-tenth of one percent," corrected Shock.

"Well, then, back to my question. What are you doing? And he's one of the most wanted dudes in the country, and if they find him here with us you and me are gonna be spending the rest of our days under the watchful eye of the federal government. And that is not a good place for any man to be, especially Black men, and old ones at that. I don't want that for my golden years. Do you?"

"I made his daddy a promise."

"But *he* ain't Ty Nash. What do you owe *him*?"

"Don't matter what I owe or don't owe him. I gave my word to a dyin' man, the best friend I ever had, and I mean no disrespect to you on that. But me and Ty went through shit together, well, that's all I say 'bout that. And he woulda done the same for me. No lie. So that's all there is to it in my book."

Jackson sipped his tea and shook his head in frustration. "You worked your ass off building all this up and you're gonna risk throwing it away over some white dude you don't even really know and probably don't even like."

"I knew him as a boy. I just now got to know him as a man. And what I know is he's done everythin' I asked him to do. He's gotten the shit kicked outta him, by me and by you. He coulda quit. Give up. Lord, most days I was hopin' Walter would quit, and then he go on about his business and I could go on about mine. But he didn't. He got back up, wiped off the blood, and got back to work. Remind me of his daddy, no lie. You got to respect that. Least I do. And his daughter is dead. I know it, you know it. And the truth is Walter knows it, but he can't admit it, not yet. What father could?"

"Everybody loses folks, Isaiah."

Shock frowned and shook his head. "Uh-uh, not like that they don't."

"Okay, you train him up and then he leaves here, goes after these folks, and gets killed. What have you really done for him?"

Shock set his drink down and leaned back against his pillow. "What I'm givin' him is a chance, a fightin' chance. Dude is an underdog, sure; you think I don't know that? You think *he* don't know that? But when I'm done with him the man will have a shot. That's all you can ask for from this life. It's what I asked for. It's what you asked for. It's what all folks ask for."

"Most don't get it. Especially folks like us."

"Which means the ones that do get it, they got to go for it. Otherwise you just pissin' in the faces of all those that ain't never got a fair shake."

"You gonna help him after he's all trained up?" asked Jackson.

"I'm gonna do what I need to do to keep my promise to his daddy. And that's all I got to say 'bout that."

Jackson grimaced. "He run into these boys you told me about, he's gonna die. You can build the dude up but you can't make him into a killer, Isaiah. He'll be going up against dudes been doing this their whole life. How can you not see that? You're leading a lamb to the damn slaughter."

"You'd be right, 'cept for one thing."

"What's that?" Jackson asked sharply.

"I knew that boy's daddy better'n anybody. Man had a motor that ain't never quit. You don't think the goddamn Vietcong ain't spent their whole lives learnin' how to kick the shit outta people? Kill 'em with their thumbs, not have one ounce of compassion if you in the other uniform? But Ty Nash survived all that shit I don't even know how, and he pulled me along for the ride, or else I'm not gonna be here with you. From small observations he would build big decisions that saved our butts time and again. Attention to detail, discipline, figurin' shit out, gettin' the job done. That's stuff Walter's been doin' for decades, just while sittin' in a chair and wearin' a suit. But even as a youngster I saw something special in him. He was thoughtful, observant, hardworking, and he figured shit out. Now, if Walter has even a little bit 'a Tiberius Nash in him, he may surprise me. *And* you."

Jackson shook his head. "I just don't see it."

"Well, then come with me and maybe you will *see* it."

Shock led a curious Jackson over to the training center. Before they got there they both heard it. Jackson glanced at his companion in surprise, but Shock didn't look surprised at all.

They stood in the darkened doorway and watched Walter Nash going full bore at the boxing dummy: knife and elbow strikes, knee crushers, head slams. Then he dropped and did push-ups, rose and did pull-ups. Then he jumped rope. Then he slumped to his knees, breathing harder than anyone probably should. Then he rose and did it all over again.

As Shock and Jackson slowly walked back to their quarters Jackson said, "Maybe that boy does have a shot."

Shock eyed him. "I ain't never bettin' 'gainst nobody got Ty Nash's blood in him."

CHAPTER

65

VICTORIA STEERS LEFT HER PENTHOUSE in Hong Kong on a cloudy morning, was driven to the airport, and was wheels up an hour later in her Bombardier Global 8000. She was dressed in her finest clothes. Her hair hung straight and her makeup was simple, but it caused her facial bones to stand out and increased the width and power of her eyes.

She had been looking for Walter Nash for a long time now. Though she had been pressuring Rhett Temple to find the man, she had no confidence in his ability or real desire to do so. She had employed private investigators, corrupt police, and savvy street criminals in America to track him down, and none of them could find a trace. It was immensely upsetting to Steers and had also resulted in her superior in this affair losing some confidence in her. He had not come right out and said it; he was far too nuanced for that. But his underlying message had been clear: Walter Nash was a problem that needed to be set right. And as time passed, she felt that they were no closer to finding him. He did not have close friends or acquaintances. His parents were dead. His wife had no idea where he was. Leads had been followed up, questions asked, people bribed and threatened, and, still, nothing. He had truly vanished.

Perhaps, in his despair, he killed himself. But he was an intelligent, resourceful man, perhaps with hidden financial resources. Such a man could lose himself in the wide horizons of the world. And as we created the image of his daughter saying what she had, he could have changed himself completely in the time that has passed.

Hours later Steers was still thinking over this problem as the jet began its descent into a rugged and mountainous area of southeast Asia. The runway was private; the facility next to it was even more so.

The Bombardier touched down in stiff crosswinds coming off the nearby mountains, requiring one go-around and then a turbulent sideways approach before touchdown. The nervous flyer Steers did not seem to notice. She was anxious, but it had nothing to do with the difficult termination of the flight.

She walked off the jet while her armed retinue stayed on board. This was not her doing. This was on orders from one more powerful than she.

A waiting car whisked her away to the one-story building that had a central block and two long wings, as well as numerous ancillary structures. Two twelve-foot-high fences topped by concertina wire encircled the compound. Armed guards patrolled the perimeter as did a platoon of fearsome dogs, a daunting mixture of Dobermans, Rottweilers, and Akitas.

Steers was cleared through security, and she found herself walking rapidly down a long, antiseptic hall behind a bulky, wide-hipped guard who, if he had recognized her name on the visitor's pass, had made no sign of it.

He had just instructed her in his native language, "Come this way! Now!"

Steers was led down one of the wings of the building, through two more barred entry points, and finally found herself standing outside of a solid metal door with a slot in the bottom for meals to be passed through.

The guard unlocked the door and motioned her in. He barked, "Ten minutes."

She passed through. The door slammed behind her and she heard the lock turn. The space was six by six, no windows, one bunk, one foul toilet, and a chair bolted to the floor.

And her, the occupant, officially Prisoner Number 113.

Steers had waited patiently for her superior to hold up his end of the bargain and allow her visit here. She knew he had probably delighted in thinking of her impatience.

How a worm squirms on the end of the hook before its death.

Masuyo Steers was in the chair, sitting stiffly. Her legs and arms were shackled to a bolt in the floor. She was in her seventies now, gray haired, wrinkled face, small limbs hung off her shrunken body. She looked defeated, void, unaware of anything at all around her.

But when Masuyo's eyes fully opened, an observer would forget about the withered frame and the gray hair and the shackles. The woman's eyes held a force that could not be questioned. They showed a person very much alive, in the moment, and, most important for Steers, a woman who was undaunted.

Masuyo said, "The guard's name in his language means 'fat,' which fits him. I tell him this in my mind. If I had the means I would tell it to his face a moment before I slit his throat. Do you think of such things, Victoria? Tell me that my daughter, my only surviving child, does."

"Do they listen in here?" asked Steers in her mother's native tongue.

"They see no need. They are all-powerful here. Confidence is one thing, arrogance quite another."

"That is good," said Steers as she lifted her head and met her mother's luminous eyes, replete with spirit and barely suppressed rage. "And I think of such things, often."

Masuyo nodded. "I know they brought down our plane. The news reached me in here. Killed Joseph, almost killed you. You survived, as you always have. Through four siblings who wanted nothing other than to bloody your throat. But you prevailed. Some ask, would Masuyo have preferred the quick death? Masuyo says, no, she prefers to live so that one day she may kill those who wronged her. I wait for that day. Do you wait for that day, my daughter?"

"I wait for that day."

"You must have pleased those who rule here for them to have let you see me."

"I did."

"There is no mirror here. Have I changed much?"

"Not your spirit. That has not changed. I see it in your eyes. I hear it in your voice. The rest, it does not matter."

Masuyo lifted a shackled hand, and Victoria drew closer so that her mother could touch her face.

"You are very lovely, my child."

"I take after you. I have my mother's spirit and her spine."

This answer seemed to both delight and sadden Masuyo.

"In the crash of a plane, the damage must be severe." She drew back her daughter's sleeve and saw the warped skin there. "All of you?"

"No, only some. But…enough."

"You have survived the fires of hell, my child. This is your reminder."

Steers nodded. "That is how I view it."

Masuyo tugged the sleeve back down. "You know that they are almost certain I will die here."

"*Almost* and *certain* are not the same," replied Steers.

"I have waited years to be able to hear you say that, my beautiful child."

Steers gripped the hand and pressed it against her chest, over her heart. "I keep you here always, Māma. Always."

Masuyo then pressed her daughter's hand against her chest. "And you here, xiă gong zhǔ."

Steers drew back and bowed her head.

"Your business goes well?" asked Masuyo, though in a way that demonstrated that she already knew the answer.

"I only enjoy the fruit of your labors."

"You have done well, Victoria. You have exceeded all our dreams."

"But the price is heavy."

"The price is always heavy, until one decides to stop paying it."

"And this is possible?"

"It is inevitable," said her mother.

"Your speech surprises and also encourages me."

"The place where one is born does not dictate all outcomes. One grows and changes, or one's life is empty and of no value. You do not have such a life. I do not have such a life."

"Plans need to be made."

"Follow the heart, Victoria, and it will set you, and me, free."

"You are wise."

"I am old. If I am not wise, then it is my fault."

"I will see you again, Māma."

"Until then."

Victoria rose just as the guard pounded on the door and called out, "Time."

He opened the portal and Victoria stepped through. She took one last look at her mother and then settled her gaze on the guard.

The fat one. Yes, indeed, she thought contemptuously. But also tactically, for gluttony and greed went hand in hand. And because opportunities were everywhere and one needed to be ready to seize them.

He said, "You will follow me to the exit. Now."

She surprised him by saying, "There is no need. I know the way. Now."

As she moved off, she thought that she did indeed know the way. Now.

CHAPTER

66

"BYRON'S BROTHER RUNS A BARBERSHOP. Taught him all he knows 'bout cuttin' hair, right, Byron?" said Shock.

"Yep, but this here job won't take much skill," replied Jackson.

Nash was seated on a stool with a towel around his shoulders. Shock and Jackson stood next to him, the latter with an electric shaver in hand. Nash had grown the trim beard and goatee that Shock had requested. And now, after his work was done for the day, Nash had been told that they had other changes to him that needed to be done.

"All of it?" said Nash.

"All of it," replied Shock.

"Why not leave a little? I'll still look different."

"I need the canvas."

"The what?" said Nash, startled.

"The *canvas*. You'll see, Walter."

"I'm not sure about this."

"Do you trust me or not?"

Nash sighed and nodded at Jackson. Five minutes later all he had left was scalp.

Jackson said appreciatively, "Not a bad dome you got, Walter. I seen worse."

Shock looked more closely. "That's good, smoother the better."

"You mentioned a *canvas*?" said Nash.

Shock went to a cabinet and pulled out a set of binders. He brought them back to a small table, and all three men sat around it. Shock opened the first binder and slid it across.

"Let me know when somethin' tickles your fancy."

"Wait, are these…tattoo designs?" said Nash, glancing sharply at him.

"Skin art, they call it. Amazin' shit they can do these days. I've got some old tats from Nam. Man, they did not hold up all that well. Or maybe *I* didn't. Your daddy had tats, too."

"I know. I saw them. A knife on his right arm, an eagle on his back, and a spear on his left arm. But why tattoos for me?"

"They don't change just your skin and appearance. They change how someone *perceives* you, I mean, below the skin. Mild-mannered businessman disappears when we get some of this shit on you."

"Can't it be fake? Or how about a tat sleeve?"

"Fake comes off. You need to be the real deal or nothin', man."

"So where on my body?"

Jackson snorted. "Might be easier to say where *not* on your body."

Nash touched his hairless head. "Wait, *this* canvas!"

"Ain't nobody gonna think you Walter Nash when you inked all over."

"But won't that take a long time?"

Shock shook his head. "Nope. Can do it all in one day."

"How?"

"General anesthesia. Four ink artists, nine hours. Good to go."

"General anesthesia! Am I going to a hospital?"

"I've got an anesthetist lined up. And a nurse. They'll come here."

"I'm a fugitive."

"They got their own troubles."

"Including the anesthetist?"

"Especially him. Now, you just got to pick out your designs. But we doin' the back, legs, arms, chest, head."

"Is this really necessary?"

"Naw, man, not less you wanna live. Your call. No lie."

Nash looked woefully down at the binders and started to slowly turn the pages.

* * *

He'd wanted to choose the knife, eagle, and spear like his father's, but Shock had, quite rightly, vetoed those choices.

"Don't want to make it too easy for 'em, Walter."

Thus he'd selected a roaring, fanged lion, his mane spread wide, for his back, and a dragon for his right arm and shoulder—the dragon's head covered the delt and the rest of the creature slid down the arm all the way to the back of his hand. For the chest and abdomen he'd chosen a huge scales of justice with the blindfolded Lady Justice holding them. Another symbol. On each thigh was a shield, like that carried by an ancient warrior. On each calf was one of a pair of dice. Every step he took Nash figured he was gambling whether he was going to live or die.

Finally, for the tat that would run from the top of one ear, over the crown of his head, and straight down to the top of his other ear, Nash had not picked from the binders. After some deliberation, he had drawn out a length of thick, steel-blue chain edged in gold. It had three kinks in it equidistantly spaced. The kinks were roughly in the form of hearts. He knew what they meant; that was enough.

Then came the day to be inked.

The artists had placed the chosen designs from the binders plus Nash's rough sketch for his head onto iPad Pros. They had then customized each design after back-and-forth discussions with Shock, who was acting as Nash's intermediary. After final approval, these designs were then printed out on transfer paper using a thermal printer that used heat to transfer the image, giving it crisp, clean lines and guaranteeing the integrity of the final images. Nash learned that ink was not actually used in this process, but rather carbon-based paper that reacted to heat to create the stencil, actually burning the design onto the stencil paper; it had four layers, including a yellow sheet that held the original in place while it was in the copy machine. Cosmetic grade dyes were used because they were safe for the skin and were also smudge-proof.

Nash had to make sure his skin was well hydrated and clean. A mild soap had removed oil and dead skin cells. He had applied Hibiclens all over his body twenty-four hours prior to the procedure. It was the same product and process hospitals used before surgery. His skin was then shaved, and a layer of stencil gel was applied to his body; it enabled the ink to adhere better to the skin. The transfer papers holding the designs were precisely placed onto the skin and then peeled off, leaving the actual design in place on his body exactly where it would be inked for permanence.

Shock explained, "For large tats, like these, you can't have no mistakes. Get in there with your tattoo pen and go from memory, things can go sideways fast. With the designs planned out, printed out, and applied directly to the areas the tats will be goin', makes it a whole lot easier and safer to bring out the pens then. And my guys are good. They don't just ink it on. They mold it to your body. Fittin' it not just to size and space but how your body moves with it there, muscles and all."

"So you've done this before? For your clients?"

"Oh yeah. For those that needed to disappear."

"Why would law-abiding clients need to disappear?"

"All depends on how you define *law-abidin'*," Shock had replied. "And right now, leastways in the eyes of the law, that definitely don't include you."

Nash was wheeled into a small room where the anesthetist and a nurse were waiting. They didn't really look at him. They asked a few basic questions and that was it.

Shock said the artists were waiting in the other room and would begin their work once Nash was fully under.

He whispered to Nash, "They ain't never gonna see your face, Walter, just the skin they be inking, so don't worry."

Nash had said to the anesthetist, "Do I count backward from ten to one?"

"If you want," said the doctor indifferently.

At nine, Nash's eyes closed and he was out for the count.

He never heard the artists come in, or felt the stencils being lay-ered over his body, or anything else, really. When he woke up, just over nine hours had passed.

The nurse checked him out. The doctor checked him out. And then they both left with their fees paid, in cash.

The artists had also already left, with their fees also paid and no photos allowed of the work they'd just done. Shock had thrown in an extra twenty percent so there were no hard feelings, since the art-ists liked to put their work online to solicit other clients, Nash had been told.

It was now just Shock and Nash left in the room.

When Nash was sufficiently recovered from the anesthesia, Shock gingerly helped him up.

Nash groaned. "Damn, I feel like I was just run over by a truck."

"Well, man, they done a number on your body packing all that into one day. You gonna be sore and hurting for a while. And your skin will feel like someone used a cheese grater on it."

Nash winced and bent over for a few moments, clearly in pain. "You didn't mention this part of it, Shock."

"Well, you might not 'a done it if I had."

Shock helped him over to a full-length mirror, then handed him a hand mirror so he could see his back. "Check yourself out, dude. Impressive."

To Nash it was like he was staring at another person. It obvi-ously wasn't simply the hardened muscle he'd acquired that made him look like an anatomical chart, but the tats had changed every-thing about him. Even the chain with the kinks. While not large, they had done something to him, his...presence. It was altered, markedly so. He touched his nose where Shock had broken it nearly a year before in the boxing ring and then manually reset it. It had firmed up at a slightly different angle and slope and also changed much about his appearance. He was sure that even Judith would not recognize him.

"Holy shit" was all he could think to say.

"Yeah, I hear you man," said Shock. "Now you got to shower, but don't let the water hit the tats too long. You gonna use Saniderm, it'll help you heal faster. I'll help bandage you up. Good for twenty-four hours and then another shower. Then we'll bandage you up again, and you wear 'em for five days. Saniderm really reduces the scabbin' and peelin'. But it still gonna itch a little, Walter. But you *cannot* scratch. No lie."

"What do I do then?"

"Just slap it, baby. That's all. Just *slap* it."

"How'd I do when I was under?"

"Okay. Only thing they was worried about was you goin' into shock."

"Into shock!"

"Tats that large are a major assault on the biggest organ in the body, your skin. But it was cool, no problems. Your vitals were perfect the whole time."

"Why didn't you tell me that might happen?"

"Hell, it might 'a made you so nervous you *woulda* gone into shock."

Nash showered, and Shock helped him apply the Saniderm and bandages. Then he redid them twenty-four hours later. On the fifth day the bandages came off, and Nash was able to admire his tats once more.

When he flexed his arm, the head of the dragon seemed to move. The same with the lion on his back, which seemed to roar when he manipulated his traps, lats, and rhomboid muscles.

When he eyed the scales of justice on his chest and abdomen his mood grew somber.

Will I ever get justice? Will Maggie?

The shields on his thighs made his skin look metallic. The dice on his calves seemed to shimmy as he walked or flexed his muscles.

He dipped his head slightly and then turned it side to side to study the chain and kinks in the mirror. They obviously represented him and his family, still tied together in love no matter what. With this thought tears leaked down his cheeks. He brushed them away, and went to do his work for the day.

He felt like a new man.

And damn if Walter Nash wasn't.

CHAPTER

67

DUDE IS REALLY BRINGING IT lately," said Jackson. "I mean, even more than usual. Think he can see the end of the tunnel coming. Maybe with a train coming, too," he muttered under his breath.

He and Shock were in the kitchen of the training facility having their dinner. There was a TV show on to which they were only half paying attention.

"Must be the tats and the bald head," quipped Shock. He rubbed his scalp. "Worked for me," he added with a laugh.

"Seriously, though, he's looking like a real weapon now."

"Told you, man. He's learned way more than folks I've been drillin' for ten years."

"But he's never killed anybody, Isaiah. You and me know that's the real deal. And I don't think the boy's there. I really don't. He was hammering me today, but when I pretended that he'd really hurt me, he pulled back; probably didn't even know he had, but he did. That ain't good if he's going to do what he needs to do."

Shock sat back, his gleeful expression melting away. "I know. I saw that shit, too. And I'm not sure what to do about it. It's not like I can call a friend and have him come here so Walter can kill him for real."

Jackson shook his head. "Please don't tell me that over a year's worth of fifteen-hour days has been for nothing."

"I can't answer that. Not yet."

"Where is he now?"

"Went for a run."

"He worked his ass off all day. And he went for a run?"

"What did I tell you 'bout his daddy's motor? See, I think that acorn fell right at the base of that mighty oak."

"Well, let's hope he can make it the last mile, which is the only one that matters."

Shock nodded and glanced over at the TV when a news anchor abruptly interrupted the program that had been on.

When Shock saw the picture that was on the screen, he forgot about everything else.

* * *

Nash was running on the track that encircled the facility. One time around was half a mile. He had done it six times and didn't really feel tired. He had never been in this kind of physical shape before, and it was like he awoke each morning with a sense of renewed purpose bolstered by a nearly inhuman amount of energy. He had turned forty-one months ago and he felt like he was twenty-one.

Each night he still diligently checked all the news feeds and social media platforms for any possible news about Maggie. He had also kept tabs on the investigation around Barton Temple's death. He was now convinced that Rhett had been behind it. He had inherited billions from his father, and Nash had also learned that Rhett had gained control of the board and reinstalled himself as CEO after pushing Elaine Fixx out. She had then taken over Nash's old position, or so the business news had dutifully reported.

He outmaneuvered his father and Fixx somehow. But then kept Fixx on for some reason.

He wasn't speculating here about Rhett outsmarting his father. Barton had told him that at his death Nash would become the CEO with Fixx as the backup. Barton had then confided in Nash that he had taken pains to have the necessary legal documents drafted and executed to carry out that wish.

If Rhett had managed to undo all that, then Nash had to reevaluate his appraisal of the man. He clearly was cagier and more strategic than Nash had given him credit for. If they were to meet up again, Nash would need to build that reevaluation into his own strategy.

Nash had, despite Shock's warnings, communicated with Agent Morris on several occasions. He felt guilty about disobeying his friend's wishes, but Nash was, if nothing else, a practical man. He needed information, and only the Bureau could provide it.

The FBI agent had expressed his belief in Nash's innocence and, more important for Nash, kept him up to date on Steers and company. However, he also told Nash that others at the Bureau considered Nash toxic to their efforts. It also seemed that Victoria Steers was still trying to find him, Morris had written. And there was no indication that the woman was going to stop. He had also informed Nash that with Rhett back in charge, Steers's focus on Sybaritic as a criminal tool remained undiminished. Thus, the FBI was looking for another way in, but as yet had been unsuccessful. He had also told Nash that the financial misdeeds he had found before Maggie had been taken had led to quite a bounty of additional intelligence and several search warrants that had produced still more evidentiary progress. Steers was also aware of this, he had said, but there was nothing she could do about it directly.

When Rhett had been reinstated as CEO, Nash had told Morris about his suspicions regarding Rhett and his father's death, writing that Barton had told him that he was to be the CEO at his death. He also told Nash that he didn't trust Rhett at all. So Nash informed Morris that Rhett had the strongest possible motive to kill his father—money and power. And it could be that Steers had worked with him to get it done. Since it had come out that Barton was terminal with cancer, Nash reasoned that Steers might have been nervous that he might make a mistake, or even confess his misdeeds as his time on earth drew to a close. Morris had thanked him for this analysis, and promised to push it up the chain. Nash had then asked Morris another question, having to do with his wife.

Has she been seeing Rhett?

Morris had sent a one-word answer: Yes.

At his place?

Morris had given the same answer.

Finally, he had asked about Maggie.

Any hope that she's still alive?

Pointedly, Morris had not answered him, which was an answer in itself.

Nash ran on as the wind picked up and a few drops of rain fell. He looked up at the darkened sky and it struck him, and not for the first time, how his entire life had changed, irreversibly. Daughter gone and probably dead, wife sleeping with another man, his career ended, his body and looks changed beyond all plausible reckoning. And his being a notorious fugitive, with the closing act on this drama having yet to be written. He had wanted to be out there looking for Maggie every day, though he had no way to really do that. One step out of place and he would be in prison.

Before you can accomplish the impossible you must achieve the possible.

He knew that both Shock and Jackson were happy with his progress in all ways save one: *They don't really believe I can kill someone.*

He had pulled back when pummeling Jackson today. He had sensed real pain and then realized only later the man was faking it, just to test him.

I believe that I can kill if absolutely necessary. My mind has gone there, or at least close to there, and I'm confident my body will follow. It has to.

The rain picked up and he increased his pace, making it inside right before the downpour hit. Smiling at his timing, he went to the kitchen for his final meal of the day.

Shock and Jackson were sitting at the table. Their attention was riveted on the TV.

When they heard him come in, they turned to look at him, the misery on their faces something to behold. But Nash was not paying attention to them.

A picture of his daughter was up on the TV screen, and the news anchor was reporting how the remains of Maggie Nash had been found in a remote area of…

Nash didn't take in the location because he could not pull his eyes or his mind from his daughter's face. He knew the picture. It was when they had gone to France together to celebrate Maggie's high school graduation. Nash had actually taken the photo, right outside a restaurant in a small, lovely village in Provence. Maggie had later posted it online. It had been one of the most wonderful days Nash could ever remember. They had been so happy, so thoroughly happy. Everything was right with them and the world. Everything.

And now?

His mind came back into focus when the news anchor uttered grimly, "The police are looking into whether Ms. Nash's father, Walter, who has been a fugitive from justice for well over a year now, had any involvement in her death." A picture of the old Walter Nash came up on the screen. It looked nothing like the current version of the man.

The anchor provided a tipline number for viewers to call with any information that could help locate him.

Shock said in a trembling voice, "Walter, I am so sorry. I—"

Nash didn't wait to hear the rest of it.

He turned and left the kitchen without his final meal. He was no longer hungry.

He had known that the odds were very much against his daughter being found alive. But now, with the fact of her death indisputably established, it was the difference between being hit with a bat and being blown apart with an atom bomb.

As he walked slowly to his room the rage that had simmered just below the surface all this time suddenly became the sole element of his being.

The transformation of Walter Nash was now complete.

First had come the physical piece.

Then the mental one.

And now my soul has gone through the ultimate metamorphosis.

Because one minute ago I just lost my humanity.

Forever.

CHAPTER

68

A MONTH AFTER LEARNING OF HIS daughter's death, Nash looked down at his hands. When he had been hired at Sybaritic, FINRA regulations required a fingerprint-based background check. Now whatever he touched with his hands could leave behind a trace that could then be compared to his fingerprints in a database. And his real identity would be revealed regardless of how much the rest of him had changed. He could not bench-press his fingerprints into a different mass of arches, loops, and whorls.

To counteract that he had used first a brick and then a pumice stone on the finger pads of his hands. Shock had told him that his prints probably would be no good for the authorities to take for up to two weeks, because the pumice and brick rubbings temporarily reduced or even erased the ridges necessary for adhesion of the printing ink. It was painful, but far less painful than being in prison. However, the skin would grow back, requiring him to keep doing it.

If he were caught he would have to explain about the condition of his fingertips, and his ready explanation was that he was a bricklayer. He had learned how to do that at Shock's direction. Apparently, there was little that the man had not done in his long life. However, the better strategy obviously was not to be caught at all.

The days were growing shorter, and gloomier. And his daughter's meager remains were long since buried. He had watched on TV as a local station covered the funeral service. He saw Judith walk into and out of the church, the same one where his father's service had taken place, then watched her at the cemetery. She looked heavier and older, like a ghost of herself. He also saw many people from Sybaritic Investments.

Including Rhett Temple. He was right next to Judith, his hand on the small of her back, guiding her where she needed to go. A staunch friend, the news anchor said, since her husband—the cause of all this misery—had gone on the run.

Yes, staunch friend. And lover. And criminal. And all-around piece of shit.

Then Shock had walked in and turned the TV off.

"Enough," he had said to Nash. "Enough, Walter." And Nash had not disagreed. It *was* enough, all of it.

Nash now had a new driver's license, an American passport, a Social Security card, a checking account, and credit and debit cards Shock had made up for him, all under the name Dillon Hope.

"These are as solid as they come, Walter. You can fly with these babies, even international, no lie."

"How were you able to do that?"

"You think folks in the right places can't be bribed? They make government wage, man. Not much left over in the kitty for fun. Some computer clicks on the old databases and, presto, you got Dillon Hope, a living, breathin' man with a past. Don't matter the background checks they do, whatever level, you will be good to go. Cost a packet. That's why I asked for some of the money the government paid you, so I could get the best stuff out there."

"Speaking of, I need to pay you for all this."

"No, Walter. I ain't lookin' to profit off this. And hell, your daddy already left me a quarter million bucks. I was already set for retirement. Now I'm more than set. And Byron's got himself a nice federal pension. We good, man, but thanks for the thought."

"Where'd you get the name Dillon Hope?"

"Knew a dude named Dillon back in Mississippi. Good man."

"You still in touch?"

"Naw, some assholes killed him when we was in high school 'cause he was gay."

"And the surname, Hope?"

"I thought that would be self-evident."

Shock gave him a flash drive with his full background from birth to present.

"You got a personal security employment background with all the certifications, clearances, bells and whistles. And, hell, with all I taught you, Walter, you can do that job no problem. Now, anybody calls or emails to verify anythin', you are good to go. Don't ask how, but let me just say that AI has been a boon to those lookin' to jack up fake CVs and backgrounds. Just memorize what you need to and then get rid of the flash drive. Your old man once told me you got a photographic memory, so it should be no problem."

"Thanks, Shock. And speaking of photographs..."

He took out one from his wallet. It was the picture he'd found in the safe, of his father and Shock in Vietnam.

He handed it to Shock, who grinned and said, "Damn, I remember that day. We'd taken back a pile of high dirt the North Vietnamese had grabbed from us the day before. And they'd take it back the next day, and on and on it would go. But right when this picture was taken, for just those few minutes, life was good. Life was sweet, man." He turned the photo over and read off the words written there.

"Woodstock." His expression bittersweet, he added, "We heard all 'bout that festival, man. Hendrix playin' his white Fender Stratocaster, upside down, Joan Baez, Richie Havens, the Grateful Dead, the goddamn Who. We woulda loved to have been there instead of Nam."

He handed the photo back, but his eyes told Nash that Shock was still back in 1969, for better or worse.

"I want you to keep the picture, Shock," he said, passing it back.

"What? Why?"

"It's part of *your* history. And Dad would have wanted you to have it."

Shock nodded. "You know who you look like now?" He tapped the image of Tiberius Q. Nash on the photo.

"I don't think anyone can really be him," replied Nash.

"You don't have to be him, Walter. You just got to be you. But havin' some of your old man in you ain't a bad thing, especially where you headed now."

Nash then decided to broach a subject that had perplexed him for decades. "I heard him call you the N-word, Shock. More than once. Didn't that...bother you?"

Shock looked off for a moment, then drew a breath, straightened up to his full height, and looked at Nash. "Let me tell you somethin' 'bout your daddy. My second Purple I caught a round from a Vietcong sniper. In and out, but it hit somethin' bad and I was bleedin' out like a muther. Your father covered me with his body and still managed to shoot the dude out the tree. On the chopper ride to the field hospital he was right there next to me. Keepin' me alive as much as the medics were. They only had one bag 'a plasma on the chopper to put in me and that wasn't nearly enough. I was dyin', but your daddy said not to worry, that he was gonna give me his blood when we got to the field hospital, even though he'd recently taken a round in his leg and still wasn't all the way healed yet. So's we got to the hospital. And let me tell you, the U.S. Army back then was not known for its progressive stance on race. The doc on duty, I found out later, was some KKK asshole from Arkansas. He flat-out refused to let a white man donate blood to a colored, and they had no colored blood to give me, he said. And without that, yours truly was leavin' this world. And you know what your daddy did?"

"What?"

"He pulled his .45, held it against the doc's head, took out a fucken grenade and held it in his other hand, and said we was both niggas with nigga blood in our veins and that if they didn't put his blood in me, he was gonna spill *white* blood all over the floor, startin' with the Klan doc."

"My God, what happened?" asked Nash.

"Never got a transfusion faster in my whole damn life." He suddenly shivered, like Shock was actually reliving the memory rather than simply recalling it. "Your daddy's blood saved me, Walter. And because of what he done, I will always have a part of your father in me. And that is a damn honor."

"Was he written up for that? Or court-martialed even? But, wait, he couldn't have been. He stayed in the military and got an honorable discharge."

"He probably woulda ended up in the stockade, but everybody in that place was too damn scared to report him."

"God, Shock."

"Your daddy risked jackin' his military career *and* losin' his liberty by doin' what he done for me. Man walked the talk so's this here colored boy could live."

"But to not give blood to a wounded soldier regardless of their race?"

"Nam was one messed-up place, Walter. All the grunts were on drugs—shit, the Army gave 'em to us to keep us fightin' harder and longer. And mor'n half the docs and nurses was takin' 'em, too. See, when you get dropped into a world that ain't really a world, but just shit and chaos every minute of every day with violent death tacked on? You need crap to get you through it, and the pills and the powder and the juice did the trick, at least for a little bit. But then if you ain't in reality to begin with, what's the fucken difference?" Shock paused and closed and then opened his eyes and let out a long breath. "But I always knew where your daddy was comin' from. And he the only white man I truly felt that 'bout. And it wasn't just Nam. You think where we grew up in Mississippi was some hotbed of racial equality? By the time I was sixteen your daddy had saved my ass probably half a dozen times from crazy, liquored-up white boys with guns who figgered I'd breathed long enough on this earth. And he almost got hisself killed in the process. So after all that, I didn't care what he called me. And it was a two-way street, 'cause *I* saved *his* butt in Nam. So I called him anythin' I wanted to and I damn sure did, includin' a fucken *idiot* for how he dealt with you."

His eyes glistening, Nash said, "Thank you for telling me, Shock."

"Now let me *tell* you one more thing, and it's important. Real important."

Nash looked at the man, all attention.

"I trained you as best I could in the time I had. You can take out ninety-nine and nine-tenths of the guys out there, Walter, and I'm not exaggeratin' 'cause that shit don't help nobody. But the one-tenth? They *will* be a problem for you. And the one-tenth is what somebody like Victoria Steers will be bringin' to the party. So here's what you got to do when you got them comin' at you." Shock paused, no doubt for emphasis. "You got to use everythin' at your disposal, Walter. Anythin' you can reach that can be a weapon, you go for it. And here's the other thing: Some of these dudes are, well, for want of a better term, *honorable warriors*. They conduct themselves a certain way even when they tryin' to kill you."

"How does that help me, knowing that?" said Nash.

"Here's how. The last thing *you* want to be is honorable. No bowin' and shit like that. No quarter. It might give you the second you need to walk away. So what I'm tellin' you, Walter, is to cheat your ass off to win. Ain't nobody gonna hold it against you. You hear me? You do what you got to do and to hell with everythin' else. Promise me?"

Struck by the man's heartfelt tone and intensity, and his voice full of emotion, he said, "I promise, Shock."

"Now, there's somethin' else you need to consider. It ain't nothing physical. It's up here," he added, touching his temple.

"I've worked on my mind sets, observation, and situational awareness, and I lost my humanity when I found out Maggie was dead. I can kill someone, Shock, *trust* me."

"Ain't talkin' 'bout that." Shock looked at him so intently Nash's pulse quickened. "Thing is, you never know when you might get snatched," he said. "And Steers won't be messin' 'round if she the one doin' the snatchin'. That woman will torture your ass like it ain't nothin'. And when it comes to torture, ain't nobody got nothin' on them muthers."

"So what can I do about that?" asked Nash. "I can't necessarily stop it."

"No, but you can *prepare* for it, choose how you want to handle it, react to it."

"How?" asked Nash curiously.

"Your daddy was held as a POW by the North Vietnamese for two months. Did you know that?"

Nash shook his head in surprise. "No, I didn't. He never said."

"Yeah, well, Ty don't like to talk 'bout shit where he thinks he failed. But he didn't fail. It was just bad timin'. Anyway, after he escaped he told me how he'd hung in there when they was torturin' him."

"How?"

"When we was growin' up in Mississippi, your daddy found this big, old horse roamin' his parents' farm. Nobody knew where that damn critter come from. Now your daddy, he was maybe fifteen, he took ownership of that horse, feedin' it and groomin' it and fixin' up an old shack on the back of his parents' property like a stable. He would ride that thing bareback for miles and miles. Or sometimes I'd see 'em walkin' together 'cross the fields. Your daddy seemed to be talkin' to that creature and it seemed to be talkin' back. I was with your daddy pretty much every day back then. And so was that there horse. He named him Sunshine, 'cause your daddy say whenever he was with that horse the sun was shinin' on him no matter if it was rainin' or thunderin' or whatnot. So when your daddy was a POW and they were doin' shit to him, he told me he'd close his eyes and make his mind believe he was ridin' Sunshine 'cross those fields back in Mississippi. And no matter what them muthers did to him, he didn't break, didn't even really notice. 'Cause he was with Sunshine. He told me that. And then he got loose, killed all his guards, and hightailed it back to our side."

"What happened to Sunshine?" asked Nash.

Shock shook his head sadly. "Your daddy joined the Army and I went off to college. When we both come back on leave his momma told him Sunshine got out and was hit by a truck. Had to shoot the thing, put it out of its misery. Your big, strong daddy cried for a week. Nobody's fault, just happened. Hell, I think Sunshine was out lookin' for your daddy. I tell you this, Walter, so you can find *your* Sunshine, 'cause maybe you gonna need it one day."

Nash thanked him, then did the last thing he needed to do before leaving. He got some soap and water and massaged his finger, lubricating it thoroughly. And then, with Shock's help, he tugged and pulled until he got it free.

Then Nash handed his wedding band to Shock.

"It'll be here waitin' for you, Walter."

As Nash had started to leave, Shock said, "One last thing."

Nash turned back. "Yeah?"

"I'm proud of you, Walter Nash. No lie. Truth, *bro*."

And now Isaiah York's large eyes held a cluster of tears.

* * *

Nash had set up an auto pay for the credit and debit cards coming out of a new account he had established under the name Dillon Hope and in which he had deposited the FBI funds. He had no expenses other than food and gas and wherever he would be staying. The physical address attached to the account was a rental owned by a shell company that was connected to one of Shock's friends.

Shock had also provided him a flash drive with intel on Steers. Some of it he already knew, but parts of it were new to Nash. When he'd asked Shock how he had come by it, Shock told him, "You don't want to know, but I had to call in every marker I had. Victoria Steers is a damn enigma, but maybe a little bit less so after you read that."

Byron Jackson had driven him to a town near the state line.

And now Walter Nash was on his own.

69

THE FOLLOWING MORNING, NASH, DRESSED in jeans, a white sweatshirt that pulled tight against his hardened physique, secondhand work boots, and a ball cap with the American flag on it, drove down the highway in a Ford F150 pickup truck he had purchased in the town where Jackson had dropped him. He was currently headed to his old hometown, and the butterflies in his stomach were nearly incapacitating. But when he thought about the images from Maggie's funeral service, the butterflies vanished, replaced by something difficult to precisely describe, but that did not lessen the hold it had over Nash's emotions. It was not about simply justice, but maybe something approaching righteousness, augmented by an overwhelming desire for revenge.

He arrived back in town that evening and rented a room at a motel not that far from his old childhood home. The old Walter Nash would never have chosen to stay in such a place, where there were racks of hard-ridden motorcycles and old cars and trucks, and pot-smoking folks in ripped folding chairs sitting outside, and women wandering around who looked like they would show you a good time in return for some drugs, booze, and/or a meal.

It also demonstrated how much he had changed that the woman managing the place looked him up and down and said, "We don't want no trouble, mister, and you got that look about you."

"No trouble," Nash said back.

"You got weapons?"

He just stared at her.

"Well, you just keep them out of sight. I run a nice, clean place, okay?"

"No trouble," repeated Nash, which got him an exaggerated eye roll from her.

He parked in front of Room 106. A rusted outdoor barbeque grill was located on the grassy area in front of the horseshoe-shaped motel building. On the grill an old man was roasting sausages and burgers. The aroma made Nash hungry.

He locked his door behind him and tested the deadbolt to make sure it held.

He didn't unpack his bag but did unlock the small, hard-sided gun case Shock had given him. Inside was a Glock nine-mill, and a seven-shot Beretta.

He broke down both weapons and then rebuilt them, all in the dark. It was a confidence-boosting exercise. He locked them away and opened the other pack that he'd brought with him. In it was surveillance equipment that Shock had also provided him. He inspected each piece and then put it away.

In the bathroom Nash checked out his new face and again marveled at how his hairless scalp, beard and goatee, and his broken nose had so transformed his appearance. The chain-link tattoo on his head seemed to give him a tangible tether to the earth, though one part of the chain, Maggie, was now gone.

He then stripped down to look at his body tats. They were all growing on him. When he expanded his back the lion seemed to roar. When he flexed his delt and arm, the dragon and its tail oscillated. However, Lady Justice etched across his chest and belly did nothing. Her image just seemed to stand there...waiting. The thigh shields simply looked cool. The die tats on his calves added a bit of whimsy to the overall impression. Taken together it was...well, weird as shit, like he was looking at someone else. Which, Nash supposed, was the whole point.

There was a bar a few blocks down the street that also served food. He got some cash from an ATM and then ventured inside the half-full bar, where beer-drinking working men who looked and dressed like him were scattered around. Toughened but clear-eyed women were also there scoping the men out, each probably looking for someone...acceptable.

Nash sat at the far end of the L-shaped bar away from everyone and ordered a beer, a burger, and onion rings. He was now 215 pounds of tatted flesh, bone, and muscle; it rode like body armor on his tall frame. He would have been nervous as hell coming into a place like this as his old self. Now, he was not anxious.

Well, maybe just a bit—it was his nature, after all.

After he finished his meal he turned on his stool and studied the crowd while sipping his beer. He immediately recognized two guys; they were the same young men who had been working on the Dodge Charger in his parents' old neighborhood and had scowled at him in his fancy Range Rover. One of them noted his staring and whispered to his mate.

Nash was afraid that they might have recognized him, but when they sauntered over the first one said, "We ain't never seen you here before."

"I've never been here before," Nash said.

The other man, larger than his friend but several inches shorter than Nash, glanced at the stool Nash was on and said, "You know you got to pay to lease that real estate."

Nash looked mildly interested. "You mean the barstool?"

"Yeah, the barstool!"

"Who do I pay?" asked Nash.

"Uh, that would be us, dumbass."

"How much?"

"Two hundred," said the bigger man.

Nash graced him with a look. "And of course I get a receipt with your signature and an itemized accounting as to what the payment is for?"

The man held up a fist near Nash's chin. "*This* is your receipt. You want a taste of it?"

Nash shook his head. "Sorry. My accountant says I always need proper documentation for any business-related expenses. Otherwise you can't deduct them and if you try, the IRS will perform an audit on you, and that is an expensive proposition. You don't want to go there if at all possible. And I think it is absolutely possible *not* to do so right here and now."

The two men glanced at each other in confusion as Nash finished his beer and stood, towering over them both.

"Where you think you're going?" said the smaller man.

"I had my beer. I tried to have some peace. I didn't get it, so now I'm leaving."

"Not without coughin' up—"

The smaller man couldn't finish because Nash had gripped his wrist and torqued it to an incapacitating angle with long, sinewy fingers that were now as strong as steel. The fellow dropped to his knees gyrating, his mouth open, his tongue dangling, but no sound coming out; his eyes bulged in agony. His friend swung an arm back to clock Nash, but Nash performed an elbow strike on the man's neck right between the C4 and C5 vertebrae. As the man began to collapse, Nash grabbed him, guided him around, and dropped him on the stool. The man fell forward and unconscious onto the bar.

"No charge on that prime real estate," mumbled Nash.

He looked down at the gyrating smaller man before glancing around to see if anyone was taking notice of this virtually silent confrontation. Everyone seemed to be going about their drunken business in the darkened bar.

Nash eased the trembling smaller man back to his feet, pulled him close, and punched him in the throat with just the right amount of force, not too much and not too little. The man fell unconscious both from the punch and the relief from Nash letting go of the crushing pressure on his wrist. Nash set him on the stool next to his knocked-out friend, and then leaned them into each other like two pillars on a house of cards.

When a waitress eyed him, he said, "Seems the boys have hit their limit."

She did an eye roll and turned back to her work.

Nash paid his bill in cash and left a nice tip.

The bartender eventually wandered over to the pair and noticed they were not conscious.

Outside, Nash drew a deep breath. He should have felt proud of that moment, which validated all his hard work, but he didn't. He felt like an idiot for bringing unwanted attention to himself. But they had started it. And he had ended it as quietly and discreetly as possible.

But there was something else, even more disturbing.

I actually wanted to kill them both. I could see myself doing it, in fact. And I could have, so easily, in a dozen different ways. And they would have died so quietly.

And the old Nash, resurfacing briefly, was appalled by these thoughts.

He slowly walked back to the motel, climbed into his pickup, and drove to his father's old neighborhood.

CHAPTER

70

THE LIGHTS WERE ON IN the house, and Nash watched as Rosie Parker moved across the front picture window. For a moment it was as though Nash had slipped back in time and he was returning home from his paper route and glimpsing his mother headed to the kitchen to start his breakfast. But his mother was dead, he was no longer a child, and this was not his home.

I don't really have a home, not anymore.

He walked up to the front porch with his cover story rehearsed. This would also be a good test, and hopefully a source of information.

He knocked, and a few moments later Parker answered the door. She had clearly taken Nash's advice on getting some new clothes, and the slacks and colorful sweater rode well on her long, lean frame, which, he was glad to see, had filled out a bit. And she was wearing her hair in a new style that Nash thought attractively enhanced her features.

"Yes?" she said, looking nervous. Nash realized he probably looked intimidating to the woman just by his appearance. And at this hour of the evening it likely amplified her apprehension in a neighborhood that Nash was aware had its issues.

He took off his hat and said in a voice very much unlike his own, "I'm Dillon Hope, ma'am. I'm the son of one of Ty Nash's old Army buddies. I told my old man if I was ever passing by here I'd say hello."

Parker's features softened. "Oh, I'm so sorry. I'm afraid Mr. Nash died quite some time ago."

"Oh, damn. My pop will sure be sad. He told me lotta stories 'bout Ty Nash."

"I'm sure. He'd been sick for a long time and was in a lot of pain."

Nash looked over her shoulder and saw a blown-up photo in a frame on the wall of his father and Shock in their Army uniforms. He pointed. "My daddy has some pictures from when they were all in Nam."

Parker turned to look and her face crinkled in pleasure. "He was one handsome man, Ty Nash."

"My daddy said he was the best soldier the Army ever had. And that man there next to him, Isaiah York? He said the same 'bout him, one helluva soldier."

"Oh, so you know him?"

"Shock? Oh yeah. He came by to visit us. He was Ty's best friend, my daddy said."

"Yes, he was. I haven't seen him since Ty's funeral," she added wistfully.

"He's probably still getting over Ty being gone. Well, I guess I'd better be heading on..." He hesitated and glanced at her with a hopeful expression.

Parker said, "Look, um, would you like to come in? I can make some coffee? And we could...talk?"

"Well, that'd be real nice, ma'am. Thank you."

"You can call me Rosie, Dillon."

She led him into the kitchen and made them both coffees.

"I heard Ty's wife, Nikki, died years ago," he said as she set the cup down in front of him.

She sat across from him, cradling her coffee. "Yes, she did. I met Ty when he came to the VA for treatment. We...well, we became friends and then more than friends. We were together for nearly two years before he died."

"Well, I'm sure you were a real comfort to him. So, you here alone then?"

"Yes, my mother lived here with me, but she passed away not long after Ty did."

"Sorry to hear that."

"She had a good, long life. I guess it was just her time," added Parker sadly.

"You keep in touch with Ty's family then? My pop said he had a son—name 'a Walter, I believe. Thought Pop said he lived around here somewhere."

Parker shot him a surprised look. "You...you haven't heard?"

"Heard what?"

"About Walter Nash. It was all over the news."

"I've been working outside the country the last couple years or so. I'm afraid I'm a little behind and such. What happened? Did he die, too?"

Parker shook her head and told him everything, including Nash's being accused of molesting his daughter, the death of the security guard, and, finally, the discovery of Maggie's remains.

Nash knew all this, of course, but when Parker had talked about Maggie, her accusations, and then her death, he had to glance away for a couple of moments as he felt himself being overcome with emotion.

Composing himself he said, "Jesus, his daughter. Do you believe he did all that?"

Parker gazed at him sternly over the rim of her cup. "Not for one minute. The man I knew, the man I *respected*?" She shook her head. "I've run into molesters before. A man at the VA. Not a patient, one of the orderlies who worked there. He was a pedophile. I suspected right away. Some children in the apartment building where he lived..." She took a sip of coffee and said quickly, "Anyway, it's ridiculous to anyone who knew him. And it made me so mad that people just accepted that he was a monster, including his own wife."

"But you said there was the video with his daughter."

"Videos can be manipulated. I'm no expert on it, but I at least know that. These days you can make anyone say anything and

it's not true at all. But with Walter they just believed it. It was...
unforgivable."

"You said he disappeared? I guess that didn't help his case."

"What else could he do?" She glanced out the window. "And
when they found Maggie's remains?" She shook her head sadly.
"And they just blamed that on him, too, although there was no evidence. None at all."

"So what do you think happened then?" asked Nash. He
respected this woman greatly and really wanted to hear her opinion.

"I think somebody framed Walter, that's what."

"But who, and why?"

"He worked at this big, fancy company. Lots of money whirling
around there. Then the man who owned it all ups and jumps off his
balcony, or so the police said."

"Good God!"

"And then that man's son, Rhett Temple? Well, he's now very
cozy with Mrs. Nash. I saw them together at the funeral service for
Maggie. And I saw them once when I was downtown. They were in
his car driving into a parking garage at one of those big, expensive
residential buildings. I bet he lives there."

"Damn, you think they're...you know?"

"I wouldn't be surprised at all," she said primly. "It's just all so
wrong."

"I wonder what happened to Walter?"

"I don't know. I just hope he's out there somewhere trying to...
oh, I don't know, figure it all out. He was real good at that. He helped
me so much. Got me all set in life with this house and my finances
and everything. So kind, so...capable. I...I miss him."

"Sounds as though you thought a lot of him."

"I did. I *do*. And Ty would have known if his son was some sort
of monster like that. But Ty died with his son's name on his lips. He
loved his boy. So that's *all* I need to know."

Nash again had to look away at these comments because he had
suddenly teared up.

After a few more minutes of conversation he rose to leave. "Well, thank you, Rosie, for the coffee. And the talk."

She gazed curiously up at him. "You know, you look familiar somehow. Have we ever met before?"

He gave her a lopsided grin that was hiding more than a little anxiety. "Hell, in this crazy old world, who really knows?"

CHAPTER

71

THE PLACE WOULD NOW ALWAYS be hallowed ground for Nash. Fifteen miles away from her home Maggie's remains had been found in this wooded area off a rural road that very few people would ever go down. It had been a hunter, in fact, who had found what was left of her, the news had said. Out searching for a deer he'd shot, he had come across something that he thought were animal remains, until he had seen the bones of a human hand.

Maggie's hand, thought Nash as he pulled his truck to a stop behind some trees and well away from the spot where it was reported her remains had been discovered. He got out and walked into the woods. The police had long since finished their forensic search of the area and had left with the remains of his daughter. A DNA test had confirmed it was her.

Remains of a daughter. Something no parent should ever have to contemplate.

The now big, strong Walter Nash stopped and leaned against a tree, trying hard to keep his legs from buckling.

She had apparently been killed not too long after the video was posted. As Parker had noted, the police suspected Nash had found and killed her, then dumped her body here to rot. They had found bones, some of her beautiful hair, and two of her teeth. The rest, the police speculated, had been taken away by animals over the long passage of time.

That thought made him nearly vomit. As he was looking around for the actual spot where she had been found, he heard a car approach and Nash froze.

He quickly took up an observation post behind a large clump of holly bushes and waited. He thought it might be the police coming back for another look, but that didn't make much sense, not after all this time. Maybe it was whoever had killed Maggie. His fingers curled into fists at the thought.

At first he didn't recognize the person who stumbled into view a few minutes later.

The woman had on a hat pulled low. She was dressed in a billowy skirt. And despite the relative warmth of the night, she wore a heavy jacket. Her heeled shoes were not meant to be walking around muddy forest grounds. They sunk into the wet dirt, forcing her to tug them off and continue barefoot.

As she removed her hat, Nash saw that it was Judith. She staggered up to a certain spot and dropped to her knees. She settled her hands together, as though in prayer. A moment later she let out a scream the likes of which Nash had never heard before from either human or beast. It seemed to be the release of her very soul. She fell forward onto the dirt and clawed at it, her cries rising higher.

Part of Nash wanted to rush out, take the woman in his arms, and comfort her. Under any other circumstances, he would have. The tears slid down his cheeks from witnessing a mother's complete and devastating agony.

And she believes I abused and then killed our daughter and then dumped her here. Married for over twenty years and she could think I was capable of that.

Judith lay there prone in the dirt until the sobs ceased, until the fingers stopped clutching at where her daughter's remains had once been.

Then Judith slowly rose, picked up her hat and shoes, and said, "I'm so, so sorry, Maggie. I love you so much. I—" She couldn't finish. She turned and staggered back out of the woods. A couple of minutes later Nash heard a car start up, and he stayed in hiding until it had driven off.

He came out from behind the bushes and walked over to the

spot where his wife had been sprawled. That was when he saw what she had left there. There were actually several items: A bracelet that Maggie had given her. A picture in a frame that Maggie had drawn for her when their daughter had been a young child. A pom-pom that Maggie had used when she'd been a cheerleader in high school. They all looked weathered, indicating they had been here awhile.

This was a shrine, Nash concluded, that his wife apparently visited regularly.

And then he saw it, off to the side. The bits of fresh dirt showed that this was the object Judith had left here just a few minutes before.

It was the necklace she wore around her neck, with the locket on it.

He squatted down, picked it up, opened the locket, and looked at the picture of his daughter from the day she had been born. He had both taken the picture and purchased the locket for his wife. She had worn it every day since then.

Until today.

His tears dripped down on the picture while he stared at his beautiful and now-deceased child.

Later, back at his motel room, Nash pulled up a corner of the tattered rug and hid the locket and necklace there.

He spent the next few hours going over the flash drive that Shock had provided him with intel on Victoria Steers. Nash decided to set this up as a business problem to overcome. That put him more in his comfort zone. His prior research had revealed the types of business maneuvers she had used to launder funds through Sybaritic Investments. He had to think of a way to get back into those databases. It would not be easy because he had long since lost all security privileges there.

What he really needed was Agent Morris and the FBI to come back into the picture.

With that thought in mind Nash sent Morris a message: Can we still work this? I need to prove my innocence and I have every incentive in the world to bring down Rhett Temple and Victoria Steers.

He waited a half hour for a reply but got none. Restless, he once more drove out in his truck and headed downtown despite the late hour.

He parked across the street from the building where Rhett had his penthouse. He had been there several times for company functions and twice with Judith for dinner. With what he knew now had gone on between them, he wondered if they had snuck a kiss or an intimate touch while he was in the next room and they had been together in the kitchen supposedly getting the food plated. The thought sickened him.

He crouched lower when a car pulled down the street, traveling fast. It was Rhett's Porsche and the top was down. He was driving and there was a woman beside him. Her hair was swirling with the wind, but Nash had no problem recognizing Elaine Fixx.

The Porsche slowed to pull into the underground parking garage, and then the door closed behind the vehicle.

Nash imagined them getting out of the car and riding up to the very top, where they would get off at Rhett's penthouse and... Well, he doubted they were going to be discussing mergers and acquisitions at two in the morning. And she was married. Rhett just seemed to relish that sort of thing.

He sat up when his phone buzzed.

Well, what do you know? thought Nash.

Special Agent Reed Morris had messaged him back.

72

NASH QUICKLY SENT BACK A REPLY. He was driving with his AirPods in when Morris called him.

Morris said, "I won't ask where you are because I don't want to know. But first of all I want to express how sorry I am about your daughter, Walter. I have kids. I can't imagine what you must be going through. I just…"

Morris paused and Nash thought he could hear the FBI agent take a heavy breath that might have disguised a sob.

"Thank you, Reed. I appreciate that. Now I just have to hold those responsible accountable."

"Wait a minute. You're not thinking of going after Steers alone? That's suicide."

"I have no other choice. I don't see any other way to get to them."

"Losing you was a big setback. Everyone at the Bureau working on this was really impressed with what you had uncovered. And I won't deny that we've lost some morale and momentum."

"Then give me a chance to get it back."

"You're a wanted man. You can't exactly fly off to take on Steers."

"I will do what I need to do."

Morris didn't reply immediately. "Officially I'm not supposed to have any further contact with you."

"And unofficially?"

"You lost your daughter because of us, so screw my career," Morris retorted.

The two men remained silent for a bit until Morris said, "Give me some time to pull stuff together. I don't want anything else to blow up."

"I think certain things are going to blow up regardless of what we do or don't do."

"You're probably right," conceded Morris.

"Elaine Fixx has my old job at Sybaritic. I know her. She's good, smart, ambitious. And married. But she's having an affair with Rhett Temple."

"How do you know that?"

"I still have some contacts," he said vaguely. "Now, I told you that Barton Temple had me lined up to take the CEO slot when he died. Fixx was the backup because Barton did not trust Rhett to handle things after he was dead."

"So how did Rhett get his old job back? We tried to find out, but they're not a public company, and we couldn't get a search warrant without showing our hand. You got any ideas?"

"The board appoints the CEO. The majority of the shareholders appoint the board. Barton held a majority position in the Sybaritic stock. Rhett had some of the ownership, too, but not nearly enough to pull off his return. If Barton left the stock in trust for his other children? He had to do so with Angie Temple, his oldest child, who has an intellectual disability. Rhett might have found some way to gain control of any such trusts and with that the shares. Then he would be able to control the board, and name himself the CEO."

"But Barton was married. Wouldn't the widow have been left some of the stock, or be named as a trustee or hold a power of attorney for the disabled daughter?"

"Mindy was Barton's very young third wife, and she's all about spending money, not taking responsibility for someone else's children, who are all older than she is. But if she did have any of those rights, Rhett might have found something to blackmail her with or done a deal with her. Mindy then could've transferred any power of attorney or stock rights she had to him."

"Devious son of a bitch!"

"And on top of it I think he killed his father, but I already told you that."

"So why did you bring up Elaine Fixx?"

"She might be a possible ally for you, if it can be worked right."

"So, do you need anything? I wouldn't blame you if you don't trust me."

"I'm good. You do what you need to do, and let's regroup when you're ready."

"You know, Walter, you sound different. More... assured."

"But I also know that right now I am the world's biggest underdog."

Nash clicked off and kept driving into the rim of darkness.

CHAPTER

73

THE NEXT MORNING NASH WORKED out in his motel room using only his body weight. He then honed his close-quarter-combat skills against an imaginary opponent before disassembling and reassembling his weapons with his eyes closed. Nash knew he would have to find a gun range to keep up his skill set.

After that he went for a HITT run of five miles, alternating between sprinting and jogging, backward and forward. He had never felt lighter on his feet, or heavier in his heart.

I had a child and now I no longer do. My life is pretty much over, but I can get this done.

Back at his room he showered, and, since it had suddenly turned warm and humid, Nash changed into a tank top and cargo shorts, and walked to a local diner to get breakfast, leaving his guns locked up back at his room. He sat in the rear of the diner with his back to the wall and observed everyone coming and going as he assessed threat levels. He studied where every exit was along with possible weapon sight lines. He had never thought about any of this before, but now it was second nature.

When a police car pulled up in front and two officers came in to eat, Nash's gaze went to his phone and stayed there.

You look nothing like one of the most wanted men in the country, so just chill.

To prove this point, when one of the officers walked past him, probably to use the restroom down the hall, he stopped, glanced at Nash, and smiled.

"Nice tats," said the cop.

Nash looked up, and eyed the sword and shield tattoos on both the man's exposed forearms. "Yours too. Good ink."

The cop smiled again and headed on.

Nash didn't leave until after they did. As he was walking back he thought, *That was a victory, not a close call, Walter. Or Dillon, rather.*

He drove to the Sybaritic building and parked across the street. An hour later Rhett came driving up in his Porsche and entered the parking garage. Fixx was not with him. Nash assumed she had probably returned to her own home after the previous night so the two could keep up the subterfuge of just being work colleagues. He again wondered where Fixx's husband was. He had met the man at some company functions. He had struck Nash as a volatile sort who might lash out at any man bedding his wife.

Well, what husband wouldn't? I wanted to kill Rhett. I still do.

Twenty minutes later Fixx drove up in her red BMW and entered the parking garage.

Nash figured there was nothing more to learn here since he couldn't go into the building, throttle Rhett, and make him tell the truth. He instead drove out into the hills to Barton's estate. Well, not Barton's anymore. He wasn't sure who had inherited it. The gates opened as he neared them, and Mindy drove out in a four-seater Mercedes-Benz Cabriolet with the top down. He now thought he had his answer as to who had inherited the property. He also received some additional intel when he saw the car seat in the back with a baby in it.

Years back Barton had informed Nash about his vasectomy. They had been in Saudi Arabia on a business trip and a drunken Barton had let it slip: "I'm done with that shit in my life, Walt. You were smart to only have one."

Well, I don't have her anymore, thanks to you and your family.

Since Barton couldn't be the father of the child, Nash wondered who was.

His first thought clearly was Rhett. That also might explain what had happened to Barton, if Rhett was sleeping with the man's wife and Barton had perhaps found out.

He drove back to the motel, sat down with his computer, and again went over the flash drive on Steers that Shock had provided.

As with any due diligence on a business deal, you learned new things, possibly important things, on the second, third, and fourth passes.

Victoria had risen to the top in her quest to be the head of the Steers crime family. But the real question was: What had happened to her parents? There had been no sightings of either the mother or father for years, according to the FBI.

Had Steers killed them, too?

He next looked on the flash drive files at a list of aircraft owned by the Steers family. Jets had to be registered, and over a thirty-year period the Steerses, through their various companies, had owned multiple planes, both turboprops and jets. A shell company owned by an org affiliated with Victoria Steers had recently purchased a Bombardier Global 8000, a top-of-the-line private jet that could fly over halfway around the world on one tank of fuel. He next went back and compared the ownership of the various aircraft from each year. He discerned very quickly that there was a pattern here where the Steerses would sell the plane after roughly five years and purchase a newer model, as, no doubt, tastes, technologies, and wealth levels changed. They seemed to favor Gulfstream and Bombardier aircraft.

And that's when Nash noted one anomaly. Years ago the Steerses had owned a Learjet 75, a popular midsize aircraft. There was no paper trail of the aircraft's being sold or otherwise disposed of, even as new jets were bought and older ones sold. Yet any record of the Learjet 75 had simply disappeared off the books a number of years before. But a plane couldn't just disappear, could it?

He had the tail number and went on a database that he had learned about when Sybaritic had invested in a private jet company.

He stared down at the screen when the results of his search on the tail number had come up.

Nearly ten years ago, total hull loss. With the result the plane had been scrapped.

There were very few ways an aircraft could suffer a total hull loss.

And a plane crash was right at the top of that very short list.

He searched the news from ten years before and going forward for any story about a plane crash involving the aircraft. He found nothing. How the hell did you cover *that* up?

Could Steers's parents have been on that flight? And had it been sabotaged? Or shot down? If it had been something normal, there would have been no need to cover it up.

He messaged Morris with this information and then turned to the rest of the material on the flash drive. He found nothing else compelling, then checked his phone for the location of the nearest gun range. There was one about four miles away. He called, made a reservation, changed into jeans and a T-shirt, and drove there.

The owner, who was heavily tatted himself, asked about the chain-link designs on Nash's head.

"Personal" was all Nash said in response.

He laid his Glock and the Beretta on the table, put on safety goggles and ear protectors, carefully loaded his guns, and spent the next hour practicing his technique and aim. After he was done and had checked his targets, the owner, a fellow in his seventies with a Vietnam veteran's cap, strolled over.

"Damn fine shooting. And I was watching you, your stance and technique are textbook. You military, right?"

"My old man was. He taught me."

"Well, he taught you damn good. What was his name? Maybe I know him."

Nash almost said *Ty Nash*. "Jimbo Hope."

"Nope, don't know him. You from around here, fella?"

"Just passing through, but I like to keep my skills up."

"Smart man. Dangerous out there, you know."

As Nash packed up his weapons he said, "Yeah, I know."

CHAPTER

74

NASH TOOK UP HIS SURVEILLANCE spot outside of Rhett's penthouse for three nights in a row with no hits. But on the fourth night, at around one in the morning, Rhett showed. Sure enough, Elaine Fixx was right there with him. The car pulled into the underground garage and the door clanked down.

Thirty minutes later something intriguing happened. A van pulled down the road, did a U-turn, and parked across the street and farther down from where Nash was and killed its lights.

Nash slid down lower, pulled out a pair of night optics, courtesy of Shock, and took a gander.

Two men were in the front of the van. They looked big and tough and focused, like they were on a job. As Nash continued his observation, two other men in the back leaned into view and engaged in animated conversation with the driver and the passenger. They were all attired in black and they kept their gazes continually on Rhett's building. One of them bent down and picked something up. It was a baseball bat.

Okay, this is looking promising, thought Nash. When Nash had seen them together before, and being aware of Fixx's husband's volatile nature, a possible plan had formed in his mind. He now just needed a catalyst. And this might be it.

An hour later Rhett's Porsche pulled out of the garage, with Fixx once more in the passenger seat. The car turned left and Rhett gunned it.

As soon as the Porsche passed Nash, the lights on the van came on and it slid in behind the Porsche.

Nash fired up his truck, did a U-turn, and joined the chase.

They quickly left the city and headed up into the surrounding hills. As they kept going, Nash had a good idea where they were headed: the Temple estate. He wondered if Rhett had any clue about the tail, but he doubted it. He was probably fully engaged with Fixx. He wondered why Rhett would be bringing Fixx to the house where his stepmother was living, arguably with the child fathered by her stepson. But then again, Rhett had never been known for his logic or for common sense. Rhett was all about Rhett. And, in truth, it was a huge house; they could be in one part of it and no one the wiser.

When the Porsche made the last turn prior to the straightaway leading to the Temple property, the van sped up, hurtled past the Porsche, and cut it off, nearly running the other car off the road.

Nash had already killed his headlights. He slowed to a stop as he saw the four men emerge from the van. Two held baseball bats; the other pair wielded knives.

Nash grabbed a collapsible metal baton from his bag and quietly climbed out of the truck as the men surrounded the Porsche.

"Out of the car," barked one of the men.

Rhett said, "Look, I don't know what the hell—"

The man cracked the Porsche's windshield with one swing of the bat. "Out, now!"

A trembling Rhett slowly opened his door and stepped out, holding up his hands defensively. "Please, I—"

"Shut up," exclaimed the same man.

Fixx stayed in her seat, also shaking with fear.

"Out, bitch!" screamed the man. "Now!"

She climbed out of the car and stood trembling next to Rhett.

"Who *are* you?" asked Rhett. "I don't have any money on me, but I—"

"I told you to shut up!" The man looked at Fixx. "Ain't you married, slut?"

The blood drained from the woman's features. "Oh my God, did Roger—"

The man waggled the bat in Rhett's face. "Hope you had your fun with her tonight, asshole, 'cause it'll be the last night you'll be able to get *anything* up."

Rhett backed away. "Please, whatever he paid you I'll double, no, triple it. Just—"

The man punched him in the gut with the head of the bat.

Rhett collapsed to the asphalt struggling to breathe while Fixx screamed.

"Okay, I think you made your point."

They all turned to look at Nash, as he stepped from the edge of the deeper darkness and into their view. Nash held the baton out of sight while he eyed the four men and thought through his possible tactics and strategies, as Shock and Jackson had instructed him. This would be the second time he would deploy his new skills for real, but the two jerks back in the bar hadn't been wielding bats and knives. Still, there were always ways to overcome challenges if you stuck to what you had been trained to do, and allowed some latitude for any surprises that might crop up.

"Who are you, *hotshot*?" the same man, and the clear leader of the foursome, called out. He was nearly as tall as Nash, in his late forties, and overly bulky. When he moved, he did so jerkily. Bad hips and a bum right knee, Nash concluded. The man to his right was far shorter and muscle-bound. That would impede his flexibility and adaptability in close-quarter situations. The last two men were carbon copies of the other, six feet lean, around twenty-five, and they moved with catlike grace and power. They were also the ones armed with knives. They might pose a greater challenge than the other pair, Nash concluded, as, on a nod from the leader, they headed toward him.

Nash replied, "Good Samaritan. I suggest you get back in your van and head on."

"Four against one, dipshit," said one of the young men advancing on Nash.

Well, it's not four on one anymore, because you just separated yourself from the wolf pack. And I thank you in advance for your overconfidence.

When the pair were close enough they both held up their knives in a threatening manner. The same one said, "Where you wanna be cut—"

The one rule Shock had drilled into him above all others was *Don't waste time jawin'. Just fucken do it while they be gabbin' showin' off how tough they are.*

Nash smashed the first man in the kneecap with the baton and then jacked him with a punishing palm strike to the nose that knocked him out. As the man fell backward Nash whipped the baton around and took out the other man's knife, and hand, at the same time. Howling with pain, the injured man bent over and got Nash's size-twelve boot in his throat for his trouble. He stumbled backward gagging, and Nash helped him along with a sharp, direct punch to his sternum and another punch to his jaw. The man's eyes rolled up in his head and he collapsed into a deep sleep.

Two down for the count. Nash slowly advanced on the remaining twin problems.

Dollars to donuts they are going to do the stupid thing and rush me when they should use Rhett and Elaine as pawns to make me drop my weapon, or leave.

They rushed him.

The bat swung at Nash's head, but he was no longer there. The man with the bad hips and bum right knee stumbled awkwardly past him. Nash hooked the man's left leg with the baton, lifting it off the ground, and then swung around and used his boot heel to stomp the man's Achilles, driving it far beyond all tearing points. The man cried out and went down, clutching at his limb and moaning.

Nash eyed his remaining opponent, who was brandishing the bat but looking increasingly frantic, since he was the last *obstacle* standing.

"I'll make a deal with you," said Nash quietly. "I won't beat your brains out if you collect your friends, load them in the van, and drive away." He held up the baton. "So what will it be? Three...two..."

The man dropped the bat. "Okay, okay, shit."

Nash helped the man load his injured and/or unconscious comrades into the van, and then watched as they drove off.

Rhett, who had recovered from being gutted by the bat, hurried over to Nash, "Jesus, man, how can I ever thank you? You saved my butt."

Fixx came up and put her arm through Rhett's. "*Our* butts."

Nash noted that neither of them showed any hint of recognition toward him.

"Glad I could help," Nash said in the low, slow, throaty drawl he had adopted as his new manner of speech.

"Seriously, can I pay you? You deserve it. That was amazing."

"Not necessary. I was just helping out folks who needed it."

"How did you learn to do all that stuff?" asked Fixx.

"I'm in the private security business. High-net-worth individuals who need protection." He eyed the Porsche and then Rhett. "I don't know you, mister, but I would advise you to get some professional folks covering your six in case something like this happens again."

"My father had a team, but I let them go after he died. They were loyal to him, you understand."

"I understand."

"I was thinking about hiring a new team. I just haven't made a decision yet."

"Well, be extra careful until you get a new team on board." He started to walk off.

Take the bait, take the bait, Rhett.

"Wait, what's your name?"

Nash turned around. "Dillon Hope."

"You're obviously a pro at what you do."

"I take pride in it. I train for it. And I keep my skill set up-to-date."

Rhett took a card from his pocket and walked over to him. "Look, come and see me tomorrow at my office. Ten sharp. This little episode showed me that I *do* need protection."

Nash looked down at the card. "Let me email you my CV, Mr. Temple. You should check me out before hiring me."

"Good idea. My email's on the card."

"Okay, I'll see you at ten, Mr. Temple."

"Make it Rhett."

"If I'm going to work for you, sir, it's Mr. Temple."

Rhett looked at Fixx and grinned. "I'm liking this guy more and more."

"Can you drive with your windshield like that?" asked Nash.

"We only have a short way to go. Thanks again, and I'll see you tomorrow, Dillon."

"I'll follow you until you get to where you're going safely, Mr. Temple."

When they got to the estate gates, Nash honked and drove off.

I'm in.

CHAPTER

75

THE RAINDROPS HIT LIKE PISTOL shots against the roof under which Nash was trying to sleep. It was three in the morning when a bolt of lightning smacked down and lit the world outside his window, as though dawn had galloped ahead by several hours.

He rose and stared out the window at the rivulets of rain S-curving down the glass.

In his mind's eye he went back through every physical strike he had made against the men in saving Rhett and Elaine Fixx: ruined knee, crushed nose cartilage, destroyed hand, damaged esophagus, cracked sternum and jaw, snapped Achilles, and probably a blown-out psyche of the last guy.

He had observed, planned, adapted, and executed with near perfection.

But even though I had a good reason, I hurt those men more than I needed to, in order to get in good with Rhett. My old self was not cut out for this. It is not who I am. No, correction, it is not who I was. It is who I am now. I have to accept that. I never thought I could change who I was. But life gave me no choice. I have never felt so powerful... and powerless.

He leaned his head against the glass and felt the coolness of the storm that was exerting its full power just an inch on the other side.

I am changed on the surface. I am changed below the surface. I have no more surfaces that have not been altered. I am no longer Walter Nash 1.0. Like Shock said, I'm a completely different person, inside and out. But maybe, just maybe, there's a bit of Walter Nash 1.0 left.

He took out the locket from under the carpet, opened it, and stared down at the picture of his daughter on the day of her birth. It was a risk to keep this memento, he knew. But one look at her face gave him the resolve to carry on. And he needed that, very much.

He dropped back into bed holding on to the locket, slept hard for three hours, got up, did a particularly rigorous workout, and later sprinted through the wet streets until he thought he would heave. He showered and dressed, had breakfast at the same diner, and presented himself at Sybaritic Investments at 9:58 in the morning.

Ellen Douglas, the cookie-lady receptionist, greeted him, though she offered him no treats. He eyed her and she stared back at him, showing no inkling that she might be looking at the former number two in the entire corporation.

"Mr. Temple will be with you shortly, Mr. Hope."

"Thanks."

Two minutes later Rhett appeared dressed in a white silk shirt, tailored tobacco-colored slacks, and chic brown lace-up shoes, with no socks visible.

Nash had on a cheap off-the-rack two-piece suit, a skinny tie over a white shirt, and new black shoes, all of which he had purchased in the small town where Byron Jackson had dropped him off.

"Come on back, Dillon."

"Yes sir, Mr. Temple," replied Nash.

In Rhett's office, Nash sat while Rhett paced on the other side of his desk. The sun had come out from behind the gloom of clouds and exquisitely lit the office. For Nash, all shadows with their gray tints were gone, leaving all important objects in sharp, true relief.

I hope.

Rhett faced Nash and put his knuckles on his desk. "You look like you could bench-press a truck."

"The importance of brute strength is pretty much overrated. The most dangerous man I ever met was half my size with very little muscle."

"So what made him dangerous?" asked a puzzled Rhett.

Clearly thinking of Shock's story about Peanut, Nash replied, "He'd kill anyone without a second thought. Just made him faster and more efficient."

"Is he still around?"

"No."

Rhett started to say something, but then noted Nash's grim expression.

"Okay. Um, I checked out your CV. Impressive, very impressive. Bottom line is, I want you to be my bodyguard. But we need to get some things straight."

Nash said nothing; he just studied the other man.

Rhett sat down and drummed his fingers on his desk. "I lead a complicated life."

"I've never guarded anyone whose life wasn't."

"I may take it to another level. First, you cannot go everywhere with me. *And* you can't meet some people that I have to sometimes meet with."

"Are these places dangerous to you?"

"Why do you ask that?"

"I can't protect you if I'm not there."

"It's just the way things are," replied Rhett.

"FYI, whatever I see or hear, if it doesn't pertain to your protection, I don't remember it."

Rhett took a few moments to absorb this. "I...will take that into account."

"So where do we go from here?"

"What are your salary requirements?"

Nash told him, using the information that Shock had provided. "I like to remain an independent contractor. Easier for you and me. I handle my own taxes and everything else that way. You just pay the biweekly fee. Direct deposit is fine."

Rhett nodded. "Seems more than fair. My father had his guys on as full-time employees, health care, 401(k), the works. And I think you could have taken out those lazy assholes single-handed. Okay, my assistant will get you all signed up." He looked over Nash's clothes. "And I'm going to send you to my tailor. You have to look the part if you're going to be with me. All on my dime."

"Yes sir."

"Is that truck you were in last night the only vehicle you have?"

"Yes."

"I'll issue you a company car then. You like Porsches?"

"I don't know. I've never driven one."

Rhett grinned. "You'll like it." He paused. "The lady I was with last night?"

"Yes?"

"She's not my wife. I'm not married."

"But from what I heard last night, she is."

"Yes. But between you and me, it's not going to last. I'm not talking about her marriage. I'm talking about her and me."

"Yes sir."

"My father's security team was quartered at his estate in the hills, where we were headed last night. They also traveled with him."

"That's normally how it's done, sir. Security is no good if they're not with you."

"I'll arrange a room for you at the estate. Sometimes I'm at my penthouse here in town. If I'm there, you'll stay in a condo I own in the building, one floor below me."

"Understood."

"My stepmother, Mindy, lives at the estate as well, as does my older stepsister, Angie. She's got mental and emotional issues, and mostly stays in her room."

"Okay."

"Mindy has an infant daughter. She was my father's third wife," he added.

"And your father? You said he died?"

"Yeah, he killed himself, long story," Rhett said tersely. "We'll get you all set up and everything with the paperwork and all. Take about a week. I'm not going anywhere, so don't worry about my safety during that time." Rhett put out his hand. "Welcome aboard, Dillon."

It was all Nash could do not to crush the man's soft, manicured hand in his hard-earned, callused one.

"Thank you, Mr. Temple. *Really* glad to be aboard, sir."

A WEEK LATER NASH DROVE HIS new silver Porsche Boxster up the winding hills to Rhett's estate. He keyed the code he'd been given into the call box, and the gates swung inward. He drove through and parked next to a pale blue Porsche 911 S/T. If this was Rhett's ride, Nash figured, then the other convertible was still in the shop having its windshield repaired. Or maybe he'd scrapped it and just bought this one. Or five of them.

Billionaires were definitely not like the rest of humanity.

When Nash stepped out of his car he buttoned the jacket of his new, tailored, sleek black suit courtesy of his employer. Nash's white shirt gleamed against the sharp sunlight. The bump under his jacket heralded the presence of his Glock in a shoulder holster. The backup Beretta rode snugly on his ankle under his flared pantleg.

A man dressed in butler's livery answered the door, introduced himself as Colin, and led Nash up to the top floor, where Rhett was seated behind a desk in his father's former office. In a chair in front of him was Mindy, her sleeping daughter in her lap. The butler withdrew, and Rhett introduced Nash to his stepmother.

Nash looked at the baby and said, "What's her name?"

Rhett answered. "Amanda, Mandy for short. Your idea, right, Min?"

Nash knew that Amanda had been the name of Rhett's mother, to whom the man had been very close before her untimely death.

"Yes, it was," said Mindy in basically a mumble. She eyed Nash. "Rhett said you're here to protect us?"

"Well, me mostly," said Rhett. "Trouble seems to follow me."

"Your father had a team of four," she pointed out.

"And they still couldn't stop him from killing himself, could they?" replied Rhett, drawing a dark look from her. "So for me it's quality over quantity, and Dillon here has proven himself in that regard. When he's staying here, he'll be in the room across from yours. I gave you his cell number. Anything seems off, call him. Or just knock on his door," he added with a smile.

"Is there some specific threat?" Mindy asked. "Should I be worried?"

Nash spoke up. "Anyone with your level of wealth needs to be aware of the threat *potential*, Mrs. Temple."

"Just make it Mindy. I'm not formal."

"Actually I would prefer Mrs. Temple, if you don't mind, ma'am."

"O-kay," said Mindy.

"Man's a straight-up pro," said Rhett. "We're lucky to have him."

Mindy stared at the tats on Nash's head, but didn't comment. "Is that all?" she said instead. "I want to put Mandy down."

"Sure, go right ahead with the little cutie," said Rhett distractedly. She rose, looked at Nash, and said, "Nice to meet you."

"You too, Mrs. Temple. And I'm truly sorry for your loss."

"Thank you." She shot a glance at Rhett before hurrying off.

Rhett pointed to the French doors behind him. "My father walked out those doors and jumped off the balcony. Ended his life on the pavers. He was terminal with a nasty cancer. Wanted to go out his way. It was probably impulsive. Think it and then do it." Rhett added in a resigned tone, "I tend to be a little impulsive, too. Knee-jerk. Maybe it's in the genes."

"Can I make an observation, Mr. Temple?"

"Waiting with bated breath," quipped Rhett.

"If someone *really* wants to kill you, and they're willing to die to do it, there's not much that I or anyone else can do to truly stop that person."

"Then why am I paying you?" barked Rhett.

"You're paying me to keep you out of situations where someone like that *can* kill you. It's all odds and percentages, sir. So the more 'knee-jerk' you are, the more opportunities you give suicidal lone wolves to end your life." Nash said all of this slowly and calmly.

Rhett sat back, all contrite now. "I get that, Dillon. Good call. Okay, I'll ride with that."

"Yes sir. Me too."

77

A WEEK LATER, NASH WAS IN Rhett's office at the Temple estate discussing some security details at the property when there was a knock at the door. It was Colin, the butler. Behind him Nash saw Detective Ramos. He sat up a bit straighter and kept his gaze averted.

Rhett rose and said, "Detective? What can I do for you?"

Ramos planted his gaze on Nash. Rhett said, "My bodyguard, Dillon Hope."

Nash shook hands with him, then went and stood in the corner, while the detective sat across from Rhett.

Ramos eyed Nash again and said to Rhett, "This is confidential, sir."

Rhett glanced at Nash. "You can say anything in front of him you want to say to me."

Ramos shrugged. "Okay. Are you still in touch with Mrs. Nash?"

"I am, yes, why?" asked Rhett.

"The thing is, sir, we've seen her out at the spot where her daughter's remains were recovered."

"What do you mean you *saw* her?"

"We've kept an eye on the place from time to time, just in case anyone shows up there. Killers sometimes come back to see if they missed anything."

Nash felt his gut clench and he lowered his gaze to the floor. *If they saw me…?*

"I didn't know she was doing that," said Rhett, looking genuinely concerned.

"And another thing. She's apparently leaving items related to her daughter there."

Rhett leaned forward. "Items related to her daughter? What sorts of things?"

"A pom-pom, a framed picture, that sort of thing."

Rhett sat back and adopted a weary expression. "Look, I've tried to get her to seek counseling, but she refuses. I'll keep trying."

"I just worry that her, well, *obsession* might lead to something... personally destructive."

"Understood. I'll do whatever I can. Anything else?"

"Yes, we discussed a long while back that the pathologist suspected that your father's death was not a suicide, but a homicide."

"I'm not convinced of that. And you never said why the pathologist concluded that."

"There were marks around the neck, and the hyoid bone was fractured."

"Excuse me, the hyoid bone?"

"Yes, when it's damaged or broken, it usually means someone was strangled. Now, they ran some additional tests recently and because of backlogs and paperwork snafus I just got those results, which is the reason I came to see you."

"What results?" said Rhett dully.

"It took specialized testing by an outside expert, but it has now been determined that one of the marks on your father's face was not caused by the impact with the ground. It was blunt force trauma caused almost certainly by a fist. This was determined by an exacting examination of the indentations of the skin at that spot, the manner in which the facial bones were damaged, and the like. It was difficult because the impact with the ground tended to cover up any such underlying and preexisting injuries. That was why additional testing was called for. And it took a great deal of time. We even had to have the body exhumed."

Rhett looked outraged. "You exhumed my father's body? Without telling me? Or getting my approval?"

Ramos didn't look so deferential to Rhett right now, Nash noted.

His look was one of professional stiffness. "It's a homicide investigation, Mr. Temple. We didn't *need* your approval."

Rhett immediately backed down. "Right, of course. I'm sorry if I implied that you did. I'm just...this is just so out of left field. So you think someone struck my father and then strangled him, breaking his hyoid bone?"

"Yes sir."

"Did he die by strangulation?"

"No. The impact with the ground killed him. That was conclusive."

"So what are you envisioning actually happened?"

"He was beaten or strangled until he was unconscious, and then he was carried through those doors and thrown off the balcony."

"It would have taken a strong man or men to do so. My father was not small."

"Yes it would."

"And this supposedly happened with his team of bodyguards nearby, my stepmother two floors below, and the butler nearby in his room?"

"You suggested that Walter Nash might have had reasons to kill your father."

It was fortunate that neither man was looking at Nash. It took all his willpower not to pull his weapon and shoot Rhett in the head. He did his four-and-four breathing and became a statue once more.

Yet as he looked at Rhett, he saw something he had seen before in the man when he had been involved in business negotiations. *He sees an opportunity and he's about to go for it.*

Rhett said smoothly, "As I told you before, I gave Nash a big raise and other perks right before the disgusting truth came out about his daughter. I did so because my father ordered me to. It had nothing to do with Nash's business performance. Between you and me, he was actually pretty mediocre at his job. I had to step in quite often to rectify some of his poor decisions. He was probably consumed with all the heinous stuff he was doing to his daughter."

"I'm sure," commented a clearly interested Ramos.

During this exchange Nash had fixed his gaze on a spot across the room. It was a painting of a dog running across a field with a little girl trailing behind. He imagined the girl was Maggie, and the dog was his beloved labradoodle, Charly.

That was when Nash realized he had found his Sunshine, like his father had when he'd been a POW. He calmed dramatically.

Ramos continued, "You said before that you suspected that Nash was blackmailing your father."

"Yes. With him being terminally ill he might have been about to expose Nash."

"Right, but did Nash know that your father was dying?"

Nash glanced at Rhett to see the man's reaction to this query. Once more, he was observing a man who had been caught in a lie and was now searching for some plausible answer that would legitimize his false narrative. He had seen Rhett do this many times when confronted by his father over some mistake or bad business decision. Rhett normally tried to shift any blame to other parties, sometimes including Nash.

"I…I'm not sure. But Nash was very resourceful and could have found out. Or, hell, my dad could have confronted him and told him what he was going to do. That was the way he was. My father got in your face. And with what happened with Maggie, we know what Nash was capable of."

"You really think he killed her, too?" said Ramos.

"Who else? And you told me you had evidence against him, right? Hair and stuff?"

"Yes, his hair and clothing fibers were found in her bed. They matched hair from his hairbrush, and the fibers were from clothes we found in the bottom of one of his drawers. And to your point about him being involved in Maggie's death we found a hair fiber with her remains. It matched samples we had taken from Nash's hairbrush."

"And there was evidence he was involved in that other murder, right?" said Rhett. "You told me and Mrs. Nash about it."

"That's right, his shoe prints were found at the scene of the crash where the security guard was run off the road and killed."

"Okay, I truly believe you have your man. Now you just need to find the scum."

Nash thought about his hairbrush and the missing clothes and shoes. The frame had been well done, he had to admit.

Ramos said, "FYI, we checked your alibi with Laurel Burke a while back and she confirmed you were with her the whole time."

"That's right. And I had no reason to kill him."

Nash drew his gaze from the painting to his new boss. *Except for billions of reasons.*

Ramos said, "Now, this is delicate, but do you think anyone here at this house could have been working with Nash to kill your father? Because, as you alluded to, it seems like more than a one-person job."

Nash once more could tell that Rhett was thinking quickly to deliver falsehoods to the detective that would support his supposition of an "inside person."

"Well, to be frank, that's one reason I let my father's old security team go. I...well, I just didn't trust them."

Ramos nodded in understanding. "I thought you might say that. And we will run those leads down. Now, this is even more delicate. Your stepmother?"

"Yes?"

"Any, um, concerns there vis-à-vis your father's death? I'm assuming she inherited a great deal of money."

Nash listened to this particular exchange intently. This might tell him a lot, considering that he well knew how Rhett's mind worked, especially if he sensed personal danger.

Rhett was already shaking his head. "None. Mindy was devoted to my father. She had his child. And he was terminal. If she wanted him dead so she would inherit, well, all she had to do was wait a few months."

Ramos nodded. "I thought so, too, but I just wanted to get your opinion. In fact, full disclosure, we asked her about you and she told us she believed you had no involvement in your father's death. And she confirmed that you were not here that night."

"Well, it's the truth," declared Rhett.

"I won't take up any more of your time, sir. Just following up."

Nash had swiftly processed all this. Rhett had not thrown Mindy under the bus, which would have been his first instinct. But something had prevented the man from defaulting to his usual ploy of blame shifting. The reason hit Nash before Ramos had even finished speaking.

She was with Rhett when Barton died. They're covering up for each other.

As Ramos rose to leave, Rhett said, "Any word on Nash?"

"Unfortunately no. It's like the man has vanished into thin air. But we'll keep you in the loop."

After Ramos had left, Rhett said, "It's time to go to the office. I have someone to deal with today, and I want you there with me, Dillon."

"Yes sir."

As they walked from the room Nash looked at the little girl and her dog, running free and deliriously happy.

The exact opposite of his reality.

YOU'RE DEMOTING ME? AGAIN? ARE you serious?"

Elaine Fixx was standing behind the desk in Nash's old office and looking incredulously at Rhett.

"Just back to your old position, Elaine."

"But why?"

"Well, if it wasn't enough that thugs hired by your husband nearly killed me, then there's also the fact that you have no experience as a senior executive."

Fixx glanced over at Nash, who stood fixedly by the door. "Look, Rhett," she said pleadingly. "I talked to Roger. I told him if he ever tried something like that again that he would go to prison."

"Oh, he's *going* to prison. I've sworn out a complaint with the police. And then I'm going to sue his ass off."

"What?"

"You couldn't think that I would just let him walk on this, right? I'd probably be dead if it weren't for this guy," he added, pointing at Nash. "I engaged a PI firm. They've traced the idiots who jumped us and they turned on your hubby. He's going to have a few years of solitude to reconsider the error of his ways."

"But I . . . I was the one who drove him to this by having an affair with you."

"Well, that's between him and you. My concern right now is your position at this firm. So you can clear out of here and go back to your old office."

"And who's replacing me?" she said bitterly.

"I've actually arrived at the conclusion that I can wear both hats."

"*You're* taking Walter's old job?"

"You make it sound like he was something special?"

"Well, he was."

Rhett drew closer to her. "You keep up that attitude, you won't have any job here at all, sweetie."

She glanced nervously at Nash. "Rhett, does this mean that you and I ...?"

He looked at her condescendingly. "Of course it does, Elaine. But with your hubby going to prison, you'll find someone, I'm sure of it." He looked her up and down like he was appraising a product at the store. "Just don't let yourself go. Men don't like that."

"I'll get my things boxed up," she said, staring at her shoes.

Nash watched as the man had the gall to pat the woman's bottom. "Come on, quit with the pouty face. And who really knows about us? Nothing is permanent, right? So the fun times might come back. All depends on you and your *performance*."

He walked out and Nash started to follow. But as he saw the tears sliding down Fixx's cheeks he pulled some tissues from a box on her desk and handed them to her.

"Here, ma'am. Are you going to be okay?"

She snatched them from him and said angrily, "Better go catch up with your asshole boss, you son of a bitch."

Nash turned and left.

* * *

That evening, Nash stood next to Rhett as they rode the elevator to his penthouse. When the doors opened directly into Rhett's home, they stepped out.

Nash pulled his weapon while Rhett took a quick step back as the woman came into view.

She was petite and slender. Her hair was long and white, although she was only around thirty-five, Nash assessed, as he kept himself between her and Rhett.

"Who in the hell are you?" barked Rhett.

"My name is Lynn Ryder."

"How did you get up here?" Rhett demanded.

"The man at the front desk was persuadable."

"Persuadable how?"

Ryder shifted her gaze to Nash. "There is no need for guns."

Nash didn't lower his weapon.

She turned back to Rhett. "Our mutual acquaintance sent me. To assist you in the task she has given you and for which there has been no resolution."

"What task?" asked a still-confused Rhett.

"To locate someone important to *both* of you? He has unexpectedly gone missing?"

As he realized what the woman was referring to, Rhett let out a breath and said to Nash, "It's okay. She's cool. I...I know her boss."

They all moved into the front room with views of the cityscape. Nash had reluctantly put his gun away, but kept his gaze locked on Ryder.

She eyed Nash and then looked back at Rhett, who glanced at Nash. "Dillon, you can go to your place. I'll call when I need you."

"You're sure, Mr. Temple?"

"Very sure."

With one more look at Ryder, Nash nodded and left them. Right before he entered the elevator, he touched the side of a tall, wooden pedestal that held the statue of a miniature horse in full stride. Then he got on the elevator and used his security card to go to the floor below.

He put his AirPods in and dialed up an app on his phone. The voices came through loud and clear on the listening device he had stuck to the back of the pedestal.

He got to his apartment and continued to listen. The conversation was brisk and businesslike, especially from Lynn Ryder. A couple of minutes later he heard the elevator coming up and then a few moments later going back down.

Two minutes later Rhett texted him: Be ready to go in half an hour.

Nash sent a message to Agent Morris detailing the latest with Elaine Fixx, and providing her contact info.

Then he wrote out for Morris the new information on the police investigation into Barton Temple's murder that he had learned from listening to Detective Ramos.

Last, he compiled a comprehensive brief for the FBI agent on what had just taken place between Rhett and Victoria Steers's agent, Ryder. He figured Morris would be especially excited about that one.

Nash had also heard the marching orders Rhett had been given by Ryder, and figured what his part would be in where he and Rhett were going.

He wants me to help him track down...me.

79

"EVERYTHING GOOD WITH MS. RYDER?" Nash asked as he and Rhett headed out in Rhett's Porsche.

"Look, she's part of what I talked about before. Where you can't really be."

"You're the boss. So, where are we headed now?"

"A friend's place. I haven't seen her in a while and I want to check on her."

A bit later Nash tensed as they turned down the road to his old neighborhood. He then noticed that Rhett had a security strip on his windshield that allowed him to get through the gate without the guard having to let him in.

Things definitely have changed in that regard.

The closer they drew to his old home, the more nervous Nash became. He knew that he looked nothing like his old self. He had obviously fooled Rhett, and Rosie Parker, and Elaine Fixx, Ellen Douglas the receptionist, and Detective Ramos, who, in varying degrees of familiarity, knew the old Nash. But none of them were Judith. And Nash was suddenly afraid that despite everything he had done to make Walter Nash disappear from the face of the earth, it might all be blown up in a couple of minutes. Would Judith be able to see beneath the tats and muscles and broken nose? The anticipatory dread was eating away his gut lining.

They pulled into the front of Nash's old home and he had to disguise his surprise. The dead grass was nearly calf high and there were more weeds in the flower beds than plants.

"Who lives here?" he asked.

"My friend Judith. She's Walter Nash's wife."

"Okay."

Rhett had a key and used it to unlock the front door.

Another change, thought Nash, willing himself to remain calm.

"Judith!" Rhett called out as they went inside. He turned to Nash. "I tried phoning and texting, but she usually doesn't answer."

Nash was busy glancing around, and while not exactly surprised by what he was seeing given the abysmal state of the landscaping, he was still taken aback. Kept immaculate by his wife when they had all lived here, the place looked like several people were squatting in his former home. There were overflowing plastic bags of trash everywhere, along with piled-up Amazon and pizza boxes. Plates of dried food were stacked on the dining room table. More trash bags were piled up in the hall. Clothing and shoes were strewn about. The smells all around them had a fuggy, unsettling odor.

"Is she...okay?" Nash asked.

A worried-looking Rhett said, "Not really. Give me a sec."

He jogged up the steps to the second floor while Nash went into the kitchen and found it just as foul as the rest of the rooms he'd seen. Judith clearly had fired the cleaning service they'd used. When he looked out the rear window he saw that the pool, which should have been closed by now for the season, was full of debris and the water dark.

He opened the door to the garage and spied Judith's Mercedes. His heart fell when he looked at Maggie's BMW.

"Hey, Dillon!"

Nash took the steps two at a time and arrived in the master bedroom following Rhett's cries.

"Yes, sir?"

He found Rhett in the sitting room, where he was kneeling next to Judith, who was sprawled on the couch, half-clothed. Her hair was unkempt, and Nash saw that his once fitness-obsessed wife looked bloated, her skin pasty and blotched.

"Is she all right?" he asked, trying to keep his voice level and calm.

"She's breathing okay but her pulse seems weak. And I can't get her to wake up."

Nash looked around and saw the bottle of prescription pills. He picked it up.

"Ativan," he said as Rhett looked up at him. "She might have taken too many." He knelt down and helped Rhett to lift Judith to her feet.

"Let's walk her around some to see if she'll rouse," Nash suggested.

They did so, taking turns calling out her name. After five minutes of this, Judith finally stirred. She looked first at Rhett and then at Nash, who would not meet her eye.

This was the ultimate test, he knew. If anyone could see past his transformation, it would be Judith. But then again, she seemed so out of it that any sort of recognition on her part would probably be impossible.

"I'll go down and make some coffee," said Rhett. "You stay with her and try and keep her awake."

He left. Nash put his arm around Judith's waist and used his strength to hold her up, which was easy despite the weight she had put on. He was amazed at how fleshy she had become, and he wondered if it was simply bad food and no exercise, or whether something else was going on.

Was she retaining fluids? Did she have a kidney issue?

He spied the empty wine and liquor bottles that were piled in one corner of the room and thought that too much alcohol was a big part of the problem his wife was facing.

"Ju— Mrs. Nash? Stay with me. Stay awake, okay? Let's go. You can do this." He was modulating his voice dramatically to keep it as far away from his actual tone as possible.

When she seemed to be slipping back into a deep sleep, he picked her up in his arms and shook her. This caused Judith to rally, and she clutched tightly to his shoulders.

"Who the hell are you?"

He glanced down to see that she was staring up at him.

"I...I work for Rhett Temple. He's downstairs making some coffee. I think you took too many pills, ma'am."

"There's no such thing as too many pills. There's only too *few* pills, that's a thing." She belched heavily and pushed against him. "Put me down. I feel sick."

He did so but when she started to heave, he snatched her up and carried her to the bathroom. He supported her over the toilet as she threw up twice. He figured that might be a good thing, to get some of the medication out of her system.

When she was done he grabbed a washcloth and wet it. He ran it over her forehead and face, and across the back of her neck.

"Are you feeling better now?" he asked.

She nodded and, with his help, slowly stood.

He led her back into the sitting room, where he helped her down onto the couch. She leaned back, and tucked her bare feet beneath her.

"Who are you again?"

"He works for me, Judith," said Rhett as he came in with a large mug of steaming coffee. "Here, drink this, you'll feel better. And here are some peanut butter crackers."

"I threw up, Rhett."

"I'm sure. Here, drink it and eat some crackers."

She took several sips and managed to eat two of the crackers.

Rhett and Nash stood back and watched her as she ran a hand through her dirty hair and then looked up at them guiltily. "I didn't have a very good day, Rhett," she said in an almost schoolgirl voice that made the hair on Nash's arms tingle.

Rhett sat down next to her and gripped her hand. "Yeah, I can see that." He snagged the bottle of pills. "I'm taking these with me, Judith. This is the *second* time. You can't keep doing this. Something bad will happen, honey."

"Something bad *has* happened!" she exclaimed. "Maggie is dead!"

"I know, I know," he said soothingly. "And I'm so sorry. So very sorry for it all."

Judith set her cup down, leaned over, and put her face in her hands. "I don't know how much more of this I can take, Rhett, I really don't."

"I offered to get you help a dozen times. I know people, good people, who deal with this sort of thing all the time. They can help you, Judith."

"I don't want any help. I don't *deserve* any help."

"None of this is your fault. It's his fault, your husband's. This whole fucking nightmare is down to Walter, not you."

Nash glanced out the window and in his mind's eye he conjured the painting of the girl and the dog. But Nash wasn't sure how much more of this *he* could take.

"I've been thinking about that."

Nash shot her a look because her voice had suddenly become more like the old Judith—focused and firm.

She took several more sips of coffee, ate another cracker, and composed herself.

"You've been thinking about what?" asked Rhett, with an edge to his voice that Nash did not care for at all.

"The night Maggie disappeared, we had an argument."

Rhett looked up at Nash and said, "Dillon, go wait outside."

Nash glanced at Judith and then nodded and walked out. But he didn't go far and he left the door open, so he could still hear their conversation.

"An argument? About what?" asked Rhett.

"She knew I'd been with another man. She didn't know it was you, but she knew that I'd had sex. And do you know what she told me?"

"What?"

"That I didn't deserve Walter. That he doted on me, loved me with all his heart. That he was too good for me."

"I'm not following—"

"Why would she have said those things if he was going into her bedroom and doing all those awful things to her? Why would she have gone online and said he was abusing her just a few days later? Why didn't she tell *me* that the night of our argument? She could have opened up, told me the truth. But she didn't. Why!"

Rhett said nervously, "I don't know, Judith. These things are complicated. She could have been in shock. She could have been confused. Sexual abuse by a parent can do funny things to you, or so I've been told."

Judith shook her head before looking directly at him. "Do you know what I think?"

"What?" said Rhett with a tightness to his voice.

"I think Walter was telling me the truth when he denied abusing her."

"Then why did he run?"

"Because I called the police."

"Are you saying your own daughter was lying about all of it? Is that what you're saying!"

She let out a sob and dipped her head. "I don't know. I just don't know. I can't figure out that part, why she would, why Maggie would…"

Rhett said gently, "Look, you just need to get some rest. And no more pills."

She shot him a pleading look. "Do you…do you have the other stuff?"

"You can't combine it with Ativan, Judith. It could really screw you up."

"But you will get me some more?"

"Yes, yes I will."

"Promise?"

"Promise."

Outside in the hall, Nash, who had heard most of this, felt his hands turn to fists.

Do not kill him. Do not. Not yet.

Rhett said, "Judith, I also came by because I had some questions to ask you."

"What questions?"

"If you really think Walter is innocent, the best thing we can do is find him. I can get him a great lawyer."

"But I don't know where he is," she said.

"But you could have some information that might help us locate him. You said he left here with a bag?"

"Yes."

"You know him better than anyone. Do you have any idea where he might have gone? A favorite vacation spot? A place where you two were thinking of buying a second home?"

She shook her head, looking exhausted. "No, nothing like that. You know he didn't take many vacations, and we never saw a need for a second home."

"Okay, how about friends or other people who might have helped him?"

"He really didn't have any friends. But his father was living with a woman named Rosie Parker. She lives in their old house where Walter grew up. He was going to meet with her in connection with his father's will. She might know something."

Rhett rose and went over and quietly shut the door. When Nash heard him do this, he quickly retreated down the stairs.

Rhett returned to Judith and sat next to her. "Good, good, see, you *do* have information that's useful," he praised. "What else? Anything, even if it seems unimportant."

She took another drink of coffee and sat back. "The guard at the gate told me that a big Black man on a Harley had come to visit Walter here shortly after his father's funeral. Walter didn't seem pleased, the guard said. But then Walter never mentioned it to me. What happened between them, I mean."

"What was the Black guy's name? Do you know?"

"I'm not sure. I seem to remember...something." She brightened. "Shock, that's it. Shock. Walter told me about him. His stupid nickname and all. And he said some terrible things about Walter."

"Wait, this was the same guy you told me about before? Who insulted Walter at his father's funeral service?"

"Yes. It has to be the same person."

"And how did Walter know this *Shock* person?"

"He and Walter's father served together in Vietnam. Walter probably doesn't know this, but I saw a picture he had in his study. I'm not sure where it came from, but I know he picked up some things from his father's house after the funeral. His father was in the photo, and a big Black man. They were obviously in Vietnam at the time. The man must've been this Shock person. I mean, it was taken a long time ago, but I'm sure it was the same man who was at the church."

"Do you know his real name?"

"No."

"Do you have the picture?"

"It's not in the study anymore. I looked but it's gone."

"Do you mind if I look?" asked Rhett.

"No, I suppose not."

"You stay right here and rest."

Rhett walked over, opened the door, and called out to Nash, "Dillon, come up and stay with her. I need to look for something in the study."

Nash, who had heard none of the latter part of Rhett and Judith's conversation, hustled up the steps from the kitchen. "Yes sir."

The last thing Nash wanted to do was let Rhett search his study, but there was really nothing he could do to stop him without giving everything away.

He entered the room and sat down across from Judith. She closed her eyes and appeared to be dozing. He was so focused on what Rhett might find that he didn't notice her staring at him until a couple minutes later when Nash looked up to find her gaze full upon him.

She said, "What do you do for Rhett?"

"Personal security."

She nodded, running her gaze over him. "You look like you can do that well. You look very strong and...capable. My husband was very capable, just not in the same way." She focused on his scalp. "What are those things on your head?"

"Tattoos."

As Judith looked at them, something tangible seemed to pierce the druggy façade around her brain, but then it faded away and her expression became distant.

Nash shouldn't have, but he had to. "I...understand that you lost a child?"

She refocused on him. "Yes. People think my husband killed her."

"What do you think?" asked Nash.

"I..."

Before she could finish Rhett burst back into the room holding a piece of paper. "Bingo."

"What is it?" asked Judith, as Nash looked on uneasily.

"A letter Walter's father wrote to him, I guess right before he died. I found it in a desk drawer. His father said if Walter ever needed help that this *Shock* guy would be there for him. So all I need to do is find out his real name. Hey, this woman friend of his?"

"Rosie Parker?" said Judith.

"Yeah. Do you have the address?"

"Yes. We dropped Walter's mother off there numerous times over the years."

She gave Rhett the address, and he input it into his phone.

He sat and gave Judith a quick hug. "Okay, let me get a cleaning and landscape crew over to get this place back right. Please, Judith. I offered before but you kept saying no."

"Let me think about it, Rhett. I'm just so tired."

"Okay, but no more pills?" She nodded, and he looked at Nash. "Let's roll. Maybe we can find this Parker person at home."

Rhett hurried out the door. As Nash was leaving Judith gripped his hand. He looked down at her.

"I should have believed my husband. I... when I saw my daughter, what she was saying."

"I can understand, ma'am. It must have been overwhelming."

"But it shouldn't have been hard," she replied as tears started trickling down her cheeks. "I'd been married to him for twenty years. I knew Walter, the sort of person he was. He would never... do... that." She looked up at him. "I wish I could tell him so."

"He may know, ma'am."

"How?" she said fiercely. "How?"

"You say you knew him?"

"Yes."

"Well, it sounds to me like he also knew you."

She held his gaze for a few seconds before saying, "Thank you for helping me... when I was... sick."

"No problem, ma'am. All you've been through, well, it's understandable." He looked in the direction of the door, then knelt down in front of her and gripped both her hands.

"I don't know what happened to your daughter, but I do know that she would not want you to do anything... to hurt yourself. So, please, just be okay, all right? I know things seem really dark right now. But sometimes the light is just a few feet away."

She squeezed his hands and nodded. "What's your name?"

Despite everything, Nash almost said *Walter*. "Dillon, Dillon Hope."

"Thank you, Dillon."

Rhett called out to him from the main floor. "Let's go, Hope!"

Nash rose, gave Judith one more meaningful glance, and then hustled out.

As the Porsche drove away, Judith stood at the window, watching.

80

Nᴀsʜ ᴡᴀs ʙᴇʜɪɴᴅ ᴀɴᴅ ᴛᴏ the left of Rhett as he knocked on the door of Nash's childhood home. He heard footsteps coming and tensed. He had formulated a plan, an absurdly tricky one timing-wise, and he just hoped to hell it worked, or else it was all over.

The door opened and there she was. She looked at Rhett first and then when her gaze caught on Nash, he immediately shook his head and mouthed the words, *You've never seen me.*

She froze but only for a moment.

"Yes?" she said, looking back at Rhett. And then Parker flinched, and Nash knew it was because she had just recognized a man whom Nash now knew the woman loathed.

"Are you Rosie Parker?"

"Yes. What is this about?"

"Walter Nash worked for me, and we were trying to see if we could find him."

"Well, if the police can't, I'm not sure how you can."

"Might we come in?"

Her eyes drifted to Nash, who once more shook his head.

"No, I'm getting ready to go out. I don't have time."

"Okay," said Rhett as he took the letter out. "Walt's father wrote him this letter before he died. He said that if Walt ever needed help he should get in touch with a guy named Shock, who was apparently his father's friend. He's a big Black guy. Do you know him?"

Parker again looked at Nash, and he shook his head.

To her quick-witted credit, Parker also subtly moved to her right to block the view of the framed photo on the wall that Nash had

seen on his last visit here, of Ty Nash and Shock. "I don't know anyone named Shock."

"But that was just a nickname."

"I still don't know him."

"But I understood that he was at the funeral service. This big
Black guy who said some nasty things about Walt. That had to be
this Shock guy. Weren't you at the funeral?"

Parker didn't chance looking at Nash again. "Of course, yes,
that's right, a tall Black man. He did say some terrible things about
Walter at the service. I guess I'd just blocked it out of my mind. It
was awful."

"But you don't know who he is?" asked Rhett.

"No, I mean he's never been around here before. Ty obviously
knew him, but I only knew Ty for two years before he died. I didn't
get a chance to meet most of his old friends."

"Did his father ever mention any of his son's friends?"

"They were estranged. Ty never spoke about him."

Rhett looked crestfallen and slipped the letter back into his
pocket. "Yeah, Walt did mention that to me. Okay, um, well, I guess
that's it." He handed her a business card. "But if anything should
occur to you, please call me. I will make it worth your while."

She nodded curtly and shut the door.

Once they were back in the car Rhett turned to Nash. "Did it
seem like she was acting a little odd?"

"Well, I think *I* would have acted a little odd if someone had
shown up on my doorstep and started asking those sorts of
questions."

"Yeah, I guess you're right. But that's okay. My private detectives will be able to track this Shock guy down."

"And then what?"

"And then we pay him a visit."

"You want to find Nash so the cops can arrest him?"

"If he did what he's accused of, he should be in prison."

"How often do you go over and check on his wife?"

Now Rhett gave Nash a dark stare. "You just pay attention to your job, Dillon. And I'll worry about everything else. Understood?"

"Understood, Mr. Temple."

Rhett glared at him for a moment before gunning the engine, and the Porsche's turbos accelerated the car like a badass with a purpose.

CHAPTER

81

RHETT DROVE THEM TO THE estate in the hills and not back to the penthouse. Nash walked to his room two doors down from Rhett's bedroom and across the hall from Mindy's. He had passed her in the corridor, where she gave him a half-hearted smile.

He opened the closet and saw three suits in different colors hanging there, along with shirts. There were shoes underneath that fit his feet perfectly. Rhett had taken care of all of this, and had tailored clothing for him both here and at the penthouse. The drawers were filled with underwear and socks, other accessories, and more casual clothing.

Nash had no idea how much it had all cost, but with Rhett what did it really matter? He was in the rarefied position of never being able to spend even the interest on, much less the principal of, his wealth.

Nash took a few minutes to send off a long communication to Shock bringing him up to date on how they knew about him, and also that Nash was now Rhett's bodyguard.

Just lay low until you hear from me. And I'm sorry to have brought this on you.

Shock's almost immediate response was telling: Don't worry about us. How are you doing? You ever need us, we are here for you.

I'm fine. Thanks for everything, Shock. I would not be here without your help.

Nash got up the following morning, put on his workout clothes, and headed to the gym complex. He did weights, cardio, stretching, and yoga. Then, using an imaginary knife, he practiced disabling and/or killing a boxing dummy that was a twin of the one at Shock's facility.

After two hours the sweat was pouring off his shirtless torso.

He sat down on a bench, toweled off, and looked up when she said, "Impressive."

Mindy was standing in the gym doorway dressed in a silver leotard and black leggings. She was barefoot. Her hair was tied back and she was holding a rolled-up yoga mat. "I think you killed that poor dummy like a hundred times."

He finished toweling off and stood. "Yeah, well, just part of the business."

"Turn around."

"Excuse me?"

"Your body art. Just want to see if it's on both sides."

He turned around and she said, "Wow, the lion's muscles ripple when yours do. And the dice are cool."

He turned back and eyed the yoga mat. "You finished or just starting?"

"I did my yoga in the studio next to this room. Barton built out this wing for me."

"I'm lucky to have access to it." He paused. "Mr. Temple said it was okay, but if—"

She waved this off and said, "This house belongs to Rhett. I'm just here because he lets me." Mindy ran her gaze over him again. "Rhett told me about how you saved him. What were you doing there at that time of night? Not many people come up this far into the hills."

This was actually an excellent, probing question. He wondered if Rhett had tasked her with asking it. And it did not appear that she had seen him in his truck when he had previously observed her and Amanda driving out of the gates in the Mercedes.

"I was just passing through the area, taking in the views, but then I noticed this van clearly tailing a Porsche. I've been involved in those scenarios before, and my professional antennae started buzzing."

"Lucky for Rhett. But his dick is going to get him killed one day. Or *night*."

Nash did not want to take the bait on that comment. "How's the baby?"

"Mandy's doing fine." She eyed his empty ring finger. "You have children?"

Nash almost answered, *I did*. Instead he said, "No. Never married either."

"Until I met Barton I didn't see myself walking down the aisle."

"Where did you two meet, if you don't mind me asking?"

"He financed an independent film, and I was working on the set as part of the crew. We hit it off, and I went from working paycheck to paycheck as a hair and makeup stylist to the wife of a billionaire."

"Must've been quite a transition."

"Everyone thinks I married him for his money." She paused and her look seemed to challenge him to make a comment. "And I did. I mean who wouldn't? He was nice to me for the most part, but he just wanted young arm candy to show off and I was it. And now I get to live here." She eyed him haughtily. "I guess you think that makes me a shitty person?"

"I think everybody has to do what they have to do, Mrs. Temple."

She smiled. "I'm beginning to like you, Dillon. And *I* have a tattoo."

"Oh really, where?"

"I'd have to *strip* to show you." She said this in a way that told Nash she would be happy to do so.

"Well, I better go hit the shower," he said quickly. "Mr. Temple might need me later."

"Why do you call him 'Mr. Temple'?"

"He's my boss."

"Well, maybe *I* should start calling him that too, then."

She turned and walked slowly off.

* * *

That night someone knocked on Nash's door. It was Rhett, looking triumphant.

"My detectives got back to me. The guy 'Shock' mentioned in the letter I found? His real name is Isaiah York. He and Ty Nash grew up together in Mississippi. They also fought in Nam together, like Judith said. York has a condo in town and a business address in another state. They checked his condo. Turns out he hasn't been there for a very long time. So we're going to hit his business. He might be there, or at least we might find a clue as to Nash's whereabouts. We're wheels up at eight, so be ready to go at six thirty."

After he left, Nash emailed Shock and told him to go deep underground. Then he got into bed but barely slept, thinking about how quickly all of this might go irreversibly sideways.

But the other thing he could not stop thinking about was… Judith. She might have cheated on him, but she was still his wife. And he still cared for her.

Just hold on, Judith. Please, just hold on.

82

RHETT'S BRAND-NEW DASSAULT FALCON 10X jet lifted off right at the stroke of eight in the morning. On board were Rhett, Lynn Ryder, and Nash, with one flight attendant and a pair of pilots.

Nash was sitting at a table with Rhett, while Ryder sat in a forward seat staring out at the gloomy morning as the aircraft cut smoothly through the low cloud ceiling.

They were all served breakfast and coffee at an accelerated pace because the flight was only about ninety minutes. Nash recalled that, with necessary stops in between, and the ubiquitous traffic snarls, it had taken him and Shock nearly fifteen hours to cover the roughly seven-hundred-mile drive to the training facility. As soon as they dropped below the clouds once more on their descent, the landing gear came down. A few minutes later they were taxiing to a stop at a private jet park where a sleek, black Cadillac Escalade was waiting. Rhett took the wheel, while Nash rode shotgun and Ryder occupied a rear seat.

"Ms. Ryder has arranged for some manpower to meet us there," said Rhett.

"You expect trouble?" asked Nash.

"We expect anything," interjected Ryder tersely.

It took another forty-five minutes to get to their destination. The road in was very familiar to Nash, but he looked around with what he hoped was a sense of seeing it all for the first time.

"Isolated, no prying eyes," he noted.

Rhett nodded. "I think that's our people right up there."

He indicated the SUV parked by the side of the road about a hundred yards from the automatic gate into Shock's training center.

Rhett stopped next to them and they got out. Three men emerged from the SUV; they looked hardened and capable. They were also all Asian, Nash noted. Ryder was clearly in command, giving them instructions in what Nash recognized as Japanese. They climbed back into their vehicles and drove to the gate, where one of the men in the other SUV hit the call box button. There was no answer, as Nash knew would be the case.

"Nobody home," observed Rhett. He eyed Ryder, who was already on her phone.

Another man from the other SUV got out and nimbly scaled the wall. Three minutes later the gate slid open and the vehicles pulled in.

They all got out and looked around at a space that Nash had been intimately familiar with for well over a year. He took great care not to show recognition of any feature, and just pointed out elements that were visible to the naked eye. But he also knew that Shock had security cameras hidden everywhere.

"Okay, let's get inside and start the search," said Rhett.

"This facility has to be alarmed," noted Nash. He had figured it would be a beneficial point to raise to divert any suspicion away from him, although he hoped no one had any.

"Good idea," said Rhett. He looked at Ryder. "Can we get inside the building without calling all the cops down on us?"

Ryder pointed to one of her men and again spoke in Japanese.

The man went to the main door of the building, which Nash knew housed the living quarters. From a gear pack the man drew out a small electronic device and ran it along the perimeter of the door-jamb until it started to beep. He next took a spray can from the gear pack, inserted a very thin flex straw in the nozzle, and shot this spot with the contents of the can. The substance came out as stark white and seemed to harden immediately. He waited for ten seconds, then took a long, thin strip of metal from his pack and inserted it between the door and the doorjamb at that same spot, carefully sliding it back and forth. He examined this area with a lighted flex scope with a small viewing screen attached. Apparently satisfied, he pulled out a pick gun from his gear pack, inserted it into the lock, and popped it. He opened the door, and no alarm sounded.

As they passed through, Nash looked at the collapsible dome-shaped sensor affixed to the topside of the doorjamb. It was still in the unreleased, pushed-down position despite the door having been opened. It looked like it had been glued into place. And the thin metal piece, Nash figured, had been inserted to clear away any of the glue-like substance so that it wouldn't impede the door opening.

"Search everywhere," ordered Ryder.

As they began to do so, Nash suddenly thought of something. The cabinet in the room that held the tattoo binders. If Shock had left them. If they saw the—

Shit.

He walked there as quickly as he could, opened the cabinet, and saw that the binders *were* still there. He started going through them, while two of the other men came in and started to search other parts of the office.

When Rhett came in about a half hour later Nash was closing up the cabinet.

"Anything?" asked Rhett.

"Just business documents, and promotional newsletters I guess they send out."

At that moment Ryder hurried in and held out an iPad. "We found these prints in one of the bunk rooms. They match Nash's."

"So he was definitely here then," said Rhett.

"But he's not here now," pointed out Ryder. "We *have* to track down this Isaiah York. He has to have another place somewhere."

"And no mention of that in those binders you looked at in that cabinet?" asked Rhett. "Another property? Another address? On some of the promo materials you mentioned?"

"No, and I went through every page."

"Shit, okay, let's regroup."

Nash side glanced at Ryder when the woman ventured over to

the cabinet door and opened it. His hand eased to his gun. *Okay, this might be it.*

And that would have been it if the man who had stayed outside on watch had not phoned Ryder, even as loud noises from outside reached them in here. She answered, listened for a few moments, and said to the others, "Sirens and alarm lights are going off outside. There must have been a trip sensor somewhere. We need to leave. Now."

Nash thought that a trip sensor would have no doubt sounded a long time ago, but he was not arguing with Ryder's command to immediately vacate the premises.

They all rushed to their vehicles and drove off. As the sirens grew louder, they reached a side road that carried them on a macadam path through a forest of mostly evergreen trees.

"GPS says this winds back to the road we originally came in on," said Rhett, who was in the lead of the two-vehicle caravan. "We should be okay."

And when the sounds of the sirens faded, they all let out a collective breath of relief.

However, Nash's was longer and more sincere than the others.

Ninety minutes later the three of them plus the team of Asians were cruising at forty-one thousand feet.

It didn't make Nash feel any better when Ryder was on the phone the whole time. And whenever she glanced at him, it was not with a friendly expression. But then again, he had concluded she never looked friendly to anyone.

He kept his fingers only a few inches from his gun the entire trip, while he noted that Rhett had his eyes closed, but did not appear to be sleeping. Nash wondered what would happen if he had to end up shooting everyone except the pilots and flight attendant. Maybe he could then hijack the plane to Cuba.

I might just take being in Witness Protection and stocking shelves at a dollar store in Idaho over this.

83

LATER THAT NIGHT NASH PERCHED on his bed at the Temple estate and stared down at the email he'd received from Shock on his phone.

> We was watching all of you on the cameras. When the lady went for the cabinet I triggered the "sirens" I got up in the trees around the place. And sorry about the damn tattoo binders. When you alerted us that they were heading our way we had to really hustle to clean up the space. I thought Byron had gotten them and he thought I had taken care of it.

He messaged Shock back. It worked great. And thanks.

Nash heard a noise out in the hall. He went to his door and opened it just a crack.

Lynn Ryder was gliding down the corridor. She stopped and knocked on Rhett's door. He opened it and she slipped inside.

Nash grabbed the small bag holding his surveillance equipment, quietly left his room, and crept into the empty bedroom next to Rhett's. He attached a listening device to the adjoining wall, donned a pair of earphones, and instantly heard their voices.

"She is not pleased," said Ryder.

"But we're making progress," retorted Rhett.

"The progress is not fast enough."

"Then what exactly would you suggest?" said Rhett heatedly.

"It is not my place to suggest. It is your place to act. Nash has already caused damage. He got into restricted databases. The FBI has executed search warrants. People have been detained and held for questioning. International law enforcement agencies are engaged and coordinating. This is serious."

"Well, it was *her* goddamned fault that Nash got away in the first place."

"Do you wish for me to report to her that you said so?"

Nash thought he could hear the clink of ice in a glass. He imagined Rhett taking a sip of whatever he was having in order to give him more time to think of an adequate response. Nash had seen him do that in business meetings, and in encounters with his father.

Rhett said, "I think that the last thing we need to do right now is fight amongst ourselves. We're only going to get through this by working together. And I've got a lot on my plate and things keep being added to it. Hell, now even his wife thinks Nash is innocent."

"Excuse me?" said Ryder.

Nash felt his heart skip a beat.

Rhett must have sensed that he had said something potentially dangerous because he immediately began to backtrack. "It's nothing. Just saying stupid things."

"Has she said these stupid things to the *police*?" asked Ryder.

"What? No, no, she wouldn't. I'm sure of it."

"There is only one way to be *sure*," said Ryder.

Now Rhett was pleading. "She's out of her head, okay? She takes pills. No one will believe her. Least of all the police."

"So she takes pills? That is good to know. And useful."

"No, wait. Please. Just leave her out of this. She is not a danger to us, I promise."

"Your promises mean nothing to me, Mr. Temple."

Nash heard Ryder leave. Then Rhett said, "Shit, I'm sorry, Judith."

Nash poked his head out the doorway and saw Ryder walking down the hall. She was already on her phone. The Asian men had not come to the estate with them, but they had to be staying nearby, he knew. And he felt certain that she was contacting them right now.

Nash closed the door, grabbed the listening device, slipped it and the earphones into his pocket, and stepped out into the hall.

"Who you?"

Angie was staring at him from across the hall in her bedroom doorway.

"I'm...I work for Rhett."

"Et?"

"Yes."

She nodded. "You want tea?"

"I..." Nash looked up and down the hall. The last thing he wanted was to waste time with tea. But if he refused, and Angie got upset and made a ruckus? He had met her once before when he and Judith had been invited to dinner. Barton had mentioned that little things could set Angie off, and it would take a great deal of time and effort to calm her down.

"Sure, that sounds nice."

She smiled and opened her door more.

While Angie fiddled with tea cups, he sent a message to Agent Morris and explained what had just happened.

Judith is in great danger. You have to get her out of there. Now!

When he didn't get a response, Nash grew agitated.

Angie brought over his tea and cookie. He thanked her and drank it, and ate the cookie as fast as he could, even though it was stale and bitter.

"Tars," she said, pointing at the ceiling littered with glittery stars. "Bootiful."

"Yeah, they are," he said, his heartbeat hammering in his ears. Then he remembered something that Rhett had done when Barton couldn't get Angie to go to sleep when he and Judith had gone there for dinner. He said, "Night-night-night, Angie. Time to go night-night-night."

She smiled, nodded, got into her bed, and closed her eyes. "Night-night-night-night," she said.

Nash was out the door a second later. His Porsche was parked in the motor court. He looked back up at the dark façade of the house. This was a big risk, but he had no other options. He manually opened the gate, put the car in neutral, pushed it out past the gates, and closed them. Then he hopped in when he hit a downward slope, started the engine, and drove as fast as he could to his old home.

He had lost Maggie. He could not lose Judith.

84

FORTY MINUTES PASSED, AND IT seemed like forty years, until Nash reached his old neighborhood. He had no way to get through the security gate, so he parked down the street, nimbly hopped the fence, and made his way in the darkness to his old home. He got in through the same back door into the laundry room that Maggie's kidnappers had forced. The mingled smells of dirty clothes, detergent, and bleach hit him. The alarm was not set, though he remembered the passcode if it had been.

He took the steps two at a time and found Judith lying in bed. But this new version of Judith did not sleep nearly as soundly as the old version.

She called out from the darkness, "Who's there!"

He could see her shadowy image as she sat up in bed. It was only now that he realized he needed to tell her something.

"Mrs. Nash, I was here earlier, with Rhett Temple." He drew closer.

"What do you want?" she said, drawing up the sheet to cover her, as she stared at him.

"You were right. Your husband was framed."

The sheet came down a bit. "Who are you?"

"I . . . I work with the FBI."

"But I thought you were working with Rhett." She paused. "Wait, you think—"

"Rhett let it slip to some dangerous people that you believe that your husband is innocent. These people do not want you raising that concern with the police."

"So they plan on killing me?" She said this so lucidly that Nash nearly forgot that his wife had handled with dignity and aplomb many crises in her life, including the tragic and untimely deaths of her parents in an accident. But the twin tragedies of Maggie and him had simply been too much for her.

"Yes. I'm here to get you to safety."

"Do I have time to dress and collect a few things?"

"Please hurry."

She took all of three minutes and joined him back in the bedroom. He held her hand to steady her as they swiftly moved down the stairs.

They had just reached the lower level and were about to exit the home through the door Nash had come in when he heard the noise.

He drew his gun and told Judith to get behind him. Nash calmly lined up his muzzle directly at the back door. As it was pushed open, Nash took aim. The man coming through had on a black ski mask and was holding a knife, so this was clearly not the FBI; they would have come in the front door with lots of guns, badges, and noise.

The moment of truth was here.

Obstacles, Nash. Not human beings, obstacles. Like Dad said.

Nash shot the intruder in the head and he tumbled down dead even as Judith screamed. The door was then kicked fully open and two more men burst in. This was the team of Asians who had accompanied them to Shock's place. They had no doubt recognized Nash, which meant he had to kill them or else it was all over. But that was far easier said than done.

Before he could fire again his gun was smashed out of his hand by a spin kick executed to perfection by the first man. This was followed up by a hard leg strike against Nash's shoulder by the same man. He tumbled backward and slammed into Judith. She went down, slid across the floor, hit her head on the baseboard, and fell unconscious.

Nash had no time to see how she was because the second man was now coming at him with twin knives, whirling them at incredible velocity. Nash grabbed a plastic laundry hamper off the washing machine and used it to block the knife strike. He finally managed to get the blades stuck in the side webbing of the basket and then Nash twisted them out of the man's grip. But the man came at Nash again, kicking and punching, and Nash was barely able to deflect the blows.

Nash knew he was not going to be able to hold out for long, especially since the other man was attempting to circle behind him in the confined space. Their martial arts skills were greater than his, he had to concede. Sometimes, it was as simple as that.

Then Shock's entreaty came back to him.

Do whatever you have to do—cheat or anything else to walk out alive.

Well, he had one advantage. He knew this particular battlefield better than his opponents.

Nash grabbed the iron off the shelf, and when the man put up his hands to block the object he believed Nash was about to hurl at him, Nash tossed it through the window instead. As the bewildered man took time to process this, Nash snatched a washcloth off a stack on the dryer, scooped something from the shattered window with one hand and lifted a bottle of bleach with the other, his fingers dexterously twisting the top off. He turned and fed a face full of bleach into the eyes and open mouth of his startled attacker. The man gagged and ripped at his pupils, at the very same time that Nash took the jagged piece of glass from the broken window, which he was holding with the washcloth, and slashed it violently across the man's sinewy neck. It severed both the left and right jugulars, sending blood spewing across the room.

The second man screamed in fury as he rushed forward. Nash dumped the rest of the bleach on the floor, and when the man hit the slickened spot his legs flew up and he landed hard on his back on the floor.

Nash dropped to his knees, drew the Beretta from the ankle holster, and shot the man in the face, twice, just to be sure.

Then, it was over. Nash stared down at three men, all of whom had lost their lives solely due to him. He felt his knees weaken and his gut lurch as he eyed the blood, the bodies, the...destruction he had wrought. He lowered the gun and closed his eyes.

Four breaths in, hold for four, four breaths out, and hold for four.

Repeat. It got Dad through his combat. It will get you through...
your combat.

When he heard the rush of footsteps coming toward the door Nash's eyes popped open and he pointed his Beretta at the opening.

"FBI!" called out a voice. "Show yourselves. Now!"

"Agent Morris?" called out Nash.

Morris, his gun held in one hand, peered around the doorway, and shone his light around. "Who's that?"

"It's Dillon Hope. I'm the one who messaged you. I've got Mrs. Nash with me."

Nash raced over to Judith, who was just now regaining consciousness. When she sat up and saw the dead men and all the blood, she moaned and was sick to her stomach.

Nash grabbed another washcloth to help clean off her face and blouse.

Morris came farther into the room and shone his light on them. The FBI agent studied Nash but clearly didn't recognize him.

"Dillon Hope?" he said.

"Yes."

"Who are you? What are you doing here?"

Nash helped Judith up and said, "I've told Mrs. Nash that I'm working with the Bureau on this matter. And that you would get her to a safe place." He looked at the three dead men. "I think we were both a little late on that score."

"The Bureau?" Morris said, still staring at Nash before looking down at the dead bodies.

"Yes. You and I have met before, actually. Up in New York City with the deputy AG, when I was recruited for this mission. You accepted my terms, and we've been working this ever since. I've just been lying low for a bit and, um, *changing* things up."

Nash looked at him directly and cocked his head. Morris stared intently back at him and then his jaw eased down in shock as he put two and two together. Nash thought he could hear the man mutter, "Holy Mother of God."

Nash said, "It would also be really good if we could somehow show that Mrs. Nash was no longer...around, so that folks would not *look* for her."

Morris nodded, clearly trying to process all this. He finally said, "Um, okay, it will be communicated publicly that Mrs. Nash was... um, killed during the course of a home invasion. We'll sell that to the local cops."

"You came up with that quickly," said an impressed Nash.

"When you messaged me, we decided on a plan if we got here in time. I need to call in another team. I'll be back in two minutes."

After he left, Judith looked at Nash and said, "I'll be safe. But will you?"

"I'll be fine. I'm just glad this all worked out and that we were able..." Here Nash stumbled and couldn't finish.

She looked at the men on the floor. "You saved my life." She gave him a searching look and then glanced away when Morris came back in.

"Okay, the team will be here ASAP and we'll get this done." He said to Nash, "You'd best be on your way...Agent Hope."

Nash looked at his wife, wanting more than anything to tell her who he really was.

All he said was, "Good luck, Mrs. Nash."

She gave him a hug and a kiss on the cheek and stared deeply into his features.

In fact, Nash felt like he was being x-rayed.

"Thank you, Agent *Hope*."

After he left Morris said awkwardly to her, "Um, he's a good man, quite capable."

Judith gave him a contemptuous glance and said, "What do you expect from a fucking Eagle Scout?"

CHAPTER

85

I STILL CAN'T BELIEVE IT," SAID Rhett. It was the next day and he was at his estate in the hills. Nash and Ryder both sat across from him in his father's old office. They had all seen the news reports of the violent incident at Nash's old home. "You sent a team there. And none of them came back. And yet Judith was killed?"

Nash said, "If you want my opinion, your guys are in custody and being questioned right now by the Feds."

"I disagree," said Ryder quietly.

"Then where are they?" retorted Nash. "Why haven't they reported back?"

Ryder did not answer. She simply studied her phone.

Nash continued, "This is classic FBI playbook. They feed out to the news what they want and leave out all the rest."

"You have experience with the FBI?" Ryder said sharply.

"Every person working in the personal security sector for high-net-worth Americans has dealt with the FBI," Nash replied. "You ask me, they had an informant that tipped them off that something was about to go down with the woman. They didn't get there in time to save her, but they got your team as the consolation prize." He glanced from Ryder to Rhett and then back at the woman.

Nash had arrived back at the estate last night—he hoped unseen—but, wanting to divert any suspicion, he had decided to go on offense and put Ryder on her heels with what had happened.

"That is absurd," retorted Ryder.

"The conditions on the ground say otherwise," countered Nash. "Unless all your guys turned traitor at the same time."

Ryder suddenly looked both confused and fearful, and Nash could understand why. Victoria Steers certainly would not want three of her men in the custody of the FBI.

"But Judith Nash has been eliminated," Ryder pointed out. "Let's not overlook that."

"Seems to me like you sacrificed two knights and a bishop to gain a rook," interjected Rhett. "Admit it, Lynn, it's a shitshow. And it doesn't get us any closer to finding Nash."

Before Ryder could say anything in response, her phone buzzed. She looked at the text. After she read it she glanced up. "*She* wishes to see us, Mr. Temple."

Rhett turned a shade paler. "Where and when?"

"Who are we talking about?" asked Nash, though he well knew.

"We are to go to her. In Hong Kong."

"Who?" Nash demanded again, but Rhett held up his hand.

"Why does she want to meet?" he asked Ryder.

"She has been made aware of the latest developments and wants to hold a council of . . . war. She requires your presence."

Nash said, "Mr. Temple. I need to come with you."

"No," said Ryder sharply. "Only Mr. Temple is allowed."

Rhett said forcefully, "No. If he doesn't go, I won't, either."

"She said—" began Ryder.

"I don't care, okay?" blurted out Rhett. "My father was murdered. Maggie and Judith Nash are dead. Nash himself is God knows where. And now your guys are missing. There's a rat somewhere. I feel it. I'm up to my neck in shit right now, lady, and you've done nothing except make things worse. So it's both of us, or you can fucking go alone."

Ryder stared hard at Rhett, as though she believed her gaze alone could slay him. Then she drew a breath, tapped in a message on her phone, and sent it off. Thirty seconds later the reply dropped into her inbox.

"It is approved," she said. "Her jet will fly us to LA and then on to Hong Kong."

They all went to pack and get ready.

Nash sent a secure message to Morris about all of this and got a reply back.

Please do not get on that damn plane.

Nash's reply was just as quick.

Please take care of Judith. And if I don't make it back, tell her I tried my best.

* * *

After the refueling stop in LA, Steers's sleek jet charged into the sky.

Nash stared out the window as he left America beneath him. He reflected for a few moments on what it must have felt like for his father, at the tender age of eighteen, to be flying halfway around the world to fight in a war where someone you knew would die pretty much every day, and your own odds of survival were never very good.

Nash seriously doubted he would be coming back alive from *his* war. Yet he also doubted that Victoria Steers and Rhett Temple would be among the living if he had any say in it. And he would do all he could to make sure he did.

I know I'm tilting at windmills, although my enemies are anything but imaginary. But sometimes an eye for a damn eye may be the best you can do.

Yet if the hell he had endured had taught Nash anything, it was that the only things that really mattered to him were his family. It was an easy thought to articulate, but far harder to actually live day in and day out. Now he regretted every second he had been on the road for business and missed anything happening in Maggie's life, because he would never get an opportunity to have a second chance with her.

Just like with my father.

And after seeing Judith descend into the depths of despair after losing her daughter, Nash understood that his cold, focused, and aloof nature might very well have driven his wife into the arms of someone like Rhett Temple.

I failed the people I was supposed to take care of. But I may have gotten a second chance to make restitution, at least in a small way. And I will sacrifice everything I have, including my life, to make it right. Or as right as I can make it, because nothing will bring Maggie back. And Judith will never be the same.

But I will try my best.

And I'm Ty Nash's son.

So bet against me at your peril.

ACKNOWLEDGMENTS

To Michelle, thanks for always being the rock for me to hold on to.

To Grand Central Publishing, for supporting me every step of the way for thirty years.

To Aaron and Arleen Priest, Lucy Childs, Lisa Erbach Vance, Frances Jalet-Miller, Kristen Pini, and Natalie Rosselli. No one does it better.

To Mitch Hoffman, who keeps getting better with each book.

To Pan Macmillan, who for me has always been the gold standard in publishing.

To Praveen Naidoo and the wonderful team at Pan Macmillan in Australia and New Zealand. We truly enjoyed our visit and getting to meet all of you in person.

To Tracey Cheetham, a special shout-out for being every inch the publicist extraordinaire.

To Caspian Dennis and Sandy Violette, for always being there for me.

To Scott Collin, for an awesome education on tattoos.

To Tom DePont, for help on all the financial aspects of the story.

And to Kristen White and Michelle Butler, who continue to make me look good in all respects.

CAN'T WAIT TO SEE HOW
NASH'S STORY CONTINUES?

TURN THE PAGE FOR
A PREVIEW OF

HOPE RISES

COMING APRIL 2026

CHAPTER

I

WALTER NASH WAS JOLTED AWAKE. The jet he was on en route to Hong Kong had encountered some rough air. He turned to see his employer, Rhett Temple, sitting next to him.

Nash's now alert gaze then moved to Lynn Ryder, who was asleep in a forward seat on the privately owned plane soaring westward toward Asia. Ryder was in her thirties with long white hair that was either colored or natural, he didn't know which. She was also an emissary for Victoria Steers, one of the most ruthless criminals in the world. They were currently aboard Steers's jet and were traveling to see the woman, at her behest.

He next glanced out the window, and reflected back was his image. That spurred Nash to *reflect* on his life over the last year and a half. He used to be a mild-mannered, law-abiding business executive, tall and skinny, with no discernible muscle, a full head of hair, and nary a tattoo within a mile of him. Out of necessity Nash had shaved his head, grown facial hair, and transformed himself into a muscled, tatted, fighting machine, complete with a new identity: Dillon Hope, personal security expert. No one—not even his wife, Judith—now recognized him.

He had gone from reviewing business plans and acquiring companies and flying on corporate jets, with not a whiff of intrigue or danger in his life, to playing a deadly game of cat and mouse and having to fool everyone around him into believing he really was Dillon Hope. Because he knew that Lynn Ryder and Victoria Steers wanted nothing more than to kill Walter Nash.

I truly am living in the upside down world. And I seriously doubt
I will ever get back to my world. But I have got to see this through.

He turned to Temple, the CEO of Sybaritic Investments, Nash's former employer. The man had been across the aisle when Nash first shut his eyes, and Nash wondered why he had changed seats. It was a small detail, but Nash sensed that seemingly trivial acts clearly mattered right now.

As Dillon Hope, Nash had dexterously placed himself in a position to be employed as his old boss's personal bodyguard. The ruse had worked, and Nash's life had changed to an even greater extent, as he was now firmly residing in the enemy's camp.

Speaking in the slow, deliberate tone he had adopted as Hope's voice, Nash said, "Is there a problem?"

Temple replied quietly, "Look, Dillon, it's delicate, but Victoria Steers is not, well, completely on the up-and-up."

"Okay," said Nash cautiously. "Meaning what, exactly?"

"She's...well, dangerous. And I don't want you to slip up and get yourself in trouble when you meet her."

Nash thought it far more likely that Temple didn't want Nash to slip up and get *him* in trouble with the villainous Steers.

Though he well knew the answer, Nash asked, "Exactly how is she not on the up-and-up *and* dangerous?"

"She's into drug distribution on a global scale. And she has people killed."

Nash stared back in feigned astonishment at his boss. Then, in keeping up the subterfuge that he had no idea who Steers was, he asked, "What the hell, Mr. Temple? Why is a rich guy like you involved with her?"

"It's a long story, Dillon. My father...he was working with her to recoup his fortune and he got me involved. I wish I had an out, but I don't. I really don't. Trust me, I've tried."

"So she wants to meet? Why?"

Temple leaned in closer and said in a near whisper, "The FBI has, well, tried to make some inroads at my company, finding a mole—a spy there, so to speak."

Nash let his jaw go slack. "The FBI! Jesus, Mr. Temple, I didn't sign up for this."

"Then you shouldn't have come," said a voice.

Both men looked up to see Ryder awake and staring at them from her seat. She had obviously overheard at least part of their conversation.

She walked down the aisle until she was standing in front of them. "In fact, as I made very clear, I did not want you to come."

Nash glanced at Temple before saying, "As his personal security guard, I insisted on coming because I was concerned with Mr. Temple's safety. But, frankly, I might have declined if I had known *all* the facts."

Ryder gave Temple a withering look as she said to Nash, "And now that you have been provided *some* facts, we will see what happens when we arrive in Hong Kong."

She walked back to her seat.

Temple glanced at Nash. "Dillon, I'm sorry you got caught up in all this. I really am."

He returned to his seat, where he closed his eyes and started taking deep, calming breaths.

Nash looked out the window, his thoughts as black as the darkness outside.

Well, Nash, this might be the end of you. But if I go down, I'm taking others with me. Starting with Victoria Steers.

CHAPTER

2

A MAN WAS WAITING FOR THEM in the airport with Lynn Ryder's name on an iPad. He led them to a large Mercedes passenger van in the parking garage. There were four men there in addition to the driver. Nash could see that all of them were armed. After their bags were loaded in they were driven off, one sturdy guard on either side of both Nash and Temple. They passed through a tunnel under Victoria Harbour and emerged into daylight on the other side. After negotiating a series of surface roads they reached a high-rise building in the Hom Hung neighborhood, located in the southeast section of Kowloon Peninsula. Nash recognized the area because he had stayed nearby on a previous trip while working for Sybaritic.

The Mercedes parked in the building's underground garage.

A glass elevator carried them into the sky.

Temple looked nervous, Ryder confident, and Nash, despite his anxiety level riding pretty high, did his best to appear calm.

The doors opened directly into an entry vestibule, where two armed men appeared. They expertly searched Nash and Temple, and promptly confiscated Nash's two guns and both men's phones.

"I want those back," demanded Nash. However, nothing was returned.

They were escorted into a large room with floor-to-ceiling windows and sweeping views of the dazzling harbor. Ryder took a seat next to a large chair set in the center of the room, while Nash and Temple were directed to two seats across from her.

Nash's gaze took in every aspect of the room, especially the armed men. What Nash was observing was not good, since he had no weapons and the exits were guarded by men who did. And he was in a foreign land that was controlled by China. None of that boded well for him.

Then she came into the room.

Prior to this Nash had seen only a photo of Victoria Steers, briefly shown to him during a previous meeting with the FBI. Steers was the product of a Chinese mother and an English father. Tall and wiry, with long black hair and porcelain skin, Steers glided across the floor dressed in sleek dark clothing that covered all of her body except her neck, face, and hands. She carried no weapon and did not look particularly threatening, yet at her appearance every hair stood up on the back of Nash's neck.

When he eyed Temple, he noted that his boss was staring at Steers with palpable fear.

Steers smiled at Ryder. "Thank you, Lynn, for all your good work."

"Of course, Ms. Steers."

Then Steers looked at Temple. "Mr. Temple, would you introduce me to your colleague, whom *you* insisted accompany you on this trip despite objections."

Temple cleared his throat and said, "This is Dillon Hope, my personal bodyguard."

"Your personal *bodyguard*? Do you have something to fear, Mr. Temple?"

"Everyone has something to fear, Ms. Steers."

She glanced at Ryder before saying, "I also understand that Mr. Hope has been told of our *private* business?"

Temple's lips curled in displeasure in the face of Ryder's smug features.

"He had to be told *some* things, Ms. Steers. But he is a professional, and everything will be kept in the strictest confidence, I can assure you."

Steers did not appear to be listening. "You bring a stranger to my home? *And* reveal some of our business to him? In my estimation you have performed acts that are *truly* unforgivable."

"I was told you had approved it," Temple added, with a sharp glance at Ryder.

Steers seemed to ignore this as well. "I was also informed that Mr. Hope is discomforted by the business between us."

"Look, he can be a real asset to you," said Temple. "He is top notch. I've seen that for myself."

"I have many *top-notch* people in my employ already, Mr. Temple. I require no others."

She slowly withdrew her searing gaze from him and swung it around to Nash. "However, Mr. Hope, now that you *are* here, it will be interesting to see if you *can* become an asset. I trust you understand all that this entails?"

"I do. Thank you, Ms. Steers," Nash said, though every muscle in his body was tensed to respond immediately in the face of her threatening phrasing.

If I can just reach the man who took my guns...

As though she were reading Nash's mind, Steers held out her hand.

One of the guards produced a Glock 9mm and placed it in her palm. She gripped it, checked the mag, and racked the slide, loading a bullet.

As she looked at them Temple went rigid in his chair, and Nash felt his butt cheeks involuntarily clench.

"A good choice in a personal sidearm, Mr. Hope," she said. "However, I prefer a Norinco NP42 Mini. But then again, I like to buy local."

"The Chinese also make good weapons," he said.

"Indeed they do. They made *me*, after all. I also understand that three of my people are now in the hands of the FBI. That is a decided setback that I find unacceptable. Accountability must be served."

At this abrupt segue, Temple glanced anxiously at Ryder and blurted out, "I had *nothing* to do with that. That was not my call. I argued against it, in fact."

Steers said menacingly, "You disavow all responsibility for this debacle? Is that really what you are telling me?"

Temple sputtered, "I didn't mean...I just wanted to point out that..." He glanced at Ryder and saw her smug look deepen even as he squirmed.

Before he could say anything else, Steers raised the pistol, causing Temple to put up his hands and flinch backward.

Steers then pointed the gun at Ryder's head and fired. The woman fell to the floor, blood sprayed all over her clothing and white hair. Some of the blowback had dotted Steers's cheek, hand, and sleeve. One of the guards hustled forward and used a wet cloth to thoroughly clean her off. Two other men rushed in, wrapped Ryder in plastic, and carried her out. The chair in which she had been sitting was also removed and the marble floor underneath the chair thoroughly mopped. Temple and Nash appeared stunned, while Steers had her eyes closed, her expression placid.

When all traces of the woman had been removed, Steers opened her eyes and studied the two men. "Death can be awkward," she said. "And unpleasant."

"Yes, it can," said Nash evenly.

"And also *necessary*," she added.

Nash did not reply to this.

She looked at Temple. "My people being in the custody of the FBI is...not...good."

"No," said Temple quickly. He still looked horrified by what had just happened.

Steers once more turned to Nash. "I trust that you understand the implications of what has just transpired, Mr. Hope?"

"I'm afraid I don't know what you're talking about," said Nash cautiously. "You mean Ryder's death?"

"You disappoint me. I thought it rather obvious." She held up the pistol. "You and your weapon have just committed a terrible crime in Hong Kong. And though Hong Kong does not have the death penalty, China does, and it exercises no hesitation in employing it. It is done by lethal injection, or else they shoot you." She handed the gun to one of her men. "That choice will be theirs. But you also have a choice to make." She glanced at Temple. "And as an accessory, Mr. Temple, your fate will not be much better: life in prison. But again, you have a choice as well."

Nash drew a shaky breath. "You mean we can *choose* to work with you?"

She shook her head. "To work *for* me."

"And if we refuse?" said Nash, already knowing the answer.

"Then steps will be taken demonstrating that my colleague's murder occurred in China, and all necessary evidence to implicate both of you in her death will be provided; the rest is assuredly known to you. One of you will be executed, and the other will spend the rest of his life in a Chinese prison." She added coolly, "I think I would prefer death, actually. The Chinese are often not kind to their own law-abiding citizens. And they are completely ruthless to their criminals." She glanced at Temple. "And Americans in particular are not at all popular in China at present."

"To work for you doing what exactly, Ms. Steers?" asked Temple in a tremulous voice.

Nash thought he knew the answer. But it would turn out that he could not have been further from the truth.

She said, "My mother is being held in a prison in another country. And you both are going to help set her free."

ABOUT THE AUTHOR

David Baldacci is one of the world's bestselling and favourite thriller writers. A former trial lawyer with a keen interest in world politics, he has specialist knowledge in the US political system and intelligence services. His first book, *Absolute Power*, became an instant international bestseller, with the movie starring Clint Eastwood a major box office hit. He has since written more than fifty bestsellers featuring, most recently, Travis Devine, Mickey Gibson, Amos Decker and Aloysius Archer. David is also the co-founder, along with his wife, of the Wish You Well Foundation, a non-profit organization dedicated to supporting literacy efforts across the US.

Killer twists. Heroes to believe in. Trust Baldacci.

THE ONLY MAN FOR THE JOB

Discover David Baldacci's gripping series, featuring undercover operative Travis Devine.

Meet Travis Devine. Framed. Blackmailed. Accused of murder. It's just another day on Wall Street for the 6:20 Man.

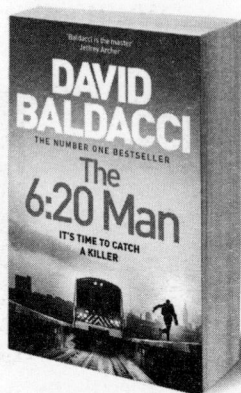

The 6:20 Man is back! Can Travis Devine solve the haunting murder of a high-ranking CIA agent before his own time runs out?

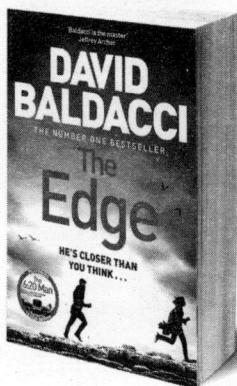

Trying to escape a skilled predator who wants him dead, Devine finds himself on a job perhaps even more dangerous than the one he's running from . . .

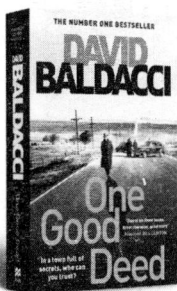

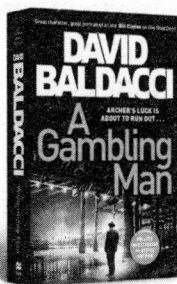

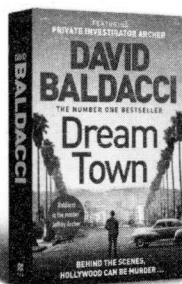

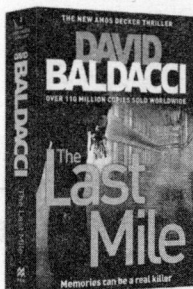

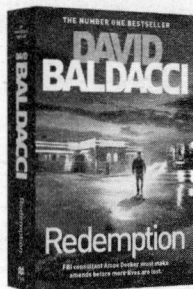